THE WOMAN WHO TO

Fiona was born in a youth hostel in Yorkshire. She started working on teen magazine *Jackie* at age 17, then went on to join *Just Seventeen* and *More!* where she invented the infamous 'Position of the Fortnight'. Fiona now lives in Scotland with her husband Jimmy, their three children and a wayward rescue collie cross called Jack.

For more info, visit www.fionagibson.com. You can follow Fiona on Twitter @fionagibson.

By the same author:

FIONA GIBSON

The

WOMAN

WHO TOOK A

CHANCE

avon.

Published by AVON
A division of HarperCollins*Publishers*
1 London Bridge Street
London SE1 9GF

www.harpercollins.co.uk

HarperCollins*Publishers*
1st Floor, Watermarque Building, Ringsend Road
Dublin 4, Ireland

A Paperback Original 2022

1

First published in Great Britain by HarperCollins*Publishers* 2022

ISBN: 978-0-00-838602-3

Typeset in Sabon by Palimpsest Book Production Limited, Falkirk, Stirlingshire

Printed and bound in the UK using 100% Renewable Electricity
at CPI Group (UK) Ltd

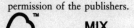

MIX
Paper from
responsible sources
FSC™ C007454

This book is produced from independently certified FSC™ paper
to ensure responsible forest management.

For more information visit: www.harpercollins.co.uk/green

'No one meets in real life, Mum.
It's all algorithms now.'

Prologue

The fear of redundancy is like a spot brewing on your chin. Although you try to ignore it you know it's still *there*, simmering away under the surface.

With that spot, you find yourself obsessively charting its progress. You wrestle with the urge to poke at it and find yourself arranging your social life around it. You almost wish it would peak, or even explode dramatically – because at least then the worst would be over.

That's how it feels when your industry is in crisis. I am a flight attendant with BudgieAir, an airline firmly aimed at your cheap and cheerful holiday market. It's all I had ever wanted to do, since I was a little girl – to work for an airline, wear the smart uniform and fly all over the world. So I'm clinging on to the hope that we'll weather the current financial storm and I'll continue to demonstrate the safety procedures and hand out packets of pretzels with a big, bright, BudgieAir smile.

And, as a bonus, perhaps that menopausal spot currently brewing on my chin might *not* peak after all, but be magically reabsorbed by my face during the night.

CHAPTER ONE

Bare feet. There's a lot of them about on this Palma–Glasgow flight. They're propped up on bulkheads, dangling over armrests and jutting out into the aisle. There are gnarly toenails, bunions, several cases of severe sunburn and some of these feet are, I have to say, not the *freshest* I've encountered. I serve teas and coffees, politely ask passengers to put their socks back on and catch Freddie demonstrating his patented method of upselling our airline's mascot.

Blue velour with plastic feet and a wind-mechanism, Billy Budgie is available to purchase on every route – just ask your friendly flight attendant.

There are gales of rowdy laughter as he slips into his sales routine as follows:

1. Home in on a particularly high-spirited group.
2. Demonstrate that two budgies, when wound up simultaneously, can be set loose to copulate on a tray table.

3. Rack up a heap of sales as each party member buys two budgies *each*.

It's hard to believe that, in the golden age of air travel, flight attendants once served martinis and roast beef dinners on real china crockery. These days it's vodka and tonics and super-heated cheese toasties in cellophane bags. But there's still a thrill to it; a kind of glamour I suppose. After nearly three decades in the job I still experience a frisson of pleasure as I clack across an airport concourse, fully made-up with not so much as a single *pore* scandalously naked. I feel right, somehow, when I'm wearing one of our few approved lipstick shades.

'What about your human rights?' my daughter Hannah exclaimed, when she'd just reached her teens and was appalled to learn that my employer dictated my choice. 'I mean, what if you don't want to wear lipstick?'

'Well, we're expected to,' I said.

'Oh my God. That's ridiculous.'

'I know, love, but it's part of the job to look polished – to send out the signal that we're a team,' I explained, and that's exactly what we are: an army of highly trained individuals in our crisp white shirts, fitted blue suits and jaunty blue and yellow silk scarves at the neck, bearing our chirpy budgie logo. Yes, I know we'd be just as capable of calming nervous flyers and attending to minor medical scares with our faces bare. But our super-groomed appearance acts as a kind of *armour* – like an armadillo's horny plates. With my heels on and my hair pinned up in its chignon, I am armed to deal with the backchat, the enthusiastic drinking, the flare-ups and occasional punch-ups, the sub-blanket fumbling and couples attempting to cram themselves into

4

the loo together – because we'd never notice, right? Or we'd believe the guy who says, 'I'm just going in to help her get something out of her eye.' For a while, among my colleagues, it was a euphemism for sex; i.e. to the friend who'd just started seeing someone: 'Has he tried to get something out of your eye yet?' 'No, but I think it might be on the cards for Friday night.'

So yes, this job can be challenging but we're trained to manage even the most demanding of passengers in the most pleasant way possible. *Smiles cost nothing so we give them for free.* That's one of the little phrases that was drummed into us during training, along with MEFS: *Make Every Flight Special.* And I try to, I really do – even today when the woman in seat 32A starts to sand at her bare heels with a pumice.

'Excuse me,' I start, 'would you mind not doing that in-flight please?'

'What?' She glares at me.

'Doing your feet—'

'I'm *exfoliating* them.'

'Even so,' I say brightly, 'I'm afraid we have a no bare feet policy on board.'

'Jobsworth bitch,' she hisses as I stride away.

I gather that there's less of this kind of behaviour on the classier airlines, where passengers just want to snooze, or prepare for meetings, and alcohol is consumed with restraint. However, I have never been tempted to work for anyone else. BudgieAir is where I started, along with a brilliant bunch of new recruits – including Freddie – who became my best friends. We work hard but it's not *all* graft; we have our parties, our awaydays and the camaraderie is like nowhere else. We also have our annual awards ceremony

5

when the flight attendant who's sold the most Billy Budgies that year wins an amazing holiday. That's why it's such a big deal, flogging those darned toys. Last year Freddie won, and the year before it was me. While he and his husband took their prize trip the following month I *still* haven't redeemed mine. It's a week for two on the Greek island of Santorini in the honeymoon suite of a spa hotel.

'It does look very honeymoonish, Mum,' Hannah remarked, when I suggested we went together.

'You don't have to be newlyweds to go there,' I pointed out. 'I mean, there's no *rule*.'

'I just think you should save it for someone special,' she insisted. Who was more special than her? I asked. My friends have been the same. It's been all, 'Oh, no, Jen. Don't waste it on me!' Like I need to be in an intimate relationship with someone to fully enjoy going on holiday with them.

''Scuse me,' a passenger calls out now, waving a pastry in the air. 'What's in this exactly?'

'That's a sausage roll,' I reply, 'so it'll be sausage meat, sir.'

'Is it?' he splutters, sunburnt head glowing. 'It's like eating a fart.'

'Oh, I'm sorry. It's premium sausage meat from naturally reared pigs—'

'Yeah, right,' he snorts.

'—But if you're not enjoying it,' I add, 'I can exchange it for anything else in its menu section.'

Clearly primed for confrontation, he seems taken aback. 'Oh, can you? I'll have the cheesy thingy then.'

'No problem, sir. I'll be back in a minute.' I whisk away the substandard pastry and Freddie winks as I pass. It's always a treat to find we'll be working together. I felt lucky, back in the early Nineties when we trained together, and I still feel lucky now, at fifty years old – even as the foot-sanding woman glares at me as she disembarks.

'Have a great day,' I say cheerily, ever polite and professional with my BudgieAir smile: the brightest smile in the sky.

I catch up with Hannah when I'm home. My uniform has already been swapped for tracksuit bottoms and a saggy sweater, my make-up thoroughly cleansed away. She's on her way home from work, walking from Mile End tube station to her shared house; it's when she tends to call. My only child left home three years ago, jumping straight from college here in Glasgow to a junior job with a podcast production company in London. She has already been promoted to an assistant producer role. Although I miss her terribly I couldn't be more proud of her.

'I've got a date tonight, Mum,' she tells me.

'Really? That's exciting. Who with?'

'Just someone I've been chatting to.' I catch the smile in her voice. 'You know what?' she adds. 'You should do something fun to take your mind off stuff at work.' She knows all about our rival airlines shedding staff and, in some cases, ceasing to operate. No one's been gloating about this. We're horribly aware that, while a determined beach lover will always prioritise their fortnight in the sun, post-pandemic an awful lot of people are choosing to stay closer to home. Who'd have imagined that drizzly Britain, with our chips and midges, would be so appealing?

'Like what?' I ask, although I know exactly what she's hinting at. Lately, my daughter's been on at me to at least be open to meeting someone. There's been the *very* occasional adventure over the years, on a layover far, far from home. This industry is rife with flings and shenanigans in resort

7

hotels around the world. But it's been at least a couple of years since I've even *kissed* anyone properly, and apart from a brief relationship three years ago I've been single for pretty much forever.

Hannah's dad and I weren't even together in the conventional sense – although I do count Rod as one of my very best friends. We'd been great mates, and flatmates for a time, at college. Sometimes that had tipped into flirtation but he was never short of attention from girls so I assumed he just regarded me as a friend. Then a few years on, we'd got it together after a party. Although we'd done a great job of laughing it off as a mad, drunken thing, that wasn't quite the end of it. At twenty-six, I was accidentally pregnant.

The truth is, being Hannah's mum and managing my work roster have consumed just about all of my energy over the years. And I've been happy, mainly, being able to do my own thing and not being answerable to anyone. However, things have felt a little different since she left home. We were always super-close, and I suppose it's hit me that now it's just me, who hasn't had a proper boyfriend since before Hannah was born. And maybe that *is* a little weird.

I also suspect that, since she moved out, Hannah's been worried about me being lonely. Maybe I am, very occasionally, when I'm not working over a weekend and everyone is busy doing cosy family things or going on dates or visiting the garden centre or whatever it is that normal, fully functioning people do. On occasion, Rod has teased me that I am actually married to BudgieAir, leaving no space for anyone else. And perhaps he has a point.

'You know what I'm talking about,' Hannah says now. 'Get yourself out there, Mum. It doesn't have to be anything serious. It can just be a bit of fun.'

'Oh, I don't think so, love,' I say firmly. 'With work and everything, I hardly have a minute—'

'You've always said that,' she teases. 'You've always blamed your job for never getting around to meeting anyone. But you know what?' She pauses. 'I don't think that's the real reason anymore.'

'What *is* the reason, then?' I'm intrigued as to what she has to say.

'It's doing it online, isn't it? Meeting someone through an app or a dating site—'

'Well, yes,' I say. 'I hate the thought of being judged by a little profile, and all the swiping and that. Which probably means I don't want it enough, doesn't it?'

'But that's how it happens these days,' she insists. 'It's what people *do*, Mum. I don't see why you're so resistant to it.'

I love our chats, and of course I don't mind my daughter talking to me as if I had been stored in a freezer since the era of dial-up internet and only just been thawed out. 'For your generation maybe, but not for me, Han. And people must still meet in the normal way.'

'This *is* the normal way now,' she insists.

'It seems so contrived, though.'

'It's just convenient and efficient. And it works! That's the whole point of technology, isn't it? To make life easier and better?'

'I'm not sure if it *is* better,' I start.

'Of course it is,' she says firmly. 'Imagine . . .' She pauses. 'Imagine you still had to write letters to people instead of messaging them.'

'Letters were nice,' I say, frowning. 'I loved having pen pals when I was a kid. I had Val in France and Bonnie in

9

Pennsylvania and a nice boy called Gino in Venice who I was completely crazy about—'

'That's sweet,' she says with a chuckle. Then: 'Remember that castle in the Highlands that you and Dad took me to when I was little?'

'Uh-huh?'

'And they had massive copper pans and a mangle in the kitchen?'

'Yeah?' I think I know where this is going.

'So, you're saying that instead of having a washing machine you'd rather wash your clothes in the sink and then mangle them?' Hannah retorts.

'I'd love that,' I tease her. 'It'd seem wholesome and quaint. Next time you come home there'll be a gap where the washing machine used to be and I'll have a huge, bulging bicep from all the mangling—'

'Great arm workout,' she sniggers.

'See? The old ways have benefits . . .'

'Are you still running, by the way?' she asks.

'Um, I wouldn't exactly call it that, but yes.'

'That's a really good thing to do. For stress, I mean,' she adds gravely. Since when did twenty-three-year-olds start counselling their mothers? 'And you really should get on some dating apps,' Hannah adds. 'How's it going to happen otherwise?'

I stretch out on the sofa and extract a cookie from the jar on the floor. 'I might just . . . *meet* someone one day?'

'Like in the films?' She is referring to the romcoms we used to love watching together, when it was just me and her, snuggled up with Meg Ryan, Jennifer Aniston and Owen Wilson – all our favourites – with a duvet across our laps and a plate of hot buttered crumpets between us. When it felt like nothing bad could happen.

'Like, she's in a bookshop,' Hannah reminisces, 'and she turns around and there's this hot man just standing there . . .'

'Or she's in the supermarket,' I add, 'and she collides with his trolley—'

'There was a lot of colliding in those days,' she says, sniggering.

'Well, there was no Tinder then. People had to crash into each other . . .'

'With an armload of books. She was *always* carrying books—'

'Or a Christmas tree.'

'Yeah.' She laughs. 'Oh, Mum, I loved all that and honestly, I wanted to believe it too. But be realistic. There's a far higher chance of liking someone you're matched with, rather than some random stranger you've just bumped into in real life.'

'That's kind of sad,' I announce.

'Why is it sad?'

'Because it makes it seem like nothing ever happens by chance anymore. Like there's no . . .' I hesitate, fishing for the right word.

'Magic?' Hannah suggests.

'Yeah, that's it. *Magic*. And I can't believe it doesn't exist—'

'It doesn't, Mum. Trust me. No one just happens to meet the love of their life in the street—'

'You mean I can't just wander around with a Christmas tree?'

'In May? If you want to look weird, yeah!' She's laughing

11

now, and there's a jangle of keys as she lets herself into her shared terraced house. I picture her flinging down her bag, catching up with her housemates in their cluttered kitchen and rushing upstairs to get ready for her date.

'Where did it all go, Han?' I ask her, sensing a pang deep in my gut.

'Where did what go?' she asks.

'The magic!'

She pauses and I hear her gently closing the front door behind her. 'We don't need it anymore, Mum. Magic's obsolete. We have algorithms now.'

CHAPTER TWO

Here he comes – the hot runner – bounding around the corner as if it's no effort at all. I replay yesterday's conversations with Hannah. *Hear that, honey? I keep spotting an extremely eye-pleasing man IN REAL LIFE.* I should get myself a pile of books! Or a Norway spruce!

Maybe I'm over-reacting to the sight of a pleasant-looking male, due to not having experienced anything remotely resembling a sexual frisson since that balmy layover at Hotel de Buenos Amigos in Malaga two years ago. But my regular sightings of this lean silver fox are at least livening up my otherwise torturous morning runs.

It goes like this. Pre-spotting Foxy I'm slumping along, thinking I might cut this thing short. But now miraculously, having sighted him, I instantly perk up on this cool May morning. *Look at me,* I'm trying to project. *I'm a proper runner, just like you, bounding along simply because I love it so!*

Some mornings he's out running with a friend but often, like today, he's alone. He's getting closer now. With my earbuds plugged in, I try to steady my breathing and look as if this is no effort at all. We smile and nod in recognition, the way runners do, as we pass.

God, he's dishy, as the teenage magazines used to say: well over six foot with one of those lean, lithe runner's bodies and a warm, wide smile. I can imagine him in an advert for a citrussy cologne for the mature man. Or cookware, maybe. He'd look good in a stripy apron, brandishing barbecue tongs, grappling a sausage.

Pushing such lewd thoughts aside I head home and get ready for work. When I started in this game it had taken what felt like forever to get out of the door. But these days I can go from zero to flight-ready in twenty-five minutes. Manicured, mascaraed and still feeling buoyant after my silver fox sighting, I drive out to the airport for one of those flights that goes like a dream: happy crew, everything running on time, passengers lively but untroublesome. There's a quick turnaround in Alicante before the home leg to Glasgow, where I grab an Americano and a bag of mini dark chocolate florentines – but only because they're on offer – to snack on as I make my way to the car park.

Once home, I call Mum, who lives a little further out in the suburbs, before Rod arrives with his grimy canvas tool bag. He lives a ten-minute drive away and is dropping off a blowtorch I've asked to borrow. I'm planning to strip down and repaint a pink wooden chair that Hannah reclaimed from the street. She went through a phase of dragging in abandoned furniture, with the intention of up-cycling it, but rushed off to London before any upcycling could be done.

Like me, Rod has been mainly single throughout our parenting years, apart from a two-year relationship with

Nesta – a history lecturer at Glasgow university – which ended mysteriously a couple of years ago. He didn't seem to want to discuss it. It was never on the cards for me and him to become a proper couple, even when we'd discovered I was pregnant. In a wave of thorough grown-up-ness we'd sat down and discussed how we'd do this thing; how we would raise our baby without living under the same roof.

We both felt it would be ridiculous to force ourselves to be together when we could do things *our* way. It wasn't the 1960s after all. Yes, I loved Rod, and he was (and still is) attractive – and very occasionally I'd yearn to snuggle close and even kiss him and, okay, sleep together again, because who could mean more to me than him? We were *friends*, I'd remind myself firmly – united forever by the daughter we'd made. And I wasn't prepared to do anything that might risk spoiling that.

'I'm really not sure about lending you this,' he remarks now, as if I am nine years old. 'Why can't you use paint stripper instead?' He rakes back his tousled salt-and-pepper hair and pulls the blowtorch, plus scuffed plastic goggles, from the bag.

'Because this'll be much quicker and it's better than those horrible chemicals,' I say.

Rod looks unconvinced. 'Okay, but don't put it anywhere near your face—'

'Oh, shouldn't I? I was planning to scorch off my facial hairs!'

'Yeah, I've heard that's the best way.' He grins and peers at me more closely. He has dark chocolatey eyes, a pleasantly worn-in face and wears old faded jeans and T-shirts with their logos almost laundered away; ironic, as he runs his own successful T-shirt printing company. 'You've got one right there, poking out of your chin,' he adds, smirking. 'Want me to get it for you?'

'No thanks,' I yelp, springing back.

'I'm surprised it's not picking up Radio Moscow . . .'

'It does at night. That's why I've left it.' Rod sniggers, and as he proceeds to instruct me on the blowtorch's usage, I make a mental note to perform a thorough check for further hairs in fierce daylight before my shift tomorrow. These menopausal sproutings are sneaky: easily missed when you look in a mirror, yet glaringly obvious to anyone else.

'Are you sure I can't I strip the chair for you?' Now Rod is eyeing the blowtorch again as if it's a hamster, and he's not sure if I'm up to looking after it properly.

'No, I'll do it,' I say firmly. 'I need a project to keep my mind off all this work stuff.'

'Oh, God, yeah.' Rod gives me a sympathetic smile. 'Macramé might be safer, Jen,' he adds.

'I'm perfectly capable of operating a simple tool, thank you.'

He pulls a wry look as he shrugs on his jacket. 'So you've used a blowtorch before, have you?'

'How hard can it be—'

'*Promise* you'll wear these, then?' he cuts in, indicating the safety goggles on the table.

I nod. 'I promise. Now you can stop implying that I'm a silly, fluffy little woman who can't operate a potentially lethal flame-throwing machine.'

'Would I *ever* do that?' Rod snorts, aware that he exasperates me sometimes. Yet it's comforting to know that he cares enough to worry about me setting myself on fire – and

16

anyway, this joshing is a ritual we have always had. If we were polite and respectful I'd worry that something was wrong.

As Rod hugs me briefly, getting ready to leave, my phone pings with a text notification on the table. I pick it up and frown as I read Freddie's message: *Have you seen email, Toots? Call me asap.*

Something thuds dully inside me. 'What is it, Jen?'

I'm aware of Rod speaking but I can't respond as I open my emails. I'm vaguely conscious of him looking concerned as I scroll through them. There are several from high street stores, including one from Ann Summers, who I must have bought something from back in the Stone Age, and now they're flagging up their 'vibrating crotchless thong – 50% off!' Don't they realise that having my underwear doing anything as untoward as vibrating would probably trigger a panic attack?

Onwards I scroll until finally I spot it:

From: *EDavenport@BudgieAir.com*
Subject: *IMPORTANT ANNOUNCEMENT*
BudgieAir
Budgie House
36–40 Beak Street
Leeds LS7 9PJ

Dear Jennifer,
 It is with enormous sadness *and regret that I write to inform you that BudgieAir is shortly to be put into administration. Therefore your position is redundant from immediate effect.*
 For further information please consult the Frequently

Asked Questions (FAQs) on Budgie World or call the redundancy helpline number below.

May I take this opportunity to thank you for your loyal service to BudgieAir and wish you the very best for your future.

Yours sincerely,
Elizabeth Davenport, CEO

BudgieAir. The brightest smile in the sky!

CHAPTER THREE

Helpline lady: *Hello, can I help you?*
Me, trying to form words: . . .
HL: *Hello?*
Me, frantically clearing throat: *Hellurghhurgh.*
HL, brightly: *Hi, how can I help?*
Me: *Erm, I've been trying to get through all morning . . .*
HL: *Yes, we've been really busy today I'm afraid. Have you received your email?*
Me: *Yes, um, it came yesterday . . .*

In fact the period between reading it last night and finally getting through to the helpline at lunchtime today has been a blur. Rod was incredibly kind, staying with me until I seemed to have gathered myself together. However, after he'd gone I sat up alone, drinking heavily, reading that damned email over and over. To further crank up my malaise I am now suffering from one of those nerve-shredding, mental-collapse-type hangovers.

19

HL, still perky: *I am sorry. Where are you, love?*
Me, voice wavering: *On the scrapheap.*
HL, sounding taken aback: *Erm, I mean, whereabouts were you based?*
'Were'. Christ – past tense already.
Me: *Glasgow.*
HL: *Cabin crew?*
Me: Yes. *For twenty-nine years.*
HL: *Oh, that is a long time, love. It's very hard, I know.*

She sounds older, I think; a kind middle-aged lady with a soft Yorkshire accent who uses a teapot, with a crocheted tea cosy, rather than the bag-in-mug method (I catch myself; of course I am middle-aged too).

Me: *Well, I took a couple of years out when I had a baby but it's all I've ever done and I just don't know . . .*

I blink away tears and try to wrestle my emotions under control. Christ, this hangover's evil. After I'd finished the wine, I made inroads into my dusty collection of spirits. I woke up this morning wearing yesterday's tracksuit bottoms and my bra.

HL: *It meant a lot to you. I can understand that.*
Me, quietly: *Yes.*
HL: *Okay, so the first thing to do is sort out your redundancy entitlement—*
Me: *I was obsessed with flying, ever since I was little girl, even though I'd never been on a plane before. I mean, we didn't have those sorts of holidays. We went camping in the Highlands or, or—*

20

HL, cutting in swiftly: *You'll find the link to the government's site in the FAQs. There's everything you need to know about—*

Me: *Then my dad bought this sailing boat on a whim and made me and Mum and my brother go out on it, and he took us on this terrifying trip in a storm –* Stop it! Stop rambling to this stranger, you lunatic! *– and we sailed through Corryvreckan. Have you heard of that?*

HL: *Erm, I don't think so . . .*

Me: *It's off the west coast of Scotland.*

HL: *Really? That sounds nice—*

Me: *Corryvreckan? It's not nice at all. It's terrifying. It means 'cauldron of the speckled seas'—*

HL: *Oh!*

Me: *There are actual whirlpools. It's the most dangerous bit of sea around Britain.*

HL, sounding baffled: *So why would anyone go there?*

Me: *Dad thought we might see minke whales.*

HL: *And did you?*

Me: *No. We didn't see anything apart from my brother being sick and Mum crying and the boat nearly capsizing. They got divorced soon after—*

HL, cutting through my insane rantings: *So, as I was saying, you'll find everything in the FAQs . . .*

Me: *Like it's that simple!*

HL, sounding startled: *Sorry?*

Me, hyperventilating now: *It's not all there, is it, in the FAQs? A new job's not there. Any chance of finding anything else I can do at fifty years old isn't there—*

HL: *FAQs means Frequently Asked Questions . . .*

Me, too loudly: *I know what FAQ means!*

HL: *There's no need to take that tone.*
Me: *I'm not taking any tone—*

Stop ranting, I order myself silently. This isn't her fault. She's just a lady at a call centre doing her job.

HL, whose 'tone' has veered towards the decidedly brittle: *It would help if you could remain calm.*
Me: *I am calm. I am.*
HL, inhaling audibly: *Okay. So with all your experience you're perfectly placed for other client-facing careers . . . What if I don't want another client-facing career? . . . And you might want to start thinking about your transferable skills.*
Me, trying to steady myself with calming breaths and wondering if, in fact, I am still drunk: *Uh, yes, I'll do that.*
HL: *In your line of work you have so many. What comes to mind, off the top of your head?*

I look around my living room, my gaze landing upon my shoulder bag, which for some reason is lying on the floor, its contents strewn: screwed-up tissues, a lidless lipstick, a pressed powder compact (cracked, perhaps stood on?), a sole Lindor chocolate, loose chewing gum pellets, the wrapper from one of those rocky road bars from the airport kiosk (which I am apparently addicted to) and a tampon which, considering that my last period was nearly a year ago, is probably as redundant as I am.

Me: *I'm organised.*
HL: *Great. And you've held down a highly responsible role . . .*

Now I've calmed down slightly, I'm detecting an acrid smell – like something burnt. Did I blunder out for cigarettes last night? Surely not; I quit smoking twenty-four years ago when I found out I was pregnant. Maybe I burnt some toast? Still clutching my phone, I stride through to the kitchen where various sticky-looking bottles are still sitting out: raspberry gin, watermelon vodka and strawberry tequila – all pink and marketed as 'ladies' drinks', grabbed on special offer at duty-free around the world. Empty crisp packets, broken pretzels and several smeared wine glasses litter the worktop (how many drinking receptacles does one person need?), plus a block of cheddar, which appears to have been hacked at with a blunt instrument. It looks like the scene of a teenagers' illicit party, before the rapid clearing up that's necessary before the parents come home.

Helpline lady is chattering on about how I might 'use this time to retrain, to up your skill set'. I'm trying to listen, but finding it hard to focus as I prowl around my flat, investigating the source of the smell. I step into Hannah's old bedroom. Something has definitely happened in here because the pink wooden chair – the one she dragged in from the street – has been repositioned to the centre of the room. Curiously, it looks as if someone has tried to burn it. No, they *have* burnt it. I blink at it, trying to work out what has happened here. Rod's blowtorch is lying on the floor beside it. There are no goggles in sight.

HL, continuing: . . . *So, what I suggest is, in your own time* – 'Please get off the line' is what she means – *start to think about what you have to offer. It's important to be open-minded and think outside the box . . .*
Me: *I'll do that. I'll think outside the box.*

23

HL, cheerily: *Great! And we're planning some online sessions to help with dusting off your CV, making a good impression at interview, that kind of thing. So do keep checking the site.*

Me: *Yes, I'll do that.*

HL: *Well, thanks for calling. I wish you the best of luck. Goodbye.*

I don't know what I expected – a miracle maybe? – but I'm awash with disappointment as I march back to the living room. So this is it, I reflect as I gather up all the detritus from my bag. After nearly three decades of flying I am officially grounded, without the faintest idea of what the heck to do next.

CHAPTER FOUR

Rod comes over again late that afternoon. Dear, caring Rod, who doesn't witter on about transferrable skills but just listens patiently and tries to reassure me that everything will be okay. However, I did know he'd lecture me if he saw the state of Hannah's chair, with one of its arms and its whole seat blackened. So, prior to his arrival, I opened all the windows and shoved the offending item back into position in a corner of her room, with an embroidered throw draped over it (not that Rod is likely to go in there but I don't want to risk it). I have also put away his precious tool, plus the booze bottles, and tidied up my entire flat. Finally, like someone banishing all traces of evidence at a crime scene, I showered thoroughly in case the smoky smell had stuck to my hair. By the time he arrived, no one would have guessed I was drunk and in charge of a blowtorch last night.

'The helpline lady told me off about my tone,' I tell him, as we drink tea.

'What kind of tone did she expect you to have?' he asks loyally.

'I know. It wasn't as if I was shouting or anything.'

'I'm sure you weren't.' He casts me a quick I'm-sure-you-were-actually look. I smile, grateful that he's here, and not just because my fellow redundant budgies have scattered far and wide (Freddie and his husband have headed up to their little cabin up north – 'Need to get away from all this, Toots,' he'd said – and our best friend Leena has gone to lick her wounds at her sister's down south). I'd have called Rod anyway. He's like that familiar sweater you pull on, knowing it'll always feel comfortable and right.

Rod sets his mug on the kitchen table and twitches his nose. 'Did you do some drunk cooking last night?'

I frown. 'No, why?'

'I'm sure I can smell something. A kind of burnt smell.'

'That's probably just my toast from earlier.'

He gets up from the chair and scans the kitchen like a man from the gas board – is there still such a thing as the gas board? – trying to ascertain whether there's a leak. 'I can definitely smell something, Jen.'

'It's probably coming from outside,' I say, glancing at the window, which is still open. Rod juts his head out in order to continue his investigations, then turns back to me.

'No, I don't think it is.'

'Let's not worry about it,' I say quickly.

He frowns, as if it's still bothering him as he pulls on his jacket. I follow him out into my unlovely magnolia hallway.

'So, what're you doing tonight?'

'I'm not sure. I don't think anyone's around.'

'Give me a call if you like, if you're fed up.'

'I will, thanks.' I smile. 'And thanks for coming over.'

'No problem—' He breaks off as his gaze slides towards

the door of Hannah's room; the door I'm cursing myself over for leaving open. Because the smell is definitely still evident here and, like a sniffer dog at the airport, Rod is hot on the scent.

I trail in after him as he heads straight to the chair in the corner and whips the throw off it. 'What're you doing?' I exclaim.

'For God's sake, Jen,' he mutters as he examines the scorched wood. 'That's bloody dangerous, what you've done here—'

'Yes, I know.' I stare, contrite, at my feet.

'I shouldn't have trusted you with it!'

'You're like an angry science teacher,' I mutter, 'when someone's been running amok with a Bunsen burner.'

'Yeah, because you have! I'm taking it back—' He looks around the room. 'Where is it?'

'Don't take it. I'll be much more careful next time.'

'Please, just give it to me—'

'You're going to confiscate it?' I ask, aware that perhaps I am not being entirely reasonable.

'How can I confiscate something that's actually mine?' His mouth starts to quiver as he tries to trap in a laugh which, ridiculously, triggers my tear mechanism, as if he's laughing, cruelly, at me – which of course he isn't. His face falls. 'Oh, Jen. I'm sorry. Don't get upset.' He steps towards me but I skitter back, away from him.

'I was drunk. I know it was a completely mad thing to do.' I shove back my lank and unwashed long hair and rub at my face. 'I'm a disaster,' I go on. 'I'm an idiot. I know that. I just don't know I'm going to do—'

'Hey, hey, hey . . .' Now his arms are around me and he's pulled me to his chest, and I'm properly crying like a big weeping kid onto his soft T-shirt that smells so comfortingly of him.

'I didn't wear the goggles,' I choke out. 'I didn't take the proper safety measures.'

He pulls back and looks at me with such kindness that it triggers a fresh sprouting of tears. 'That's because you're a reckless maniac.'

'I know,' I choke out. He perches on the edge of our daughter's bed that's still made up with her favourite duvet cover – geometric spirals of purple and blue – and motions for me to sit next to him. I plonk myself down and blot my wet eyes with my sweater sleeve.

'You know what I think?' he says gently.

I shake my head.

'I think you should get away for a little bit.'

I look at him, knowing he means well but that's not what I need. 'I'm hardly in the mood for a holiday,' I murmur. 'Although I do still have that Santorini prize. I wonder if they'd let me exchange it for money now that I don't have a salary anymore? I could do with it. I wonder how much it's worth—'

'Never mind that now,' Rod says firmly. 'I didn't mean a holiday anyway, unless you want that.'

'No, I really don't.' I shake my head.

Gently, he pushes a strand of hair from my face. 'I just mean a little break from this place . . .' His gaze rests momentarily on the blackened chair. 'How about a few days away with Han? Don't you think that'd do you good?'

'Oh, I don't know if I'm up to a trip to London,' I say quickly.

'You'd be fine.'

'I'm just not sure I'm in a fit state to be out in public,'

I add. 'And anyway, she's probably busy.' A trace of self-pity has crept into my voice.

'Well, you could ask her at least, couldn't you?'

I rub at my eyes as we get up and head into the hallway. 'I can't stop crying, Rod. I mean, I keep having these outbursts when I don't expect them. And I wouldn't want to make an arse of myself in front of Hannah and her friends, all those gorgeous people from her work—'

'You don't have to see them, do you?' Rod suggests. 'It doesn't have to be a big social thing if you're not up to it. You could just hang out with Han and eat nice food, maybe see a film or something. Keep it low-key.' His presence is having a calming effect now, like tea and toast and a hot water bottle in a furry cover; all the comforting things. Sometimes I don't know where I'd be without him.

'I'm just not sure I'd be much fun,' I say.

'C'mon,' he says, giving me another hug at the door. 'You don't have to be fun. You're not a party entertainer, are you? You're her *mum*.'

CHAPTER FIVE

It's not just Hannah and me in the bustling bar in Hackney where I find myself the following Friday night. There's also Indie, a producer at the podcast company, plus Cass, the 'audio geek' and Jacob, the assistant, whose boyish enthusiasm lends him a puppyish air. Everyone is in their twenties. They're at the start – not the abrupt end – of their careers.

Hannah had asked, tentatively, whether I was up to an evening with her friends. 'I'd love that,' I'd said, not remotely in the mood for a group thing but realising that their Friday night out has become something of a fixture, and not wanting to seem lame. And now, at a table crammed with cocktails and dishes of chips and dips and toasted cornbread, I'm glad I did.

Although everyone's been hugely sympathetic about my redundancy, I haven't wanted to dwell on it tonight. For the past week I've felt sick with fear – not only over my precarious financial situation (I've never been sensible enough to amass more than meagre savings) but also because, without my job, I don't know who I am. But Rod was right,

I realise now. Getting away was precisely the right thing to do. It certainly feels better than drowning my sorrows at home and spending hours on calls with friends, lamenting our situation and endlessly speculating on whether a buyer might appear, magically, for BudgieAir – literally out of the blue. We haven't yet been able to accept that it's over; that our beloved airline will go the way of Woolworths and Pick 'n' Mix counters, to gradually fade away into the past. But here in London, with Hannah and her friends, I've managed to shove the wretched business to the back of my mind, at least for now.

'I've been saying you should start dating, Mum,' she says, and everyone nods in agreement, insisting how easy it is, how it can just be fun.

'Oh, I don't know, Han.' I look around the table. 'I've never done it online or with an app or anything like that.'

'Why not?' Jacob asks, looking genuinely curious.

'Mum's literally had her head in the clouds for the past thirty years,' Hannah says with a chuckle.

I grin. 'She's right really. That's why so many flight attendants end up with other flight attendants or pilots. There's hardly a chance to meet anyone else.'

'That never happened to you?' Cass asks, leaning forward.

I shake my head and sip my deliciously sharp concoction of gin and fresh lime. 'It can all get a bit messy if it doesn't work out and you still have to fly together.'

'You should try some dating apps,' Indie says firmly. 'Everyone does it.'

'Yeah, even my mum,' Jacob explains, and I can't help smiling at that. 'She's having a brilliant time,' he adds. 'Honestly, she's the expert on it. You should talk to her about it—'

31

'And Mum's got this prize that she's never taken,' Hannah cuts in. 'A holiday for two in a honeymoon suite in Greece—'

'I've told you, I want to take you!' I exclaim.

'No way,' she says, laughing, as she turns to Jacob. 'What am I going to do with her, Jay?'

It's something of a relief when the conversation swerves onto workplace gossip. Their enthusiasm is infectious, and I'm fascinated to see Hannah in her natural habitat, with her friends. She seems to have grown up even more – even though we FaceTime regularly – since she popped up to Glasgow for a visit back in February. There's a new assuredness about her after three years in London; enough time to establish new friendships and put down roots of her own. She is tall, like her dad (at barely five foot four I only just made the minimum height requirement for flight attendants) and has cut her once long, light brown hair to a jaw-length bob and dyed it a glossy cherry red.

Now the talk has turned to everyone's love lives. All four are casually dating; no one seems concerned with meeting a serious partner anytime soon. It all seems wonderfully free and I feel flattered that they feel able to chatter away with me being here, as if I am just a normal person – rather than a parent. It's just gone nine-thirty when I sense a slight change around the table as Jacob comes back from having nipped outside, presumably for a cigarette. Now he and Hannah are whispering and sniggering conspiratorially while glancing towards the main door.

'What're you two up to?' I ask, buoyed up by three cocktails now.

'Nothing,' Hannah says blithely. I catch her exchanging glances with Indie and Cass and sense that something is afoot.

Indie adjusts her chunky spectacles and laughs. 'Tell her, Han.'

My daughter glances at Jacob, her face breaking into a wide grin as he swivels towards the door again, clearly struggling to maintain a neutral expression. They're all in on some plan here, and with a bolt of alarm it hits me what they're trying to do.

No, please not that. It's only a week since I lost my job, and I'm not sure I can handle it.

'Han, what's going on?' I ask lightly.

She smiles, feigning innocence. 'What are you talking about, Mum?'

'Come on, darling. I know there's something. Please tell me what it is . . .' I'm trying to be brave, and bracing myself for the fact that this lovely evening might be about to take a terribly embarrassing turn. I scan the room, barely aware of the server who clears our table, and another who brings us a fresh round of cocktails.

I glance down as he lifts each glass from his tray. There are six this time, rather than five. 'Han, this isn't funny,' I blurt out with a note of panic.

'Mum, just relax!' Hannah commands.

I inhale deeply and sip my drink in the hope that it will steady my thumping heart. *Please don't say they're setting me up.* If they are, who the hell is it? Some older man they know through their company? Or – God forbid – one of their dads?

'Erm, I think there are too many drinks here,' I start, but Hannah grabs my hand across the table and beams at me.

'No, there aren't,' she says firmly. 'And please stop looking so panicked, Mum. There's just someone coming who we'd like you to meet.'

33

CHAPTER SIX

Fabriana, 61

She swishes in with long silver hair flowing, wearing a neat back leather jacket, a snug-fitting soft cerise sweater and a knife-pleated black skirt, plus boots. Reed-slim, she must be nearly six feet tall. The clientele here are pretty much Hannah's group's age yet heads swivel as she passes.

'Hey, lovely!' she exclaims as Jacob leaps up and embraces her.

'Hey, Mum. Really glad you could come.' He grabs her a chair from a nearby table.

'Me too.' Fabriana beams around at us all through Jacob's speedy introductions; it seems she's met only Hannah before tonight. I have already gathered that Jacob hadn't nipped out for a cigarette, but to invite her to join us. 'Everyone calls me Fabs,' she explains with a dismissive flap of her hand as I try not to seem too overawed, as if I meet women like this all the time. It turns out that she's a model, originally from Argentina, but had met Jacob's father (whom I quickly learn has been long out of the picture) here in London, where she has lived for thirty years. 'My career's had a surprise resurgence,' she says with a throaty laugh, when I ask her about it. 'With the whole diversity thing they're all desperate to wheel out the old codgers like me.'

I smile. With her husky tones she manages to make *old codgers* sound highly alluring and sexy.

'I'd hardly call you that,' Hannah insists.

Fabs chuckles. 'Well, I count my lucky stars every time a job comes in.'

'Mum was in the *Sunday Times* last week,' Jacob announces proudly, 'and the Marks & Spencer Christmas campaign . . .'

'I'm just having a lucky streak,' she cuts in. 'Give it a few months and it'll be adverts for stairlifts and incontinence pads.' We all laugh as she takes an enthusiastic sip of her whisky sour. Jacob is obviously familiar with her preferred tipple. 'Anyway,' she adds, turning to me, 'd'you know what my dream job was, when I was a little girl?'

'No?'

'An air hostess,' she announces, adding quickly, 'although I'm pretty sure you're not meant to call them that?'

'Oh, it doesn't matter,' I say. 'We tend to say flight attendant, or cabin crew, but it's all the same thing and anyway,' I add with a shrug, 'I'm not one anymore. I worked for BudgieAir and they've just gone under. So I'm a *redundant* budgie.'

She nods gravely. 'You're grounded, darling. Yes, Jacob told me. I'm so sorry to hear that.'

'I'll survive,' I say.

'I'm sure you will.' She takes another sip from her glass. 'He also said you're thinking about dating? Getting on the websites, the apps, all of that?'

'Oh, I'm really not sure—' I start, taken aback.

'Trust me, it's the best way,' Fabs says firmly, whipping out her phone from her black patent bag. We all huddle round as she flips from app to app and site to site; there's a dazzling array and, unsurprisingly, a whole stack of fawning messages.

'My God,' I murmur, peering at the screen. 'There's so much here. So much to keep on top of. It must be like having another job.'

She chuckles. 'It's best to spread yourself around, so to speak. To cast the net widely. If you were looking for an outfit for a special occasion, would you go to just one shop?' Actually, yes. Having to maintain such a high standard of grooming for flying has made me extremely laissez-faire in my approach to fashion. But I understand her logic, and as she flicks through the profiles of some admittedly attractive men, my interest is piqued.

'I'd never get this kind of response, though,' I remark.

'Why not?' She frowns at me.

'Because you're . . . well, you're you. And I'm *me*.'

'Don't be crazy, Mum,' Hannah retorts.

'You'd get tons of attention,' Indie insists.

'But what if I didn't? Or what if I got the wrong kind of attention, like the penis pictures you hear about—'

'Who says that's the wrong kind of attention?' Fabs asks with another husky laugh. 'I got one of those last Christmas and the thoughtful man had tied a bit of tinsel around it. Very festive, I thought.' She turns to me and beams a big, bright smile. 'I'm telling you, Jen, you need to get yourself signed up. You're in for *such* an adventure.'

*

36

She regales us with tales from her dating life as we leave the bar and head for a jazz club a few streets away. As Indie and Cass decided to call it a night, now it's just Hannah, Jacob, Fabs and me.

We hear about the man who'd recorded seven albums of himself playing his banjo back in lockdown and expected her to listen to them all. ('Darling, I don't have time in my life for *one* album of banjo music!') Then there was the driving instructor who kept prefixing things unnecessarily with the word 'woman': 'You know when men do that?' she continues. 'It was all, "I used have this terrible *woman*-boss. She stressed me out so much I went to the doctor – it was a *woman*-doctor . . ."'

'No one says *man*-doctor,' Hannah retorts.

'Exactly,' says Fabs with a snort. Then there was the man who was clearly married, as he would only call her when he was out of the house. 'When I challenged him he insisted he *was* at home, when there were clearly audible traffic noises . . .'

'Mum, you're meant to be encouraging Jen,' Jacob reminds her. 'Not putting her off.'

'Oh, I've met some lovely ones too,' Fabs says, her dark eyes shining. 'But it's kind of boring to talk about those.' In fact, I can't imagine anything Fabs talked about being boring. She has the kind of rich, expressive voice that could make a boiler instruction booklet sound fascinating. 'Didn't you meet lots of men through your job?' she asks. 'Through travelling, I mean?'

'Once in a blue moon,' I tell her. 'And I did have a sort of relationship, if you could call it that, a few months after Hannah left home . . .'

'Was that through work?' she asks.

'Um, no.' I grimace at the thought of it. 'He came to sort out an issue with my flat.'

She leans closer, eager for details. 'A plumber?'

'No,' I say, laughing now. 'I was doing a lot of long haul at the time and I kept seeing the odd mouse when I came back. I'd set traps and Rod, Hannah's dad, had offered to lend me his cat for the odd overnighter—'

'Well, *my* cat,' Hannah cuts in with a grin.

'Yes, love. Your cat. But I decided to contact the council instead, and they sent a man over.'

As Hannah falls back into her chat with Jacob, I tell Fabs about handsome, flirtatious Marc with his kitbag of poisons, which he'd tipped into trays and hidden behind the kickboards in my kitchen. She sniggers as I describe how, while I made him coffee, he said, 'You need to figure out where your entry points are and plug them with steel wool.'

'Erotic,' she exclaims.

'It really was. Then he said he thought I had an infestation and he'd be back in a couple of weeks to check the bait.'

While Hannah and Jacob are locked in conversation, I tell Fabs how he'd asked me for a drink on his next visit and we'd started seeing each other. Admittedly, we hadn't had tons in common but we did have fun, and the sex had been exciting enough to propel me into buying an extensive array of lingerie. 'Rod thought it was hilarious,' I add, 'that I was seeing someone from the environmental health department.'

'Pretty useful, I'd say!' she says.

'If you're prone to rodent visitations, then yes.'

'So, what happened?'

I shrug. 'After four months or so he stopped calling and just ignored my messages. So I s'pose you'd say he ghosted me.'

'That's *so* rude.' She frowns as we arrive at the small basement club, tucked away down a narrow side street. 'There's no excuse for that.'

'Oh, I was soon over it,' I say truthfully as we trot down the iron staircase together. 'And the good news was, the mice cleared off too.'

Inside the club a woman in a black sequinned dress is crooning Billie Holiday songs backed by a jazz band in Forties-style suits. The venue is charming despite being worn around the edges – or perhaps because of it. The four of us find a table towards the back of the room and sit in rapt silence, sipping yet more cocktails, until the band takes a break.

'So, d'you have any tips for Mum?' Hannah asks Fabs.

She considers this for a moment. 'The main thing is to be specific about the kind of man you're looking for. It's far better than a scattergun approach.'

'But I thought you'd signed up to lots of different sites?' I remark.

'Yes, but they're all specialist ones,' she clarifies. 'I meant, home in on those who share your interests. That way, you know you'll have something in common and you're more likely to get good matches.'

'What kind of specialist sites,' I venture, 'if you don't mind me asking?'

''Course not,' she says. 'I love dancing competitively, so there's that – and horse riding and wild swimming. And I read a lot, so I'm on one for bookish types, and I love going to art galleries, so—'

'Is there really a dating site for horse lovers?' I exclaim.

'There's one for pretty much everything,' she insists. 'And

the good thing about signing up to a whole range is that you can leave certain sites alone for a while.' She smiles broadly. 'It's like EU fish stocks. You have to let them replenish.'

Jacob breaks off from his conversation with Hannah and looks round at us. While the two of them have been chatting away, Fabs and I seem to have paired up, like two strangers at a wedding reception, when you're overjoyed to have found yourself seated next to a prospective new friend.

'We're not in the EU anymore, Mum,' Jacob reminds her.

'It's the theory I'm talking about,' Fabs retorts. 'Stocks can dwindle.'

'And you can end up rooting about among the bottom feeders,' he remarks, and we all laugh.

'What kind of specialist sites could you sign up to, Mum?' Hannah asks.

I try to dredge up some thrilling hobby that I might share with potential matches. 'Honestly, I have no idea.'

'Well, what d'you love more than anything else?' Fab asks.

'Eating?' I reply, meaning it as a joke.

'There you go, then,' Fabs says with a note of triumph. 'That's a starting point . . .' She whips out her phone again and prods at it impatiently with a scarlet nail. 'No signal down here. Oh, I wish we could get you signed up now—'

'This might not to be best time,' I venture, thinking: why can't I horse ride or dance competitively? Christ, I'm fifty years old! What have I been *doing* with myself all these years, apart from working? What transferable skills do I actually have? As the band reappears, I glance at Fabs with her wide, red-lipsticked smile. She is clapping now, radiating joie de vivre as she swings round to murmur into my ear. 'Promise me you'll sign up and tell me how you get on?'

'I promise.'

'And you're up for adventure?'

'Yes,' I say, giddy from the cocktails and just *being* here – 400 miles from my everyday life.

'And let's stay in touch,' she adds. 'I want to hear about *everything*.'

I can't help smiling at that. And as the singer steps back onto the stage, her dress a twinkly constellation under the dim lights, I'm propelled back to the magical night when I won the Golden Budgie award; when I thought my life was the best it could possibly be. I can hardly believe I'll never board another BudgieAir flight, and that that part of my life is over. But maybe there *is* something out there for me – something new and different and maybe even a little scary, in a good way, to shake things up. It won't give me my job back but maybe, until I figure out what my future holds, a little adventure is precisely what I need.

CHAPTER SEVEN

I'm always fantastically impressed whenever Hannah takes me to a delightful coffee shop off the beaten track. But this is her home and of course she knows all the interesting places. On this gloriously sunny Saturday we stop off at a Lebanese café for lunch, where Hannah insists I must try the char-grilled chicken and pickles crammed into warm flatbreads.

In the afternoon we wander around a gallery of contemporary paintings bursting with colour and joy, where I buy art postcards to bring home and lose in a drawer somewhere. Later, as the afternoon slips towards a cooler evening, we sit on a bench and tuck into some kind of sensational focaccia/pizza hybrid covered in melting goat's cheese, roasted red onions and thyme. Clearly, I am *carbing* my way out of redundancy gloom.

For the evening part of our itinerary Hannah has wangled free tickets for the theatre (such a pleasure to follow along with her plans, without having to make decisions about anything). The play is a creepy horror and is utterly gripping. At one point I even scream.

'That was amazing,' I enthuse as we leave. 'I was terrified!'

'So I noticed,' Hannah teases. 'And so did everyone else.'

I chuckle. 'Sorry about that.' I look at her as we step into the tube station. 'I can understand it with films, the way you get swept along and forget everything else.'

'It's the suspension of disbelief, Mum.' She smiles as we travel down on the escalator. 'I love seeing you like this,' she adds. 'All happy again, I mean.' She pauses. 'I've been worried about you, with all the job stuff. Since the redundancy especially. But I know you're going to be okay.'

'Do you?' I ask, smiling too.

'Yes, Mum,' she says firmly as we step onto the train. 'I really do.'

Later that night, tucked up again in Hannah's bed – she's insisted on giving me her room, while she sleeps on the sofa bed in the living room – I notice that Fabs has texted me. *So enjoyed meeting you last night. You might not be flying anymore but I know you will again very soon!*

Thank you, I reply. *You can't imagine how much you've lifted me.* If dating were as easy as this, I reflect as I click off the bedside lamp, I'd sign up instantly.

'So, what d'you reckon about checking out some dating sites?' Hannah asks next morning as we browse the flower stalls at Columbia Road market. 'Some niche ones, I mean, like the ones Fabs is on?'

'I'll think about it,' I say. The heady scent of char-grilled lamb drifts from a Turkish café, and as the crisp, bright morning slides into a golden afternoon, we can't resist tacos at a cheery Mexican place decked out with tissue paper garlands.

All too soon, we are picking up my wheeled case from her house, and she's accompanying me on the tube to Euston station. 'This has been brilliant,' I say as we make our way across the crowded concourse.

'I've loved it too, Mum. What did you like best?' She grins, catching herself sounding as if she's the mum.

'Everything,' I tell her truthfully. 'Hanging out with you. The market with all those lovely flowers. Meeting your friends. Meeting Fabs. The jazz club, the theatre and all the amazing food we've had . . . What was that called again, the flatbread and garlicky chicken?'

'Shish taouk.' We head down the slope towards the barrier where I fish out my ticket. 'Wish you were staying longer,' she adds.

'Me too. But you're working tomorrow—'

'You could've found stuff to do and then met me after-wards. Or you and Fabs could've hung out together.'

'I know, love. But when I booked my ticket I wasn't sure whether I was up to a London visit at all. It was Dad who persuaded me.'

'I'm glad he did,' she says. 'Give him a massive hug from me.'

'I will.' Hot tears spring into my eyes as we hold each other. 'I hate saying goodbye,' I add.

'Me too. I love you, Mum.'

'I love you too,' I say, wiping at my eyes and mustering a big wide smile as we let each other go, and I join the surge towards the train that will take me home.

It's fine, I remind myself as we pull out slowly from the station. It's the natural way of things that children grow up, fly the nest and make lives for themselves. Sometimes, it niggles me that I could have done better, as a mum – on the practical front at least. Hannah would be invited for

44

tea at friends' houses and I'd pick her up and see the results of their baking sessions set out on three-tier cake stands. There would be flapjacks and fairy cakes and, on one occasion, a gingerbread house with an intricately decorated exterior plus a rustic perimeter fence constructed from those Matchmaker chocolates that look like twigs.

In response – fuelled by a rare competitive urge – I'd supervised as the then seven-year-old Hannah and her friend Kaya had baked a chocolate sponge.

'That looks fantastic,' Kaya's mum enthused when she arrived. 'I didn't know you baked, Jen!'

'The girls made it,' I said.

'We used a cake mix,' Hannah explained, innocently.

Kaya's mum frowned. 'Oh, did you? I never use those. You never know what's in them, do you?' Well, you do actually, I thought, *because there's an ingredient list on the box*. Yet somehow, despite my shortcomings on the domestic front, Hannah has turned out just fine; a happy young woman doing a job she loves – which is, of course, as much down to Rod as anything I've ever done.

The train carriage is quiet, so I lift my laptop from my bag, figuring that I really should focus on my own job prospects now. I brought it with the intention of writing my CV and browsing job recruitment sites on the journey. But my head is too filled with my weekend with Hannah, and Fabs urging me to have adventures of the dating kind. So instead I google combinations of dating, food, and appetite.

Fabs was right; there are *tons* for singles who love their scoff. As the train rattles northwards I discover that they seem to fall into distinct sub-sets: the dietary choice sites (paleo lovers, gluten avoiders, vegans and raw-food-only

45

types); then the serious foodies drawn by their love of restaurants featured in the Sunday supplements. While I love to eat out, the idea of 'embarking on a food lover's voyage of discovery' is off-putting, as is the slogan: *Because you have impeccable taste.* Because I don't really. Yes, I loved the seafood feast we all devoured at a rooftop restaurant for Freddie's birthday last summer – but in the right circumstances (i.e. just home on a wet night, having tumbled off the return flight from Bangkok) there's nothing I love more than Dairylea slathered onto white toast.

When I try key phrases like 'loves food' and 'big appetite' in conjunction with dating, it propels me down a murky alleyway loosely entitled 'men who love big women'. Words like 'curvy' and 'buxom' spring out – which makes me wonder whether this is for me after all.

But then, I'm enticed by the idea of reporting back to Fabs that I've made some headway with this project. And the thought of having something fun to occupy myself, amidst the job hunting, definitely appeals. 'So, what are you looking for really?' Hannah had asked over coffee this morning, before her housemates had started to appear in the kitchen.

'Someone nice and non-weird, who I can have fun with,' I told her. And maybe it really is as simple as that. To have someone to do things – and share things – with.

I fetch a white wine from the shop and start to read up on the big sites; the ones with millions of members. I read accounts of online dating from women of my age and upwards, and learn that it's not unusual to be inundated by messages from much younger men; guys in their twenties, who profess to love older women – finding them sexy and smart. But whilst that might seem flattering, I'm not sure

I'd know what to *do* with a man of that age. What if he wanted to go clubbing? That was never my thing, even when I was younger; I far preferred sitting around a pub table with my friends, all chatting, laughing, drinking and shouting over each other.

I loved all the attention I was getting from younger men, one glamorous woman in her fifties explains, in an online discussion about midlife dating. *But then it dawned on me that it was a kind of fetishisation. Either that, or they simply wanted to tick off having done it with someone old enough to be their mum.*

I shudder and sip my not-quite-chilled-enough wine. The thought of seeing anyone who Hannah could potentially date is beyond awful. And I'm strongly averse to the idea of being on some bloke's to-do list: *Visit the Pyramids. Take a flying lesson. Shag an older bird.*

As a distraction I check my phone and spot a message from Freddie:

Seen the latest email from our dear former employers?

My heart lurches. Maybe a last-minute buyer's been found and we're not all redundant after all? But that hasn't happened. Instead, it's this:

From: EDavenport@BudgieAir.com
Subject: IMPORTANT ANNOUNCEMENT

Dear Jennifer,
    As you will be aware BudgieAir is now in receivership. I am writing to let you know that, if you have been in receipt of a prize of any kind, such as a holiday, this must be taken before December 31 of this year. Your flights will now be redeemable with EuroAir.

47

However beyond that date, prize holidays will no longer be honoured.

There are no cash alternatives to any prizes of this kind.

Yours sincerely,
Elizabeth Davenport, CEO

BudgieAir. The brightest smile in the sky!

There are plenty of people who'd come to Santorini with me, I remind myself. Leena would love it, and maybe Freddie and his husband Pablo could come too? We could go as a gang and hang the cost of the extra flights and another room. What would be more cheering, given what's happened to us all this year?

Now I'm thinking: or maybe I should ask Rod? No, that would feel *too* weird, I decide, almost immediately. We've been away with Hannah plenty of times, the three of us tucked up in tents and tepees and even budget hotel rooms – but Rod and I don't have a holidaying-together kind of relationship. Perhaps I could tempt Hannah? I picture us pottering around markets, tucking into perfect Greek salads and those delicious cheese pies, and sipping wine on the balcony overlooking the turquoise Aegean Sea. In all my years of flying I've never become jaded about going away. Beachside restaurants, cocktails, soft golden sand and sparkling seas; I love all the holiday things. Then I remember how adamant she's been that I must save it for 'someone special' – and anyway, tying her down to a holiday has been impossible since she moved away.

Sod it, I think. There must be *someone* who'll come on holiday with me. All in a rush, I go ahead and book the hotel, using my prize voucher – picking a week in October, not for any carefully thought out reason, but because it's fully booked until then. It's obviously a pretty special destination, judging by the rave reviews I'm now reading. I see now that some couples actually arranged their wedding dates around the honeymoon suite's availability.

It's even more beautiful than we'd imagined, I read. *It was blissfully romantic spending our days on the hotel's private sun-drenched beach.*

Well, Greece is still lovely slightly out of season, I remind myself. The tourists have dwindled and my currently unchosen holiday companion and I will be able to explore those ancient whitewashed villages without stepping aside to let the crowds go by. It'll be heavenly!

In a rush of enthusiasm, perhaps fuelled by tepid wine, I wonder now if these events were in fact *meant* to happen simultaneously; the email issuing a deadline to redeem my prize, and being harangued into dating by Hannah and her friends. Heck, maybe it's a sign that I should fling myself into this new adventure, with the aim of selecting a delightful man to take to Greece with me? I'm certainly not looking for someone to marry. Christ, no; but then, the suite's not only for honeymooning couples. It's just romantic and special.

A kind, sweet and sexy man with a valid passport is what I'm looking for, I decide. Perhaps he's out there right now, dithering over whether to sign up, just as I am, and we're destined to meet? Stranger things have happened. Who'd have imagined I'd have ended up dating the mouse man from the council?

I browse some more, focusing now on sites for 'mature daters': the 'silver singles', all of that. While they hardly have the pizazz of horse riding or wild swimming, I'm starting to warm to the idea of this grown-up age bracket. After all, I'm *in* it, even if I don't feel that way sometimes, and at least the men here won't be looking for younger women (which I've gathered is another common feature).

I buy another wine and read the success stories that feature on these sites. There are widowed people who'd never expected to meet someone special again, and others who had been single for decades, then dipped in a toe into the dating world and found someone wonderful. There are photos of couples in their fifties, sixties and beyond, looking blissfully happy at outdoor café tables and walking hand in hand on beaches. The overriding impression is that it's all very heart-warming, and no one would scream in horror on glimpsing a stretch mark or a sturdy bra.

There are still worrying aspects – such as, what if no one is interested in me? Or if I only attract the secretly marrieds and the penis pics?

No one meets in real life, Mum. It's all algorithms now. Hannah's right; I know it's smart and efficient, and that somehow I've failed to keep up with modern times. While I've hopped around the world, giving out smiles for free and clip-clopping through the distinctly unreal atmospheres of airport concourses, real life has marched on.

I continue to pore over the sites as if I'm cramming for an exam on twenty-first-century courtship rituals. So what if some creep sends me a dick pic? It won't jump out and bite me. I can just delete it. And if I don't enjoy the whole online experience, I can delete my profile too, and that'll be that.

It's not like the army, I remind myself. I won't be obliged to sign up for five years; there's no *commitment* needed here.

As I sip my wine and munch on my Mini Cheddars, a slightly different-looking site catches my eye. It looks less glossy and slick than the others. It could have been designed a decade ago and I'm wondering now if its retro vibe is in fact deliberate. There's something cosy and friendly about it, and it's aimed at daters of forty-plus.

Some of its members are featured. There's a couple in chunky sweaters and bobble hats, snuggling up together on a craggy rock in the Highlands. There are stories of couples who fell in love at first sight, and others whose relationships grew gently over time, from friendship to deep, lasting love. There's even a pair pictured strolling hand in hand along one of the famous volcanic black sand beaches . . . of *Santorini*. So I absolutely have to sign up, right?

With my heart thumping excitedly I start to create a profile, typing with the intense focus of writing a job application. The miles fly by, the Mini Cheddars are guzzled and the last drops of tepid sauvignon have been tippled from a plastic cup. And by the time we pull into Glasgow Central station I have completed my profile, selected my photos and am a fully paid-up member of maturematches.com.

CHAPTER EIGHT

Helpline lady: *Hello, how can I help?*

Me: *Hi, I just wondered if there's any new information coming up on the site?*

HL: *About your redundancy entitlement?*

Me: *No, I've checked that out already.*

After ranting away the first time I called, I've forbidden myself from complaining to this woman about the paltry payouts, and the stark fact that mine won't last me more than a few months. She didn't dish out the money, I remind myself.

HL: *Right. So all that's in order?*

Me: *Yes thanks. Well no, not really. I had to anaesthetise myself with a bottle of wine when I found out how tiny it was . . . Stop it! It's not her fault!*

HL: *I'm sorry, I—*

Me: *No, I'm sorry. That's not why I called. It's just, the last person I spoke to said something about online sessions to help with CVs and interviews – that kind of stuff?*

HL: *Yes, that was me.*

Me: *You're the same person? Sorry, I thought there'd be lots manning the phones—*

HL: *There are lots of us. But I remember you.* Did a beleaguered edge creep into that soft Yorkshire voice?

Me: *Really? Well, I'm actually calling about the CV advice you mentioned. I haven't been able to find a link to the online training session. And I wondered if I'd missed it.*

HL: *No, it's up there already.*

Me: *Oh, all I could find was a five-minute video of a woman saying really basic stuff, like make sure your information's up to date and your CV is nicely presented.*

HL, **after a pause:** *Yes, that's it.*

Me: *That's IT?*

HL, **tone firmer now:** *Yes.*

Me: *But . . . she said something about printing it out on a clean sheet of paper?*

HL, **tersely:** *Hmm-hmm?*

Me: *Um, well, I might be a little out of touch, but surely everyone emails their CV these days?*

Perhaps I'm wrong, I'm thinking now. Maybe you're expected to hand-deliver it, written on parchment, in a horse-drawn wagon to make yourself stand out?

HL: *Well, yes. But maybe they were just trying to cover all bases—*

Me: *If I do send out a printed version, it's kind of obvious, isn't it? That it should be on clean paper?*

And not splattered with chicken grease or have bits of jam doughnut stuck to it, I want to add, but stop myself.

53

HL: *You'd be surprised what people don't know.*

Me: *Really?*

HL: *Oh, yes. When I worked for another company we were still getting CVs sent in by post, and you wouldn't believe the state some of them were in.*

Me: *Really? I just thought it was a bit patronising, as if anyone might think that printing out their CV on the paper lining from a cat litter tray might get them the job . . .* I'm losing it again, I realise. Talking to this mild-mannered lady in a call centre in Huddersfield or wherever seems to send me a bit mad. *I'm sorry, I don't even have a cat, and I don't know if you put lining paper in litter trays. My daughter's cat lives with her dad and she won't use one. She does all her business at the bottom of the garden. The cat, that is, not my daughter—*

HL, **sounding bemused now**: *You get litter tray liners but they're not paper. They're a kind of polythene.*

Me, **chastened**: *Oh.*

HL: *So you wouldn't print out your CV on one of those.*

Me, **after a deep breath**: *I'm sorry. I know it's not your fault that BudgieAir went bust or that the CV advice on the website was rubbish. So I'll get on with writing it now, which I should have done yesterday. I had hours on the train and instead I was, well, I was doing other stuff—*

HL: *Applying for jobs?*

Me: *Actually, I was writing my profile for a dating site.*

HL, **brightening**: *Really?*

Me, **wondering what possessed me to tell her that**: *Yes.*

HL: *That sounds exciting!*

Me: *Well, that's what I'm hoping. I've never done it before. I'm probably the last person on earth to have never tried it. Anyway, sorry for ranting. You must be so busy taking calls—*

HL: *It's fine. You've cheered me up actually. I've had a pretty awful weekend . . .*

There's a small sound, like a barely audible gulp, or maybe it's just something in the background? She clears her throat.

Me: *Are you . . . okay?*

HL, briskly: *I'm fine, love. Can I give you some links to some better advice for updating your CV?*

Me: *Don't worry about that. I can find stuff myself. Are you sure you're all right?*

HL: *Yep, absolutely.*

There's another sound that's definitely a gulp, then silence; in fact, I wonder if she's cut me off. Who could blame her?

Me, cautiously: *Hello?*

HL: *I'm fine, love. I, er . . . I've just broken up with someone, that's all.*

Me, startled: *Oh God. I'm sorry—*

HL, all in a rush: *It's fine. It was long overdue and it's not even that. Can I help you with anything else today?*

Me, after a pause: *D'you mind me asking what your name is?*

HL: *I'm Sally.*

Me: *I'm Jennifer but everyone calls me Jen.*

Sally: *Hello, Jen. Now it's my turn to apologise, blurting that out.*

Me: *That's quite all right. You do sound a bit upset.*

Sally: *Well, yes, because he took my cat—*

Me: *Oh, that's awful!*

Sally, sounding riled now: *I thought he'd run away. My cat, I mean—*

Me: *He didn't tell you he'd taken him?*

Sally: *Not at first, no. He said he was coming round to pick up his stuff while I was at work. But Mr Sox isn't his. I found him in my shed as a newborn feral kitten and I've had him for fourteen years. And Gavin never wanted anything to do with him. He's not even that keen on animals. He just took him to spite me—*

Me: *You must've been so worried . . .*

Sally: *I was. Hours I spent, pacing the streets, asking neighbours and putting notices everywhere because it wasn't like him, you know? He liked going out, he loved prowling about in the neighbouring gardens, but he'd never not come home for his dinner. I kept picturing him lying somewhere, injured or dead . . .*

Me: *Your ex can't just do that, can he? I mean, how can he take something that belonged to you, or was owned jointly—*

Sally, dully: *Well, he has.*

Me: *But surely that's not allowed? I mean, if someone took the ironing board, you'd have a right to—*

Sally, shrilly: *He's a cat, not an ironing board!*

Me, mortified: *Yes, of course. And I'm not suggesting he's a thing. Like I said, my daughter has a cat. Casey's quite an old girl too. Hannah adores her—*

Sally: *You do get very attached.*

Me: *Yes, I realise that.*

Sally, clicking back into professional mode (I'm picturing her supervisor passing by, giving her a pointed stare; but maybe it doesn't happen like that and she's just remembered that

calls are recorded?): *So if there's anything else I can help with, regarding your CV or interview preparation?*

Me: *Erm, no. I think I'm all sorted, thank you . . . and I'm so sorry that's happened to you. I really am.*

Sally, briskly, obviously keen to wind this up: *Great. Well, have a nice day then. Goodbye.*

I'd planned to spend the morning cracking on with my CV. However, after Sally's revelation it takes a couple of large, strong coffees for me to wrestle my mind back to the matter in hand. Another distraction – on top of my indignance over Mr Sox – is the dating site and the delights and/or disappointments that might await me. However, I've made a firm vow not to be one of those people who obsessively checks for likes or messages in a needy way, as if I have nothing else to fill my empty days. Because my days are *full*. At least they will be once I have a respectable CV to send out. Then it'll be a whirl of interviews and a new job to start, and instead of that BudgieAir schedule dominating my life, I'll have regular hours and a shiny new workplace where no one will moan about their sausage roll or vomit into a little waxed bag. (Well, they *might*, but it won't be my responsibility to deal with it.)

Installed in front of my laptop now, I gawp at the blank screen, as if trying to stare it into submission, and figure out what to put on my CV.

Name: Jennifer Morton
Employment history: 1992 – one week ago: BudgieAir cabin crew
Interests: Eating, drinking
The end

Aware that that won't do at all, I try to recall my school exam results (as the certificates are lost), wondering if anyone really needs to know that I barely grasped the concept of photosynthesis thirty-three years ago yet managed to scrape a biology pass. While I do remember that I did better in English, French and history, things become a little woolly around home economics – although I have a disturbing recollection of incinerated rock cakes (more boulder than rock) and that when one was knocked one off the counter it actually *crashed* to the floor, like a missile, causing the teacher to scream. As for PE, 'Jennifer tries hard' was as good as it ever got on my school reports.

As the BudgieAir site has been spectacularly unhelpful, I google advice on writing a CV. A certain phrase keeps cropping up: 'How to make yourself stand out'. I have never *wanted* to stand out. I have been one of an army of hundreds of flight attendants, all identically dressed and adhering obediently to the strict rules about the height of our heels and the opacity of our tights. I never minded any of that. I liked that feeling of belonging, of being part of a team and knowing exactly what was expected of me.

When it came to writing my dating profile there was no shortage of tips on how to make myself 'stand out' in that way too. ('Make sure your unique personality shines through!') Part of me still wonders if it's better to let things happen naturally, and just meet someone in real life; yet I'm aware that if I sit around waiting for a job to 'happen naturally' I'll still be unemployed at seventy with my utilities cut off and having to forage for food in the nearby allotments.

Crunching on a biscuit, I browse websites offering career

suggestions for former flight attendants, which utilise our 'transferrable skills':

Hotel receptionist
Office manager
Personal assistant
Customer service manager
GP's receptionist

'Think outside the box,' Helpline Sally urged me the first time we spoke. So mentally, I add a few of my own:

Purveyor of upcycled furniture
Blowtorch operative
Alcoholic

Deciding that that's enough for one session, I switch my attentions to my emails instead, spotting one from the site.

Hi Jennifer,
  Here's your daily customised selection. You have 24 matches!

Wow! So many! Well, of course there are, I tell myself. That's what it does. It takes your keywords and there's some unfathomable jiggery-pokery like when you briefly check out underwear online, then every time you check your social media there's this great sea of knickers, until you google an embarrassing minor ailment and then you're hounded by itch-alleviating bum ointments for evermore.

It's algorithms. That's what they do.

But hang on; there's more. I see now that I have likes –

actual likes, from people who *like* me! While I was sleeping, or perhaps hearing about the outrageous catnapping of Mr Sox, my profile was being perused and the little heart was being clicked. And now seven messages are waiting for me!

CHAPTER NINE

From Pete, 51: *Hiya.*

That's it. That's all he's said. Am I supposed to reply with a 'Hiya' too, or more of a 'Thanks so much for getting in touch, Pete. Hope you're well? I'm well. Let me tell you a bit more about myself . . .'

Nice Benny, 55: *Hey there.*
Dean: *HEY.*
TomBola, 54: *Great profile!*
Maz, 57: *Hi there a bit more about me what's your fav food I like fryed rice.*
Well, I like fried rice too (would that be enough to form a connection?) but now I can't shake off the image of him forking it into his face. Moving swiftly onwards . . .
Joel, 58: *You look nice massage me.*
Maybe he meant 'message'? Easy to mistype, of course.
Big Mac, 53: *Hi, tell me your favourite fantasy.*

I beg your pardon? I might possibly share it if someone were to press a knife to my throat but otherwise, no. Is this as good as it's going to get? I try to shrug off a niggle of disappointment as I skim the rest of the messages, which are all in a similar vein. Maybe this is the way it kicks off around here? With the message equivalent of a grunt?

Moving on to my matches, I study their profiles with a growing level of gloom. Dutifully, I'd filled out all of the questionnaire's sections and hadn't realised you could miss bits out. But here we have:

Dennis, 56. Height: *I'd rather not say.*
Occupation: *Computing.* Interests: *DIY, eating out.*
Luka, 58. Height: *5'8".* Occupation: *Retail.* Interests: *I'd rather not say.*
Smithy, 59. Height: *I'd rather not say.* Occupation: *I'd rather not say.* Interests: *I'd rather not say.*

Why all the secrecy? Maybe Smithy reckons he'll snag plenty of dates by looks alone. Yet his profile has only one photo (you can include up to six) in which he appears to be asleep with his head lolling back on a sludge-brown sofa. Or perhaps he's dead?

Is this it for me then: someone who's unwilling to divulge anything meaningful about themselves, or an actual corpse?

Leena reckons you should 'never judge a man by his sofa' when we meet up with Freddie later: three redundant budgies trying to boost each other as we embark on our job-finding missions. But naturally, my first steps into online dating must be discussed first.

'I'm not,' I insist, twirling a fork in my noodles. 'I'm

trying to be open-minded. But, y'know. I'd prefer them to be *alive*—'

'So picky, Jen,' Freddie sniggers as he flicks through my matches. I was relieved when they'd come back from their respective trips. There's a kind of comfort in knowing that they're around; that we're all in this together.

'If he won't divulge his height he's *tiny*,' Leena observes.

'Yes, possibly.' I pause. 'But I s'pose it's fair enough, not wanting to put your occupation . . .'

'If you're a judge or the chief of police,' agrees Freddie.

'It's this "Interests: I'd rather not say" bit that sounds creepy,' I add.

'They're just being lazy,' Leena suggests.

I look at her over the cluster of condiment bottles on the table. 'But how much effort does it take to put "baking" or "gardening" or something innocuous like that?'

'What did you put on yours?' she asks.

'Travelling,' I say with a rueful smile.

'And "I'd rather not say" doesn't suggest they enjoy baking or gardening, does it?' asks Freddie with a frown. 'I mean, it doesn't sound innocuous. It sounds more like they collect swords or axes or Nazi memorabilia—'

'Oh, God,' I groan. 'I don't know how I'm going to find my way through this.'

'There'll be some lovely people out there,' Leena says firmly. 'Some people just hate writing about themselves. They're terrible with words. Just message a few, give them a chance. It's a numbers game—'

'But you've stopped,' I remind her. 'You got sick of it, you said.' It's true; she tired of men implying she was 'too old' at forty-eight, or for them to look nothing like their photos, when they actually met. I'm aware that all of this

63

goes on: the ageism, the lying, the profile photos taken a decade ago before the belly expanded and the hair turned grey. I suppose I've been hoping the Mature Matches community might be a more honourable sort.

'I'm just having a break,' she says. 'But I'll do it again, definitely.' Leena looks around at us, long chestnut hair gleaming, make-up as immaculate as she wore it for work. 'You've only just signed up,' she reminds me.

After our table's been cleared we study my matches again. Apart from the possibly deceased Smithy, several others are lounging on sofas in various degrees of consciousness. One unsmiling man is sitting in front of a shelf bearing a gigantic pot of antiseptic cream. Big Mac's toilet is clearly visible behind him, and Luka's sole photo – badly blurred, his face frozen in shock – might have been taken during his arrest.

'What gets me,' I remark, 'is these are the *best* photos they had.'

Now Leena and Freddie want to see *my* profile, prompting Freddie to observe, 'I like this photo especially, the one where you're ramming pizza into your face.'

'I'm not ramming it into my face. I'm holding it midway to my mouth.' I look at them and grin. 'I thought I looked happy in it. It was when I was with Hannah in London—'

'You do look happy,' Leena insists.

'You look gorgeous,' Freddie says loyally, giving my arm a squeeze. 'You're going to be massively popular on here.'

'Well, I read that it's a good idea to include an action shot,' I say, chuckling now, 'and it was all I had.'

Now the talk veers towards our quests for gainful employment. As we vent our frustrations at BudgieAir's paltry support, it turns out that all three of us have called the helpline and been advised to 'think outside the box'.

'They're just paying lip service,' Freddie remarks, 'so they can say they're' – cue eye-roll – 'supporting us through this difficult time.' We agree that support has in fact been lamentable, and I tell them about my own recent call, regarding Sally and Mr Sox.

'If a pet's jointly owned,' Leena says, 'surely it's a matter of sorting out official custody, like with kids?'

'I'm sure it's not *quite* like it is with kids,' I say.

'Poor woman,' Freddie adds. 'Taking call after call from distraught people like us, then going home to her cat-less house. If me and Pablo broke up I'd fight to the *death* for Max.'

'That'll never happen,' I insist truthfully, as I can't imagine Freddie and Pablo ever breaking up, let alone feuding over their little Cairn terrier in the way that my parents wrangled over their every possession when they divorced. The wrecked outboard motors at the boatyard were clearly Dad's but Mum reckoned they 'had value'. I have only ever lived with my parents, then flatmates and, of course, Hannah. So there have never been any possessions to squabble about.

Later, when I'm home, I wonder if I am in fact cut out to share my life with anyone – at least in a couply kind of way. I've grown extremely used to doing my own thing, being answerable to no one. And while I've had responsibilities – being a mum, and holding down my job all those years – I wonder if my family and friends are really all I need in order to feel truly fulfilled and happy.

Maybe, if I can't persuade anyone to come with me, I could go to Santorini alone? I quite like the idea of wafting around the hotel in a floaty sun dress and an elegant straw hat, bare-legged and brown, attracting curious glances from the staff.

Who is she? they'd murmur on spying me appearing for breakfast. *Why is she staying in the honeymoon suite alone? She's so mysterious and self-assured!* I'd lounge in the poolside bar in the evenings, sipping wine, picking at olives. *Maybe she has a lover who's joining her later in the week?* Now I'm trying to convince myself that all this would be great – even being constantly asked by fellow guests *why* I was alone, because people are at their most inquisitive on holiday. And now I'm imagining having to avoid those people who were grilling me in the bar, perhaps with an air of pity, to the point where I'd be forced to barricade myself in my suite and have all my meals sent up there.

Imprisoned, that's how I'd feel, locked up in my ivory tower! What's wrong with me? I wonder now. A proper grown-up woman would be able to enjoy holidaying alone. It would be *enriching* for her. But then, holidays designed for singles tend to have activities factored in, like yoga or painting or sailing, and the activity that comes to mind in the case of a honeymoon hotel suite on a stunning Greek isle is 'sex'.

I sit up late, browsing profiles on the site, realising that certain categories are definitely evident here. There are the professionals in their crisp white shirts, often photographed in an office setting and keen to emphasise that they're solvent and extremely hard working, 'but now I'm ready to enjoy more leisure time with a like-minded lady'. However, they are far outnumbered by the outdoor crew; the ones snowboarding or straddling enormous motorbikes, or clinging to mountainsides or the ropes on a yacht.

There's a scuba diver in a wetsuit and a full-face mask. Other men are on horseback, skis or at the helm of a speedboat. Less glamorous perhaps, although still active at a push, another man is balancing on a stepladder, changing a halogen lightbulb in a kitchen ceiling – showing nothing but the back of his head. What's he trying to say with that? 'I'm happy to change your bulbs for you?'

I'm wondering now if there are any nice, normal men who aren't half-dead on their sofas, posing in their flashy offices, skiing off precipices, flaunting their toilets or attending to mundane domestic chores. But then, as Leena pointed out, I've only just signed up, and maybe some of these strangers are perfectly lovely people who just aren't terribly good at putting dating profiles together. And maybe I should give them a chance.

CHAPTER TEN

If online dating is a numbers game, I've decided to adopt a similar approach in my search for work. And so pretty much all of last week was spent applying for literally any job that seemed vaguely relevant. I've left my flat only to buy essential provisions and to visit Mum, having decided to *blast* the job market and find something (anything really) as soon as I can.

It's not that I don't care what I do. I've always loved to work, to feel useful and to be able to provide for Hannah and me, so she could go on that school trip to France and we could have treat days out, all of that, beyond the basics. But I have never had a possible alternative career simmering away at the back of my mind. There's been no plan B. And if I'm going to be able to pay my bills and mortgage and hang on to this flat, then I'll have to figure one out pretty sharpish (of course, as my brother would undoubtedly point out, I wouldn't be in this mess now if I'd planned for the future, and *invested*).

I've pinged off my CV to hotels, restaurants and retail chains; to media companies, advertising agencies and recruitment consultancies; anyone, in fact, who is looking to take on a corporate receptionist or 'front of house' type person, which seems to be the logical destination for a grounded flight attendant.

'The right person will meet and greet our high-net-worth clients with the ultimate professionalism,' reads one job spec. 'You'll have a warm, confident manner and be immaculately presented.'

I check my reflection before venturing out in public on this chilly, pale-skied Monday morning. I'm only going out for a run but I am alarmed to see another wiry black hair sprouting defiantly out of my chin. And how speedily eyebrows grow out when left untended! My flight-ready brows were permanently plucked to an arch and lightly pencilled in. My grounded brows are creeping beyond their boundaries like untended lawns. Just over a week since I came back from London and my face seems to have re-wilded already.

I jog along with my earbuds in, and the running app woman enthusing, 'Soon you'll be running easily for a whole fifteen minutes!' I'm glad someone's excited because it doesn't seem terribly impressive to me. But at least I'm making progress, I remind myself when I let myself, panting, back into my flat.

Immediately, before I've even showered, I check my messages from the site.

Maurice, 55: *Hi fancy a chat?*
Laszlo, 60: *Hey! :)*
Benjamin, 51: *Nice photos u have.*
Seamas, 60: *Hiya like to meet?*

Occasionally, over the last week, I've sent the odd equally brief message. E.g. *Hi, I am fine thanks. How are you?*

—*Great. Where u live?* Then, gallingly: *What are u wearing?* And on it's gone. Maybe this isn't the right kind of site for me? Fabs stressed the importance of signing up to several, and at her dating peak Leena was on Match, Bumble and Hinge simultaneously. I had no idea how she was also managing to hold down a full-time job, and I'm not sure I have the dedication to continue with this one, let alone multiples. But then, just as I'm dithering between poring over yet more job ads or gazing, lustfully, at photos of Santorini's beaches, I find myself diverted as a man named Stephen has just messaged me.

Hi Jennifer,

I see you're a newbie here like me. Really enjoyed reading your profile and thought I'd tell you a bit more about myself as I kept my profile pretty brief. Like you, I live in Glasgow. I'm divorced with two grown-up kids (who keep reminding me that they are grown up and don't need me to hover about, 'supervising', when they're just boiling spaghetti).

Am I one of those tedious blokes who goes on about his kids all the time? Probably! As for me, I am a lawyer specialising in family law, a partner in a practice. By the time I'd graduated I thought law wasn't for me, that I'd made a mistake – but here I am, twenty-five years on and I love it actually. Or rather, I love it mostly.

I'd love to hear a bit more about you. There's some-thing so sunny and positive about your profile and you really jumped out for me.

Really hope you'll get in touch.

Kind regards,

Stephen

Well hello, Stephen-the-lawyer. You sound nice. I don't write that, of course. I don't write anything until I have reread his message carefully, on the lookout for signs of weirdness (there are none) and then checked out his photos. That's photos *plural*; there are five.

Good things about Stephen's photos: they are in focus. His eyes are not only open but also radiate kindness and warmth. His smile seems genuine, crinkling those attractive eyes, and in one picture he's been caught mid-laugh. Whenever I've been photographed laughing I look insane, all teeth and flared nostrils, like a horse – but here is a man who can appear *dashing* while finding something hysterically funny.

His hair is short and dark, peppered with grey at the sides. There's no toilet in shot. His photos have been taken in sunny locations: in a park, by a river, on a beach. Stephen doesn't look like a man who's spent the past decade slowly rotting on his sofa.

I pause for a moment, and after a couple of false starts I reply:

Hi Stephen,
Lovely to hear from you. Yes, I'm a newbie too and am curious to see where this takes me. Until recently I was a flight attendant but my airline has just gone under so I'm figuring out what to do next. I guess my job filled up most of my life. So this is the first time I've really thought about dating and maybe meeting someone.
I'd love to hear more about you. What do you do in your spare time?

My heart quickens as I press send. It's nothing, I tell myself. It's not like I've committed to anything. Anyway, he's probably one of the super-popular guys on here and I'll never hear from him again.

Twenty minutes later another message appears.

Wow! You replied! Really sorry to hear about your airline. That must have been awful for you. I'm sure you'll find something else really soon. (I'm always so impressed by the highly capable and unflappable nature of flight attendants!)

Unfortunately, spare time is pretty rare at the moment but I do love to get out of the city and head up to the Highlands whenever I can. Nothing crazily ambitious – just a bit of hillwalking and enjoying the scenery. It's good for the head, I think.

I'm also getting into photography, he continues, *and finding my way around a DSLR camera with mixed results. Enjoying the challenge though. I also love films and reading. But then everyone says that don't they? Maybe I'm a clichéd middle-aged bloke, or just normal? You decide! :)*

What do you enjoy?

Better hold off replying, I decide. Can't appear too eager. Instead, as instructed, I message Fabs to update her on developments. *He sounds promising,* she replies. *What about the others?*

—*Not too keen on the others.*

—*Don't put all your eggs in one basket!* she warns, and I smile at that. *It's a numbers game,* she adds.

—*So I've heard. I'll keep at it! What are you up to today?*

—*I'm on a shoot for a knitwear company. Nasty stuff. Cowl necks and atrocious waterfall cardigans. But it's okay,*

I'll keep smiling! And she attaches a selfie in which another person's hands are visible: a make-up artist, dabbing at her face with a cosmetic sponge. She wishes me luck, adding: *One word of caution, darling. Don't message right away. HOLD BACK.*

So, obediently, I turn my attentions to the job sites, reminding myself that this, too, is a numbers game. So I mustn't feel despondent that, so far, my applications seem to have disappeared into a black hole. A little later another selfie appears of Fabs wearing an 'atrocious waterfall cardigan'. She looks stunning in it.

—*Hideous huh!* she has written.

—*It hurts my eyes! :) Seriously you look amazing.*

—*You'd better not be messaging that lawyer right now.*

—*Of course I'm not,* I fib, adding a winking emoji and turning my attentions back to the matter in hand.

CHAPTER ELEVEN

You don't sound like a cliché to me, I type. *And yes, you do sound normal. What do I enjoy? Well, work took up a lot of my time, and family life before my daughter left home. But I've always loved exploring our city, going to exhibitions etc.*

I pause, aware that I have slipped into trying to create a persona for myself: someone who 'goes to exhibitions etc'. And while I'd love to be that person who's always seen the latest show of gritty 1960s street photography, or the Tracey Emin exhibition everyone's raving about, I rarely get around to actually doing that. So I delete that sentence, writing instead: *I've started running although I'm not obsessive about it . . .* Understatement of the decade. *And I've got into up-cycling vintage furniture,* I continue, getting into the flow now. Well, what the hell. Stephen-the-lawyer is unlikely to demand a demonstration of my paint-stripping skills. And it sounds better than, 'Right now I'm spending a lot of time munching crisps and biscuits and drinking cheap wine.'

What else to put, in order to seem like a fully functioning

woman with a vibrant life? *And I love to read too,* I add. *Maybe I'm a cliché? You decide :)*

As I send it a violent shudder runs through me. That 'mirroring' thing, repeating what he'd said; I'd hoped it would come across as funny but now I'm aware of an unpleasant sensation, as if a tiny piece of foil has wedged itself into a back tooth.

After putting my laptop and phone away where I can't see them, I spend the rest of the day knocking my beleaguered flat into shape. This culminates in me gazing at my BudgieAir uniform which still hangs in my wardrobe. I don't *want* to look at it. Yet for some reason I can't stop staring at the sky blue jacket and skirt, hanging there smugly, reminding me of the good times we had together. The silky blue and yellow scarf with its pattern of budgies in flight, which I keep loosely wrapped around the hanger, seems like a particularly cruel touch.

Should I upcycle it? Hack at it with scissors and turn the jacket into some kind of bizarre jerkin, or pass it on to someone to use as fancy dress? I shut my wardrobe firmly and am soon settled back at my laptop again, probing around on yet more job sites, when my brother messages me.

Hey, how's things? Fancy a quick chat?

Phil always does this; wants a catch-up when it's morning in Sydney and my night-time here. I suspect he's also the only man alive who prefers FaceTime to an audio call, and I'm pretty sure it's to display the backdrop of what he terms his 'yard', but is actually a vast garden with a banquet-sized table, multiple gazebos and a gas-fired barbecue the size of a steam locomotive.

'Haven't heard from you in a while,' he says now, looking

extremely tanned in a T-shirt that's as crisply white as his teeth.

'There's been quite a bit going on,' I tell him.

'Ah, yeah. I heard your airline went under?' As soon as Phil had settled in Sydney his speech acquired an upward swoop so everything sounds like a question.

'Yep, that's right.'

'I've been meaning to call, sis. But it's been mentally busy here?'

'Yeah, well, I've got to find something else as soon as I can.'

A breeze ripples his hair as he sips coffee from a tiny white cup. I'm sure Phil was starting to go grey at one point, but from what I can make out he's back to his youthful light brown again. 'So no other airlines hiring?' he asks briskly.

'Not at the moment, no.'

'The whole industry's a bit fucked, isn't it?'

'Seems like it . . .'

'Change of direction then, eh!' he announces. 'Could be exciting. Shake things up a bit. Any thoughts?'

No, Phil. My brain is a void. 'I'm applying for a whole range of things really,' I murmur, unkeen to get into the details.

'Great. Wise move. So, what else have you been up to?'

Drinking. Working my way through entire packets of biscuits. Staring bleakly at my uniform. 'Apart from applying for tons of jobs, not much.' I'm certainly not going to tell him about signing up to a dating site.

'Are you going to be okay, money-wise?'

'Oh, I'll be fine,' I reply firmly.

'You must let me know if you're not?' He's slipped into his mildly irritating paternal mode now, perhaps to assuage his guilt at not contacting me as soon as news broke about BudgieAir's demise. Just eighteen months older than me, Phil has always assumed the superior role.

'Honestly, I'll be all right. Thanks anyway, though. So, how are things with you all?' He fills me in on the family news, which always involves his wife Loretta and their teenage sons, Marlow and Rohan, frolicking about on their boat and attending lavish parties.

As a young man, Phil left Scotland to go travelling straight after college. I had no idea how he could eke out a living selling leather thong jewellery and scraping barnacles off boats in his drifter years, but he survived somehow (assisted, I'm sure, by his good looks and easy charm). Eventually he wound up in Australia where he met the dazzling Loretta, a model-cum-actress, to whom he's been married for twenty years. They are something of a golden couple out there, featuring in the gossip pages from time to time, and have two teenage surfer dude sons. My brother's wealth has been amassed partly through Loretta's family money, her substantial earnings through her modelling and acting careers, and the commercial casting agency that Phil set up. It's about 'celebrity talent procurement', as he terms it. They match celebs with brands, negotiating eye-watering contracts between A-listers and the products they've been signed up to promote. He's currently planning an event centred around projecting an up-and-coming star's face onto the Sydney Opera House.

Phil makes it over to the UK once a year, cramming his visits with meetings in London but always managing to squeeze in a few days with Mum. Like a child desperate for her birthday to arrive, she tends to build herself up into a state of feverish anticipation whenever he's coming. (One time she'd had the living room redecorated and Rod quipped, 'When's the marquee arriving?')

'I see you're drinking already,' he teases now. Phil's other job is to monitor my wine consumption.

'Phil, it's ten o'clock at night. I'm unemployed. Of course I'm drinking!'

'No need to jump to the defensive,' says the man who has an actual wine cellar, with hundreds of ancient bottles laid down for unspecified future occasions. If they were mine, I'd worry that they were going off and be forced to drink them all.

We move on to talking about Mum. Phil tends to keep up to date via me, as the only way of contacting her is by her landline and she rarely answers it. 'She seems okay,' I start. 'But you know, she *is* different these days—'

'She's still out and about, though? Doing her own thing?'

'Well, yes. But there's something going on. It's hard to describe but I can just sense it.' There are 10,000 miles between us but I can detect his interest waning, or perhaps he just doesn't want to hear about Mum's decline. 'I took her to the cinema a couple of weeks ago,' I continue. 'Normally, you know, we'd just go in and sit down and she'd be all happy and excited. But this time the adverts had already started and as we stepped into the dark she seemed terrified, like she couldn't adjust. And she gripped tightly onto my arm and I had to guide to her seat and—'

'I think you're reading too much into that,' Phil cuts in. 'That's just a normal, getting older kind of thing, right?'

'Maybe,' I say, 'but I have to check her fridge these days too. Last week there was off bacon and a rotten lettuce . . .'

'So *you* never find the odd disgusting old thing in your fridge?' he teases with an infuriating laugh.

'That's different, Phil—'

'She's not doing anything dangerous, is she?'

'I don't think so, no.'

'Not wandering the streets in her nightie?' That seems to be the classic signifier that all is not okay; the nightie-wandering thing.

'No, she hasn't done that. At least, not as far as I know.'

'And that neighbour – that woman – still looks in on her, doesn't she?'

'That woman' who happens to live next door and pops round for a chat most days? 'Kirsten. Yes, she does. She's brilliant actually.'

He turns away, as if someone's called him, and now Loretta's face has appeared: a vision of sunshine and honey tan and a big, dazzling smile. 'Hey, Jen! How's it going?'

I edge my wine glass out of sight. 'Great, thanks. How are you?' There's a bit of chitchat, and Loretta explains that they've just splurged an enormous amount of cash on a DJ set-up for Rohan – 'Because they're all DJs these days, aren't they?' she trills, rolling her eyes.

'Yes, of course they are!'

'He's really good, though,' Phil cuts in. 'I mean, really, *really* good . . .'

'And we've just bought a puppy,' Loretta announces. There follows a kerfuffle as she rushes off to find it and then re-appears, clutching the tiny bundle of white fluff to her face.

'Oh, how lovely!'

'She's a Maltese Shih Tzu and we've called her Nico.'

I coo over her some more, and Loretta announces, 'You should get one too, Jen.'

Phil has disappeared from view now. I can sense my smile congealing in preparation for Loretta saying something about my situation because she always, always does. 'You've never been able to have a dog, have you?'

'Well, no—'

'Being on your own and working so much. I always thought that was such a shame for Hannah . . .'

'Hannah has a cat,' I offer weakly. 'She lives at Rod's—'

'Still, maybe you could get one now!' As if this is an unexpected bonus of losing my beloved job after twenty-nine years. Thankfully, she has to rush off now, and is quickly replaced by my brother's big, beaming face with the blaze of pink bougainvillaea behind him.

'Better get on,' he announces, 'and let you get some sleep. You look knackered, sis.'

It's the anaesthetising effect of corner shop wine. 'Yes, I am actually.' Loretta reappears, waving goodbye frenetically, then they're gone.

A weird silence settles. I'm not jealous of my brother; truly, I'm not. And normally I'm fine after our catch-ups because I have never wanted his life, as I've always been perfectly happy with mine.

But it feels different tonight. Phil and Loretta bursting into my flat to enthuse over their brand-new puppy and imply that I'm a crap mum, whipping up the stale air before rushing off again, has left me all off-kilter. As if Hannah missed out because we didn't have a pet living here! As I tip the dregs of the wine into my glass, another cat flickers into my mind: Mr Sox, snatched away from the woman who loves him. It occurs to me that Stephen might have heard of situations like this one, but is it the done thing to ask a lawyer for advice unofficially? It's worth a try, I decide. But as I go to message him I see that he has messaged me.

—*You sound like you have a good, full life. So how are you finding the site so far?*

—*I suppose I'm taking it cautiously. My daughter's been on at me for years to try online dating and when I lost my job she reckoned I could no longer trot out my old excuse.*

—*Which was . . .? That you had no time for it?* I smile at that.

—*Exactly, yes.* I pause, then: *How about you?*

—*My life was feeling a bit all-work-no-play. A bit empty I guess, if that doesn't sound tragic. So I thought I'd give it a try . . .* We chat on and on, batting messages back and forth as we share our favourite TV shows, films and books, all that. While not everything matches it's far more pleasant than being ticked off for drinking by my brother.

—*Can I ask you something work-related? A legal thing I mean?* I venture finally, fuelled by wine.

—*Sure, no prob.*

—*When my friend and her partner split up he took her cat . . .* I can hardly admit that it's a woman I've spoken to twice on a helpline. *It was definitely her cat, not shared,* I continue, *and she's devastated. Is there anything she can do to get him back?*

A few minutes' pause and then:

—*I haven't dealt with anything like that personally but one of my colleagues might know. Let me ask them.*

—*Thanks, I'd really appreciate that.*

—*No problem at all. You sound like a lovely caring person. Would you like to chat on the phone sometime?*

The phone? Hannah's told me that no one communicates with actual voices anymore!

—*Sure, that'd be nice.*

But what if he's weird? Then I can block him, I remind myself.

As we exchange numbers any lingering irritation over Phil and Loretta seems to dissipate, and instead I'm aware of a glimmer of hope that something good might be happening to me.

Of course, I don't really know Stephen. All I've had to go on are those five photos and his messages. But he seems kind and considerate and, well, normal, I think – and although it feels maybe a bit *too* easy, I have a good feeling about him.

Maybe algorithms are the way to go after all.

CHAPTER TWELVE

Apart from a carton of milk that's definitely 'on the turn', plus a cucumber that turns out to have gone to mush when I poke it, all seems fine at Mum's neat suburban bungalow later in the week.

I'm not proud of my secret cucumber prodding, but needs must. I bin it sneakily and pop out for fresh milk. Once I'm back again we settle with a cuppa and chat. As a younger woman Mum was pretty formidable, prone to angry outbursts and bouts of sulking that could go on for days. I knew she was highly regarded at the hospital where she'd worked as a midwife. However I got the impression that she had struggled with being a mum, at least when my big brother Phil and I had grown from being pretty compliant children, wary of rocking the boat and upsetting her, into teenagers who were less willing to abide by her rules. By the time I'd reached my late teens she and Dad were consumed by a bitter divorce with protracted arguments over what seemed like their every possession. The doll's house he'd built for me ended up being shattered during a particularly furious row.

When the dust had finally settled Dad got together with sweet, loyal, scrub-faced Barbara, who he'd known for years at his allotment. They were blissfully happy until Dad died of lung cancer five years ago, and his broken-hearted wife passed away a few months later. Meanwhile Mum had met Brian McGuire, a florid bear of a man, who enjoyed a full cooked breakfast – with fried bread – every day of his life. I had to admire his dedication to saturated fat, especially being married to with Mum, who has always been wedded to her low-fat yoghurts. But then Brian died too and for the past couple of years Mum has lived alone.

At seventy-nine she has become gentler and sweeter, less prone to irritation and dark moods. I've been telling myself it's an ageing thing; a natural softening of those spiky edges. But in the past few months I've started to wonder if something else is going on. Although I've told her about losing my job she hasn't seemed to understand the implications ('Oh, I'm sure you'll find something else') and today, as we finish our tea, a small silence falls.

'Shall we have a look at your garden, Mum?' I suggest.

'Oh, yes.' She brightens. 'It's looking lovely. Come and see!'

'Can I drop some shopping off for you this week?' I ask as we head outside and park ourselves on her bench.

'No need for you to do that.' She pats my arm. 'You're busy with work and Hannah.'

'I'm not working at the moment,' I remind her, 'and Han's in London, remember, Mum? She's all grown up now. She doesn't need much from me anymore.'

'Girls always need their mummies,' she says with a sparkly laugh, and I smile too, despite the fact that Mum had never used the word 'mummy' once I'd left primary school, until recently. She says it quite a lot now. *If a mummy can't treat her daughter then it's a sorry old world!* (When she'd picked up a tub of curious chocolate-coated wafer snacks for me from the corner shop). *Come on, you can tell Mummy!* (After she'd asked, with a playful glint, whether I was seeing anyone.) Mum never used to express one iota of curiosity about my life, not until . . . well, until she turned into the softer, twinkly person she is now. And it should be a lovely thing, and I should be able to enjoy it but I can't ignore a small niggle of unease. She doesn't even drink anymore, which is a relief, actually – the Gordon's gin and chardonnay having been replaced by copious quantities of Irn-Bru.

The chatter is easy now as I admire her herbaceous border in the bright, early June sunshine. Kirsten has appeared in her garden with her pug, Brad, trotting along at her heels, and we catch up on news. She has been Mum's neighbour for ten years and is unfailingly kind, dropping in on her regularly, and even more so since I mentioned that I was a little concerned.

'Hey, Jen,' Kirsten says. 'How're you doing? So sorry to hear about your job . . .'

'Oh, thanks,' I say. 'I'm sure I'll be all right, though. I'm bound to find something else.' In her late fifties, Kirsten works in a discount supermarket and has brought up her five children single-handedly. I lose track of how many grandchildren she has, although I was stunned to discover that her family birthdays average at two a month. She never misses one and seems to spend copious amounts every time.

'Had any interviews yet?' she asks, pushing back her thick, shoulder-length blonde hair.

'Not yet, no. But it's early days.'

She nods sympathetically. 'It's a tough time to be looking.'

'Jennifer only ever wanted to fly,' Mum tells her with an indulgent smile.

'Yeah, I know.' She smiles at Mum. 'You were lucky too, Mary, that you did what you loved all your working life.'

'Oh, I loved it,' Mum says, referring to her years as a midwife. 'I still get letters about it, you know.'

Kirsten and I exchange a quick glance, and she comes out her back gate and in through Mum's to join us, with Brad still pottering along at her side. *What d'you think's going on with Mum?* I try to transmit as Mum reminisces about one of the hospitals she worked at, and how 'baby charities are always writing, you know, to say thank you for everything I've done.' While most of the time Mum could pass as perfectly fine, these 'spirallings', as I think of them, are starting to happen more often. When a seemingly ordinary conversation scoots off down an altogether different track, as if she's misread the road map and then it's caught by a gust of wind and flies out of the window. Now she's off talking about a ward sister she worked with, possibly back in the 1960s, and with whom she had some kind of feud: 'But of course, I was right all along. Everyone knew that. She was a right old busybody, that one!'

I catch Kirsten's eye, and there's a flicker of understanding which I interpret as, *Yes, I'm worried about her too.*

Mum stops abruptly as Brad nudges at her ankle with his nose. 'What does it want?' she snaps, as if she has never met him before. I know she looks after him occasionally when Kirsten's regular dog walker has let her down. She even buys him treats, little one-calorie biscuits ('Don't want him getting fat! Kirsten's put on weight, have you noticed?') and a doggie selection box at Christmas.

'He just wants a bit of attention, Mary,' Kirsten says, but

Mum glares down at him and steps away. Clearly feeling thwarted, Brad starts to bark indignantly until Kirsten scoops him up into her arms. 'Anyway, I'll let you get on,' Kirsten says quickly, adding to me, 'You've got my number, Jen, if you need anything anytime . . .'

'Yes. Thank you.' I smile gratefully and wait until she and Brad have disappeared back into their own garden, and then their house, before turning back to Mum. 'I thought you liked Brad?' I say gently.

'It's quite an annoying little dog. I've always thought that.' Her eyes narrow and she turns to glare at Kirsten's flouncy blinds and cluster of porcelain ornaments in the window as if unspeakable acts go on in there. A little while later, as we hug goodbye, I wonder if Phil is right and this is pretty normal and I'm just reading too much into things, over-worrying. I can see my brother's eye-rolls whenever we discuss Mum – because of course it's tiresome, being given accounts of rotten bacon and bizarre behaviours from your sister, harbinger of bad news.

I guess it's no fun being forced to think about your mother's ageing brain when you're focusing on projecting a stunning young actress's face onto the Sydney Opera House.

CHAPTER THIRTEEN

Ralph, 50

Bob, 52

Mum's doing great really, I try to reassure myself as I haul myself out for a run next morning. At least, we're not at wandering-out-in-her-nightie stage. Perhaps that won't happen. And maybe Phil's right and I over-worry, which is natural, of course – as I am the one who's physically closest to her.

At just gone nine a.m. my thoughts turn to the handsome runner, who I haven't seen for a while. This is his time to be out, I realise now: fox o'clock. I don't actually fancy this man in any real, hoping-for-something-to-happen kind of way. I'm not that deluded and, anyway, there's bound to be a stunningly attractive partner at home. He helps to motivate me, that's all.

Swerving into the park now, I circuit the pond under the watchful gaze of the regal swans. All the while, I'm on the lookout for Foxy with the keenness of a bird-watcher primed to spot a crested tit. I'm still using the running app, and I try to focus on the woman's perky tones: *You're doing so well! You should be feeling really proud of yourself!* Along the tree-lined pathways I plod, feet slapping down hard, my breath coming in ragged gasps. I leave the park and force myself up the slight incline, which has somehow turned into a steep hill, past the grand sandstone villas towards my less salubrious neighbourhood with its jumble of grocery stores and takeaways.

And there he is, in the distance, heading towards me! The neighbourhood fox! On spotting me, his face breaks into a grin, and as we're just about to pass each other he calls out, 'Haven't seen you in a while. You're doing great!'

'Thanks,' is all I can manage. But I'm still smiling inanely as I let myself into my flat.

There are further sightings and hellos over the next couple of weeks as June brings a spell of glorious blue skies and sunshine. Curiously, my enthusiasm for running seems to have cranked up several notches. At least, it's not as torturous as it once was. In fact it's helping to keep my spirits up as, date-wise, Stephen and I still haven't managed to meet up. He's cancelled twice – 'So sorry, Jen, the last thing I want is to mess you around' – blaming his workload, although we have chatted on the phone. He is very well spoken; not unfriendly but with a slightly brisk edge. So far I've learnt that he grew up in Edinburgh, went to boarding school and studied law here in Glasgow, where he's lived ever since.

Meanwhile, job-wise I've had another flurry of rejections, and as I start to wonder if Stephen is in fact stringing me along, I find myself agreeing to meet a man called Ralph from the site.

His messages haven't been particularly interesting and he hasn't given much away beyond the very basics (never married, no kids). Perhaps they'd just landed in my inbox at the right time, when I was *receptive* (or desperate for a bit of fun?). Anyway, at least he'd seemed normal and non-weird, so why not? I'd reasoned. As Leena has suggested, some people are better face to face.

So here we are now, in a bland city-centre coffee shop on a Friday afternoon. Ralph is wearing a paisley-patterned shirt that I recognise from the Ted Baker window and is heavily doused in pungent aftershave. While he seems pleasant enough there's definitely no spark and I don't fancy him. We certainly won't be skipping off to Santorini together. But that's okay, I decide. I'm just having a coffee with a man. It's no big deal.

Then he leans towards me across the table and growls, 'Y'know, most women of your age have really let themselves go.'

And that's it – a red flag, as Hannah calls it. When suddenly, out of nowhere, something feels terribly wrong. Apparently, on a recent Tinder date the guy had been curt with the bartender because his glass was still warm from the dishwasher. *You're not expecting me to drink out of that, mate!* he'd barked. Well, that had been that for her.

'Really?' I say now. 'I don't think that's true actually.' Already, I am trying to figure out how quickly I can get the hell out of here. I'd rather be scrubbing my bathroom floor than doing this.

'Oh yeah, all the ones I've met have,' Ralph continues, 'apart from you. I don't know if it's the menopause or what it is. It's like they just stop caring.' *And you, sir, are quite the catch!* He smiles, clearly pleased with himself, revealing two rows of tiny grey teeth. In his profile picture he'd had his mouth closed, and it had obviously been taken some years ago because the sandy hair has faded and the face has plumped and sagged a little. I don't have an issue with ageing, because I too have plumped and sagged – but I haven't tried to trick anyone.

Now he's chuntering on about his electric radiator business. 'They're the way forward,' he insists, and at one point he asks if *I'd* be interested in a radiator, 'because I'd be happy to come round to your place and take a look, if you like?'

'No, I'm fine for heating, thank you.'

He rubs at his chin. 'If I came round, though, I could advise you on the most economical type.' I glance at the café door, yearning to propel myself through it. 'You might be better with a wall-mounted model,' he adds with a leering grin.

'My flat's perfectly warm, thanks,' I say politely. I still haven't managed to shake it off, this burning need to be pleasant at all times. *Sorry, sir, the bar is closed now as we'll be landing shortly. No, I can't serve you just more drink. Could you please sit back down and clip on your seatbelt?*

'That's the thing, though,' Ralph is saying now. 'There's a thermostat so you can control the heating to exactly how you want it.'

I know what a fucking thermostat does!

'Sorry, I've really got to go,' I explain as soon as we've finished our coffees. What exactly am I apologising for?

'Well, this has been nice,' he says, flashing his pebbly teeth again as we step out into the hazy afternoon. 'If you fancy meeting again sometime—'

91

'I'm sorry, I'm in a real hurry,' I bark, dashing off like a coward and aware of him standing there, staring after me, bewildered. Christ, there must be a better way of ending a bad date than actually fleeing.

In order to steady myself I walk home instead of taking the subway, enjoying the soft rain that starts to fall as I cross the pedestrian bridge. *It's a numbers game,* Fabs told me. So later I arrange another date, with a sporty-looking, dark-haired chap called Bob, who has a whole raft of hobbies: football (playing and watching), golf, gardening and playing the drums. This varied mix suggests a well-rounded individual with a full life, and I find myself looking forward to our drink a couple of nights later.

As soon as we've greeted each other in the pub, he launches into telling me all about fencing, which at first I'd assumed was fencing-the-sport, but it turns out that Bob used to travel the country building fences for farmers, but now it's more lucrative to erect them around prisons. 'My last one was over a mile long,' he says proudly.

I try to look suitably impressed, which seems to encourage him to talk more about prisons, in great detail, about the people who work there and the daily routines of prisoners, and that they have 'all kinds of programmes and courses like, y'know, if you want to write your life story, or do poetry, or something like that?'

And then it strikes me: *Bob has been in prison.*

'It was just a few months when I was a daft young lad,' he says when I pluck up the nerve to ask him about it. 'I'd got in with a bad crowd, nothing serious or violent or anything like that.'

'What was it, then?' I ask.

'Theft,' he replies.

'What kind of theft?' It feels important to know.

'Just whatever was there,' Bob replies with a shrug, and it dawns on me that he doesn't mean shoplifting (because surely no one goes to prison for that), or even cars – but people's *homes*. I'd always imagined that, by the age of fifty, I'd have my life pretty much sorted out. But here I am, sitting in a nondescript pub with an actual burglar.

It was decades ago, I remind myself as Bob tell me more about his past; how his late father was 'in the trade' too and it would be mainly cameras, jewellery, stuff like that, 'and the occasional pet, I'm ashamed to say.'

'Pets?' I exclaim, fortifying myself with a gulp of wine.

He nods. 'I know it's bad. There was quite a market for dogs at the time, though. Pedigrees, obviously. Some of them were worth well over a thousand quid.'

'But how could you steal a pet,' I venture, 'without it going completely mad?'

'There were ways,' Bob says, shifting uncomfortably now. 'If you were friendly it'd just go with you without a fuss.' He pauses. 'I'd do anything to undo all of that, to be honest. D'you mind if we talk about something else?'

'Of course not,' I say, still shell-shocked as our conversation shifts to lighter subjects: the city we live in and our favourite places to go. Then, clearly keen to stress that his old ways are firmly behind him, he swerves our chat back to his fencing business again.

More drinks are ordered. I might not fancy Bob, and I'm pretty sure he doesn't fancy me either, but I'm learning such a lot about cast-iron construction and prison food (back to jails again!) which he describes in great detail: cereal and milk for breakfast ('The milk was never quite cold enough'), a sandwich and crisps for lunch and something hot like a stew with potatoes for dinner, in a plastic tray with divided compartments. It sounds a bit like BudgieAir food. Definitely tipsy now, I am about to mention this, but would Bob be offended by the suggestion that there are similarities between incarceration, with all liberties taken away, and being aboard a Palma-bound flight? Then all of a sudden he's checking the time on his phone and saying he has to dash, and this has been nice, and am I okay getting home?

'Yes, of course,' I say, getting up from my seat.

'Great. See ya then,' he says with a quick smile. Then, as if he might turn into a pumpkin if he's in my company for a second more, he zooms off into the night.

CHAPTER FOURTEEN

'Bolter Bob', Rod calls him, when I describe the date two days later. Then there's 'Posh Stephen' (the elusive lawyer) and 'Radiator Ralph', who's been bothering me with further messages and finally had to be blocked. Having taken a keen interest in my dating endeavours Rod seems to enjoy giving my 'suitors' – as he calls them – amusing nicknames. But then, as Marc had always been referred to Mouseman Marc ('He's just employed by the council,' I'd retorted defensively), I shouldn't be surprised. Of course, when Rod was last in a relationship I didn't refer to his girlfriend as 'Lecturer Nesta' or 'boffin Nesta who's basically a reference library in human form' or anything like that. She was just *Nesta.*

'I'm finally meeting Stephen tomorrow night,' I tell Rod now as we sit and drink tea on the step overlooking my shared back garden. It's a crisp, sunny Sunday afternoon and a line of jewel-coloured washing flutters in the light breeze.

'On a Monday night?' He grimaces.

'Yeah.' I pause. 'D'you think there's still a hierarchy of nights out, or is that just old-fashioned?'

'Fridays and Saturdays still probably have the edge,' Rod replies, 'but I don't think there's any *stigma* about a Monday . . .'

'No, I don't think so either,' I say firmly.

'Well, I hope it goes well,' he says. I glance at him, surprised by the absence of teasing. Then: 'Which site are you on again?'

'Mature Matches.' I'm braced for some ribbing – but still none comes. 'Why d'you ask?'

'Just interested, that's all.' He shrugs.

I peer at him. His wavy salt-and-pepper hair is all over the place, crying out for a trim but kind of suiting him too. I have only once seen Rod all spruced up and fresh from the barber. It was for his father's funeral; his mum had died a few years before and he'd been especially close to both of them. Hannah had too. They'd been wonderful, doting grandparents. My heart had crumpled at the sight of him being so stoical and brave, the eldest of four brothers, yet also looking like an overgrown student in a proper grown-up's suit.

As I study his face, his apparent curiosity starts to make sense. 'You're not thinking of signing up, are you?' I ask.

'I was thinking of maybe giving it a go,' he says quickly, 'but obviously I wouldn't want to be on the same one you're on.'

'Really? Oh, you should!' For some reason, this revelation has knocked the wind out of me, although I'm trying not to show it. I don't know why I'm so shocked. After all, everyone does it, as Hannah's been so keen to point out. I got over those earlier occasional yearnings for Rod a long time ago, having reminded myself that there was too much at stake and I'd only regret it bitterly, if I launched myself at him on a wine-fuelled evening. In fact, those feelings are buried so far in the past that these days, shamefully, I almost forget he's a sexual being, with *needs*; an adult man who might want to find a partner at some point. He's been single for so long, I guess that seems like his natural state. Even when he was with Nesta, who was a perfectly lovely woman, if slightly distant, they never lived together and seemed intent on leading pretty separate lives. For instance, his Christmases were always spent with me and Hannah at Mum's (she's always insisted on hosting it) while Nesta visited her own parents.

It's occurred to me that perhaps the way we are together has somehow got in the way of him fully committing to someone. But then, when I suggested that he needn't feel obliged to spend Christmas with us – that he could be with Nesta, or she could come to Mum's – he looked bewildered and said, 'Don't you like the way we do it?' *No, I'm just saying Nesta might like you to spend it with her.* 'Nesta's fine,' he insisted.

'I'm just considering it,' he says now, in an airy tone, 'seeing as you've been having such a heady time with it.'

'Hardly!' I say. 'But you should do it, Rod.'

'You reckon?'

'Yeah! You'd be snapped up in no time.'

His brows shoot up and he colours slightly. 'What makes you say that?'

'Just . . .' I pause, trying to figure out the right way to say it. 'I just know you'd make a wonderful partner for someone.'

'Why, *thank you*,' he says, hamming up the gratitude, and we both laugh. 'Show me, then,' he adds.

'Show you what?' I blink at him. 'You mean my profile? No way!'

'No, I mean your many suitors.'

I exhale heavily, fish out my phone and bring up my daily matches. Every day I'm presented with a new selection, like those ever-changing hotel breakfast buffets from the days before anyone worried about fellow guests breathing all over the scrambled eggs and poking at the pastries. No matter how vast those buffets were – and Hannah and I *loved* them – your choices generally fell into distinct groups. There were the hot dishes, the virtuous cereals and fruits, the comforting croissants and Danish pastries, and the quirky cured meats and cheeses and even pickles (what?!) that no one ever seemed to want.

Similarly, my daily selection seems to include the following categories: those slick professionals with their high-standard photos and lack of grammatical mistakes; the aforementioned sportsmen brandishing their oars and ice picks; and the barely conscious (including sofa snoozers).

'Who's messaged you?' Rod asks, peering at my phone.

'Hang on, let me see . . .' I open the message. 'Mr Marmite. He's forty-seven. I haven't seen him before—'

'Did you put your real age?' Rod asks.

'Of course I did,' I retort. 'Why would I lie?'

'A lot of people do,' he says with a shrug. 'Men especially. A third of them shave a few years off—'

'Do they?'

'—But a fifth of women do it too, apparently. And loads of people use photos that are at least five years old—'

'You seem to know a lot of statistics,' I remark, placing my mug on the step and studying his face, 'for someone who's only *considering* doing it.'

Rod shrugs. 'Um, I s'pose I've looked into it a little bit.'

Now it dawns on me. 'You've signed up already, haven't you?'

He gazes around the garden as if Mrs Kadir's fluttering washing is suddenly fascinating to him. 'Rod?' I prompt him.

'I might have,' he says, setting his mouth in a fine line.

'Which one is it? Please tell me!' It takes some wrangling to extract the information and, thankfully, it's not the same one as me. 'Why didn't you say?' I ask.

'There's nothing to tell really,' he says. 'I mean, I haven't met anyone yet . . .'

'You should,' I say firmly.

'Yeah, *okay*, Jen. I will in my own time. Anyway, what does Mr Marmite have to say for himself?'

Still reeling from his news, because Rod has never expressed the slightest interest in dating (maybe Hannah's been on at him too), I angle my phone so we can read it together.

Hey Jennifer,

Interesting profile pic you have there with the pizza slice. Fancy a chat about your thick v thin crust preferences and your favourite topping?

We check his profile.

Height: *5'11"*. Occupation: *IT/computing.* Interests: *I realise this is the bit where I'm supposed to say kayaking or hoofing up Ben Nevis on a weekly basis but my lack of action photos might alert you to the fact that you're more likely to find me in the kitchen. And not just at parties. I love to bake bread. Yes, I am one of those guys – the sourdough squad. If you like the sound that, or just fancy a recipe, why not get in touch?*

'He sounds all right, doesn't he?' Rod gives me a quick look.

'He does actually.' We check out his photos together, poring over the jovial headshot (reddish hair and a cheery face with a wide, clearly genuine smile). There's also a couple of pub pictures with other, similarly jolly-looking blokes in shot, and another in which Mr Marmite is presenting a presumably home-baked loaf on a board, like a *Bake-Off* contestant.

'You should message him,' Rod suggests.

'Oh, I don't think so.'

'Go on. He sounds just your type.'

'I don't really have a *type*,' I point out truthfully.

Rod gives me a sly smile. 'But look at that loaf. Imagine it, hot from the oven, crust all *crusty*, inside all soft and squidgy, just the way you like it . . .'

'I'm not sure I could take that level of excitement.' I chuckle as we make our way back inside and head upstairs to my flat. 'Anyway, I have that date tomorrow night,' I remind him, 'and I think I'll see how that one goes before I jump into anything else.'

'Why, though?'

'It just seems simpler that way,' I reply.

I'm conscious now of Rod fixing me with one of those looks that suggests he knows what I'm thinking, that he can read exactly what's going on in my head. 'You really like Posh Stephen, don't you?' he murmurs.

'I don't know about that,' I say firmly, sensing myself flushing for no good reason and aware that I'm being ridiculous in building up this date into some momentous event. After all, Stephen could easily turn out to be a dud. I know from Leena and Fabs that, despite how lovely someone seems in their photos and messages, it's entirely likely.

'Oh, c'mon.' Rod fixes me with a look. 'I can tell.'

'I s'pose so,' I admit.

He's grinning now as we step back into my flat. 'Does your heart do a little skip when you see a new message from him?'

'Stop it,' I say, giving his arm a playful push.

'It does, doesn't it? I can see it in your face . . .'

'Okay,' I exclaim, laughing and conscious of my simmering cheeks. 'Yes, it does, all right? It sounds a bit pathetic, I know. But at least it's cheering me up . . .'

His smile flattens and concern flickers in his dark eyes. 'No luck with your job applications? Sorry, I haven't wanted to keep asking. I figured you'd tell me if you'd had good news.'

'Oh, don't worry. It's fine.' I shrug. 'I had five rejections last week, that's all. And a phone interview, and another one on Zoom, but I didn't get them—'

'I know it's tough.' He squeezes my hand.

'Yes, it's pretty crap really. Not exactly good for the self-esteem.'

'You'll find something soon,' he says. 'You're so experienced, so employable and good at what you do. You've got so much to offer, Jen.'

'Do I, though?' I shrug, hating myself now for fishing for reassurance and praise.

''Course you do,' Rod exclaims. 'And maybe, when things pick up, airlines will start hiring again?'

'Let's hope so . . .'

'You could find yourself working for one where you don't have to flog those little plastic toys—'

'Hey, I happened to be good at that!' We both chuckle. 'That's what I keep telling myself,' I add. 'That the industry will recover and this is just a little blip.' I pause. 'But sometimes, y'know, I just wonder if this is it, if I'm over the hill—'

'Don't be crazy. Over the hill? Jesus . . .'

I lean into him for a hug. 'Well, you know how it is. It's bloody scary, not knowing what the future holds. So I guess I've been overly fixating on Stephen's messages, and I'm excited to have something to look forward to at last. That's all it is really.'

'Yeah, I get that,' he says gently. Then he smiles and his deep brown eyes glint with mischief. 'Shame he's actually eighty-two with bits of old hamburger rotting in his beard.'

CHAPTER FIFTEEN

Stephen, 54

There's no hamburger beard but there is an umbrella, which he's in the process of pulling down as he hurries into the pub. An umbrella! Mum is the only person I know who uses one. She insists on carrying it on the wildest of days, buffeting and blowing, as if closing it would be a sign of letting the weather win.

'Jen! Sorry I'm late.' He has a lovely face, I decide immediately. Striking, actually *beautiful* eyes that hover between hazel and green and a strong, elegant nose. He's clean-shaven, as he is in his photos, and I can't imagine he's lied about his age because, if anything, he looks younger in real life.

'Don't worry,' I tell him. 'I've only just got here myself.'

He indicates my glass of wine. 'Can I get you another?'

'No, I'm fine, thanks.'

A quick half-smile and he's off to the bar, returning with a beer. 'Lovely to meet you at last.'

'You too,' I say.

There's a small pause as he settles in his seat. He looks dapper in a casual navy blue shirt and smart jeans and I'm wondering now if I've overdone it by wearing a dress, and heels – for the first time since losing my job.

'So, how's your friend getting on?' Stephen asks.

'Which friend?' I ask.

'The one with the cat?'

'Oh, yes!' In my fizzle of nerves and excitement I'd forgotten about that. 'I don't think there's been any change in the situation,' I say quickly.

'Well, I spoke to my colleague,' Stephen says, 'and she said it's usually sorted out between the two parties, depending on who's provided most of the pet's care. Things like, whose name is registered at the vet's? Who spends the most time with it and who chose and bought it?' He stops and sips his beer. 'A solicitor can work through all of that.'

'That's good to know,' I say, a little taken aback by this gush of information.

'Believe it or not, a pet is actually classed as a possession,' he continues, 'like a car or a TV.'

'Really? I'll pass that on.'

'I hope she manages to sort things out,' he says. He seems a little on edge, maybe because he was running late or perhaps this is his first date from the site. 'Keep me posted,' he adds, 'with what happens . . .'

'I will,' I say, keen to move on now because, the longer we discuss it, the higher the likelihood of my being expected to invent an entire backstory regarding my close friendship with Sally; how we'd been firm buddies for years, but drifted a little when she'd got together with that shifty bastard of a pet-thieving boyfriend. 'So, does this feel a bit weird, meeting like this?' I ask lightly.

'A bit, I suppose.' Stephen rubs at the back of his short dark hair and smiles properly for the first time since he arrived. 'I've never done anything like this before.'

'I'm pretty new to it too,' I say. 'But I guess you get used to it. So my friends tell me, anyway.'

He nods. 'Mine too.'

I sip my wine, warming to him as he seems to relax a little. His wet umbrella is propped up against the wall. 'Have you been under pressure,' I ask, 'to get yourself out there? By your friends, I mean?'

'Just a bit.' He chuckles and his handsome face softens, and he starts to ask me about my life. He wants to know about my family, and the job I loved for all those years, and he is kind and sympathetic about my redundancy. He even asks about my parents, and seems to enjoy hearing about Dad's devil-may-care sailing adventures up and down the West Coast. And when I tell him about Mum, and how I'm worried about her, there's no hint that this is a subject that really shouldn't come up on a first date.

I like him, I decide. He seems keener to ask me about my life than to talk in any great detail about his, but that's refreshing, I decide. Mouseman Marc had a tendency to chatter on rather too much about football, and I could only feign interest up to a point. Would a woman ever do this? I used to wonder, when he'd tell me in immense detail about the new signing to Celtic and even, on one occasion, expected me to sit with him and watch a compilation of classic goals.

Stephen doesn't seem like that at all. In fact, it takes some quizzing to encourage him to open up and, when he does, I learn that he's immensely proud of his son and daughter. 'They're both studying in Edinburgh,' he explains, 'and have pretty full lives. So these days, the best way to see them together is with the lure of an amazing meal.'

'Oh, d'you love cooking?'

He smiles and shakes his head. 'I don't seem to have the gene, unfortunately.'

'Me neither,' I admit.

'But I love to eat out and so, fortunately, do they. So we've got into this thing of trying amazing places up north, making a day of it.' As he starts to tell me about various incredible restaurants hidden away in remote locations, his face lights up and he seems to be fully alive. Not that he *wasn't* – he's no Smithy, comatose on the couch – but I can see now that this is what makes him truly happy; being up in the Highlands, eating wonderful food with his kids. 'There's this amazing place,' he enthuses, 'perched on the shore of Loch Earn. Everything's fresh and locally sourced and they're so inventive.' He pulls out his phone and shows me its menu.

Mousseline, truckle, halibut skirt. Unfamiliar terms jump out at me. 'Sounds amazing,' I say.

'Are you into food?' he asks.

'Oh, yes,' I enthuse. When he asks about my favourite restaurants I mention a couple of special occasion places I've been to with friends, or with Rod and Hannah for birthday nights out. It strikes me that I've never tried to impress anyone in this way before, and wonder what's come over me. In truth, my real favourites – the ones I associate with the best kind of nights – are a cheapie Italian and a noodle bar in the city centre. 'So, where does the hillwalking fit in?' I ask.

'That's just to make us feel like we've earned the meals,' he says with a chuckle. 'I'm not exactly a Munro bagger.'

'More of a restaurant bagger?'

'Yep, that's about it.' Stephen smiles and fetches us another round. This feels *good*, I decide, as we agree how tricky it was to write our dating profiles. 'I wanted to be as straightforward and honest as I could,' Stephen explains.

'Yes, me too. I can't understand why people use photos from years back. I mean, what's the point? I'd hate for anyone to reel in horror at the sight of the real me.'

'I can't imagine anyone doing that,' he says firmly.

As compliments go it's pretty mild, but it's sweet, and seems sincere. And this, coupled with his impeccable manners, makes me decide, as we leave the pub, that I am definitely up for another date if he wants to meet again. I like his shy smile and his enthusiasm for restaurants; the way he showed me that menu on his phone. However, being an utter novice at this I'm not quite sure how to end the night.

'It's been lovely meeting you, Jen,' he says.

'I've really enjoyed it too.' I'm about to add, 'Shall we do it again?' when the gleam of a cab's light appears in the distance.

'You take this one,' Stephen says quickly, hailing it gallantly with a wave of his folded umbrella.

'Are you sure?'

'Yes, of course.' There's a brief cheek kiss before he tugs the cab's door open for me, and it feels like he just stops short of shovelling me into it and yelling to the driver, 'Take this woman away!' As the taxi pulls out I give him a little wave, like the Queen, while telling myself firmly to *not* start overanalysing and wondering whether he'll want to meet me again.

So what if he doesn't? Maybe I'm not his type and he's

looking for a proper foodie who's familiar with mousselines and halibut skirts and that's *fine*, of course. It doesn't mean there's anything wrong with me. It was just a date, I remind myself as the taxi rattles over the bridge. There'll be plenty of others – maybe with Stephen or perhaps with other men. And of course he wasn't going to dive on me and kiss me properly. He's a proper grown-up man who sorts out people's divorces for a living. And proper grown-up men don't go around snogging women – in public – who they've only just met.

CHAPTER SIXTEEN

Helpline lady: *Hello, how can I help?*

Me: *Hi, I wondered if I could speak to Sally, please? If she's working today?*

Helpline lady, pertly: *Hold on, I'll transfer you.*

A pause, then: *Hello, Sally here. How can I help?*

Me: *Sally, it's me. It's Jennifer. Remember I've called before? You told me about your cat, and how your ex—*

Sally: *Oh! Oh, yes, of course I remember. How can I help you today?*

Me: *I just wanted to let you know I talked to someone about it.*

Sally, sounding a little shocked: *Really?*

Me: *Yes, I saw a lawyer. I mean, I went for a drink with a man last night who happens to be a lawyer. And he said a cat is classed as a possession, so when two people can't agree on who owns it, their solicitors consider the various factors and decide . . .*

Sally: *So it's just like, what, an ironing board or something? Like you said?*

Me: *Kind of, I suppose. At least in a legal sense. It's things like, who's been responsible for most of its care? And who takes it to the vet?*

Sally: *Oh, I see.*

Me: *And obviously, no one takes an ironing board to the vet.*

Sally, chuckling now: *Oh, you do cheer me up, you know. And I appreciate that. You asking him about it, I mean. I'm surprised you even remembered. You must have so much on your plate right now . . .*

Me: *Well, my daughter and her dad adore their cat. I know how they'd feel if anything happened to her. So, is he still refusing to give him back to you?*

Sally: *Yep, unfortunately.*

Me: *What would happen if you went round and demanded he gave him back?*

Sally: *I've tried that a couple of times. He said Mr Sox was out and then he shut the door on me.* A small silence hangs between us.

Me: *I'm sorry, I'm sure you're madly busy with calls . . .*

Sally: *No, it's really tailed off now so don't worry. How's the job hunting going? Did you get your CV out there?*

Me: *I did. I even managed to make sure there weren't any bits of doughnut stuck to it.*

Sally, chuckling: *Glad to hear it. Have you had any interviews?*

Me: *A few, yes. But I didn't get the jobs. I guess there are so many of us out there desperately swimming around in the job-hunting pool now.*

Sally: *You'll find something, I'm sure.*

Me: *Yeah, I keep telling myself that. And it's only been a month. I know that's not long. But my redundancy pay's come through and it's pretty paltry, isn't it?*

Sally: *I've heard that, yes . . .*

Me: *It's not going to last very long. I can't believe I've allowed myself to get into his situation. I mean, I'm not even supporting my daughter anymore. She doesn't need anything from me. Yet all these years I've been working and ended up with virtually nothing. There's no excuse. I've just frittered it all away . . . I pause. Sorry, I'm really going on . . .*

Sally, kindly: *This is the helpline, Jen. We're here to help.*

Me: *Yes, and I know that sometimes I've been a bit ranty and not very pleasant. I'm sorry.*

Sally: *You've been perfectly nice. You should hear some of the people we deal with!*

Me: *You did tell me off about my tone, first time I called . . .*

Sally: *That was unprofessional of me. It had only just happened, you see. The thing with Mr Sox.*

Me: *D'you think you'll get a solicitor onto it?*

Sally: *No, I can't face that and I couldn't afford it anyway.*

Me: *But if you won, then surely he'd have to pay the costs?*

Sally: *I can't face it, love. I'm finishing up here at the end of the week and I'll need to focus on what I'm doing next.*

Me: *Oh, you're leaving?*

Sally: *Well, I'm being made redundant. The whole team are. We were just put in place for the first few weeks after the big announcement and our time's nearly up.*

Me, a little stunned: *I'm sorry to hear that. What'll you do next?*

Sally: *Um, I could go for more call centre work but I'm thinking of something closer to home, something in the Southside to tide me over. A friend said they're hiring at a shop near me—*

Me: *You mean Glasgow's Southside?*

Sally: *Yes, love.*

Me: *I assumed you were in Yorkshire near the headquarters.*

Sally: *Well, I'm from Leeds originally but I've lived in Glasgow for twenty years. Haven't shaken off the accent though . . .*

Me: *No, you haven't. Well, er, I just wanted to pass on the cat info . . .*

Sally: *Thanks for thinking about me. Really, you're a very kind person. I think a lot of people think I'm quite mad for being so upset about it.*

Me: *I don't think you're mad at all.*

Sally: *It's just, it's been me and him for so long, way before I met Gavin. I don't have any kids. He was like my family and the flat feels so horribly empty without him.* She pauses, as if catching herself. *Now it's me, going on!*

Me: *You've every right to. It seems like such a spiteful thing to do. I really hope things turn out okay for you.*

Sally: *You too, Jen.*

Me, without thinking: *Would you like to take my number? If you want to keep in touch, I mean? I'm sorry, I know calls are monitored and you're probably not allowed—*

Sally: *Well, I—*

Me: *But I'd like to know what happens and maybe this man I've met might be able to help somehow? As a favour, I mean . . .*

Sally, sounding startled: *Oh! Um, yes. Yes, I'd like that . . .*

I'm aware, as I give her my number, this is a little bizarre and maybe she's only taking it out of politeness and not even writing it down. Like me, she's been trained to offer excellent customer support and be unflappable, whatever the situation. But she sounds so warm and kind and I'm still outraged by the cat situation. And maybe, if things progress with Stephen, he'd be willing to fire off a sole, stern letter, which might even be enough to scare the pants off her shitty ex.

Sally: *I meant to ask, didn't you say you'd a joined a dating site? How's that going?*
Me: *It's early days but this lawyer guy seems pretty nice.*
Sally: *Really? That's great. I might give it a go myself someday . . .*
Me: *You should!*
Sally, chuckling: *If you're sure they're not all weirdos and crazies out there?*
Me, like some kind of expert: *Oh, far from it. It seems like the most efficient way really. I don't think anyone meets in real life anymore.*

A new 'type' has appeared in my daily matches. As well as the slick professionals, the Mr Actives and the almost-deceased, I have noticed the 'take me as you find me' guys with their drum kits (or other assorted hobby props) and keenness to stress that they're happy doing their own thing. One of them is Mr Marmite: 'Not to everyone's taste!' I remember now that he'd already messaged me and sense a twinge of guilt at not replying, because he seems like a decent man. At least he's cheerful, unlike several of today's bunch whose profiles bear a slightly aggressive edge:

Dominik, 54: *If you like what you see then stop and say hi. What's the point of all this endless window-shopping if it doesn't go anywhere?*

Happyman, 50: *I've had bad experience with trust and am looking for woman for real relationship who won't mess me about.*

Norm, 56: *Life is for living but lot of time-wasters on here, getting sick of it tbh. And I am NOT looking for a pen pal.*

All of which are bound to have women flocking, obviously, because nothing turns us on like bitterness and sulking, or the implication that these men don't actually *like* women very much at all. There's a lot of mentions of this 'pen pal' situation, too, which I interpret to mean that they're averse to more than a couple of curt messages (maybe written communication prior to a date comes under the 'time-wasting' banner). In fact now I think about it, a pen pal situation would be kind of nice! No worries or nerves about actually meeting; just entertaining missives bouncing back and forth.

Stephen seems to enjoy messaging, and obviously puts some thought into what he writes. I feel lucky now to have met him, even if it ends up going nowhere – because at least it was a fun experience. And this 'adventure', as Fabs put it, is certainly lifting me out of my job-hunting malaise which, so far, really *is* going nowhere.

I've had another slew of rejections, and the fact that some have come with encouraging feedback hasn't really helped matters. It's not feedback I need but an actual job – at this stage *any* job – not only to get some cash coming in but also to alleviate my fear that a washed-up flight attendant is unsuited to any other line of work. All those transferrable skills I have! I'd be prepared to be an office tea lady, shunting a trolley along corridors if such a person still exists. Or is it all vending machines now, or are all beverages brought in? Yet again it strikes me that, during all those decades I've spent flying, the real world has moved on, leaving me lamentably out of touch.

'I guess we should feel lucky that we had all those years in jobs we loved,' I remark, determined to be positive when I meet Freddie and Leena for coffee later.

'D'you reckon?' Leena raises a brow.

'I do, yes,' I insist. 'You know how people still think it's glamorous, even these days—'

'Yeah, all the *travel*,' Freddie remarks with a smirk, because that's what people always say – 'All that travel! You're so lucky!'

'We did do it for nearly thirty years,' I remind him. 'I'm just saying we should be thankful for that. What about all these young people out there, trying to get their careers started?'

'You mean you're feeling sorry for young people,' he teases, 'with their perfect skin and ability to cope with hangovers and all the glittering opportunities ahead of them?'

'Well, yes. It's not always easy being young, you know.' I picture Hannah at seventeen, unable to sleep for stressing over exams, worried that she wouldn't get into college.

'But *young* is what people want now,' Leena says firmly. 'They're fresh, they're perky, they're eager to learn—'

'*I'm* eager to learn,' I say unconvincingly. 'I guess we've just got to stand out somehow. How are we going to do that?'

She smirks. 'By being thirty?'

'You're only forty-eight,' I remind her. In these desperate times being two years younger than Freddie and me seems significant.

'Yes, but we're all competing with the new crop coming through,' she says with a sigh.

I really don't like the way this conversation is going. 'We can retrain and gain new skills but there's not much we can do about our ages,' I remark.

'We can't turn back time, Leen,' Freddie adds.

She shakes her head, pokes at her phone and flashes it at us. 'What's this?' I ask.

'Bovine collagen,' she announces.

'You're not serious,' Freddie exclaims.

'I am,' she insists. 'I've ordered a bulk supply.'

'But . . . does it even work?' I ask, frowning.

'Oh, it must do. Everyone takes it these days.' She grins. 'I might have a thread lift as well.'

'*Please* don't do that,' I blurt out. 'Please don't do anything drastic to your lovely face.'

'It's not drastic,' she says blithely, tossing back her glossy dark hair. 'They just insert a kind of thread right around here' – she traces a line from one ear, looping down around her chin and up to the other – 'then pull it up tight—'

'Like the string in a drawstring bag?' cuts in Freddie. 'The kind you used to carry your gym kit in at school and it always reeked of sweaty feet?'

'It's a bit more sophisticated than that,' she announces, posting the last piece of her carrot cake into her mouth. 'You just look renewed. Like yourself, but better—'

'Kind of upcycled,' Freddie chips in, 'like Jen's famous chair?'

'I don't *want* you to upcycle your face,' I say firmly.

'Doesn't it cost thousands anyway?' Freddie asks.

'Yeah, but it'd be worth it, right? And weren't you talking

about investing some of your redundancy money in your future prospects?'

'Erm, I was thinking more about taking a course, Leen,' he remarks.

'What in?' I ask.

'Psychotherapy. Me and Pablo have discussed it. We reckon that, with everything that's been going on these past couple of years, loads of people will need emotional support. And I think it'd be fascinating.'

'You'd be brilliant at that,' I say truthfully.

'Yeah. A damn sight better than those helpline people,' Leena chips in, and I shift a little in my seat. Aware of how weird it might sound, I haven't told them about my further conversations with Sally. Of course, it's considered fine and normal to exchange messages with men who could easily have created fake profiles; yet giving my number to a call centre worker? She could be *anyone*, they'd tell me.

We've veered onto the subject of my date with Stephen last night, and pick over it in forensic detail. 'Any more lined up?' Freddie asks. 'With other guys, I mean?'

'Not yet, no. I think I'll just see how it goes with him.'

'Eggs, basket,' Leena says archly. Of course they want to see my daily matches, and Freddie homes in on their written profiles, instantly dismissing any with spelling mistakes or grammatical errors.

'You've got to have quality control,' he warns.

'If he has more than three teeth in his head I'll forgive him a wrongly placed apostrophe,' I snigger. As the three of us part, all thoughts of ageing and thread lifts forgotten now, I feel buoyed up with an in-this-together feeling. The *people*; that's what I loved most about working for BudgieAir. The friends I'd made and who will always be there, no matter what.

Emboldened now, I check my phone before stepping into the subway, with the intention of messaging Stephen; just a 'Hi, I enjoyed meeting you' kind of thing. But it turns out that he has jumped in first.

Hi Jen, he's messaged, *really enjoyed our drink last night. Let me know if you'd like to do it again sometime soon? Sx.*

CHAPTER SEVENTEEN

We meet the following Thursday, ten days on from our first date. While it hardly suggests rabid keenness on Stephen's part at least it's a step up from a Monday. However, he does mention that it's a 'school night', clearly signalling that we won't be making it a late one, which is fine with me. Already, this is starting to feel pleasingly civilised; the way mature people get to know each other. The last time I dated in any 'normal' sense I was twenty-five years old, before that night with Rod, before Hannah. Back then there were house parties with people drinking beer out of cans and snogging against wobbly kitchen cabinets or on piles of coats.

Those were my dating frames of reference; stuck in the days of phone numbers scribbled on scraps of paper and stuffed into pockets. Add in the very occasional fling, and the thing with Mouseman that ended up with us kissing on a bench at midnight after our first night out, and it's clear that I need to get up to speed with how Proper Adults go about things.

Tonight Stephen's slight shyness has all but disappeared. We chatter easily in the quiet pub, with him asking for an update on my job search and quizzing me a little about my unremarkable suburban background, and what it was like to fly all those years. And he tells me more about his hill-walking and favourite spots up north.

I'm a little apologetic about not having explored the Highlands very much, which seems pretty remiss when I grew up in Glasgow. 'You're not really an outdoor person then?' he suggests.

'I'm not *averse* to being outside.' I catch his eye and we laugh.

'I think a lot of us are guilty of forgetting how beautiful our own country is,' he remarks.

'Oh, definitely,' I say.

'I'm the same really. When I've gone away with the kids, or on holiday with someone, the obvious thing has always been to book somewhere in Spain or Greece or Italy . . .' Briefly, I wonder who these 'someones' might be.

'Have you ever flown with BudgieAir?'

'Yes, of course I have.' He grins.

'I might have served you a toastie!'

'I'm sure I'd have remembered you.' It's a charming thing to say, even though I'm not sure it's true. We have another drink, and I find myself telling him about Rod, and our accidental fling, and how we'd ended up having a baby together. I don't spell it out that we had drunken, unprotected sex. However I'm pretty sure that, as a fifty-four-year-old man, Stephen is capable of figuring it out. Nor do I add that the sensible step would have been to rush straight to the doctor's for the morning-after pill (in those days you couldn't just buy it, like a packet of plasters, at the chemist's). Or that I'd been rushing off on holiday the next morning with Freddie and a couple of others, and had just crossed my fingers and hoped everything would be all right – because really, what were the chances?

'So we've never been a proper couple,' I explain. 'But I don't regret it. What happened, I mean.'

'Of course not,' he says. 'Because you've got your daughter.'

'Exactly. And it's worked out fine with Rod and me. It's been brilliant actually, and it still is. He's always been great with a lot of the practical stuff – especially the stuff I couldn't do.'

'What kind of stuff?'

'Well, he can cook, for one thing,' I say with a smile. 'That's never been my special talent. And he got a cat because Hannah was desperate for one. She'd nagged for years, and I could never do that because of my work shifts . . .' I pause. 'But they're just small things, you know? They're not what he's all about. He's just a great, all-round dad really.'

'You sound really fond of him,' Stephen remarks.

'I am. Of course I am.'

'So . . .' He pauses. 'You never wanted to make a go of it with him?'

I shake my head. 'I know it sounds weird but I realised pretty early that it was much better that way. I mean, I had occasional thoughts, you know? "What if?" kind of thoughts, I mean.' I hesitate and sip my drink. 'But our whole situation – me, Rod and Hannah – felt so right and I never wanted to risk spoiling that.'

Stephen nods, and I allow myself to savour how easy it feels tonight to share the details of our lives. 'If you'd got together,' he suggests, 'and it hadn't worked out—'

121

'That would've been awful,' I say, cringing at the thought. 'For Hannah as much as for us.' *And I'm ninety-nine per cent sure Rod would have been horrified if I'd ever made a move* – but I don't mention that.

'Yes, I can imagine,' Stephen says. 'Well, fair play to you for being so mature and handling it all so well.'

'Oh.' I grin at him, momentarily taken aback. 'I've never thought I've handled anything particularly well. But here we are. We've all survived and she's all grown up—'

'So now it's time for *you*,' he suggests with a smile that causes my heart to lift. I'm still feeling that way – warm and happy – as we leave the pub. 'Would you like to go for dinner sometime?' he asks.

'That'd be lovely,' I say.

'Anywhere you fancy?'

'Oh, I'm happy with anywhere really,' I say quickly. 'Why don't you choose?'

He glances up and down the street. It's a warm, still June night; there's no umbrella this time. 'I'll have a think,' he says. Then, in a move that catches me by surprise, he pulls me in for a hug and we find ourselves kissing tenderly on the lips. *Oh-my-God!* my brain screams. *You're kissing Stephen-the-lawyer! You've met someone online like a proper person living her life in the modern world!* We pull apart as a cab appears which, again, he insists I take.

I kind of float into it on a cloud of happiness. And it stays with me, that giddy sense of joy and excitement as the driver chats about the weather and an annoying neighbour he has, who plays his guitar very loudly at night. Then he's moved seamlessly on to commenting about a new building that's just been constructed at the river's edge; a vast slab of glass and steel. 'My kid could do better with a box of Lego,' he announces. I hear myself agreeing – although I don't really because right now the skyline looks amazing with this bold new structure reflecting the city's night sky.

The driver chatters on, and I'm making all the right noises just as I did whenever a passenger was disgruntled that, sorry no, I wouldn't be serving any more vodka and we were all out of pretzels; until eventually I stop listening altogether and just look out at the tumbledown shops and ancient pubs with grass growing out of their guttering, and then the smart new cafés and delis on the regenerated street.

That's how I feel, I decide, as the driver takes a swift right turn; regenerated or, as Leena put it, *renewed*. She doesn't need bovine collagen and she certainly doesn't need her face hoicking up with a piece of thread. And I don't need a man to kiss me in order to persuade myself that I'm not on the scrapheap. But if this is grown-up dating, then I'm starting to like it – because, God, that kiss felt so good.

CHAPTER EIGHTEEN

Mystery Man, age unknown

I only tell Mum about my dates with Stephen the next day because I think she'll enjoy it. 'A lawyer!' she exclaims, eyes sparkling. 'Pretty keen on him, are you?'

'It's early days, Mum. We've only been out a couple of times but we chat quite a bit in between times. And I like him, yes.' I haven't mentioned that I met him online, because she'd think it was tawdry and certainly only for the desperate and possibly insane. Certainly not something 'everyone' does. 'We're just getting to know each other,' I add. 'But it's kind of exciting, you know?'

'I bet it is!' She beams at me happily. My set-up with Rod has always perplexed her; why we're not together 'properly', let alone not married. 'Wouldn't it be better for Hannah if you were?' she asked once, many years ago. 'I mean, what does she *tell* people?' Seemingly, it would have been easier for our daughter if her parents were separated or divorced, 'because people understand that, don't they?'

In truth, Mum would love to have seen me settle down with a doctor, a dentist or, yes, a lawyer, although she's extremely fond of Rod. She couldn't not be, really. He's been so helpful over the years, building so much flatpack for her that he automatically stuffs an Allen key into his jeans pocket whenever we visit her together.

'Anyway,' I add, 'it's taken my mind off the job-hunting situation a bit.'

'You are still looking, though?'

'Yes, of course. I mean, that's the priority. I have to find something pretty soon.'

'With all your experience,' she remarks, 'I'd have thought people would've been queueing up to take you on.'

I smile. 'It's a bit tricky at the moment, Mum. So many companies have gone under so there's an awful lot of us out there, looking for jobs . . .' With her interest clearly waning, she gets up from her floral-patterned sofa and goes to pick up an untidy stack of mail from the bookshelf. She frowns as she starts to rifle through it. 'Are you looking for something?' I ask.

'Just a letter.' Her forehead is furrowed in concentration.

'Oh, who from?'

'A nice man who came round to see me. I wanted to show it to you.'

'A nice man?' I frown. 'You mean someone you know?' *Who the heck is writing to my mother?*

'Yes, of course I know him,' she says distractedly.

'Who is it, Mum? Who's been round?' I'm trying to keep my tone light, to not make a big thing of it. Mum's never been one for having lots of friends or social engagements. She's not a joiner of clubs, not one to get involved in 'activities' and, apart from Kirsten next door and a couple of

125

other local ladies, her few connections seem to have gradually fallen away over the years.

'He's just a nice man,' she reiterates. 'Very polite with lovely manners. We had a good old chat.'

'So . . . is he a neighbour?'

'Erm, yes, I think he lives in the area,' she says vaguely. Although my sense of alarm is ramping up by the second, I figure that the best way to extract information is to joke about it.

'Have you been dating too, Mum?' I tease her.

She chuckles in delight. 'Never you mind!'

'Mum—'

'He was very kind and helpful,' she butts in, 'and I made him a cup of tea and he was in no rush to leave—'

'Really!' As if all of this is perfectly normal and delightful when I really want to say, 'That's nice for you, Mum. So how about you tell me where he lives so I can go round there right now to ask what the hell he's playing at?'

'He's a good-looking chap,' she adds. Now her eyes are glittering and a flush has bloomed on her cheeks as if it's Sean Connery we're talking about, risen from the dead.

'He sounds lovely,' I say, breaking a rich tea biscuit with a sharp snap. 'Maybe, if he comes over again, you could let me know?' *And I'll call the police?*

'I might,' she says with a coquettish smile. Mum is still clutching those letters and I'm willing her to put them down and go off and do something so I can rifle through them.

'Would you like me to have a look through those for you?' I suggest casually.

She frowns. 'What for?'

'Just to sort them out for you,' I reply, aware that I'm

edging towards dangerous territory now; Mum hates any implication that she can't do everything for herself.

She shakes her head, suggesting instead that we go out to admire the flowers in her garden. It's a lovely June day; bright and sunny with a light breeze. The lawn has been freshly mown by Kirsten's brother, who attends to it during the growing season. The rest – the borders and pots on the patio – Mum insists on looking after herself. 'It's looking lovely,' I say, and it is; a jumble of colour although now I notice that weeds are encroaching more than usual. Knowing she'd be annoyed if I offered to hoick them out, I decide to leave it for now. There's a hierarchy of concerns: Mum's mysterious man friend, then the fridge stuff. A few rogue dandelions don't really matter.

We sit on the bench for a while, watching the sparrows fluttering around the feeders Rod put up for her. I'm still figuring out how to find out more about this 'friend' who's been visiting, probably with an eye to making off with her valuables – but the chance doesn't come up and somehow, in between us sitting around drinking tea and heading outside, she'd managed to stash those letters out of view. While Mum might forget her PIN sometimes, and there have been a few lost door-key dramas, she clearly senses my urge to look through her post, and is having none of it.

'Mum,' I venture as I'm leaving, 'you will be careful about letting people in that you don't know, won't you?'

'I'd never let anyone in that I don't know!'

'I know, I'm just saying.' I hug her goodbye.

'I might be old but I'm not stupid,' she mutters as she pulls away from me.

'Yes, I know, Mum.'

'You're saying I'm stupid, that I can't look after myself . . .'

127

'I've never said that! Of course you can.'

She's glaring at me now, with real anger beaming from her small grey eyes. 'Hannah never treats me like this, like a silly old woman . . .'

'*Mum!*' Tears prickle my eyes as I touch her arm gently. 'Please don't say that—'

'How is she anyway?' she asks, even though I told her all of Hannah's news in the garden. Despite her brittleness as a mother, Mum has always been a kind and doting grandmother. We have managed to set up Zoom calls with her Australian grandsons but I know it pains her greatly that they are so far away.

'She's fine,' I reply. 'She's really happy in London.' This time her face softens.

'She's a clever girl, that one.'

'I know, Mum. She is.' My heart seems to clench as I climb into my car. Mum smooths down her soft white hair and turns back to her house, without waving, as I drive away. Something's going on – I'm sure of it now. My brother would have it that I'm over-reacting, making a big thing out of nothing. But for once, I'm absolutely certain that I do know better than him.

CHAPTER NINETEEN

Over the next couple of weeks several significant things happen.

I rejoin the world of the gainfully employed! It's not exactly what I'd envisaged when I'd discussed my next possible move with Helpline Sally. But I guess it could still be classed as a 'client-facing career.' Up and down the aisles I go, not with a trolley laden with fragrances and wind-up plastic budgies but a reduced-item sticker gun to mark down the stuff that's about to go out of date.

It was Kirsten who mentioned that they were hiring at the discount supermarket where she works. I'd phoned her after another recent visit to Mum's, when her little pug had again been shunned for no apparent reason, and my mother hadn't seemed too happy to chat to Kirsten either. As Mum had been on about her mysterious 'friend' again, I'd asked Kirsten if she'd been aware of this male visitor. 'No, but I'll keep a close eye – don't worry,' she assured me.

'I'd so appreciate that,' I said. 'I know you have a lot on your plate—'

'Oh, I love your mum. She's a wonderful lady. It's no trouble at all.'

I smiled. 'I suppose that's one good thing about losing my job. Being able to spend more time with her, I mean.' Then Kirsten had urged me to contact Sumi, her manager, enthusing, 'They're a lovely team there. I know you're massively overqualified for that kind of work, but—'

'I'm qualified to be a flight attendant,' I cut in, 'but people aren't exactly hammering my door down, desperate to employ me. I'm actually interested—'

'I'll send you Sumi's details and I'll put in a word for you too.'

I thanked her profusely and now here I am, doing the late shift from three to ten-thirty p.m. It feels good, doing something useful, that I'll be paid for and that provides some shape and structure to my days. Kirsten has been here on some of my shifts, which I was relieved about. But the others have been extremely helpful in showing me the ropes, and warning me about the kind of stuff that happens when you're in charge of 'the gun'.

'You'll get the hoverers,' explained Sumi on my first day, 'panting down your neck, hassling you to sticker whatever it is they've got their eye on.'

'What should I do then?' I asked.

'Don't let them pressurise you,' she warned. 'Just tell them no and if they keep on at you, walk off and do something else.' She grimaced. 'It can get a bit intense in here sometimes.'

She was right. As she described, there's a lull in the evening until around nine-thirty when the bargain hunters start to arrive. But I am unafraid of belligerent customers. After all, I have calmed down hysterical hen parties thirty thousand feet in the air. So I can handle the drunk couple who nag me to sticker the mature cheddar, and a loud man with a curious waxed moustache who tries to wrangle the gun off me. ('I've always wanted a go with one of those!')

Tonight a bald man in a shiny tracksuit lurches up to me in the cooked meats aisle. 'Sticker those for me, would you?' He jabs at the pork pies.

'Sorry, they're not going out of date,' I tell him.

'They look rotten to me.'

'No, they're fine,' I say pleasantly.

'Couldn't you just . . . do it for me?' Now he's trying on the charm with a conspiratorial wink. 'Some of the others do. They don't mind. And it's not like it's your own personal stuff you're reducing . . .'

'I'm afraid I'm not allowed to do that. But I'm about to reduce the stilton and broccoli quiches in the next aisle, if you're interested in those?'

'Do I look like I want a fucking stilton quiche?' he thunders. But he doesn't rile me, and I remain pleasant and calm as I go about my business for the rest of my shift. Smiles cost nothing, after all.

'I can just imagine you with that gun,' Rod announces next day, 'prowling around, relishing your power like a traffic warden—'

'I am not like a traffic warden!'

'—Or those litter patrollers, remember them? That guy who fined me eighty quid for dropping a cigarette?'

'You're still bitter about that, aren't you?' I ask, laughing as he hands me a mug of tea bearing his company logo. We're in the workshop-cum-stockroom behind his shop, where his T-shirts are printed and orders packaged. I know Rod's small team well and often pop in when I'm in town.

''Course I am,' he retorts. 'There was cooker lying a few yards down the road, *and* a mattress with its grubby sheet still on. And he fined *me*—'

'At least it made you quit,' I tease him.

Rod grins. 'It actually was a factor, yeah.' We recommence packing up some orders, and while I'm folding and wrapping, and Rod tapes up boxes, I fill him in on the latest developments with Mum. Marta, Rod's right-hand woman, is manning the shop and Laurence, the youngest team member, is out running an errand.

'You haven't managed to find out who this mysterious friend is?' he asks with a frown.

'No, and there's still no sign of those letters either. Remember she said he'd written to her?' Rod nods. 'I keep hoping I'll get the chance to have good hunt for her mail but she keeps an eye on me the whole time like a store detective.'

Rod rakes back his hair and looks at me. 'D'you think maybe there *isn't* a friend, and it's all in her imagination?'

'I have wondered that,' I reply.

'Or it's wishful thinking and she likes the idea of having a gentleman caller?'

'Maybe, yes.' I chuckle. He has a way of doing this; of unknotting my tensions and making me feel a lot better about things. When Hannah struggled with maths and science at school Rod would always focus on the subjects she excelled at: art, music, drama and English. We'd attend parents' evenings together and whenever a teacher made a negative remark, that Hannah 'should apply herself more' and 'has trouble grasping mathematical principles' I'd catch Rod's

132

expression; an *Oh, right, so you think you know my daughter?* look of mild disdain while I sat there wrestling with pent-up defensiveness.

'Maybe she needs extra tuition?' I suggested one time as we left the school.

'Never mind him,' Rod retorted, meaning the maths teacher with whom we'd just had a meeting. 'What was going on with his hair? D'you think I'm seriously going to worry about what a man with a comb-over says?'

'How were things generally?' Rod asks now. 'I mean, with the house and everything?'

I inhale deeply. 'I'm probably over-worrying but there are little things, you know? Like instead of her damp laundry being hung neatly on the stand, it was stuffed in a big bunch on top of the radiator. And there was a nasty-looking grey thing in a plastic bag in the fridge.' I pause. 'Some kind of meat, I think. I chucked it anyway. I wish she'd turn vegetarian . . .' He catches my eye and we smile. He knows Mum finds Phil and Loretta's vegetarianism baffling. ('They won't even eat *mince!*') 'Phil thinks I'm over anxious,' I add, 'but anyway, his life seems to be all about house-training his new puppy and there was some crisis last time we spoke because Loretta had just trodden in poo—'

'Remember when Hannah was nagging the arse off me for a puppy?' Rod cuts in.

'Yeah.' I chuckle. 'You were smart choosing a kitten instead. How is the old girl anyway?'

'Doing her usual thing, owning the neighbourhood. Brought in half a mouse the other day . . .' He stops and I catch something in his expression. There are no customers in the shop and suddenly, the place suddenly feels very quiet.

'What is it?' I ask.

'Erm, it's just, I might have to keep her out when a friend comes over to visit.' Gripping a roll of parcel tape, he smiles awkwardly.

'What friend?' I study his face, intrigued now.

'Just someone I've kind of been seeing . . .' He wraps a strip of tape across a box top but misaligns it and has to rip it off again.

'You've met someone?' I exclaim.

'Uh-huh. Yeah.' He nods.

'Online?' I ask.

'Yeah. Yeah.' Now he looks like he's struggling to hold down a wide smile.

'Oh, that's great, Rod! What's she like?'

'She's really nice,' he replies with an exaggerated shrug. 'Just normal, you know? A nice person . . .' I look at him for a moment, quite stunned by his news. As we resume packing up orders, I will myself not to fire more questions at him because maybe he doesn't want to tell me any more than this? And anyway, it's none of my business. I make tea and help myself to one of the treacle cookies he keeps in a tin.

'What's her name?' I ask.

'Gaby.' A slightly awkward smile this time. 'I wasn't expecting it to happen so fast,' he adds, flushing now. 'It's blown me off my feet a bit, to be honest—'

'Oh, I think it's great, Rod. I'm really happy for you.'

'Huh. Thanks. We're just getting to know each other really . . .'

I perch on the workbench. 'Have you told her you were fined eighty quid for dropping a cigarette?'

He laughs. 'No, I'm holding that titbit back for a bit further down the line.'

I beam at him, intrigued by his unfamiliar bluster. 'Oh, it's brilliant, Rod. I'm really happy for you.'

'Yeah, you've said.' A proper smile now, as he's relieved to have got it all out.

'So c'mon, tell me a bit more about her . . .'

He pauses as if it really matters to portray an accurate picture. 'She's really smart and good fun. A bit quirky, I s'pose. Likes to do her own thing.' He shrugs again. 'I was pretty surprised she was keen on me, to be honest.'

'Why? You're quite a catch, y'know.'

'I'm not sure about that.'

'Come on, no need to be coy.' I smile. 'So, is she gorgeous? You can say it, you know. I won't jump on you for being superficial.'

'She is,' he says, almost apologetically.

'Can I see a picture?'

'Sure.' He looks pleased now, as if he'd wanted to show me all along. Up comes her Instagram on his phone: Gaby Forest. She has a fine, delicately boned face, the kind that suits softly cropped hair like hers. Gamine is the word, I decide. Obviously an outdoorsy type, in one picture she's wearing a loose, baggy vest, khaki shorts and wellies and is sitting on a log. In another she's lounging on a rug by a camp fire in a floaty multi-coloured dress and a big straw hat.

'How old is she?' I ask.

'Forty-eight.'

'She looks great,' I say, studying the shots of her with friends now. All gorgeous in a natural, sunny-faced kind of way, they look like the kind people who'd be gathered around a garden table in a cookbook of casual feasts. There are more pictures of Gaby by herself, leaning against a

135

charming vintage bus, and sitting inside it with the door open and her long brown legs dangling out.

'Where's that?' I ask.

'Down in Dumfriesshire. That's where she keeps her vintage bus. She's converted it into a weekend home.'

'You mean she sleeps in it?'

'Yeah, if it's not being let out on a holiday rental site. It's a little sideline she has. She did it all herself – bought it as a wreck and did all the converting and fitting out.'

'Wow. That's incredible . . .' It strikes me that, before now, I had only ever seen Rod emanating pride like this when he was talking about Hannah. Like when she learnt to ride her bike – it was Rod who'd taught her – and grafted hard enough to get the grades she'd needed for college, and then landed the job in London. 'She sounds amazing,' I add. 'I bet you'd trust *her* with your blowtorch—'

'Hey,' he splutters, 'I trusted you!'

I grin at him, still coming to terms with Rod's new situation and aware of voices in the shop now as Marta chats to a customer. 'So, does Gaby have a day job too?'

'Yeah, she has her own PR consultancy, doing press for restaurants and hotels, stuff like that.'

'She sounds really impressive, Rod.' I pull on my jacket, getting ready to leave as my work shift starts soon. 'Play your cards right,' I add, 'and maybe you'll get an invite to the love bus?' I catch it again; another awkward smile, signalling that he hasn't told me everything yet. But then, why should he? He is free to do what he wants and this is thrilling and wonderful for him. 'Unless you've been already?' I suggest.

'Um, we went down last weekend actually,' he says lightly, as if it's nothing.

'You stayed there? In the bus?'

'Yeah, it's dead cosy. Kind of quirky with all these cush-
ions and throws and there's a hot tub outside.'

'A hot tub?' I exclaim.

'Yeah.' He reddens as if I'm his mum, probing too closely
into his romantic life. 'They make perfect sense, out in the
wilds like that,' he adds defensively.

'I'm sure they do,' I say, trying to keep down a smile.

We head through to the shop where Marta asks what I
think of the new display they've created. Seventies-style
T-shirts, designed by Rod with a nod to disco-style graphics,
are framed beautifully and grace the bright white walls. 'It
looks fantastic,' I say truthfully, and it strikes me how far
this place has come on. In the early days it wasn't really a
shop at all; just a workshop with a tiny counter and a
harassed Rod, who ran the place single-handedly. He'd
worked as a graphic designer on a newspaper after college,
but he'd also loved live music and lots of our old college
friends were in bands, and they were always keen for him
to design their logos and merchandise. And he had always
wanted to work for himself. So when his newspaper had
gone under he'd used his payout to buy printing equipment
and take a lease on a scruffy little unit sandwiched between
a Polish grocer's and a quaint little dancewear shop, its
window filled with sugar-pink tutus and satin ballet shoes.

Right from the off, he'd done a brisk trade with orders
for bands, local companies and charity events. But it wasn't
until he took on the bright, ambitious, six-foot Marta with
her white-blonde pigtails and boundless energy that the shop
had been transformed into the enticing modern store it is
now.

Marta and I catch up on news, and just as I'm leaving

137

Rod says, 'Sorry, I haven't even asked how it's going with that guy, Posh Stephen—'

I smile. 'That's okay. It's kind of . . . nice. I've seen him a couple of times now.' I'm aware that compared to vintage bus sleepovers that probably sounded a bit mundane. 'I've been busy with work,' I add. 'They're short-staffed at the moment so we haven't been able to see each other again—'

'But you like him?'

'Yes.' I smile. 'Yes, I do.'

'I'm glad,' Rod says warmly. 'Oh, and I forgot, I have something for you . . .' He reaches for something from beneath the counter and hands it to me.

'Oh, thanks!'

'It's a reject,' he adds, indicating where the T-shirt's colours are misaligned, 'but I thought you could use it for running?' He grins at me. 'It's got go-faster stripes.'

'Perfect.'

'Not that you need them,' he teases. 'I'm sure you're like a gazelle out there on the streets.'

I'm so tempted to retaliate by ribbing him about the hot tub. *It's funny, you saying they make perfect sense out in the wilds, because you always mocked them before. You called them sex ponds, remember? They're a swirling soup of pubic hair, you said* . . . But I don't because Marta is there, folding T-shirts neatly and, anyway, I am happy for Rod, that he has met someone wonderful. And I get the sense that he won't find sex pond jokes very funny anymore.

CHAPTER TWENTY

Stephen suggested this casual Korean place for dinner where we're presented with a vast array of tiny, beautiful dishes, all so prettily garnished and delicious. We're still getting to know each other, filling in the gaps piece by piece, like a jigsaw; discovering how our stories fit together. He chats happily about his daughter and his son, both of whom are studying in Edinburgh (medicine and physics respectively) and sound like exemplary offspring, sailing through their exams, gaining top grades, doing zillions of extra-curricular activities. 'They sound like brilliant kids,' I say. 'And so smart.'

'It's more about hard work really,' he remarks. 'Anyone can make the best of themselves if they're prepared to put in the graft.'

Well, not everyone can be a doctor or a physicist, I'm thinking. 'I guess so, but people have different qualities, don't they? And not everybody is naturally academic. I mean, I wasn't. I struggled quite a lot at school, and Hannah did too—'

'But that didn't matter, did it?' he asks, spearing a frilly little dumpling that looks like a shell. 'Because you had a clear career path in mind, and you got what you wanted. You *applied* yourself.'

'It wasn't all straightforward, though,' I tell him. 'I had a surprise pregnancy, remember?'

'Yes, of course. But you soon got yourself back on track, didn't you? You must've been incredibly driven and determined—'

'A lot of that was down to Rod,' I explain, wondering why I'm feeling prickly tonight and not just taking Stephen's compliments with grace. Maybe it's because Kirsten called this morning, to say that Mum had mentioned her 'friend' again. Apparently he'd phoned her and they'd had another 'lovely chat', during which he'd arranged to visit again soon. (When I dropped round at lunchtime to 'casually' find out what had been going on, Mum claimed that there had been no phone call. 'No one rings me these days,' she announced.)

Or maybe it's Rod and the love bus in the woods that's niggling me, for some bizarre reason? If that's it, it doesn't make any sense at all. Of course he was going to meet someone eventually. Maybe I'm just worried he's jumping in too quickly, I muse, realising how ridiculous I'm being. As if he's a fragile, inexperienced teenage boy and I'm his mum.

Relax, for goodness' sake, I tell myself as Stephen asks me more about Hannah, and which university she went to. 'She went to college,' I tell him. 'She started off doing graphics, like her dad, but then she switched to media and communications and that led to her job at the podcast company.'

'Right. She was lucky, then.' I'm not sure how to interpret

this. Is a media and communications course not impressive to him?

'I guess she was,' I say, 'to find a job she loves. And she's really happy in London.'

'What does Rod do?' he asks. For some unfathomable reason, this triggers an enthusiastic spiel as if I'm his unofficial publicist. 'The business has really grown,' I say proudly, 'because he takes such care with quality and design. It's not your cheap tat, not those rubbishy T-shirts you could split through and that fade after three washes, or the design goes all crackly and peels off.' I stop suddenly. *Stop ranting on about the quality of Rod's dyes,* I tell myself. *You're being weird,* as Hannah would say.

Now Stephen is asking me about my job. He's being attentive and interested, and maybe I'm just not used to being with someone like this. Again, I remind myself to relax. 'It's actually working out okay,' I say with a smile. 'The shift goes so quickly and they're such nice, friendly people. And it's good to feel useful again.'

He smiles too. 'I really admire you, Jen.'

'Really?' I meet his gaze. 'Why's that?'

'For picking yourself up and dusting yourself down like that.'

'Oh. Thank you!' I'm sort of pleased but wish he hadn't made me sound like a battered old pair of trainers he'd found hiding under a bed.

'I know this job won't be forever, but it's something, isn't it?' he adds.

'Yes, definitely.' I nod. 'If you're ever thinking of dropping in, make it just after nine-thirty. That's when I'm out with my gun—'

'Your gun?' He looks startled.

141

'Not a real gun,' I say quickly. 'I mean the sticker machine for marking down stuff that's about to go out of date.' I chuckle. 'There's loads for 10p if you time it right. You could probably fill your freezer for a couple of quid!'

'Really?' He laughs in a stilted way, as if I've told a joke he didn't quite get. Because of course, Stephen doesn't do his grocery shopping at places like that and he probably didn't even know about end-of-day reductions.

By the time we leave the restaurant I've managed to push all thoughts of Rod and Gaby and Mum's mysterious (perhaps imaginary?) friend out of my mind, and as we wander past the row of bars and shuttered shops I suggest another drink.

'Sure, why not?' Stephen says brightly. We find a cosy bar with tarnished mirrors and flickering candles on the old worn tables and laid-back Latin music playing quietly in the background. Although the place is busy there's one vacant table, tucked away at the back, and as we settle in with our drinks I'm thinking: I wonder how he'd react if I suggested he comes back to mine tonight? We've only had that one kiss in the street, and he doesn't seem in any hurry to move things along, which is fine, of course – respectful, I guess. Unlike Rod's hot tub scenario this feels like a slow burner but, heck, it's a Saturday night, not a school night. So why not?

Yet I don't have the nerve to suggest it. I can't face the very real possibility that he might seem a bit shocked and blurt out a polite, 'No thank you.' So instead I say, 'Can I ask you something?'

'Yes, of course.'

I clear my throat. 'Erm, I don't know how to ask this, or what the etiquette is really. I mean, I know it's different these days, a lot more *fluid*, and I'm fairly new to this thing and I know you are too—'

'Hey,' he cuts in gently. 'What're you saying? What's different these days? What's fluid?'

'Oh, you know!' I'm aware of my face glowing hot. 'The dating thing. The way people do it . . .'

He seems to be studying me with amusement, as if enjoying the show and wondering what I'm going to do next. 'So, what were you going to ask me?'

'Well, I just wondered if you're seeing other people from the site?'

Stephen blinks at me and I register his handsome features – the strong nose, the chiselled cheekbones – deciding that I really do like this man, and not just because of his eye-pleasing qualities. He's a proper grown-up who's proud of his kids, and he's decent and kind and doesn't give the impression that he'll mess me around.

'Actually,' he says, 'I'm not.' Another flicker of amusement in his greenish eyes. 'Are you?'

'Um, no, I'm not either.' We look at each other for a moment, seeming a little surprised, yet happy to have discovered a new thing we have in common.

'I'm kind of enjoying this,' Stephen adds. 'Spending time with you, I mean . . .'

'I am too.'

'Well, we've got that out of the way, then,' he says with a small laugh, and his hand squeezes mine. We stay until last orders, sitting close together and chatting easily about our parents, our childhoods, funny anecdotes from our working lives; further piecing together of the jigsaw. I tell him about the skinny teenager in a grey hoodie who'd snatched a joint of beef right in front of me last night and knocked me into a display of pineapples in his hurry to leg it out of the shop.

'God, Jen.' He looks aghast. 'Were you hurt?'

'Oh no, I was fine. I just wish I could've done something to stop him. I should've chased him—'

'That's not part of your remit, is it?'

'No,' I say, laughing. 'It's not my job to wrestle shoplifters to the ground.'

'Well, that *is* a relief,' he says, and perhaps the thought of me being shoved into a fruit display is still niggling at him, because he puts an arm around my shoulders as we leave.

Once again, I'm seized by an urge to suggest he comes over to my place sometime. No, not sometime. *Tonight*. It's simmering up in me, that yearning to feel wanted and desired and to do all those things I haven't done in so long. I am aware of my heart pounding as we scan the street for a taxi.

Ask him, I will myself. *Just say it.* Yet, even though I'm pretty sure he wouldn't be appalled and run away screaming, I still lack the nerve to suggest it.

There's a scarcity of cabs tonight and we stand for a few minutes, looking up and down the street. 'Um, I was wondering . . .' he starts.

Oh my God. He's going to ask *me* to go home with him! I'm going to have sex for this first time since Hotel de Buenos Amigos which, although it was 'only' two years ago, might as well have been on Mars for how hazy and distant it feels now. I don't have my toothbrush or moisturiser or a spare pair of knickers but, what the hell, I won't desiccate after one night without my hyaluronic lotion. And I can always rub on a bit of his toothpaste with my finger and turn my knickers inside out.

'. . . What I mean is,' he's saying, as these thoughts of knickers and night cream shoot around my brain, 'I'm pretty full on with work all next week . . .' Oh, right. So he's too busy to see me. This new revelation has the effect of a pin to a balloon. 'It gets like this sometimes,' he adds apologetically. 'It all piles up.' *Are you really not seeing other people?* I'm thinking. *Or could it be that it's not work, but dates that are piling up?* '. . . But d'you remember that restaurant I was telling you about, at Loch Earn?'

'Yes?'

'Would you like to go there for lunch next weekend?'

I almost laugh. 'It's a long way to go for lunch,' I blurt out.

'Yes, but we could make a day of it, if you'd like that? They do an amazing tasting menu and we could explore the area a bit.'

I look at him, thinking, well, that does sound lovely, but would it be an okay thing to do? I've read about it since he first mentioned it, and know it's garnered heaps of awards and is in a stunning location, perched on the edge of the loch. But I'm also thinking it really is a long way to go with a man I'm only just getting to know – and we'd be out in the wilds, miles from anywhere. And now I'm picturing Rod, warning me that Posh Stephen could turn out to be Psycho Stephen who's lured me out to a remote location, not to enjoy a tasting menu but to disembowel me in the woods. I could be discovered years from now, washed up on the shores of the loch, nibbled by fish. *Aren't there hundreds of perfectly good restaurants in Glasgow?* he'd ask. I catch myself being ridiculous when, mere minutes ago, I was itching to ask him to come home with me.

'I'd love that,' I tell him.

'Great,' Stephen says. 'I'll book it then.' He bends to kiss me and there they are again – those tiny sparks shooting around my brain. I'm still feeling all sparkly and light, filled with delicious anticipation, as the taxi pulls up and takes me home.

CHAPTER TWENTY-ONE

There's no slow, piecing-the-jigsaw-together approach with Rod. He seems to have flung himself in, seeing Gaby constantly to the point where Marta gives me a pointed look next time I pop into the shop, explaining, 'He's gone out for lunch, Jen. He said he might be quite a while.'

'Really?' I'd be no more surprised if he'd nipped out to have his entire body waxed.

'Yeah, seems to be a bit of a thing these days.' She gives me a knowing smile, and now I get it.

'Oh, I see!'

'Yeah.' She presses her lips together and grins.

'Wow.'

'I *know*,' she says, blue eyes wide, our minimal exchange being code for, *Amazing, isn't it? Rod – our Rod – who never takes lunch apart from cramming in a sandwich at the back of the shop is now gliding out for an extended rendezvous several times a week, with his new lady.*

When Hannah and I discuss this development later we both agree it's just what he's needed. On the days she was at her dad's as a child, he'd always make sure he was free to pick her up from school. But since she's grown up his working hours have spilled over into evenings and weekends, and we've teased him that he might as well live in the shop. We both know he works too hard but whenever I've mentioned it he's said, 'I'm as happy there as anywhere else.' And I wondered if his utter immersion in the business was one of the reasons he and Nesta drifted apart.

'Are you okay about it, though, Mum?' Hannah is asking now.

''Course I am,' I say, tugging a brush through my hair as I get ready for work. 'Why wouldn't I be?'

'It's just a bit . . . different, isn't it? For him I mean – meeting someone online?'

'You kept saying everyone does it,' I remind her.

'Yeah, but that was for you. This is him!'

I laugh. 'I must admit, I was pretty surprised when he signed up.'

'I couldn't believe it either,' she says.

'Maybe he'd just got to the stage where he was feeling a bit lonely, with only Casey for company?'

'Yeah. A lonely cat man,' she says with a tinge of sympathy. She adores her dad and occasionally, when she was much younger, she'd mention something about us not being together, as if she couldn't figure out why that was. As my own mother has implied, divorce is easier to explain. *We grew apart. We wanted different things,* as Mum put it to me, when she and Dad split. *And he's always cared more about that damn boat than anything else. He might as well have thrown thousands and thousands of pounds into the sea!*

There was no bitterness between Rod and me because, as we'd never been together as a couple, there was nothing to be bitter about. In fact, it was pretty obvious that we were extremely fond of each other; we had our family days out and even weekends and holidays all together, and all Hannah ever saw was us messing around and hanging around together, being Mum and Dad who obviously liked each other very much.

'Why don't you just marry each other?' she asked once, looking delighted at the very possibility.

'We love each other, honey, but just as friends,' I told her.

'But you had me!' Even at six years old she knew that babies were made by some mysterious process involving love.

'Why d'you think we should be married?' I asked, worried that she was harbouring some deep-rooted sadness over us living separately.

'Because a wedding would be fun. And I could be a bridesmaid!' I breathed a sigh of relief. 'And I don't want Daddy to be lonely,' she'd added, 'when I'm not there.' Even back then I'd figured that was one of reasons she'd started haranguing him to get a puppy, before they had compromised on a cat. She'd been worried about him being all by himself in his flat.

'Have you checked her Instagram?' Hannah asks now.

'Who, Gaby's?'

'Yes, of course—'

'He showed me, actually,' I tell her, deciding not to mention that I've studied it forensically since then. 'Have you seen it?'

''Course I have,' she says. 'He was a bit cagey about it but as soon as he mentioned her vintage bus I knew she'd have one.' She pauses for breath.

'It looks amazing, doesn't it? Kind of fairy-tale-like.'

149

'It's gorgeous,' she agrees. And now she wants an update on *my* dating adventures, and when I tell her about the planned trip to Loch Earn she exclaims, laughing, 'God, Mum. What's happening to my parents? It's like you're both embarking on these whole new lives!'

I smooth down my hair and check my reflection. No need for a French plait or a full face of make-up for my work shifts these days. 'We're only going for lunch,' I say.

'That's a long way to go for lunch . . .'

'That's exactly what I said.'

'Aw, it sounds *romantic*,' Hannah says. I know she's smiling and I'm hit with a pang of missing her, of wishing she wasn't four hundred miles away and that tonight, instead working my shift, we could be cosied up with one of our movies and toast. 'Love you, Mum,' she adds. 'Hope you have a great time. You deserve it too.'

I'm getting to know the regular customers at work. I even have favourites who are mainly elderly and far too proud to make it obvious that they're hovering, poised for the stickering, hoping to grab a bargain or two. Sometimes I give them the nod that there's a whole load of vegetables about to be reduced, or that I'm heading for the baked goods. Otherwise they might miss out, because certain customers have no qualms about barging their way towards the goodies and snatching the entire lot. Fridays can be especially hectic with customers swerving in on their way home from the pub, and tonight two grown men almost come to blows over a reduced custard tart. I have to utilise all of my BudgieAir skills to defuse the tension, guiding the 'losing' customer towards acceptable substitutes and engaging him in a bit of jokey chat.

'I saw what you did there,' says Sumi, a little while later. 'I'm so impressed how you handled those two guys.' Stephen would probably think it was bizarre to feel proud when he sorts out divorces and child custody issues for a living, but I glow with pride for the rest of my shift.

I've just finished when Fabs texts me: *I hear you're going away with someone you've met. Need to discuss!* Hannah must have told Jacob, who told his mum. Word travels fast, I reflect with a smile.

Still in the shop's car park, I fire off a quick reply: *Only for lunch. But we're making a whole day of it and I think I'm going to ask him back to mine afterwards.* Is it mad to put that? To share the details as if I'm nineteen? *Pretty excited,* I add.

The instant I've pressed send, she calls me. 'You mean you haven't done it yet?'

'No!' I can't help laughing at her directness.

'How many times have you seen him?'

'Only three.'

'How chaste you're being, Jennifer.'

'It just hasn't come up,' I say with a smirk.

'Obviously!'

'Well, I'll see how things go and I promise I'll report back.'

'Hmm.' A pause. 'Have you been to his place?'

'No, not yet. But maybe tomorrow—'

'Jen?' she cuts in. 'You don't think there's a *reason* why he hasn't asked you over, do you?'

I frown as it dawns on me what she's getting at. 'D'you mean . . . he might be married or something?'

'I'm sorry,' she says quickly. 'I shouldn't even have mentioned it.'

'I . . . I don't think he can be. I mean, we're going out for the whole day . . .'

'People can figure out alibis, darling.' She pauses. 'I am sorry. I don't want to spoil things. It's just, it's happened to me so maybe have your radar on for it?'

'Yes, I will.'

A small pause hangs. 'D'you ever call him in the evenings?'

'Um, no. I'm usually working . . .'

'Oh, of course.'

'If he is married,' I add, 'surely he'd be on one of those sites specifically for people looking for affairs? If he wanted something on the side, I mean?'

'Hmmm, maybe. But they're everywhere, those types.'

'And wouldn't he have suggested coming back to my place before now? If he just wanted a bit of illicit sex?'

'Oh, I don't know. Just ignore me, okay? Jacob's always telling me off for blurting things out without thinking, for not filtering myself. I just don't want you to be messed around, that's all.'

'No, I'm glad you said it,' I say truthfully.

'How about the other men? Who else have you been chatting to?'

'No one. It's just been Stephen lately.'

'Really?' She sounds surprised. 'Remember what I said about eggs, basket . . .'

'I'll see how tomorrow goes,' I tell her quickly, wishing I could push away the niggle of unease that's started up in the pit of my stomach. 'Am I mad for taking Stephen at face value,' I add, 'believing everything he says?'

'Not mad, darling,' she says firmly. 'But dating is an adventure and sometimes, you know, any adventure can be a bit of a bumpy ride.'

Fabs's warning lingers in my mind to the point where, just before bed, I browse my daily matches for the first time in ages. And I see that Mr Marmite has messaged me again.

Hi again Jennifer,

You didn't reply, heartbreaker you! Hope you're enjoying the site anyway. If you're ever at a loose end, and there's absolutely nothing on TV (that dates me doesn't it? Remember when there really would be nothing on TV?) then maybe you'd like to drop me a line? My name is Harvey and I'm not a weird stalker, I promise. I'm a normal bloke just doing what we all do on here. Staying hopeful but wondering, actually, if I should buy a kayak.

Maybe I should tell you a little bit more about myself? I have it on good authority that my home-baked bread is the best in Glasgow's Southside and also that I am a terrible dancer!

Love, Harvey x

I examine his cheery face, his slightly lopsided smile and tousled reddish hair. He looks like he'd be a laugh on a night out, and he's a refreshing alternative to all those men posing in executive settings, with their shiny desks and even a lectern, in one instance, or the hordes of cyclists in body-hugging Lycra. In contrast Harvey is wearing a sweater, and it looks as if his selfie was taken in his garden. At forty-seven he's also a little younger than any of the other guys who've been in touch. Feeling bad for ignoring him, I reply: *Thanks for your message. You sound like a really nice person but I'm kind of seeing someone now and I'd like to see how that goes.*

At almost midnight I'm not expecting a reply straight away. But within minutes his message appears: *Sure I can't tempt you with my hula hooping? I can keep it up for hours!*

He's added a shocked-face emoji and, boosted by a large glass of wine, I can't help laughing as I reply: *Cheeky.*

—*Sorry to brag but it literally is my only sporting 'skill'.*

—*It's probably remiss of me to pass up the opportunity but sorry, no thanks.*

—*Aw well, hope it works out for you then. He's a lucky guy!*

Is it that simple, I wonder now? Or is Stephen stringing me along and not being entirely honest about his life?

I'm going to find out, I decide. I'll assume we're going to his place, when we get back to Glasgow tomorrow. Surely we will, after a day out together, and a special lunch? Or is he planning to drop me off at my flat and drive away as if we've been on a school trip?

No, I'm going to assume it's actually going to happen, and that at some point tomorrow Stephen and I will be naked together. And that's going to need a *lot* more preparation than a Glasgow to Marrakech flight.

CHAPTER TWENTY-TWO

It's a perfect summer's morning when Stephen picks me up from my flat. As we leave the city behind us, the swooping hills are illuminated by bright sunlight. It's a classic scenic calendar vista, of the kind Mum sends to Phil and Loretta every year at Christmas to pin up in their Australian state-sized kitchen. (I doubt very much if they do.) The sky, scattered with a few tiny white clouds, is the almost impossible blue of a filtered photo.

Stephen's car smells pretty new and is pristine inside. Well, of *course* it is. A senior partner in a legal practice doesn't carry around a scattering of tissues, cookie wrappers, crisp packets and bottles of dried-up nail polish as I do. His car is for transportation only, not for copious snacking or emergency manicure touch-ups.

He puts on the radio, and an old favourite of mine comes on: 'Lovely Day' by Bill Withers. It is, I muse. We have the whole of this glorious Saturday ahead of us, which is *way* above a wet Monday night, or even a Friday, in the pecking order of dates. And as we chat easily about our respective weeks, any remaining niggles start to ease away and I remind myself that Stephen is an admirably sorted, grown-up man, undoubtedly with pensions in order and a boiler-maintenance plan. And that's why we're taking things at this stately pace, because *that's what proper grown-ups do*.

In fact, he's opening up more on our drive north than he has on our previous dates. I discover that his late father was distant and didn't even go to his graduation; 'because there was some big social event happening and that was more important to him.' I also learn that his mother, who has also passed away, wasn't overly troubled by what her only child made of his life as long as it was something she could brag to her friends about.

'I bet she was proud of you though,' I venture.

'Oh, I don't know about that,' he says briskly. 'And it didn't really worry me, once I'd got my own proper adult life started.' Maybe that's it, I decide; he's had to forge his own life without an awful lot of parental support, and that's made him a little reversed and self-contained, focused on his career and being a better parent than his own mum and dad had been to him.

I feel quite honoured now that he's finally sharing a little more, and actually a little guilty about my own dark secret: the fact that I've taken the precautionary move of stashing my toothbrush and a travel-sized toothpaste into my bag – plus my cleanser, day moisturiser, night cream, deodorant, basic make-up, clean knickers, socks, a hairbrush and condoms, bought specially for the occasion, just in case Stephen is without any, which I doubt, but I'd rather our first night together didn't feature a panicky dash to a petrol station.

I can almost *feel* the box at the bottom of my bag,

self-consciously new – in the way that white trainers glare too brightly the first time you wear them out. In fact, I did find a packet in my bedroom drawer, among the tangle of redundant adapters and cables and an unopened jar of some kind of youth-making elixir that Leena had urged me to try. But I estimated that, as they were probably even older than the spices in my kitchen cupboard, they'd be as useful as my antique dried coriander as a contraceptive and likely to disintegrate on exposure to air.

On top of all that, I have packed tweezers in case a spiky hair should sprout, like a rogue thistle, from my face during the night; and also pyjamas, which would suggest that I'm heading for Girl Guide camp rather than a potentially erotic encounter. It's that menopausal thing – those gushing night sweats. 'I'm still waking up all slick and wet,' I complained to Rod recently.

'Like an otter?' he asked, without missing a beat. So, if I do end up staying over, I'm hoping a layer of M&S brushed cotton will blot the worst of it and avoid Stephen's undoubtedly expensive Egyptian cotton sheets being turned to mulch.

Oh, and there's hair conditioner too, in my bulging bag of secrets! But only because Stephen's neat crop suggests that he doesn't bother with it and I'd rather avoid having to literally tear a comb through an unconditioned, fuzzy thatch in the morning. Of course it goes without saying that I have exfoliated my entire body, buffing it to a sheen like a car bonnet and pruned my pubes in readiness. (No fuzzy thatch there!) Although I'm pretty sure he wouldn't faint at the sight of me in my untended, natural state, I have no intention of being viewed as an object of curiosity from a bygone age like the mummified crocodile at Kelvingrove Museum.

So yes, I am fully prepared for staying over. In fact I'm wondering now, as we take the road that ribbons its way along the lochside, whether I may have overdone it a little. I watched a documentary recently about wild animals that live in the Australian bush. And I suspect great sex only happens when your pubic hair could shelter a colony of possums and your morning breath could kill a horse.

As he's timed it so we've arrived an hour before our reservation, we stroll along the shores of the loch, which glitters beneath the bright sun. The mountains are hazy purple, and we follow a path up and away from the tiny village where the restaurant is perched on the water's edge.

From up high the views are spectacular. I'm a little bowled over by being here, strolling along the bracken-edged paths with my curiously bulging shoulder bag and a man I'm warming to even more. Hunger grows in me, not just for the carnal delights I've already pictured, salaciously, in my mind but also for lunch – and by the time we arrive at the restaurant I am ravenous.

Formerly two ancient cottages, it has been remodelled beautifully, whitewashed and adorned with hanging baskets and a discreet sign over a window, etched in slate. Inside it's all knobbly bare stone walls, rustic mismatched wooden furniture and flickering candles. Most of the tables are occupied by couples, plus one family with a young daughter and grandparents, presumably celebrating an occasion. It's relaxed and casual, yet very special, just as Stephen had described.

'They do the best oysters I've ever had here,' he tells me, as we study the menus.

'I've never actually had one,' I admit.

'Really? The people who run this place have their own farm on the loch. So the oysters have had to travel less than two hundred metres to the table. Shall we have a couple each to start?'

'Why not?' I say, feeling emboldened. I am the kind of woman who goes to the Highlands for a posh lunch and eats oysters, I decide. That person who once – okay, pretty recently – ate cold rice pudding straight from the tin and strained a bottle of 'bitty' wine through a pair of tights is long gone! Now I work regular hours, serving the community, which is also enabling me to keep a closer eye on my mother and possibly even enjoy a proper relationship with a man.

My God. I might be one of those women who drops the term 'my boyfriend' into conversation without it sounding as bizarre as 'my butler'. And now I'm thinking, isn't modern dating brilliant? So easy! Why didn't I try it years ago, instead of stubbornly thinking it was 'contrived' and likely only to lead to heartache and cock shots? So far, I haven't been sent a single photo of an erect appendage. Perhaps the *members* of Mature Matches are too well behaved for that?

Glancing out over the shimmering water, where a yellow fishing boat is bobbing along, I take a moment to give silent thanks to Hannah, Jacob and Fabs for urging me to do this. And now I'm wondering if maybe one day Stephen and I will be sitting at another restaurant, not on the shores of a Scottish loch but the Aegean Sea, on the Greek island of Santorini, having redeemed my prize for being the top Budgie toy seller in the skies and – oh, our oysters have arrived!

CHAPTER TWENTY-THREE

I look down at them glistening in their shells, waiting for Stephen to demonstrate how to eat them. While I'm not a complete dunce, in that I do know you don't start hacking at them with a knife and fork like fish fingers, I'm still not quite sure how to tackle them. Do you pick up the shell and slurp the thing down? If so, what's the purpose of the curious implement – a sort of two-pronged teaspoon – that's been placed beside them?

'Let's tuck in then,' he announces. I watch what he does, taking care not to make it obvious that I'm watching. Then, following his example, I use the implement to make sure my first oyster is detached from its shell, and tip it into my mouth. *Mmm, lovely!* I tell myself, catching a glint of amusement in his eyes as I gnaw away on it gamely. Okay, maybe 'lovely' isn't the right word; it's more 'interesting' and certainly an 'acquired taste', and at fifty years old it's about time I acquired it. At least, I'm not going to be a baby and spit it back out onto the plate.

'What's the verdict?' Stephen asks.

I choke the jelloid thing down. 'Delicious!'

'You might enjoy more if you give it just a couple of little bites to release the flavour, and then swallow,' he advises.

'Hmmm, right. Okay.' I shrug off a shiver of unease at the lingering texture and taste (frankly disgusting) and the oddness of being instructed – a shade too loudly – on how to eat. As for the second oyster, rather than even *attempting* to smuggle it into my hand and drop it into a nearby pot plant, I decide there's only one thing for it, and that's to adopt the same approach as when I found myself having terrible sex with a boy I'd been seeing for a few weeks, back when I was a student. Having believed, mistakenly, that I was in love with Eliot Higginbottom, it wasn't until we were actually doing it, and he was instructing me where to position my legs (perilously close to his two-bar electric fire as it turned out) that it hit me like a lightning bolt that I didn't want to be doing this with him at all. My best course of action, I decided, was to get it over with as quickly as possible.

I know it's a *terrible* thing to do, and that young women of Hannah's generation would be appalled by the very concept of getting-it-over-with sex, and call a halt to proceedings immediately (at least, I hope to God they would), in the unlikely event that they ever found themselves in such a situation. But that's what I did then, and when Stephen asks again, 'So, what's the verdict on oysters?' I fib that they were pretty nice.

Happily, things improve from that point. We're having the tasting menu, featuring tiny slivers of salmon in gooseberry butter and lobster, which I hadn't had either, and love. Everything is utterly delicious and not remotely reminiscent of the terrible sex I had in a bedroom that smelt of fried onions in the late Eighties.

'This place is amazing,' I enthuse, glancing out at the stunning view over the loch.

'Yeah, my kids have always loved coming here,' Stephen says. 'It's been a favourite of ours for years.'

'You mean you brought them here when they were little?'

'Yes.' He smiles. 'Since they were about four or five, I guess.'

'And they liked this kind of food then?'

'Oh, yes,' he says brightly. 'They loved it.'

'Did they have oysters?' I ask, incredulously as, back then, Rod and I knew there was no point in taking Hannah out to eat anywhere apart from our favourite Italian in the city centre, with its wipeable gingham tablecloths and enormous bowls of spag bol.

'Yep, they were keen to try everything,' Stephen says.

I smile at him, still wondering how today will end, and whether my carefully assembled overnight kit will be put to good use. 'When I was a kid,' I tell him, 'if we ate out as a family it was always sweet and sour pork in a neon orange sauce.'

'Ha, yes. We had that too,' he says. 'There was a big place just off Sauchiehall Street, wasn't there?'

'Yeah, that was the one!'

'Is it still there?'

'I'm not sure . . .' We have finished our lunch and Stephen is sipping his non-alcoholic elderflower cordial. I've been spinning out a large glass of Chablis, having decided that's my limit for lunch. I don't want to be all snoozy later, when things might *happen*, and I'm not keen on looking like a lush either. Pulling out my phone from my bag, I google the legendary Chinese restaurant and show him the screen.

'Yes, that's it,' he says. We pore over lurid photographs

of the determinedly retro dishes they still offer, and then dawdle over coffee. The afternoon has turned golden and the loch gleams, its silken surface broken only by a couple of sailing boats. 'We should probably head back fairly soon,' he offers.

'Yes.' I nod. 'This has been amazing,' I add.

'I've really enjoyed it . . .' He pauses and smiles a little awkwardly. 'I was going to ask you, if you don't have to go home tonight . . . I mean, if you'd like to come round to mine, you know, you'd be very welcome.'

'Oh,' I say, sounding pleasantly surprised, as if I hadn't spent two hours this morning on extensive preparations. 'No, I don't think I *have* to go home . . .' I pause and look thoughtful as if just mentally confirming with myself that my imaginary houseplants could survive without water for the next twenty-four hours.

'Great, then,' he says. I beam at him, then get up and make for the ladies' where I stand for a moment, fizzling with delight that we are going to do it tonight because there is no secret wife at home! He hasn't been lying and setting me up as his bit on the side! I check my reflection, gratified that, while flushed with the wine and excitement, I'm still presentable. I opted for natural make-up today, which actually took three times as long to apply as my Budgie face, which I could slap on in five minutes. I'm feeling less sad about my old job these days, I realise; at least, I no longer wake up bereft that I'm not a flight attendant anymore.

My life is moving on, I decide as I leave the ladies' and stride back into the restaurant where Stephen is looking so handsome as he sits there studying his phone. I've recovered from my redundancy and instead of moping at home, anaesthetising myself with Londis wine, I'm putting myself out there and working hard, meeting people, *serving my community* in the world of cut-price groceries. And I'm dating, and it's not a dismal world of Radiator Ralphs after all!

Stephen glances up and flinches as if startled to see me there. All at once, I recognise what that was. A red flag. The warning sign that Hannah told me about: 'After one of those there's no going back.'

Quickly, he puts the phone back on the table and repositions the pepper pot unnecessarily.

I pause, wondering if I've just read that all wrong; if I have made a mistake. But I know I haven't, and that that wasn't his own phone that Stephen was studying – but mine.

'Hi.' I sit down and form a smile as I scan his expression. 'Everything okay?'

Why can't I just say it? Why can't I ask, *What were you doing with my phone while I was in the loo?*

'Yeah-yeah. Fine.' His smile is tight and his cheeks have reddened. An awkward pause hovers above us as I study him, this utterly grown-up man who sorts out people's marriages and families and lives. A well-heeled, successful, good-looking man who checks a woman's phone when she goes to the ladies'.

'Were you checking my phone just then?' I ask lightly.

'No, of course not.' His mouth twitches. 'I just couldn't help seeing a message come up,' he adds quickly. 'A text, I mean. I couldn't avoid it.'

I blink at him, figuring that of course he's right; my texts appear as notifications. Anyone can see them. The red flag flaps in the periphery of my vision, growing bigger by the second. 'So . . . you read it?'

'It was just *there*,' he says with a frown. For a moment, it's as if I've been removed from the situation and am watching as an observer; as if I am one of the young, attractive staff in the blue tunics who have looked after us so beautifully today. *Keep calm. You're having a lovely day so don't over-react. It's nothing really.*

'Oh, right.' I pick up my phone and check the message.

'I just thought it was a bit funny,' Stephen adds, 'when you said you hadn't been seeing anyone else.'

I stare at him. 'I haven't. I mean, I met a couple of people right at the start . . .' Why the hell am I justifying myself? 'But I didn't meet them again,' I add.

'So, was that message from one of them?' he asks.

'No!' I exclaim, almost wanting to laugh. 'It's from Rod, Hannah's dad. You know all about him. He's one of my best friends—'

'And a bit more than that maybe?' he cuts in.

'What?' I gawp at him, unable to form any more words and certainly not prepared to explain my relationship with Rod to him. Besides, I have already. Stephen knows all about our student days, when we were close friends and even flatmates for a spell, when Rod would routinely parcel up a lump of cheap cheddar in a tortilla wrap, shove it into the microwave and pronounce it a 'meal'. He knows about our drunken night together a few years later, and the pregnancy, and how we've been parents together ever since.

I stare at the message. It reads: *Can I nip over for blowtorch?*

The restaurant has gone very quiet – we are the only customers left – and I'm aware of my heart beating horribly fast as I place my phone back on the table and look at Stephen.

'You didn't think that was something . . . suggestive, did you?'

'Well, it seems like it.' He shrugs and his nostrils flare. 'So is it a friends with benefits kind of thing you two have?' He's adopted a blasé tone as if he doesn't really care, but would quite like to know all the same.

'Of course it's not.' I can't take my eyes off his face. In a minute he'll laugh, I tell myself. It's all been a joke, and although it's not remotely amusing I might just forgive him – because he's tried to be funny and I have already suspected that hilarity isn't his strong point. *Ha-ha, can we move on now please and also could you never again pry at my phone?*

'If there's a thing going on,' he's saying now, scowling and twiddling his coffee spoon, 'I'd rather you told me now because I've actually had some bad experiences with liars and time-wasters on the site—'

'Stephen,' I cut in sharply, 'd'you really think I'm a liar and a time-waster?'

A waitress appears bearing a stack of bread baskets. On registering the mood she turns and scoots back into the kitchen. 'I really don't know,' he replies.

I thrust my phone towards him. 'D'you know what that message is?'

'Well, I think I can guess,' he says, turning pompous now. 'It's hardly subtle, is it—'

'You think it's code for something?' My mouth quivers.

'Yes, of course—'

'Well you're wrong,' I say in the polite-but-firm voice I always used to adopt whenever a passenger refused to clip on their seatbelt during turbulence. 'That's not it at all. It's not code for anything. It just means Rod lent me his blowtorch and now he wants it back.'

CHAPTER TWENTY-FOUR

Gaby, 48

It's not just Rod who arrives next morning but Rod and Gaby. She is even lovelier in real life: long-legged and lean in faded jeans and a Breton top, with her abundant light brown hair piled casually up on top of her head.

'Sorry if we've disturbed your Sunday morning,' she says.

'Oh no, not at all,' I reassure her, wishing I hadn't run out of ground coffee and had to offer them instant, and wasn't wearing black jersey 'trousers' (actually pyjamas but hopefully they pass as proper daytime attire?) plus a bobbly grey sweater that I'd flung on hastily.

In fact I'd expected just Rod. 'Just gonna pop over,' he'd said. And I hadn't imagined that my doorbell would be buzzing within twenty minutes of his call. It seemed the blowtorch was needed urgently. Also, gallingly, he's now telling Gaby why I'd asked to borrow it, and how I'd 'attacked' that chair, nearly setting myself alight in the process and narrowly missing asphyxiating myself with

fumes. Now we're all chuckling away at my reckless inept-
itude, how I'd flung myself into a furniture restoration
project whilst heavily medicated on white wine.

When the mirth has finally simmered down I learn the
following facts about Gaby Forest. She has a twenty-year-old
son who's volunteering in Tanzania, helping to build a
school. Originally from Cheshire, she arrived in Glasgow
ten years ago as her ex was setting up a business here,
running bars and clubs. They worked together until she
'kind of grew out of it,' she explains, 'and I wanted to set
up my own thing.' Presumably she grew out of him too.
'What d'you do, Jen?' she asks brightly.

'I work at a supermarket,' I reply.

A small silence falls, because no one knows what to say
about that, and then Rod is gamely prompting Gaby to tell
me all about her vintage bus. 'You're welcome to stay in
her anytime she's not booked out,' she says.

'Thanks, that's very kind of you.' I try to appear as if I'd
be keen to do that, perhaps marinating alone in the hot tub
that she and Rod had most likely recently had sex in.

Oh, it's ridiculous to feel this way, I tell myself as Gaby
shows me her Instagram – unaware, of course, that I have
studied it until my eyeballs were almost falling out of my
head. Embittered old hag that I am, I'm now feeling weirdly
all chewed up that Rod and Gaby are about to leave for
Dumfriesshire again; that's why he needed the blowtorch.
Gaby has bought a second bus down there – also to reno-
vate and rent out – which they are planning to work on
together.

As it's *not* that I'm envious I can't figure out why I'm
feeling this way. Maybe I'm still smarting over how yesterday's date ended; with the waitress, who could clearly

sense the tension, placing the bill between Stephen and me and retreating quickly, as if it were a firework about to go off.

Gratifyingly, Stephen had looked sheepish as he'd reached for it. 'Let's split this,' I'd said.

'No, no, I said it was my treat—'

'Stephen, we're splitting it,' I'd insisted in a fierce voice that hadn't seemed to belong to me. I'd never even addressed belligerent passengers in that way.

'Okay, okay . . .' He nodded and we'd managed the transaction curtly. 'I'm really sorry,' he added again. 'It was unforgivable to look at your phone. And I'm sorry for taking it the wrong way . . .'

'It's all right,' I said, although of course it had been too late for apologies.

The sky had darkened as we'd climbed into his car, and the shimmering loch had turned amethyst beneath gathering clouds. We'd chatted a little on the journey home but it was stilted and curt. And all the while I'd thought, *You packed your toothbrush, conditioner and condoms, idiot. What made you think he was right for you?*

As Stephen pulled up at my flat I said, 'Thanks. It was a lovely lunch, but I don't think we're—'

'Okay, that's fine.' He'd clicked into professional mode and I'm sure he wasn't that cut up really. 'Bye then,' he'd added, and that was that.

Last night, when I undressed, I looked at the pedicure I'd done for him, and as I slipped towards sleep I could still taste those oysters in my throat.

Now Rod is picking up his canvas bag containing the blowtorch and goggles. 'We'll be down there for a few days,' he tells me.

'Oh, what about the shop?' I ask, as if I'm his boss and he hasn't had his holiday approved.

'He's taking a bit of time off,' Gaby says with a wide smile.

'That's great,' I say, catching his eye. 'You need it, Rod.'

'You're saying I look knackered?' he teases.

'No, of course not—'

'I think he looks great!' Gaby announces, loyally, which has the strange effect of making me jam my back teeth together. It never felt like this with Nesta although, admittedly, they seemed to mooch along together like a couple of mates who happened to share a bed from time to time, with her ticking him off occasionally for letting his hair go 'A.P.' as she termed it ('Approaching Mullet').

I liked Nesta. She was witty and smart and kind enough, in her own brusque way – but I wasn't entirely convinced that they were crazy about each other. Their relationship seemed to be focused around Nesta lending Rod an awful lot of hefty books and encouraging him to watch challenging films with her, usually featuring immense torment and pain – and *always* subtitled – as if her main role had been to expand his mind.

'I hope the weather holds up for you,' I trill, inanely.

'Thanks,' Gaby says. 'And thanks for the coffee!'

Rod and Nesta had never been like this, I realise, as Gaby clutches his hand before they've even left my flat. Of course they hadn't because I guess, back then, Rod hadn't been in love. At least not in this sort of love, when you can't stop touching or looking at the other person. When your adoration for them is shining out of your eyes.

That's what he's like now, and I'm happy for him. I really am. But it strikes me that no one has ever looked at me in that way – and Rod's loved-up state will just take a bit of getting used to, that's all.

CHAPTER TWENTY-FIVE

And I decide I'll get used to Rod's new situation by keeping busy, so busy I barely have time to think about anything other than dropping in on Mum, helping with her garden when she'll allow it, and my work shifts, and applying for other jobs (although I'm kind of enjoying working with Kirsten and the others, I'm thinking there might be something else out there for me). So yes, my life is too full to be poring over anyone's holiday photos or even missing Rod very much at all.

When I have a *tiny* peek at Gaby's Instagram, I gather that this trip of theirs is mainly about the new bus she's acquired – dented and rusty but obviously with heaps of potential and charm. Over on Rod's Facebook, he's posted a picture of himself standing in front of it, brandishing the blowtorch and smiling proudly. It's unusual for him to post anything yet here he is, looking grimy but clearly happy in the sun-dappled clearing in the woods. He's always been good at DIY, at tinkering with vehicles and fixing things up.

When he comes back to Glasgow a few days later I gather that the trip was a huge success, that the bus is 'amazing' and Gaby plans to find more old vehicles, to build an empire of buses to let out through Under the Stars, a holiday letting site, or possibly even start up a site of her own. 'Cabins, yurts, that kind of thing,' Rod explains when we speak briefly on the phone. But communication between us is more sparse these days, which is to be expected of course – and that's fine. There's no reason for us to be in each other's pockets all the time.

Meanwhile, if I find myself with even a tiny gap in the day I've started to fill it by pounding the streets, determined to complete that running programme because I'm a sorted, together woman and that's what sorted, together women do; it's the law.

Running is good, I tell myself over and over as I canter along in my leggings and the T-shirt Rod gave me with the colours all misaligned. At least it's started to feel less like a terrible torture, designed to create humiliation and pain. 'You're growing stronger now,' the woman chirps into my ears. 'You're doing great!' Amazingly, I *am* making progress, with my 'ample' chest clamped tightly by my unyielding sports bra, made from girders. I imagine it's the kind of garment that might have been worn in Medieval times, during battles, if there'd been lady knights.

I'm now greeting these bright July mornings by running new routes along wide tree-lined avenues that I'd never explored before. While it's still pretty torturous I'm starting to understand why exercise is so popular, and not just with those 'I'm so active!' types on maturematches.com. Apart from the obvious benefits – i.e. looking less of a physical heap generally – there's the occasional sighting of the dashing silver fox. Whether alone or with a running buddy, he always waves and smiles when he sees me.

Plus, I can kind of *process* stuff while I'm running. Like the fact that Mum looked confused when I dropped in to see her yesterday, as if she'd been expecting someone else. And then, although she'd insisted on making the tea, I found her gazing at the kettle as if she couldn't quite remember what it was.

There were other things too. Clearly, she had been over-buying bird seed as several huge packets were piled on the worktop, and yet more were stacked up at the back door like sandbags in readiness for a flood. And when I glanced out into the garden I saw that, instead of filling the bird feeders, Mum had strewn great drifts of seed across the lawn and a whole load of crows were out there having a feeding frenzy.

She's always loved birds, my brother said, when I messaged him. *What harm's it doing?* More concerning to him was the fact that Nico the Shih Tzu had gnawed his hideously expensive calf leather wallet. ('We're wondering if she's hit puberty already and this is causing her to behave like this?')

Meanwhile Rod has been busy too, jaunting off down to Dumfriesshire yet *again*, less than a week after his last trip. This time I barely glance at Gaby's Instagram where there are pictures of him having acquired a light golden hue, possibly for the first time in his life. In fact I hadn't realised his pale Celtic skin, that's usually hidden beneath baggy T-shirts and old, worn jeans, could tan like that.

I just hope he's wearing a high-factor sunscreen, that's all. Even in South West Scotland he could still burn himself, and I know from our trips to the seaside with Hannah over the years that he has a terribly cavalier attitude towards the sun. 'It's fine, it's just that first-day thing,' he retorted once as I dabbed calamine lotion on his sizzled shoulders during a camping trip to Perthshire. As if sunburn was a tedious but necessary part of 'acclimatising' to warmer days.

I also hope he's applying a moisturising body lotion after his hot tub session because he seems to be spending an awful lot of time chest-deep in water and I wouldn't want his entire body to wrinkle like a prune. I'm also a little concerned that he's not being quite so hands-on with the shop these days, with all these lunches and trips and no more late-night working, from what I can gather. But Marta and Laurence know everything inside out. And if their boss is too busy shagging in an oversized paddling pool to take care of business, then that's really nothing to do with me.

Thank you for your recent application for the above-named position. I regret that you have not been selected for further consideration at this stage.

Then, a few days later:

We received an unprecedented number of applications for this role and will not be inviting you for a further interview on this occasion. May we take this opportunity to thank you for your interest and wish you the very best for your future career.

I can't understand why they don't want me, when I list all my skills. I mean, I could remember that the man in seat 62B was waiting for a bacon toastie and that the woman in 92A was due change from a tenner and I'd promised to warm a bottle of baby formula for the young mum in 17C. My eyes and ears were everywhere. I could spot a couple fiddling with each other under a blanket, even when I was three rows in front and serving coffee, and although – thankfully – it never happened, I'd have known *exactly* what to do if the plane had started to plummet towards the sea.

Perhaps I'm being too fussy in today's competitive job market, especially at fifty, when there are millions of eager young people desperate to start *their* careers. Perhaps I should be more open-minded and, while I'm at it, why not have a look at my daily matches too? Now I'm thinking maybe I've been too fussy here as well. It's a tricky business, getting your personality across in just a few sentences and by completing a questionnaire. Maybe that's why so many of these men go for the 'I'd rather not say' option; because none of this really tells you what someone is really like.

As for the shabby standard of photos generally? Some people hate being photographed, I remind myself. Not Rod, obviously – at least not these days. Point a camera phone in his direction and he's beaming at it, even when he's lying on his back on the ground with the lower half of his body still under that vintage bus.

Maybe, I'm thinking now, I should get out there again and give someone a chance.

I text Fabs, who says, *Message lots more. And only meet for coffee so you haven't wasted much time.*

How's your dating going? I ask.

I've been off it for a while.

That EU fish stocks thing?

Exactly. I needed a break. But a lovely man has been messaging. Sweet, respectful, v handsome. Works in theatre, my age for a change (not younger). Almost too good be true!

175

I think of the hamburger beard scenario. *Planning to meet him?*

To check if he's for real? Absolutely! she replies, which lifts me, as at least someone I know is having an exciting life. Maybe I should throw myself back in and meet a few of those daily matches? As Fabs pointed out, it's a numbers game. And if Rod is out there having a wonderful time then surely I can too.

CHAPTER TWENTY-SIX

Adrian, 49

Maz, 57

So far Adrian, a curly-haired structural engineer, has spent roughly seventy per cent of our date staring at my chest. Hasn't he sat and had coffee with a woman before? And don't men realise that women know when they're doing that, or don't they care? 'Let me know if you want to do this again, will you?' he offers brightly as we leave the coffee shop.

'Yes, I will,' I say, wondering if there's something wrong with me as surely, at fifty years old, I should be able to tell him that that won't be happening. I'm not *fleeing* this time, as I did with Radiator Ralph. Yet rounding off a dud date is so tricky.

'I just say it's been nice, but I don't feel any chemistry,' Leena told me. And Fabs put it this way: 'I usually say I don't think we're in the same kind of place at the moment.'

The trouble is, Adrian and I *are* in the same place, hovering outside a city-centre café on a drizzly Wednesday afternoon, and although he's bored me with his political views (which don't match mine) and gawped at my tits, I still don't know how to respond when he blurts out, 'You know what, Jen? You're actually the nicest woman I've met on the site. Honestly. You wouldn't believe some of the nutters and liars there are on there, with their baggage and hang-ups and dramas . . .'

'Oh, really?' I croak.

'And the thing is,' he adds over the enthusiastic singing of a woman outside Marks & Spencer, who's belting out, 'I Will Always Love You', 'I might as well tell you now that it's a real relationship I'm looking for and not just an *oh-en-ess.*'

I stare at him. 'An oh-en-ess?'

'A one-night stand,' he announces. 'O.N.S.' He draws the letters in the air with a porky finger, and a couple of long-haired teenage girls giggle as they swish past.

'Oh, I see,' I say. 'Well, look, it's been really nice meeting you and I respect you for being honest but, um, I'm not really sure if I want anything right now. With anyone, I mean. I thought I did. That's why I joined the site. But now I kind of feel there's too much going on my life to be doing this, to be dating at all, I mean—' *Stop it, for God's sake. You don't need to tell him all this. He certainly doesn't need to know you're auditioning for someone to take to Santorini with you.* Occasionally, I find myself wishing that I hadn't won the holiday or at least that the prize had been more modest. I wouldn't have a second's thought about enjoying a few days in a cottage in the Lake District on my own; I'd potter around picturesque towns, catch up on some reading and relax.

Adrian looks crestfallen. 'But I thought maybe we could see a film sometime, or go for a dance one night? Maybe you'd like that?' *So you can stare at my tits while they're in motion, you mean? Tempting . . . but no.*

'I don't think so really,' I babble, trying to look genuinely regretful. 'It's been nice, though. Thanks.' With that, I turn and march down the street and swerve into WHSmith, as if something is happening in there – a medical emergency by the giant Galaxy bars which I, with my certificates in administering CPR and the use of a defibrillator, must attend to.

Once safely inside the store I find myself staring at a grinning man holding a huge, glittering fish on the cover of *Improve Your Coarse Fishing* magazine. I buy a women's glossy and a large bar of chocolate, figuring they're a fair reward for the hour of my life that I've just lost. And I remind myself to pick my date a *lot* more carefully next time.

And I do! After a bit of back-and-forth chat with 'fryed rice' Maz, who'd appeared in my daily matches early on, and messaged me recently, I remind myself that I shouldn't dismiss someone over a spelling mistake. He seems fun and sparky and definitely un-weird, and so we arrange to meet.

He suggests a walk in the park, picking up tacos from a nearby takeaway, which sounds appealing. And I have a good feeling about this date when the day rolls around and he spots me, waiting by the carved acorn sculpture. With a big smile and a bounding gait, he heads towards me.

'Hey, it's so good to meet you!' he says.

'You too.'

'Fancy a walk before we get something to eat?'

'Yes, it's a lovely day, isn't it? So why not?' Bright sunshine beats down on us and we fall quickly into easy conversation.

Maz is tall and wiry with sharp cheekbones, intense brown eyes and a buzz cut. I already know he's divorced with a grown-up daughter and has a signwriting business. (I'm assuming he pays more attention to spelling in his professional life than he did when writing his dating profile.) And now I'm discovering that he is also something of an 'old raver', as he describes himself with a self-deprecating grin. He's been a regular at Glastonbury and Latitude for years, and now he's telling me about acts he's seen and DJs he rates, none of whom I have even heard of, although I nod and listen as if I'm au fait with the world of dancing in fields, and let him chatter on.

'Which festivals have you been to?' he asks. I mention a tiny two-day event in South West Scotland that Rod and I had taken Hannah to when she was little. Maz hasn't heard of it. 'But you took your daughter to a festival? Respect!'

'There were loads of children there,' I explain. 'It was family-friendly with a fairground and clowns—'

'I'm always in awe of people who bring their kids along,' he cuts in. 'I mean, if I'm at a festival I like to fully immerse myself in it, you know?' His eyebrows do a little wiggle.

'What does that involve, then?' I prompt him.

'Oh, you know,' he says, chuckling, and pretty soon he's describing chemically fuelled adventures, of days and nights lost in a haze of music and dancing and copious drugs. 'You've never been tempted?' he asks.

'I'm not sure it'd suit me,' I admit.

He casts me a teasing glance. 'You never know till you've tried it.'

'I think I'd have an actual heart attack,' I say, laughing

now. Then, so he doesn't think I'm a total square, I add, 'I had space cakes once in Amsterdam. Nothing seemed to be happening so I had another one and then I fell head first into a pizza and everything went in slow motion, and my friend Freddie had to guide me all shaky and wobbly back to the hotel.'

Maz sniggers over my rookie's mistake. 'That "nothing seems to be happening" thing. Yeah, that's happened to us all.' Then he's off again, regaling me with his adventures in various European cities; the festival in Bulgaria where 'everyone was off their tits' and the night in Ibiza when 'the whole sky turned bright green'. I'm not sure I'd *enjoy* the sky being green. While I'm certainly fond of a few drinks I'm not great with reality being altered to that degree. Now he's on about the club in Berlin where 'the doorman's notorious for turning people away; he can spot a tourist who just wants to go in to gawp'. I glance at Maz, surmising that as a visitor to the city he might possibly have fallen into that category. BudgieAir passengers never seemed embarrassed about being tourists. In their souvenir caps and T-shirts, clutching novelty bottles of sangria, it was never something they tried to hide.

'*I* didn't have any trouble,' I tell him. 'He just waved me right in.'

'What?' He looks shocked, then laughs. 'I don't think it'd be quite your scene, Jen.'

'What d'you think my scene is, then?' I ask. *A sing-along? Afternoon tea with the whist club?*

Maz shrugs. 'You seem like the kind of person who might feel a bit out of place in a latex room—'

'Well, thanks.' I feign outrage.

'I'm just saying.' He grins cheekily.

181

'*Is* there a latex room?' I'm intrigued now and try to picture this fairly regular-looking fifty-seven-year-old bloke in, I don't know, a pair of shiny tight black pants and maybe a scary mask?

'Oh, yeah,' he says airily. 'There are rooms to suit all kinds of persuasions. That's why you're not allowed to take your phone in.'

'Why not?' I ask.

'Because there are people having sex—'

'Oh, I see!' Now I'm starting to sound like his shocked auntie.

'Some people stay for three days,' he goes on.

'Three whole days? But where do they sleep?'

He barks with laughter. Hardcore Maz is clearly tickled by my lack of experience of 'the raw techno Berlin scene'. 'They don't go there to sleep, Jen. No one takes pyjamas. They're there for *the full immersion experience.*'

'Is there a room where you can sit and have a nice glass of wine and a chat with your friends?' I ask.

There's more laughter at this, which abates only when we stop off at the takeaway for tacos. We eat them on a bench, warmed by the sun, then wander over to a kiosk where I ask for a coffee and Maz has a mint tea as apparently he 'doesn't do caffeine at all, it's too much for me these days'. This strikes me as curious, considering that he doesn't have a problem with guzzling down those party drugs.

I'm not sure we're each other's types, I decide as we wander towards the park gates. I mean, latex clothing for one thing. Leena had a rubber dress once, bought for her by a boyfriend (which amounted, I reckoned, to giving a present to himself) but she never mustered the nerve to wear it out. And how do you get them off? Yet despite our very different notions of a great night out, our couple of hours together have passed pleasantly. I've learnt an awful lot and he's been far more fun than Adrian-the-tits-starer. And I'm thinking now that maybe Maz and I could be friends, as long as he doesn't imagine that all my years of flying might enable me to give him some insight on how to smuggle illicit substances into the UK.

We part with a brief hug, thanking each other for a lovely afternoon.

Later that evening I'm given a short, sharp lesson on how to communicate that a second date won't be happening:

Had a lovely time Jen, great to meet you . . .

At least his reason for not wanting to meet again seems apt, given his fondness for pills:

. . . but I don't think there's any chemistry.

CHAPTER TWENTY-SEVEN

'He was here again. Really helpful, he was,' Mum says when I visit. As casually as I could manage, I'd asked if she'd heard from her friend again.

'Helpful with what, Mum?' I'm aware of anxiety knotting inside me, somewhere in my chest.

'With various things we're going to do,' she says with a coy smile as if she's seventeen and the boy she fancies at school has started paying her some attention.

'What kind of things? D'you mean jobs you need doing around the house, or in the garden? Because I can always help with—'

'Just some plans we've been talking about,' she cuts in.

'This is worrying me now, Mum.'

'Why?' she asks in surprise.

'Because I don't know this person.'

'You don't know everyone,' she says with a half-scowl.

I breathe out slowly. 'Okay, Mum. But what kind of plans d'you mean?' *The ones where he gets hold of your bank cards? Or accompanies you to the cashpoint so he can drain your accounts?* I have started to picture this 'friend': sly eyes, a mean, thin-lipped mouth, twitchy long fingers ready to thieve her valuables. Refusing to discuss it further, she changes the subject. Clearly Mum's old, steely determination is still very much there.

A few days later my work shift overlaps with Kirsten's and she beetles over towards me. 'I don't want to make a big thing of this, Jen,' she says.

Immediately, my heart seems to lurch.

'It's my fault,' she adds quickly. 'I shouldn't have asked her. I know your mum's not quite herself. But I was stuck yesterday. I'd been let down again—'

'What's happened, Kirsten?'

'—asked her if she could look after Brad, just while I was at work. You know she's done that for me sometimes?' I nod. 'It's not like she needed to walk him. She could just pop him in her garden and I'd pick up his poops when I got back . . .' She stops and her eyes fill with tears. 'I know she's been a bit funny with him lately but she seemed really pleased to be asked. Honestly, I thought it might be nice for her to have him for company, but when I got back yesterday he wasn't there.'

'Oh God! Where was he?'

'Out. He'd either got out somehow, or your mum had let him out. I've no idea. She didn't even seem to remember that she'd had him. Said she didn't know what I was talking about—'

'Did you find him?' I ask, horrified. Kirsten nods and rubs at her eyes. She's always fully done up with immaculately groomed brows and bronzer, even for work or when she's just out walking Brad.

'I went straight out to try and find him but then

185

someone called me, a woman from a few streets away. He was in her garden, sniffing around. My number's on his collar—'

'I'm so sorry,' I say. 'That's just awful.'

'I don't want you to feel bad,' she says firmly as she starts to restock the bakery section. 'That's not why I'm telling you. I just wanted you to know. I shouldn't have asked her, I realise that now. It was my mistake—'

'You're brilliant with Mum,' I say, trying to shake off a creeping sense of dread because there's no denying that strange things are happening more and more often now. The buying of copious bird seed, the 'friend' she keeps mentioning – and now this. 'Thank you,' I add.

'What for?' Kirsten asks. 'It was really stupid of me—'

'No, you're a fantastic neighbour and a real friend to Mum.' I hug her briefly. 'Honestly, Kirsten, I don't know what we'd do without you.'

'What d'you think's got into Dad?' Hannah asks when she calls next day. She's talking about a bunch of photos he's posted on Facebook from his latest jaunt down in Dumfriesshire with Gaby. He's certainly got up to speed with it lately, a decade or so later than everyone else. Rod has had a profile for years but, until this recent flurry, had hardly ever posted anything. In fact he's often declared that he can't see the point of social media at all.

'You can't see the point of it?' Marta exclaimed once in the shop. 'How d'you think we should market this business, then? Through adverts in the back of taxis?'

'I always read those adverts,' he'd said with a trace of defensiveness. But Marta had forced him to have an online presence, arranging shoots in which she modelled their

T-shirts in her own quirky, pigtailed style – and to his relief she's pretty much taken care of it ever since.

However, now it seems like he's woken up to the modern age, like Snow White arising from her enchanted slumber. Only instead of a handsome prince in the photos it's Gaby in teeny denim cut-offs and a pale pink T-shirt, looking all sunny and natural as she leans, clutching an enamel mug, against a tree.

There are also numerous shots of the coastline, all pebbly coves and rocky outcrops, and one of a sun-dappled path with drifts of wild garlic on either side. (Helpfully, he has captioned this picture WILD GARLIC!) There's another of Rod and Gaby together, beaming happily in a forest clearing. They must have asked a passer-by to take that one. It doesn't seem like Rod-type behaviour, but maybe Gaby had asked a forestry worker, or a handily passing woodland elf? While she's looking at the camera he is gazing at her in a way that makes me catch my breath.

It's a look of love, I realise. He is completely head over heels with this woman.

'Maybe he's having such a lovely time he wants to share it?' I suggest.

'It just doesn't seem like *him*, Mum,' Hannah declares.

'Well, he's probably just getting modern,' I say, phone in one hand while I brush my hair, getting ready for work.

'Facebook isn't *modern* . . .'

'It is to Dad.' I focus on my reflection. Although high-level grooming isn't needed for work these days, I do try not to look too scary, too hairy of face.

'Well, you've got to have a word with him about his swimwear,' she adds.

'Swimwear? What d'you mean?'

'He's just posted some more pictures. He's wearing those awful orange shorts with the white flowers.'

'I'll have a look. But they're just his old beach shorts, love.' I tweeze out a particularly aggressive hair, wincing at the pain.

'*Old's* the word, Mum,' she chuckles. 'He had that same pair when we went to Arran when I was about ten, remember?' We fall into reminiscing about that glorious weekend when the three of us had taken the ferry to the island, and then set up camp at Lamlash, where an elderly man had taken us out on his fishing boat and we'd caught mackerel and barbecued them on the beach. Late into the night we'd lain in our little tent, with Hannah between us, telling ghost stories in the light of our lamp.

After the call, although I really should be leaving for work, I'm seized by an urge to check out Rod's new photos. Here's Gaby, rising out of the hot tub in a bikini like a lithe, golden mermaid. And here's Rod, perched on the edge of it, smiling broadly, looking like he's lost a few pounds actually! And he's wearing those shorts, as Hannah said. Well, of course he is; he's in a hot tub. He'd hardly be wearing a duffel coat.

In another picture the two of them are clutching glasses of wine whilst up to their chests in the water. Who took these pictures? Did they take a professional photographer along with them? Thank God they're not actually canoodling (I realise my attitude is verging towards that of an angry nun) but it's still startling to see how *public* he's being about his life, all of a sudden.

Whatever Rod's doing down there in that forest is no business of mine, I remind myself. I check the time, which jolts me back to the fact that I really need to leave for work.

So I shut my laptop, telling myself that it's probably doing him the world of good. It's not that I'm jealous or sad or even feeling weird about it, not remotely. Rod is my dear friend, and a wonderful father, and of course I want him to be happy and having copious amounts of sex in an over-sized barrel in the woods.

In fact, what's really concerning me now, as I drive to work, is what to do about Mum and this friend, because now I'm starting to think, is she smitten with someone too? She never used to be like this: all flushed and giddy, seemingly thrilled by some kind of male attention. It might be imaginary; just a delicious, dreamed-up liaison that's providing her with so much enjoyment and fun. But what if it isn't? We can't just keep on trundling along pretending everything is normal, even though Mum is insistent that everything is fine, and she doesn't need any help with anything.

We'll have to get help from someone. And now, as I pull into the car park ready for my evening shift, I know exactly who that someone will be.

CHAPTER TWENTY-EIGHT

Dr Mahmoud, age unknown

'So, how long have you been having trouble with your memory, Mrs McGuire?'

'I can't remember, Doctor,' Mum replies brightly, sitting bolt upright on the blue plastic chair.

'But you've noticed that sometimes it's not been quite as sharp as it might once have been? Would that be fair to say?'

Mum beams at him – and no wonder. His manner is perfect: kind, charming, and respectful yet still authoritative. I want to throw my arms around him in gratitude; hell, never mind that. I'd take him home if I could and whisk him off to Santorini with me.

Sitting next to Mum, I observe how skilfully he gathers information. Clearly enjoying herself, Mum is wearing a smart cream blouse and black skirt under her best M&S tailored jacket, plus low heels and copious heady perfume, Red Door by Estée Lauder, her favourite for decades.

'My daughter seems to think so,' she says, leaning forward with a conspiratorial grin.

'Well, it's always good to have a check-up every now and again,' he says.

This is how I coaxed her here; by mentioning that everyone sees their GP occasionally, just as a matter of course, and perhaps the doctor might be able to suggest something to help her short-term memory, which perhaps wasn't *quite* as a sharp as it usually was? I'd been conscious of treading carefully so as not to upset or alarm her. She'd said no at first, barking, 'Why should you be involved in my medical appointments?'

I know how Mum's GP practice works, and that patients see whichever doctor is available, as is usually the way these days. But I also remembered that she'd gone in for a blocked ear and had enthused over the 'lovely' doctor, who she thought was Egyptian, and I'd gathered then that she'd had a bit of a twinkle for him. So all it had taken was for me to go to the practice's website where photos of all of the doctors were conveniently displayed. Was that him? I asked, indicating the best-looking one. Awful, I know, objectifying a man of good standing in the local community.

'Ooh, yes,' Mum enthused. 'That's the nice doctor!' After that, all I'd had to do was casually mention that it was 'normal, in fact *preferred*' for a relative to accompany the patient these days and, miraculously, Mum agreed that that would be okay. And when I'd called, the surgery's reception-ist had conceded wearily that if Mrs McGuire was *insistent* about seeing Dr Mahmoud, then that could be arranged.

After further quizzings about her general health, he has now moved on to a series of questions designed to give an indication of Mum's cognitive abilities. This is the part I've been scared about; how she'll react if she struggles with the 'test'.

'Could you tell me which season we're in please?' he asks her.

'This is summer, Doctor,' she says brightly, as if happy to assist.

'And which month is this?'

'Oh, hang on a minute . . .' She turns to me and I give her an encouraging smile: *You can do this, Mum!* 'May?' she suggests with a flirty smile.

'Not quite,' Dr Dashing says, 'but let's not worry—'

'—June? July? August?'

'Erm, yes, that's right, we're in August . . .' Mum is glowing happily as if this is a game. 'Now, can you tell me the current prime minister?' She nails this one, beaming proudly.

Dr Mahmoud asks Mum several more questions. While she can't answer all of them, she is being put on the spot. 'That nasty man with the orange face,' she says, with startling force, when asked to name the current US president.

'You're not far off,' says Dr Mahmoud, smiling, 'but thankfully it's not him anymore . . .'

'Oh, isn't it? That is good news!'

'It is, yes!' he agrees.

'I never liked him,' she adds.

'You're a wise woman,' he says, and they're chuckling away to the point where I almost feel like a gooseberry sitting here.

'Now,' he says, 'I'm going to show you three objects, Mrs McGuire—'

'Just call me Mary, Doctor.'

'Right. So, Mary, I'll show you the items and in a few minutes I'll ask if you can remember what they are. Does that sound okay?'

'Yes, that sounds *great*.' Although I'm awash with relief that this is going well, it also twists my heart to see her looking so perky and delighted, wanting to please Dr Mahmoud, to gain top marks in his quiz. He shows her a pen, a watch and a small pair of scissors, then puts them away again.

Now he hands her a pencil and piece of paper and asks her to draw a cube, and when she hands it to him proudly, like a child giving in her homework, my heart actually seems to crack.

It's just a few wobbly lines that don't look like anything. Drawing has never been her strong point, I remind myself. Now he's asking if she can remember what the three objects were. She frowns, looking puzzled. 'D'you remember the things I showed you a few minutes ago?' he prompts her gently.

Pen, watch, scissors, I try to project. 'Oh, yes.' She beams at him. 'A cup, a rubber and a telephone.'

Well, she's probably just distracted with fancying Dr Mahmoud, and having me sitting next to her; and anyway, I tell myself, I forget plenty of things. Last time I went running I'd searched and searched for my earbuds and found them in a tangled knot in my knicker drawer.

The three of us talk some more, and Mum listens with rapt attention, not even flinching when the doctor says he'd like to refer her for further tests with a specialist and a hospital appointment. His manner is so warm and kind, and his smile so pin-up worthy, Mum seems to take it all in her stride.

'Such a nice man,' she announces, virtually floating out of the surgery into the bright, breezy summer's morning, when it's all over.

'He is, Mum. He has a lovely manner, doesn't he?'

'Oh, yes,' she says happily, as if it had been a social visit as I link her arm in mine. We cross the road and make our way past the car showrooms and the parade of slightly faded suburban shops, then down the quiet residential side streets with their neat bungalows and immaculate front gardens. Someone is practising a trumpet and there's the tinny jangle of an ice cream van further down the road.

'Would you like an ice cream?' Mum asks suddenly, as the van stops. I'm on the verge of saying no thanks, but she looks so excited at the prospect that I say yes, that would be lovely. We arrive at the van, where Mum whips out her purse.

'Mum, I'll get these. What would you like?'

'No, *I'm* getting them,' she says firmly, looking up at the ice cream man with his crooked nose and sweep of black hair. There's a sparkly smile for him, too, like the ones for Dr Mahmoud, although he doesn't seem to register it. Mum, who used to rail against anyone for the slightest of reasons, now finds pretty much everyone 'lovely' and wants to be their friend. The Jehovah's Witnesses who appear from time to time are now invited in and offered tea. She'd even baked for them once; a sensational coconut and lime cake, presented on her best cake stand. A few months earlier she'd have kept them on the doorstep and told them to take a hike.

Mum is rummaging through her purse. 'I'm sure I have money here,' she mutters.

'*Please* let me get them, Mum,' I say.

'I only want to treat my daughter to an ice cream,' she announces loudly to the man, as if I am ten years old.

'Could I have a look for you, then?' I reach a hand towards her purse. She recoils, alarmed, as if I were about to tear it from her grasp.

'I've told you, I have money!' There's more rummaging, and I can sense impatient vibes emanating from the van's hatch as the man regards us with a flat expression. With no more customers approaching he's probably keen to move on. 'Here we are,' Mum exclaims triumphantly. From the jumble of store cards, booklets of postage stamps and mysterious scraps of paper she has produced a thick wodge of notes. 'See?' She holds them in front of my face.

'Okay, Mum. But be careful, that's a lot of money—'

'How much are two cones?' she asks the man.

'Three pounds,' he says gruffly. She turns her attentions back to the clutch of notes, but instead of peeling off one to give him she seems to loosen her grip, or perhaps the breeze whips them from her because now the money is blowing away in all directions.

'Oh, Mum!' I cry out as I start to chase them, grabbing a twenty-pound note from the road and another from a puddle in the gutter, and yet more as they're caught in box hedges and come to land on driveways and on neatly cut lawns. Mum seems too startled to be able to do anything other than stand, aghast, watching me.

'Blimey, love, you shouldn't be carrying that amount of cash,' the ice cream man says with a frown, as finally she is back in possession of as much of her stash as I've been able to gather up. I haven't managed to persuade her to stuff it all back into her purse yet.

'It's all right,' she tells him defensively.

'Well, be careful you don't drop it again—'

'I'd like two large cones with chocolate flakes,' she snaps at him. I catch his barely perceptible eye-roll and want to hiss, *Please be respectful and kind. My mother isn't very well.* This surge of protectiveness has risen up in me like a gigantic wave, and I fix him with a firm gaze as a twenty-pound note is exchanged for ice creams and change.

It takes quite some coaxing to persuade Mum to put her money back into her purse, and zip it up firmly. Finally, we stroll away with our ice creams, as if everything is normal and she hadn't been quizzed about which month we're in, and terms like 'dementia', 'brain scan' and 'geriatric psychiatrist' hadn't been mentioned, and I hadn't spotted a twenty-pound note snagged on a climbing rose and scurried into the garden to retrieve it.

Back at Mum's I make us a pot of tea. We drink it and nibble chocolate fingers in the kitchen, chatting easily and watching the birds through the window. Mum never used to eat chocolate. Ever-vigilant about her calorie intake, she claimed to 'not like sweet things' but today she munches away on half a box of fingers, and as well as her tea she has a huge glass of Coke – the size of those cartons you take into the cinema – which she never used to have either.

When I have a sly peek in her cupboard I spot six more boxes of chocolate fingers and several two-litre bottles of full-fat Coke. I reason with myself that it doesn't matter, not in the grand scheme of things. We're going to have bigger things to worry about than Mum's sugar consumption.

As I drive back home it occurs to me that normally I'd have called Rod straight away after a day like this. He knows about the rotten vegetables and off sausages in Mum's fridge, and her mysterious 'friend'. Even at work, he'd always pick up a call from me. We'd have had a laugh about Mum having a crush on Dr Mahmoud and flirting while trying, pretty unsuccessfully, to draw a cube on his notepad. Although I'm terrified about what's going to happen, and wouldn't have expected Rod to have any magic solutions, I'd have felt better just having talked to him. Less full of dread, I suppose; less alone.

Rod has always made *everything* feel better.

However, I can't call him this time because there probably isn't a signal down there at Gaby's love bus. Even if there is, I'm reluctant to phone him these days in case I'm interrupting something or it's clear that he doesn't want to talk.

I'm assuming he's there anyway. Since they've been working together on this new vehicle, it's seemed like it's his second home and he's been spending so much time in the hot tub I wonder if he's actually turned amphibious.

It's probably time I stopped relying on Rod quite so much anyway, I decide now, as I let myself into my flat and breathe in the slightly musty air. Maybe he's wanted some space from me all along, instead of me dropping into his shop and hanging about, drinking his tea and eating his biscuits. I know Mum has always found our relationship a bit weird, reckoning that it's neither one thing nor another and probably takes up far too much of my life. And while she might be a little hazy on the name of the current US president, I think that in this instance she's probably right.

CHAPTER TWENTY-NINE

Tariq, 50

Pascal, 55

Neil, 49

It's not just because of Santorini that I'm determined to persevere with this dating lark. In fact, as the weeks go by I'm almost reconciled to the fact that I'll probably be wallowing in the hotel's rooftop jacuzzi all by myself. (Who cares if it's decided that I was jilted on my wedding day, hence occupying the honeymoon suite alone?) No, the reason I'm keeping at it is to reassure myself that not every straight man is a tit-starer, a phone-snooper or a radiator bore, and that I'm not an undateable weirdo, too set in my ways to enjoy being with another person even on a casual basis. Plus, as I'm paying a monthly subscription to Mature Matches – when funds are tight – I might as well use the darned thing. Like when you buy shoes, only to discover that they kill your feet. 'I'll give them a proper chance,' you tell yourself, wincing in pain, 'to see if they loosen up.'

So here we go, on a dating flurry! I meet a man called Tariq for a drink and get the distinct impression that he's having a hard time not checking his phone constantly, which is sitting on the table, winking with messages, a couple of inches from his hand. When we part company after one drink I glance round to see him prodding at it, his relief palpable. 'Sorry to keep you away from it!' I want to shout, like a madwoman.

On the day I set out to meet Pascal, who I actually have quite high hopes about, a menopausal spot has peaked in the middle of my chin. Charmingly, it's the kind of raging boil you might reasonably expect at fourteen years old – not at fifty. I can't go back to Clearasil, I just can't. I'm not even sure if it still exists. Still, I reassure myself, what's an attack of midlife acne in the great scheme of things?

Fortunately, at least for the first seventeen hours or so of our date, Pascal is far too self-absorbed to even properly register that there is another human sitting across the pub table from him, let alone one with a throbbing carbuncle. At least, that's how long it feels I've been here, subjected to a lengthy discourse on his illustrious career in dentistry, and his son who has followed in his footsteps. ('The apple doesn't fall far from the tree!' he gloats.) It's all teeth, teeth, teeth as the evening slides onwards, to the point at which my own are starting to ache. Or perhaps I'm imagining it?

'Ninety-five per cent of it is about gum care,' Pascal drones on. Then: 'I could tell you about the benefits of a sonic toothbrush but I wouldn't want to bore you . . .' Really? Why stop now? By this point I'm starting to feel nostalgic for old-fashioned dating, when computers were the size of chest freezers and the internet didn't exist. If I'd met Pascal at, say, an olden-days house party, I'd have given him roughly fifteen seconds of attention before wandering off to talk to someone else.

'Avoid that blond guy by the bread bin,' I'd have warned my friends, 'unless you want unsolicited dental advice.' That was how it worked. It's occurred to me now that not only has Pascal failed to ask what I do for a living, but on the rare occasions when I've had the chance to open my mouth and actually get a word in, he's been fixating on my teeth; i.e. assessing them with a laser-like stare. I am not imagining this. I can tell when someone's gawping at my chest and it's equally obvious when someone's staring at my incisors and finding them lacking.

I don't mean *completely* lacking. I do, obviously, have teeth. They're not perfect, I'm fully aware of that; they're just your average, slightly wonky British teeth. Yet the way in which Pascal is fixating on them you'd think they were rotting pegs.

At least they're distracting him from my chin boil, I think glumly, draining my glass.

'I have to ask you, Jennifer,' he says, 'have you ever thought of having braces?'

'No, I haven't.' I smile tersely. *Have you ever thought of having an engaging personality?*

'They can completely change your whole appearance,' he explains.

'I'm sure they can.' A vein has started throbbing in my jaw.

'The modern kind are amazing,' he adds, as if I might have tumbled out of the ark, 'and they're not as expensive as you might think . . .'

200

'That's interesting,' I fib.

'We can always talk about it if you like?'

The *gall* of the man! Is that why he wanted to meet? To drum up some business? Before he can issue me with an easy payments plan I smile again, exposing my chaotic gnashers as I tell him I have to dash; there's some urgent ironing waiting for me at home. I don't actually say that. I just announce, truthfully, that I am suddenly exhausted.

'I meant to ask, what do *you* do?' he says as we leave the pub together.

'I work in a supermarket,' I reply. 'I was a flight attendant until a few months ago when my airline went under . . .'

'Oh right,' he says, trying – unsuccessfully – to stifle a yawn when the sentence is barely out of my mouth.

I'm really *not* that boring, I try to reassure myself as I travel home on the subway. Pascal might not be wildly impressed but I'm good at my job – and my colleagues and our customers seem to like me – and once upon a time, in my former career, I actually won a prize! Now I'm picturing the CEO of BudgieAir beaming from the podium in that vast conference hall, her red lipstick immaculate, her sequinned dress glittering like a disco ball.

'And now,' she'd announced, 'for our final award of the night, the one you've all been waiting for . . .' I glanced around the table at Leena and Freddie. We were all rooting for each other that night. There was no competitiveness on *our* table.

'I'm taking you outside if you win, Morton,' Freddie growled at me.

'It's you, isn't it?' I exclaimed. 'You know and you're not saying—'

'Yeah, c'mon, Freddie.' Leena grinned tipsily, clutching

her glass. 'Didn't you figure out a way to upsell?' To sell those wind-up budgie toys, she meant; his patented method.

'Don't know what you're talking about,' Freddie said with a snigger as our CEO waved an envelope in the air.

We all turned towards the stage. 'So, without further ado,' she announced, opening it and extracting a card, 'the winner of this year's Golden Budgie has achieved an *incredible* performance . . .' It was as if the entire room was holding its breath. '. . . racking up an amazing 978 sales of our beloved BudgieAir mascot. It really is an astounding result . . ,' She beamed around the fairy-lit conference suite. 'So please, everyone, put your hands together for our incredibly talented flight attendant, our very well-deserved winner of this year's Golden Budgie award . . . Jennifer Morton!'

Shooting up out of my seat, I gawped at Freddie and Leena – who were clapping and cheering – and wove my way between tables towards the stage. I'd actually won! I was good at sales – I knew that. I worked hard and performed my duties as best as I could. But in all of my twenty-seven years with BudgieAir I'd never walked onto that stage and shaken our CEO's hand as she'd presented me with a slim box, bedecked with a golden ribbon, containing the voucher for my prize. I'd never stood there, soaking up the whoops and applause, so happy and proud because I loved what I did.

And now I was fizzling with joy and prosecco as I left the stage, beaming at the sea of faces and, above them, the enormous sparkly banner displaying our company's motto, which seemed particularly apt that night: *BudgieAir. The brightest smile in the sky.*

And where am I now? Allowing myself to be bored, almost to sobs, as I endure a twenty-minute description of precisely what goes into a dental amalgam filling.

Weirdly, he appears in my dream that night. We are sitting at a table on a hotel balcony. The Aegean Sea is glittering, there is a big bowl of Greek salad on the table and the sky is an impossible blue. The scene is utterly perfect but Pascal hasn't noticed because all he's talking about is teeth, teeth, teeth.

I almost give up after that. Honestly, I don't think I have the time or inclination anymore. But the weekend arrives, and I have two days off from work and not a single plan to fill my days. Freddie is immersed in an essay for his psychotherapy course and Leena is in London for a job interview with a big hotel chain. Other friends are either busy or I know not to expect them to be available at short notice on weekends. They have partners, younger children, obligations and plans; they have *lives*. Naturally, I wouldn't think of bothering Rod these days, not now that he and Gaby seem to spend pretty much all of their free time together.

Neil it is, then. Neil who's been keen to meet for a while, and who doesn't seem weird or pompous or likely to imply that my teeth aren't fit for purpose. He has a friendly, open sort of face and says he's 'a bit ragged around the edges', which I like. There are pictures of him with jovial-looking mates in a pub garden, and sitting on a lawn hugging a boxer dog. Pets feature pretty regularly on the site, as does the phrase 'easy-going guy' (which is how Neil describes himself) as, of course, no one's going to put, 'I am a simmering heap of neuroses.' But he seems like a decent bloke, so off I go to meet him.

There he is with his swept-back dark hair (do I detect gel?) and a tufty beard, perched on a bar stool in the Drummond Arms. As soon as we greet each other I know

203

this isn't going to go anywhere. I don't know how, but I do – and so, I think, does he, as his gaze keeps flicking behind me, at other people or the sepia photos of old Glasgow scenes on the walls, or perhaps even the light fittings. Who knows? It's not that he's unattractive or conversation is awkward because we're both chatting pleasantly as if we're two passengers who have found themselves sitting opposite each other on a train.

But as raw-techno Maz said, there's no chemistry.

And yet . . . we finish our drinks and have another round, and then a couple more, and finally leave the pub at closing time. Even though I know we're not particularly attracted to each other, somehow I find myself kissing him; properly kissing, deeply and hungrily for God knows how long. *Why are you doing this?* screams my brain. Yet I keep on kissing this man because I'm drunk and I seem to have forgotten how to stop.

Or maybe it's because it feels like I haven't kissed anyone properly since 1992?

When we do pull apart, there's a mumbled agreement to message. (I know we won't.) Neil sees me into a taxi and when I get home I try to tell myself it's okay, it was just a bit of fun. It's not that I think there's anything wrong with snogging someone you've just met, or even sleeping with them if you want to. I did that when I was much younger, kissing a boy at a party or having a bit of a snog in the park on a hot summer's day. I had the odd one-night stand back then too.

But I'm no longer twenty years old with a curly perm the size of an unclipped poodle. And I'm not at a party with lots of up-for-it friends, with my future life stretching ahead of me, promising adventure and fun. I am fifty years old, having just kissed a man I didn't even fancy, while pressed up against a skip with a roll of carpet hanging out of it. And when I examine my jacket I discover that there's a rusty streak right across the back.

And that, I decide, is enough.

CHAPTER THIRTY

Weirdly, even though I'm not off the site yet, I seem to have much more free time. I'm no longer checking my matches or messages; I'm just letting it . . . *slide*, as I've explained to Fabs, when she's asked for updates.

It's a relief, I suppose. There have been huge, yawning stretches of celibacy in my life, and I've accepted that I'm in one now. It's been over two years since I slept with anyone, and sometimes I wonder if an entirely new way of doing it has been invented, and that when it finally happens for me, I'll be lamentably out of touch. Either that or I'll have forgotten the basics – in the way that algebra flew out of my head pretty much as soon as I'd left school.

'Don't worry,' Leena teased me last time it came up. 'It's like riding a bike. You might be a bit wobbly to begin with but you'll soon get the hang of it again.' The truth is, I'm not really worried because, in the pecking order of concerns, other matters rank far higher than that.

Like dropping in on Mum as often as I can, and continuing to fire off job applications while keeping a keen eye out in case airlines are starting to hire again. And running. I'm still forcing myself through the beginners' programme on the app and, by some miracle, I'm nearing the end of it.

It's a muggy Monday morning and I'm not due at work until three. Allowing myself a lie-in, I'm considering toasting some crumpets, slathering them in butter and bringing them back to bed.

Of course, there is also the option of pulling on my trainers and hauling myself out of the flat. Then I'd enjoy my crumpets even more, having 'earned' them. Minutes later, I am pounding along with my earbuds shoved in.

A whole thirty minutes I've been out. A few weeks ago I wouldn't have imagined it would be possible to propel myself forward for such an incredibly lengthy period of time. Figuring that that's quite enough for one day, I employ the technique I've devised to propel me through the final stretch home. This amounts to running with my gaze fixed determinedly on the pavement, as if on the lookout for dropped coins. Weirdly, this seems to make the finish come quicker than if I'm staring bleakly at the road stretching for miles and miles (it feels like) ahead. Onwards I batter, focusing downwards as I turn the corner and – 'Oh God, I'm so sorry!' I stagger backwards, clutching at my upper arm as the man stops and swings around to face me.

'No, *I'm* sorry,' he exclaims. 'Are you okay?' It's him. It's Silver Foxy. I slammed right into him *just like in the films!*

My face is flaming as I tug out my earbuds. 'I'm fine. I wasn't looking where I was going. I feel so stupid.'

A smile flickers at his generous mouth. 'Hey, don't worry. As long as you're not hurt or anything?'

'No, I'm okay, really.' I push back my dishevelled hair

from my clammy forehead. 'I think I'll walk the rest of the way home, though,' I add.

'Me too,' he says as we fall into step. He's wearing his usual running attire of a dark blue vest and black shorts. I am clad in a grey top and leggings that make my legs look like sausages.

'Sorry if I've interrupted your run,' I add.

'Oh no, not at all. I've already done my distance for today.'

'How far have you been?'

'Um, ten k or something, maybe twelve? I'm not sure . . .' A shrug, as if it's nothing. 'Sure you're okay? You haven't hurt your arm?'

I insist, truthfully, that I am undamaged.

'How's your running going?' he asks.

'My' running. I glow with pride. 'Loving it,' I say, which isn't *quite* the truth but never mind.

'That's great.' He flashes another smile and my stomach seems to flurry in response.

'When I'm running the last bit I always look down at the ground instead of ahead,' I add. 'That's why I crashed into you.'

'Really? Why d'you do that?' He looks at me quizzically and I realise now how deranged it must seem to a proper seasoned runner like him, who has no need for silly mind games.

'Because that way, I can't see how far I still have to go. I know it sounds a bit mad. It's a kind of trick I play on myself to make it seem less awful—'

'I thought you said you were enjoying it?' His grey-blue eyes glint with amusement.

'Erm, well, it's starting to become *slightly* less horrific,' I say with a grimace.

He's laughing now, brightening up this normally dreary street where the girl from the sandwich place is smoking outside the shop, still wearing her corporate peaked cap. Now I'm almost glad I slammed into this poor man's shoulder. 'Maybe you need a running buddy?' he remarks.

'Yeah, maybe. You seem to have quite a few.'

'Oh, they're clients,' he says quickly. 'I'm a PT, a personal trainer . . .'

'Really?' I exclaim. 'God, I can't imagine what you must think of me, chugging along, purple in the face . . .'

'I'm not here to judge,' he says lightly. 'And it looks like you're doing pretty well to me.'

'Well, I'm determined to keep at it this time. It used to be trickier, fitting it in with my work shifts. But I have regular hours now.'

'What's your job?' he asks.

'I've been working in a supermarket these past few weeks. Before that I was a flight attendant, but I was made redundant.'

'Oh, God, really?' He frowns.

'Yeah.' I nod. 'But it's okay. I've kind of got my head around it now—'

'You know, I'd never have guessed you did that,' he adds. *Aren't you too OLD?* I think he means.

'Well, yes,' I concede. 'People tend to have a preconceived idea of what a flight attendant's like, and I was probably one of the oldest in the skies . . .'

'Oh, I didn't mean that,' he says quickly. 'Not at all—'

'Yes, but people do tend to give up after a certain number of years,' I explain. 'The schedule plays havoc with your personal life. It's virtually impossible if you have a young family, unless you have a very understanding partner. And the single ones like me, well, we couldn't even keep a gold-fish alive—' I break off, alarmed by the thought that he might think I'm hitting on him. *I'm single, just in case you were wondering!*

'I can imagine.' He nods. 'You don't have kids, then?'

'I do actually – a daughter, Hannah. She's twenty-three.'

'You're kidding,' he exclaims. 'You don't look nearly old enough.'

I smile. 'That's very kind of you. But I couldn't have done that job if it hadn't been for her dad. We weren't together but he was still brilliant. He insisted I went back to flying after having her, that we could make it work . . .'

'Sounds like a good situation,' he remarks.

'Yes, it was. Anyway,' I say quickly, catching myself, 'you don't need to know all that, do you?'

'It's interesting.' He flashes another smile as we turn the corner.

'Well, I live just down here,' I tell him. 'Nice talking to you, er—'

'Jack. Jack Sander.'

'I'm Jen.'

'Hi, Jen. Good to meet you too. Properly, I mean.' His eyes catch the bright morning sunlight, and I notice how long and actually *silken* his dark eyelashes are.

'I really am sorry about slamming into you like that,' I add.

Dimples form at his cheeks as he grins. 'Don't even mention it. But maybe start looking ahead when you're running? We don't want you having an accident.'

'I'll do that, I promise.'

A small pause, then: 'D'you fancy coming out for a run with me sometime?'

'Oh, I'm not sure,' I say quickly. 'I'd just hold you back.'

'No, you wouldn't. We'd take it at your pace.'

'Honestly, I'm probably best just going out by myself,' I say, as it dawns on me why he's being so friendly. He's trying to get me on board as a client. He is *soliciting* me.

'Sure, lots of people prefer that,' Jack says lightly. 'D'you fancy meeting up for coffee sometime, then? Or a bit of lunch?'

'I should probably make it clear that I'm not looking for a trainer at the moment,' I babble, convinced now that he plans to use the convivial coffee shop setting in which to persuade me, by means of his considerable charm, to commit to regular sessions at vast expense. Why else would he have introduced himself with his surname rather than just Jack? Clearly, he wants me to google him, find his website with its various pricing structures and sign up. It's almost like that Pascal the dentist all over again. Does every man I encounter see me as a project ripe for renovation?

'No, I get that.' He beams at me, looking bemused now. 'I just meant, would you like to go for lunch sometime? There are so many nice places springing up around here. That's all I meant. Nothing to do with anything else.' He pushes a hand through his neatly cropped silvery hair.

'Oh. Oh, right. I just thought . . .' I start, flushing hot. *Get a grip. He's asking you out, you bloody dimwit.* 'Well, that'd be lovely,' I say.

'Are you free tomorrow?'

I figure, quickly, that it'll be far more enjoyable if I'm not clock-watching in readiness for my shift. 'I'm working the next few days,' I explain, 'but I'm off on Friday, if you're free then?'

'Great.' Jack fishes his phone out of his armband and we

211

exchange numbers. I'm trying hard not to hyperventilate at the realisation that this kind thing does still happen after all, despite what Hannah said.

People do still ask each other out – in real life. It can even happen in daylight, in the morning! Off he trots, leaving me striding towards my flat with a huge smile on my face. Fuelled by a renewed surge of energy I break into a canter, like an excitable pony, without the running app lady even telling me to.

CHAPTER THIRTY-ONE

Jack, 52

According to Hannah, trusting those carefully curated and filtered photos – plus a teeny bio – on a dating app is absolutely fine because everyone does that. Yet meeting a nice man while out running is weird.

'He could be *anyone*,' she warns when I tell her about my lunch date.

'He's just a nice, normal guy, Han. And it's a quaint courting ritual, asking someone out to their face. It's what people used to do all the time.'

'Yeah, I know, but—'

'And it's only lunch,' I remind her.

'Hmm. Well, good luck,' she says, still sounding unsure.

Freddie, too, is iffy about it when we meet for coffee. 'He's not some weird stalking neighbour, is he?' he asks with a frown.

Although I laugh it off I'm touched by his concern. Way back in the mists of time, he dated with enthusiasm. But these days he and Pablo – a solid, dependable customer relations guy with a bank – are the epitome of suburban domesticity. ''Course he's not. We're both *runners*,' I remind him.

'Oh yeah. I'd forgotten about that.' He smirks.

'We see each other out and about all the time,' I add. 'And he doesn't look like the type who's planning to disembowel me and feed me to his Doberman pinschers.'

'He has Doberman pinschers?' Freddie's eyebrows shoot up. He adores dogs.

'Not as far as I know. But you seem to find it exciting, the thought of me being ripped apart by ravenous hounds?'

'Just be careful,' he stresses. 'He could be—'

'He could be anyone, yes. So everyone keeps telling me.'

Yet I *am* nervous as our date rolls around – not because I fear for my safety but due to the fact that, for the first time since Posh Stephen, I am actually genuinely thrilled about a date. For one thing, as Jack and I have met in the flesh I'm pretty sure there won't be any nasty surprises.

It's only lunch, I keep reminding myself. There's no need to get myself in a tizz or make a big deal about dressing up for it. After all, Jack has seen me out running, hair scraped into a ponytail, glistening with sweat. Yet as I set off on foot on this sunny August afternoon, wearing a jade green top and jeans and barely a scrap of make-up, I wonder if I've downplayed it too much, and could as easily be dragging out the wheelie bin as going on a date. And now I'm thinking, should I have gone for heels rather than flats? Should I have made more of an effort?

Be as fresh upon landing as your first hello. That was one of the rules drummed into us in cabin crew training. There was a whole list and I learnt them diligently, keen to gain my budgie wings:

Positive, pleasant, professional.

We do our best to say yes.

And the one that beams neon-bright in my mind, as the cheery yellow facade of the restaurant comes into view:

Whatever happens, STAY CALM.

My mouth is as dry as a desert as I walk into the restaurant. There he is, sitting at the back and now jumping up when he sees me.

'Hey, you look great,' he says, greeting me with a kiss on the cheek.

'Thanks,' I say. 'You do too.'

'Well, y'know.' He shrugs and smiles. 'Thought I'd change out of my running gear.'

'Me too. I didn't want to look intimidatingly athletic.' His blue-grey eyes glint with amusement and I sense myself relaxing immediately. He's wearing smart jeans and a pale grey linen shirt, and I catch a hint of clean, woodsy fragrance as I sit down. He'd suggested we meet in this vegetarian place with its shiny white-tiled walls and vases filled with tumbly mixes of wild flowers. It's one of the crop of new, independent neighbourhood restaurants, and it's clearly popular.

'Oh, spanakopita,' I enthuse over the hubbub of chatter as we study the chalkboard menu. 'I'll go for that.'

'That's the Greek one with feta?'

'Yeah.' I smile. 'It's my favourite.'

'Bit too hefty for me,' Jack says lightly as he studies the board. A young waitress with a swingy ponytail and a French accent arrives at our table and takes our order. Jack, it turns out, 'doesn't eat much' at lunch, and when it arrives, his teeny grilled pepper salad with a scattering of seeds makes my spanakopita look vast. It *is* vast; vast and extremely delicious.

'This is amazing,' I tell him as I sip a glass of sauvignon –

also without shame, because I hardly ever eat out locally. And the fact that Jack requested only tap water doesn't mean I shouldn't enjoy wine with lunch.

We fall into conversation easily. In fact, already it's making a pleasant change to be with someone who asks questions, and appears to be genuinely interested, rather than spouting off about himself. Jack wants to know all about my current job – not that there's a huge amount to tell – and then the talk turns to flying. 'What was it like, jetting off all the time?' he asks.

'Well, it was just my job,' I say. 'I mean, I loved it. I really did. But it's not a glamorous industry anymore – if it ever was. And it was BudgieAir I worked for. We were at the less salubrious end of the industry . . .'

'So it was mostly your package holiday crowd?' he asks.

'Pretty much, yes. We had a lot of big, excitable groups and sometimes we had to keep them in order.'

'Bet that was a challenge!'

'It could be, yes.' I smile.

'I've never understood that thing of wanting to get inebriated on a flight,' he adds.

'It's overexcitement really,' I say. 'I had to remind myself of that sometimes. I mean, when you're flying all the time you forget what a big deal it can be, and that people have saved up for their holidays for months, or maybe even the whole year, and probably sacrificed things so they can afford to go away. And then, when it actually happens, they're pretty hyped up and some of them are going to get hammered.'

'I suppose you're right.' He smiles unconvincingly.

'Have you never been on those kinds of holidays?'

'They're not really my kind of thing,' he says with a shrug. 'I tend to do hikes and cycling trips. And I'd always take the train rather than fly.' Ooh, a note of disapproval there. But then, he's a fitness guy. I can't imagine him partying with the Ibiza crowd.

'So, how did you get into being a trainer?' I ask.

Jack starts to tell me about the various sales and marketing jobs he'd had, for companies he says are enormous but I've never heard of them. 'It was about paying the mortgage,' he explains. 'They weren't my passion. So I started studying sports science and massage on the side.'

'You're a masseur as well?'

'Yeah.' He nods. 'It's an important part of the whole wellness package.'

'Right.' I sip my wine. 'What kind d'you do?'

'The whole range really. Deep-tissue, Swedish, Indian head massage . . .' I try to affect a neutral expression, as if he's reading out a shopping list. He's a *little* bit flirty; at least there's no shortage of smiles across the table.

'That sounds great,' I remark.

'It is,' he enthuses. 'It's just brilliant being able to work for myself, you know? I didn't really fit into that corporate world.'

Our talk turns to our dating history. As mine is so sparse – and he knew about Rod already – it's dealt with quickly, and I'm far more interested to learn about his. It turns out that Jack fell into marriage 'way too young', and that he and his ex are long divorced with no kids. 'It was that classic scenario of growing in different directions,' he explains.

Keen to spin out lunch a little longer, I indicate the cakes sitting alluringly under their glass dome on the counter. 'Don't they look good?' I suggest. 'I'm tempted.'

'Oh, I won't bother,' Jack says with a quick shake of his head.

'Coffee, then?'

'I don't drink coffee,' he says, 'but you go ahead.' This knocks a tiny puff of wind out of my sails, but I ask for a slice of lemon cake anyway, plus an Americano – because why not?

'A hot water for me please,' Jack tells our waitress.

'Hot water?' she repeats. 'With lemon or anything?'

'No, just as it comes, thanks,' he says pleasantly. I know it's ridiculous to have an opinion on hot water drinking, I tell myself as my Americano and a generous slab of cake arrive. Plenty of people avoid caffeine, after all.

'Is that a health thing?' I ask, indicating his white porcelain cup.

'Yeah, it's good for digestion and hydration,' he replies. Then, as I start to tuck into my cake: 'Are you sure you don't want to come out running with me? Just for a nice easy jog, I mean?' Was that a red flag I caught in the periphery of my vision? No, of course it's not. He's just being encouraging; *not* inferring that I need to up my exercise quota, what with all the cheesy pie and cake I clearly enjoy scoffing.

'Maybe someday,' I say.

'I promise I'm not trying to get you on board as a client,' Jack adds with a grin.

I laugh, relaxing again now as I finish my coffee. 'You did seem keen to chat.'

'I was,' he says, 'but not for that reason.'

A small pause hovers, but feels entirely comfortable. 'Now I'm almost glad I crashed into you,' I admit.

'And I'm *very* glad,' he says, his gaze catching mine again. We ask for the bill, which he wants to pay but I insist on sharing; after all, I've had wine and cake and coffee, and he's only consumed a teensy salad and water from the tap.

218

We leave the restaurant and stroll along the bustling street lined with cafés, bars and artsy, independent shops selling craft ales and hand-made pottery. This is the newly gentrified area, where the park is filled with bearded dads with babies strapped to their chests, and the ducks on the pond turn up their beaks at cheap white sliced bread, preferring artisanal sourdough.

A few streets on, the vegan bakeries and smart new delis have given way to ramshackle grocery stores with crates of cheap fruit and vegetables piled up outside. We're chattering about our neighbourhood, and how we hope its character won't be entirely lost as gentrification continues to spread. Then the talk turns to our backgrounds, and I learn that Jack grew up craving the bright lights of Glasgow as he grew up in a small, unremarkable town in Lanarkshire.

As he suggests we detour through the park, I take a moment to reflect how well this is going. And now I'm wondering if we are going to start doing this regularly, and if our next date will be drinks or dinner? There are so many things about Jack that I like. We seem to get along, he's local (so handy!) and of course he's not exactly unpleasing to the eye. Then there's his superior fitness level (perhaps he could sort out my body?) and his massage skills (ooh!).

My mind is racing ahead now and I'm thinking, maybe *this* is the way it's going to happen for me, without any help from a dating site or app. Jack is definitely a marked improvement on my other dates, and I'm sure I could deal with his hot water drinking. (There's no law against it after all.) In fact, it could turn out to be a good thing, as his influence would undoubtedly rub off on me and I'd be less of a wine guzzler if we were together. Give it a month and I'd probably be joining him in those beverages from the kettle and my menopausal, spot-prone complexion would be saying, 'At last you've stopped filling your body with toxins, Jennifer Morton. Thank God for that.' And with the regular sex we'd undoubtedly be having, I'd be all aglow. In fact, maybe – I realise now that that one (admittedly large) glass of wine must have rushed to my head – Jack Sander is the one who'll come on holiday to Santorini with me! Oh my God, I hope his passport's not out of date. Of course it's not, I reassure myself. He runs his own business, inspiring clients and encouraging them on their 'health journeys'. He's bound to have such matters in order.

I give him a quick sideways glance as we walk, picturing him now in shorts on the beach or perhaps on the lounger next to mine next to that rooftop pool at the spa hotel. He's wearing sunglasses, I decide, and his chest is bronzed and lightly oiled, and he takes off his shades and turns to me and smiles and says, 'I'm worried you're going to burn your back, darling. Can I rub some sunscreen on for you?' And I smile and say yes please, and pass him the tube and—

'Can I ask you something?' Jack says suddenly, snapping me back to reality.

'Yes, of course.' Oh God, he's going to ask if I'd like to go back to his place right now! Will he trot out the 'Would you like to come in for coffee' line even though he doesn't drink it?

Then he says it: 'I was just wondering. D'you think it's a good thing your airline went under?'

I stare at him, assuming I misheard the question. 'Sorry?'

'I mean, are you actually quite pleased?'

'That BudgieAir went bust?' I'm still trying to make sense of this. What on earth could he be getting at? 'No. No, of course I'm not. Why d'you ask?'

'Well, maybe it could end up turning into some kind of opportunity for you?' he suggests with a raised brow.

I glance at him in surprise as we walk on, leaving the park now and climbing the long, straight hill towards my street. 'What kind of opportunity?'

'Well, to pivot,' he clarifies. '*You* know.'

I frown, genuinely uncomprehending. 'To pivot?'

'I mean, to veer into a new direction,' he says, 'like I did.'

I'm struggling with how to respond to that. 'You mean, the way you went from corporate life to being a personal trainer?'

'Yeah,' Jack says, 'and believe me, my life's so much richer for it.'

'Well, I'm pleased it turned out so well for you, but I don't think—'

'Honestly,' he cuts in, clearly warming to this topic, 'this could be your chance to change your life, and do something new and different.'

'I *am* working at the moment,' I remind him, aware of a terse edge to my voice.

'In the shop, yeah, I know that. But I'm talking about a long-term thing. Your future career. And I was wondering if it might be a chance to do something . . .' he pauses, as if searching for the right word '. . . *kinder*.'

I'm conscious of the heavy thudding in my chest. 'Kinder?' I repeat. Those feelings of excitement at possibly enjoying a massage courtesy of Jack's firm hands at some point in the future have now evaporated.

'Yeah.' He nods as we cross the street. 'You know what I mean.'

'I actually don't,' I say truthfully, 'because, when you

think about it, flight attendants tend to be pretty kind people.'

'D'you think so?' He sounds surprised. Although I'm still not quite sure what he's getting at, the mood has changed irreversibly. It's like when you've been enjoying a fabulous meal until you spot a wriggling bug in the salad. Even when it's been removed, and a fresh salad brought to you, you just don't fancy it anymore.

'Well, yes,' I say firmly. 'I mean, we pacified passengers who were scared of flying. We looked after them if they were ill. We warned them not to burn their mouths on our super-heated toasties—'

'I mean kinder to the *planet*,' Jack cuts in, turning to look at me as we walk. His blue-grey eyes look a little flinty now in the bright afternoon sunlight. 'I know redundancy's awful,' he adds, 'but when it's a company like BudgieAir . . .' He shrugs. 'It's kind of hard to be sympathetic.'

'*Is* it?' I exclaim.

'Well, yes,' he says, in an *isn't it obvious?* kind of voice. 'You can't disagree with the fact that the aviation industry is one of the main reasons our planet's fucked, can you? And budget travel's the worst—'

'Jack, I don't really want to talk about this right now, thank you—'

'—encouraging multiple journeys per year,' he charges on, 'releasing all those gases high up in the atmosphere. They're even more damaging, even more responsible for climate change than pollutants closer to earth.'

I inhale deeply, willing myself to remain calm and not to lose it with him. 'I hear what you're saying,' I mutter. 'But it's pretty personal to me. It's—'

'It's pretty personal to the polar bears whose habitat's

222

being destroyed!' he crows. 'And that's not to mention noise pollution and the manufacture and maintenance of aeroplanes. When you think about it, the carbon footprint of flying is *massive*—'

'So you're saying it's a good thing that hundreds of people lost their jobs?' I cut in sharply.

'I suppose I am.' We stop, and he looks at me and grimaces. 'Although I'm sure it's all been very worrying for you.'

'Well, it has a bit,' I say with a trace of bitterness.

'But maybe it's time we all had a reset and realise we can't just jet off on holiday without there being consequences?' he goes on, a cloud of self-righteousness now hovering over his head.

'People are always going to fly, though,' I say, impressed by my ability to appear calm when my heart is racing. 'I mean, maybe it'd be better if they didn't, and if they went on holiday on bicycles, or walked, and slept in tents or yurts and shat in a composting toilet—'

'I'm just making a point,' Jack interrupts, frowning. 'You're obviously a bright woman, Jen—' I marvel at how a seemingly innocuous statement can sound so very fucking patronising '—and I'm sure you could do something careerwise that's far more worthwhile.'

'So you're saying *I'm* responsible for climate change?'

'In a way, yes.' He seems to catch himself as we reach the end of my street. 'I don't mean single-handedly,' he adds.

'Well, thank you very much,' I say, wondering now what possessed me to fancy this man and to look forward to a sighting or a friendly wave. I blame running for this. Clearly, it must judder your brain cells around to the point where it actually sends you quite mad. In the early days, spotting Jack was the only thing that had kept me at it, pulling on my trainers diligently and setting off into the drizzle. And that tipped me into having lewd fantasies about him magically appearing in my shower like a vision, and giving me a thorough going-over with a loofah mitt to revive me after my exertions, and then being able to report back to Hannah that people *still meet in real life*. I'd become so carried away that I hadn't even considered that Jack might be a sanctimonious arse.

Incredibly, having been thoroughly lectured and patronised, I have managed to remain on just the right side of polite. It's my BudgieAir training. I've been brainwashed into being unflappable, even when under duress.

Not happy with your sausage roll, sir? I'll happily exchange it for anything else in its menu section!

'So, d'you think I can tempt you out for a run sometime?' Jack asks brightly.

I beg your pardon? 'No, I don't think so,' I say, forming a tight smile.

'Oh, right.' He looks genuinely surprised. 'Well, you can always text me if you change your mind.'

I nod quickly, just wanting to be inside my flat now, away from him. 'I'm actually pretty busy at the moment,' I say.

'Oh, right. Well, bye then, Jen.'

'Bye, Jack.' And then, before he can accuse me of wantonly destroying the habitat of polar bears, I turn quickly – I *pivot*, in fact – and stride away without looking back.

This has got to stop, I decide. No more dates. I go onto the site where there are two messages for me; one from Mr Marmite who says, *Hey Jennifer, hope things worked out for you. If ever you fancy a chat I'm still here, hanging on in there!*

He does sound sweet, and at any other time I might have replied. But what's the point? I'd only be leading him on, maybe even being one of those 'game-players' who seem to get the men on here so riled up. So I leave it unanswered and check my other message, from a man called Gavin, who's fifty, and says merely: *Hello.*

Nice to make an effort, I think, checking out his profile. There are two photos: one of him looking glum in a drab living room with a bare magnolia wall behind him, and another – taken closer up – in which he is holding a black and white cat.

It's that using an animal as a cute accessory thing, I realise now. I've seen it many times with dogs, cats and even a rabbit and a white mouse on one occasion. I'm pretty much immune to it now. However, on closer inspection this man piques my interest as I read his brief but illuminating profile:

I'm just a friendly easy-going guy, he's written, *who loves socialising, keeping fit and hanging out with my little fur buddy, Mr Sox.*

CHAPTER THIRTY-TWO

Sally, 44

'He's using him,' Sally exclaims, staring at the picture on my phone, 'as bait to reel in women.' She hands it back to me. 'Do guys do that?'

'I think it's pretty common,' I tell her as we're brought glasses of wine at one of the canal-side café's outdoor tables. Sally lives in a warehouse flat a little further down the towpath and had suggested meeting here, at her local. She was greeted warmly by staff and we've been brought complimentary hummus, toasted pitta and olives.

Sally's soft Yorkshire accent and devotion to her cat had led me to expect a homely kind of woman, short-haired in a sensible outfit from the M&S Classics range. But her dark, glossy hair is cut in a long fringeless bob, and she's wearing a yellow and black patterned dress with a Seventies vibe about it, with a bright green cardigan. Her lips are pillar-box red, her eyeliner expertly winged. She's beautiful and stylish and rightfully outraged at Gavin's appropriation of her pet.

'I don't care that he's on a dating site,' she says firmly. 'It's the Mr Sox part. I can't believe his bloody nerve!'

'It's outrageous,' I agree.

'I mean, I don't want Gavin back. That's the last thing I'd want—'

'Why did you break up, if you don't mind me asking?'

'Oh, I don't mind at all.' When we first met today, and laughed about the bizarreness of how we'd got to know each other, I warmed to her instantly. Like me, Sally fired off numerous job applications post redundancy, and decided to take a shop job in favour of more call centre work. 'It was actually because of a dating site,' she explains now. 'Not like the one you're on, though. It was one of the no-strings types for people looking for hook-ups and affairs where it's all "discreet", you know?'

I nod. 'Yes, I've heard about those.'

She sips her wine. 'I thought he was up to something when I'd lost my phone and needed to use his, and I noticed he had a Kik account.'

'What's that?' I ask.

'A messaging app where you don't share phone numbers,' she explains. 'You have a username instead. Lots of people use it for affairs, sexting, sending intimate photos, that kind of thing.'

In just a couple of months I've learnt about Berlin techno clubs, prison food and now this. My eyes are being opened in new and unexpected ways.

'So I spotted the app,' Sally continues, 'and thought, ah, right. And next time I looked he'd deleted it. That's what people do. They just have it when they need it and then they get rid of it – only that time he must have forgotten.' She pulls a wry smile and her blue eyes glint in the early evening sun. 'He's not the brightest bulb in the box, is Gav.'

I learn that Sally decided to find out precisely why he had been staying up late every night, long after she'd gone to bed as she had work to get up for, 'whereas he'd always got by with the odd decorating job. So, one night I waited until he'd gone from the spare room – we used it as a little study – to the loo. He'd minimised what he'd been looking at on his laptop but he hadn't shut it down. So I opened it back up and saw the messages, graphic messages he'd been exchanging with some woman, arranging to meet. His last message said BRB—'

'What does that mean?'

'Be right back,' she explains. 'But when he did come back I was sitting there. He nearly had a heart attack.'

'Bet he did!'

She smirks. 'He claimed it was just a one-off, he'd been feeling low, blah-blah-blah, but I know it was baloney and that was it, I threw him out . . .'

'But your cat. What happened—'

'We agreed that Gav could let himself in one day to pick up his stuff, as long as he put the key through the door. And I came home and he'd taken all his things and Mr Sox as well.'

She stresses that he'd never been interested in the cat, never showed him any affection or been involved in his care. 'He used to complain about the hair,' she adds, 'and nagged me until I bought a robot hoover and said there was a smell, which there wasn't. Mr Sox is a very clean cat.'

'And you've tried to get him back?'

'Oh, God, yes. I've been round again. He said Mr Sox wasn't there, which might've been true – he's always been a bit of a roamer, and Gav's in a ground-floor flat. He said he's taken to nipping in and out through the kitchen window onto the bin shelter out at the back. I couldn't prove he wasn't home, but I searched the neighbourhood and couldn't find him.' She exhales. 'I s'pose it was a bit hopeless really.'

'There must be something you can do,' I say.

Sally shrugs. 'I can't afford to go down any kind of legal route. And I know Gav. If things start to get difficult he'll just dump Mr Sox somewhere, say he's disappeared or something, or even worse. I dread to think—'

'Oh, Sally. I'm so sorry.'

'Hey, it's okay,' she says, briskly. 'The good thing is, it's made me realise what a vile person he is and that makes me feel grateful to be shot of him.'

'I wish I could help,' I say.

'You could *date* him, maybe?' She looks at me and grins.

'I don't think—' I start.

'Don't worry. I'm joking . . .'

I chuckle. 'Why is he on there anyway, if he's only looking for hook-ups or affairs?'

'Oh, he does like having a regular girlfriend,' she says. 'He doesn't function terribly well by himself. I've seen his place. It looks worse that a student flat. Anyway,' she adds, 'let's forget about him. How's it going with the site?' I start to tell her, and by the time I've run through my sorry line-up it's merely confirmed that I'm ready to delete my account. 'Is it really that bleak out there?' she asks with a frown.

'Seems like it, yes.'

'D'you mind if I have a look?'

'No, not at all.' I pull out my phone and bring up my

daily matches to show her, which she pores over. 'They're not *all* awful,' I add. 'I mean, there are all sorts of people on here and I don't want to judge anyone before I've even met them. I've just run out of steam with it, I think. In fact, it's just what I thought at the start, really. That it's not for me.'

'But there must be some decent guys on there,' she suggests.

'Actually, there *is* someone.' I take my phone from her briefly and show her a profile.

'Mr Marmite,' she murmurs, squinting as she reads his details and studies his pictures. 'He sounds nice.'

'Why don't *you* join?' I suggest, but she shakes her head quickly.

'I don't think so. I quite like being by myself just now.'

'You know, I think I do too.'

Sally looks at me, amusement flickering across her mouth now. 'I think you should give it one more go.'

'Oh, I don't think so,' I say.

'But this Mr Marmite sounds fun and he's kind of cute, don't you think?'

I shrug. 'I s'pose so—'

'And he's been messaging you, right?'

'Yes, a few times now . . .'

'And look, he bakes bread! He makes his own sourdough, Jen.' She grins at me and as I pick at an olive. 'Why not just see what he's like?'

I shrug and nibble a piece of pitta. 'I wonder if I'm actually not that good a judge of character.'

Sally smiles understandingly. 'I'm sure that's not true. But it must be hard to tell until you meet face to face . . .'

'Yeah.' I nod. 'I seem to have got it wrong so many times now.'

'But there's something different about him, isn't there? I mean, he sort of shines out. He seems to me like he's being a hundred per cent himself.'

'You said you'd never done this,' I say, laughing now.

'I haven't! But those months at the call centre made me a good judge of character and I could pretty much tell what someone was like within five seconds . . .'

'I'm sorry if I was a ranting idiot.'

'No, I actually enjoyed talking to you,' she says with a chuckle. 'You kind of . . . stood out.'

'I'm not sure that's a good thing,' I say with a smile.

'Believe me, it is. When you're on calls for seven hours with hardly a break, having someone going on about putting their CV on cat litter tray liners can actually brighten up your day.'

I laugh. 'Okay, so how about we make a deal?'

Her eyes widen. 'What kind of deal?'

'Well, I don't think you should give up on Mr Sox,' I say firmly.

'But I don't know what else I can do,' she insists, 'apart from breaking into Gav's place when he's out. And what if someone saw me—'

'Maybe there's another way?' I pause and look at her. 'Sally, I might not have a pet of my own but I do know how much my daughter adores her cat. Her dad does too. He'd do anything for her. There must be something you can do . . .'

'Well, maybe.' She seems to consider this for a moment. 'So, what was that about a deal?'

'You go all out to rescue Mr Sox and I might just give the site one more chance,' I tell her.

'You mean you'll set up another date?'

'I'm thinking I *might*,' I say, picking up my glass and draining the last of the crisp white wine.

She twiddles the stem of her own glass and beams at me. 'D'you even *like* Marmite?'

'Actually, I love it,' I say.

CHAPTER THIRTY-THREE

Harvey, 47

Mum never used to be particularly affectionate. Not unless Phil had arrived home on a visit – and then he'd be bestowed with fierce hugs and home-baked Victoria sponges and even the chocolate crispy cakes he'd loved as a child (never mind that he was a middle-aged man with all the top Aussie celebs' numbers stored in his phone). But now Mum seems to delight in my company. While she was never terribly interested when I was a flight attendant, now she claims to be 'incredibly proud' that I work in a supermarket and enjoys hearing about the sticker gun and the prowling customers, poised to grab the bargains.

And Harvey's face does something similar when I walk into the café, in that it actually lights up; all smiles and bright blue eyes and a hug, which feels natural and kind of right. I like him, I decide. I like this man already even though we don't know each other yet.

Having shunned Fabs's advice to just have coffee, I agreed

to meet Harvey for lunch on his suggestion, at his favourite bakery that has a cosy little café tucked away at the back. 'The hot smoked salmon's amazing,' he says, 'and it comes on this toasted brioche with some kind of sauce, but then everything's great here. I've been coming here for years.'

'It's lovely. I can't believe I've never noticed it before.'

'It is a bit hidden away.' Harvey smiles across the table. He has shortish, wavy reddish hair and those blue eyes radiate humour and kindness. He's definitely cute, but I get the impression he has no time for vanity. 'Shall we have wine?' he suggests.

'Why not?' I say, deciding that, however this goes, Harvey isn't a mug of hot water kind of man, which can only be a positive sign. A young guy takes our orders and there's a bit of chitchat with Harvey before he disappears. Then we're diving right in, skating through our basic life details at an impressive speed. I used to talk to strangers constantly at work – dozens every day – but it's taken a while to get used to this kind of date-talk, the necessary information exchange.

Harvey has had a few long-term relationships, but children didn't happen ('I'd have loved them but my nephews and nieces have kind of filled that kiddie-shaped gap') and he's been single for over a year. 'So, how've you been finding it?' I ask. 'The site, I mean?'

'Varied and interesting,' he replies with a small laugh.

'In what way?'

'Well, it's been interesting seeing the various expressions of sheer disappointment and, in some cases, horror, when they've walked into a coffee shop and seen me—' He breaks off as I laugh. 'And how they've quickly pulled themselves together and bolted their coffee down, because they had to dash off—'

'I've done that,' I tell him. 'I've been a dasher.'

'Really?'

'Oh, yes. And I've been dashed as well.' He already knows about Stephen and the oysters and how that didn't work out. Now I tell him about Maz-the-Raver and other dating highlights, which he seems to enjoy hugely. Already, it feels like chatting to a friend as I go on to recount my sole 'real world' date, with Jack Sander; how he lectured me about the planet-wrecking nature of the aviation industry, and how I blurted out that thing about the composting toilet.

'Jack Sander?' he repeats. 'Sounds like a tool. "I'd better use my Jack Sander for that" . . .' We snigger over the lameness of his joke.

'He was a bit of a tool,' I concede. 'Okay, he had a point about climate change. I do realise that. But I try to do what I can – for the planet, I mean. Maybe it's not enough—'

'Me too,' he says with endearing earnestness. 'I recycle. I don't buy fast fashion. I don't buy fashion at all, as you can see . . .' Grinning, he glances down at his checked shirt. 'And I take my bottles to the bottle bank. I mean, even when it nearly breaks my back I manage to get them there . . .'

'D'you do that thing of worrying that passers-by are noticing how many bottles you're throwing in?'

'Always!' Harvey nods. 'As if anyone's lurking with a clipboard and counting.'

'Yeah. I always feel I should shout over that I've had a party or something.' We are chuckling now at the madness of it.

'That must've been an amazing job, though,' Harvey adds. 'Flying, I mean.'

'It was really. I loved it. I mean it was challenging some-times. The passengers could be a real handful—'

'What did they get up to?'

I smile, touched by his innocent line of questioning. But of course, not everyone has shepherded boisterous hen parties off a Boeing 757 with willy-boppers bouncing above their heads. 'Well,' I start, 'there was smoking in the loo, and other stuff went on in there too . . . I'm sure you can imagine.' I grimace, and Harvey pulls a mock-shocked expression.

'You mean the mile high club? People don't really do that, do they?'

'They try to, yes. But we were primed to spot them sneaking in together. And then there was the heavy drinking, the fighting, the inappropriate grooming . . .'

'What did that entail?' he asks, looking fascinated.

'Oh, all sorts. Applying fake tan, shaving legs, even clipping toenails—'

'My God.' He splutters. 'Bits of nail pinging off?'

'Yes, frequently.'

'Wow. How did you deal with all that?'

'It was just part of the job,' I say.

He turns serious now. 'Sorry, you probably don't want to talk about all that, do you? Your old job, I mean?' Harvey knows all about my redundancy.

'It's fine,' I say. 'It's not a taboo subject.'

He nods, looking thoughtful. 'D'you think you'll ever go back to that kind of work?'

I consider this for a moment. He also knows I'm working at a supermarket and still casting around for something else. 'You know, if you'd asked me this three months ago, when it happened, I'd have said I wanted nothing more. But now . . .' I pause. 'Being grounded hasn't been all bad. I mean, there have actually been some positive aspects.'

'Like having a bit of your life back?' he suggests.

'Yes, definitely. I don't think I'd realised how much of it my job demanded. BudgieAir owned us, really, heart and soul. And now there's space for other, more important things – like spending time with my mum.' I pause and collect myself. 'It used to be a constant source of guilt with me,' I add, 'especially as she started to become a bit, well . . . not herself.'

'Oh, I am sorry,' Harvey says gently. It's as if he understands without me having to explain.

'Thank you.' I smile. 'Anyway, these past few weeks I've been able to be there for her a lot more. So, you know . . .' I hesitate again, aware of the kindness in his expression, encouraging me to go on. 'I'm not saying it was one of those it-was-meant-to-happen things, but it's been kind of handy.' Our food has arrived, and I sip my chilled wine, so glad that we arranged to meet today. He's easy to be with: a friendly, chatty, *listening* kind of man, who I can have lunch with, without feeling I have something to prove. There's no being presented with a mollusc I feel obliged to eat, wondering whether he's been in prison or having my teeth assessed unfavourably. I'm wondering now what possessed me to push Harvey aside while I met a tit-staring radiator bore and a hectoring dentist.

In fact, it turns out that he *has* been in prison – at least in a professional capacity, teaching IT skills to prisoners. 'It was great,' he says lightly, as if it was nothing remarkable at all. 'I met some brilliant people. Really interesting, decent guys a lot of them were – focused on getting educated and making a better life once they'd been released. It was just a three-month block of classes and I was kind of sad when it finished.'

The talk turns back to Mum and it strikes me that I haven't really chatted to anyone about it in detail before. I haven't wanted to burden Leena or Freddie because what could they do anyway? Hannah knows a little, but I certainly wouldn't want her worrying about strange men turning up at her grandma's door and wheedling their way in for cups of tea. And I haven't talked to Rod about it because, well, we don't seem to really talk much about anything anymore.

'I think you know when a parent's changing,' Harvey says. 'You feel it in your gut because you know them so well. You pick up the tiniest things.'

'Yes, you're right.' I tell him about Mum's mysterious gentleman caller, and her wad of cash being blown away at the ice cream van, and being unable to answer all of Dr Mahmoud's questions. 'But it wasn't really those things,' I add. 'It was subtle changes that were starting to happen.'

'I hope you're getting good support,' he ventures.

'Well, yes. Her doctor's brilliant. Mum fancies him something rotten—' Harvey chuckles, and it occurs to me how striking his blue eyes are '—and the psychiatrist was great too, although Mum was a little put out that she wasn't Dr Mahmoud.' I accompanied Mum to the appointment a few days ago. Again, there was a raft of questions and simple tests designed to assess Mum's awareness and memory function.

'How's your mum taking all of this?' Harvey asks. 'I mean, does she understand what's happening, do you think?'

'Weirdly, she seems pretty unfazed so far,' I reply. 'I'm not sure if she's just accepted it, or she doesn't believe it, or maybe doesn't know what's happening to her. I really can't tell. Whenever I broach it, and ask if she feels okay about what the doctor said, she changes the subject straight away.'

'My mum was like that too,' Harvey says. 'She's in a care home now. Dad passed away a couple of years ago—'

'Oh, I'm sorry . . .'

'It's okay. But thanks.' There's a pause that feels natural and entirely un-awkward, then Harvey starts to tell me about his mum, and how he'd been 'scared shitless about how she'd take it, when I suggested it might be best if she moved into a home . . .'

'It's terrifying,' I agree, 'and I've only had to coax mine to the doctor's so far. Did you worry about your mum settling in?'

'God, yes. She'd always been hugely sociable with tons of activities, clubs and things she was chair of. She was the boss of everything,' he says with a fond smile. 'And like most people I'd had that thing of: "We can't put Mum in home. It just isn't right." My brother and sister felt the same. We were like: "How can we take all those things she loves away from her?"' He stops for a moment. There's a glint in his eyes and I feel quite honoured that he's sharing this with me. 'But it had become dangerous for her to be in her own house,' he continues. 'She'd become obsessed with scented candles and had them burning all over the house, set a rug on fire once, and put the electric kettle on the gas rig and turned it on . . . There were so many things.' Harvey stops and pushes back his reddish hair. 'Sorry. I am going on a bit here, aren't I?'

'Not at all,' I say.

'I don't want to make you feel worse about things. About *your* mum, I mean.'

'You're not,' I insist. 'Not at all. So, what happened, when she moved into the home?'

'Oh, she loved it from day one. It was a ready-made social life right there and now she's basically running the place. The weird thing is, she loved her own house but she's never even mentioned it once. It's as if it no longer exists.'

'That's wonderful,' I say. 'So, were your brother and sister supportive throughout the whole thing?'

Harvey nods. 'We were all in it together so, as hard as it was, I never felt alone. How about you?'

We've finished our lunch now and moved on to coffees. As I tell him about Phil in Sydney, I find myself wishing that my brother and I could talk like this, about Mum in a *real* way, without him brushing off my concerns and telling me instead about some party he's planning where the caterers will supply two thousand chocolate-covered strawberries and something called 'charcoal lemonade'.

'But I don't feel cross anymore,' I add, 'that he's on the other side of the world and busy entertaining his celebrity friends. Because that's his life and he's worked hard for it. And, y'know, this whole thing with Mum has brought me and her closer. I mean, *much* closer. It's what I'd always wanted really – to feel like we had a proper connection.'

'You sound like a really caring daughter,' Harvey says, and something catches in my throat.

'She'd always been a little bit scary,' I add. 'I don't mean horrible or anything like that. Just kind of tough and a bit volatile. And now this is happening and, I don't know, I just feel like I want to look after and be close to her.'

Harvey smiles kindly. 'Of course you do.'

'Sorry, I really *am* going on . . .'

'You're not at all,' he says. 'I mean, I'm not a dad so I haven't experienced that but I'd imagine that, apart from raising a child, realising you're the one taking care of a parent, rather than the other way round, is one of the biggest challenges a person can ever face—'

'Yes, exactly,' I say.

'And at first you don't feel like you're ready, like there's been some kind of mistake—'

'God yes,' I say, amazed at how he just gets it and that this feels okay, even though we haven't talked very much about his life, his baking – I haven't even heard about his sourdough mini-empire yet! Yet I'm pretty sure that we'll see each other again, and that whatever happens this won't just be one of those dates where you think, *Well, at least it'll make a funny anecdote.* I've had enough anecdote dates.

I find myself telling Harvey about the laughs Mum and I have together these days, how she delights in my supermarket stories, how I'd told her about the man I'd seen trying to stick a label from a 20p pack of salami onto some full-priced pork chops. 'Bet you gave him a piece of your mind!' she'd exclaimed delightedly.

Harvey chuckles. 'Isn't it weird, how something can be heart-breaking and sort of wonderful at the same time?'

I nod and that's when it happens. My chest seems to tighten as I sit there opposite this kind, interesting and attractive man, whom I don't even know yet – not properly – and suddenly I can't talk anymore. Because my throat has choked up and tears are fuzzing my vision, threatening to overspill.

'Oh, Jen. I'm so sorry.' Briefly, he places a hand across the table over mine.

'No, *I'm* sorry. God, I didn't expect this to happen.' I place the flat of a hand over one of my cheeks and find it wet. 'This is so embarrassing,' I mutter, grabbing a paper napkin and blotting at my face.

'Don't worry. It's okay, really . . .'

'I'm sorry,' I repeat, blotting again – the napkin is sodden already – and inhaling deeply as I try to get a grip on myself.

'Please don't apologise,' Harvey says, his face full of concern.

I open my mouth to speak but more tears come, accompanied, startlingly, by a terrible gulping noise that seems to come from somewhere deep in my gut. While I'm aware of things being taken away from our table and a bill being brought by a smiling girl with a straight blonde fringe, I can't actually do anything apart from willing my body to stop producing this awful mess of tears and, oh God, now there's snot – copious snot, I'm amazed my body can produce so much – which I'm trying to stem with yet more paper napkins.

We leave the café with Harvey having insisted on treating us this time, but probably only because he wanted us to get out of there, his favourite lunch place, before I'd used up all the napkins and resorted to wiping my nose on my sleeve. I caught the blonde-fringe girl casting him a sympathetic look as we left, as if he'd found himself lumbered with a mad drunk.

'I'd like to make sure you get home okay,' he says now, but I shake my head firmly.

'I'm fine, honestly. It's just, I haven't really talked about any of this before. Apart from with the doctors, I mean.'

'Honestly, you don't need to explain—'

'Thank you. Thank you for being so kind.' We hug briefly. Despite Harvey's offers to accompany me, as if I might need a carer, minutes later I am travelling alone on the subway home, with my sore eyes and puffy face, thinking what a shame that happened, that his kindness turned me into a weeping mess, and my nose into a kind of snot tap that I couldn't turn off. It wouldn't have happened with any of my other dates because we hadn't even talked about Mum.

It wouldn't have occurred to me to even mention her. When a date is focused around the benefits of modern braces, or your lamentable understanding of techno clubs, it's unlikely to turn you into a sobbing wreck.

And my date with Harvey was different. It was lovely, I reflect now, as I ride the escalator back up to ground level and step out into the bright summer's afternoon. It *definitely* wasn't an anecdote date. It's just a pity that he won't want to put himself through that again.

CHAPTER THIRTY-FOUR

But I was wrong about Harvey because he messaged me that evening to make sure I was okay. I thanked him for lunch and suggested I treated him sometime. *Hope you'll feel able to show your face in your favourite café again,* I wrote.

Oh, they're used to it, he replied, *me having lunch with a friend who looks all fine and happy at the start but by the end they're weeping. Either that, or they're trying to maim themselves with the cutlery . . .*

And now on this, our second date, we are having a picnic in Kelvingrove Park. '*Please* tell me,' I urge him as I pick up a plump, glossy cherry from the punnet.

'You really don't want to know.'

'Go on. I do!'

'It's embarrassing . . .' Quick shake of the head.

'I'm sure it's not. I'm sure it's fantastically witty and clever—'

'How d'you know it even has a name?' Harvey raises a brow.

244

'You seem like the kind of person who'd name his sour-dough starter.'

'Do I? I'm not sure if I like that!'

'It's not an insult,' I reassure him as we tuck into our picnic on this breezy, turquoise-skied Sunday afternoon. While Harvey brought salami and cheeses to showcase his delicious home-baked bread, my contribution of fruit and little orangey cakes were picked up from a posh grocer's en route.

'"You seem like the kind of person who . . ."' He grins at me. 'Don't you always a worry when someone starts a sentence with that?'

'I guess so. It's often a little dig, isn't it?'

'At least, it's rarely a neutral observation . . .'

'Because none of us like being judged,' I add, 'by someone who doesn't know us properly.'

He nods. 'That's kind of what dating's like, isn't it?'

'It's felt like that sometimes, yes.'

'It's a weird thing,' Harvey observes, 'putting yourself out there, with a little advert for yourself, as if you're a car . . .'

'I haven't asked you yet,' I venture, 'what made you do it? Join the site, I mean.' I catch myself. 'That's more a first-date question, isn't it?'

'We were too busy talking about other stuff,' he says with a smile.

'I was too busy sobbing.'

He gives me a wry look. 'You were just getting it all out. No harm in that, is there?'

'I s'pose not. So, the site?' I prompt him.

'Oh, yeah. I'd been under fire from friends at work and eventually I agreed to give it a go.' He shrugs. 'I was intrigued, I suppose. I wondered how it'd work and what'd happen, and if nothing happened I could quietly delete my profile and *no more would be said*.' He grins. 'I guess it's one of those things you feel like you should try, at least once, like eating the worm out of a mezcal bottle—'

'And at least then you can say you've done it,' I cut in.

'Exactly.' His laugh is infectious and I'm aware of a warm feeling from being here in the beautiful park with him. When I started dating it startled me how self-conscious I was, how focused on what Stephen and all the others thought of me, as if it had been a job interview, even if I wasn't remotely interested in seeing them again. As I'd always felt confident in my job, it shocked me how self-doubting I could be, once I no longer had that BudgieAir scarf tied at my neck. But today, as we lounge on the freshly mown grass, I'm no longer wrestling with any of that. When Hannah asked me what I was looking for, and I said, 'Just someone nice to have fun with', I thought it sounded a bit lame. But it was true; I'd just been made redundant and I wanted something to happen to lift my spirits. And now, as I tell Harvey all of this – without even wondering what he might think of me – we find ourselves agreeing that, as a concept, 'meeting someone nice' is vastly under-rated.

'Would you say it's been fun so far?' he asks. 'Honestly, I mean?'

I pause, considering this. 'Well, today is, and our lunch was too, until all the tears—'

'I mean the whole' – eyebrow waggle here – 'dating experience.'

'Um, like you said, it's been varied and interesting.' I press my lips together, trying to trap in a laugh. 'Remember the clubber I told you about? The one who said there was no chemistry?' Harvey nods. 'He also said, "You seem like the kind of person who might feel a bit out of place in a latex room".'

He splutters. 'Damn cheek! I'd have thought you'd have fitted right in.'

'Well, exactly,' I retort, which sets us off again, laughing like teenagers.

'Where is it?' he asks. 'This latex room, I mean? We could head over but I'd need to go home and change.'

'Harvey.' Without thinking I've placed a hand on his knee. 'It's in Berlin.'

'Oh.' Then: 'I'm kind of relieved, actually. I mean, I'm sure you could pull it off – that kind of look, I mean – but I'm not so sure about me.' He glances down in acknowledgement of his T-shirt and jeans: the default casual wear of the middle-aged male. The T-shirt is plain grey, the jeans loose on those long legs stretched out before him.

'So, anyway, what is it called?' I ask.

He looks quizzical.

'Your sourdough starter.'

'Oh, are we back onto that?' A bemused smile. 'Can you guess?'

'Bubbles?' A shake of the head. 'Bread Pitt? The Beast from the Yeast?'

'Where are you *getting* these?'

I smile and push my hair back from my face. The day is turning chilly now and I pull on my jacket over my denim dress. 'Hannah and her housemates went through a sourdough phase and there were debates on what to call it. The starter, I mean. But it turned out to be like when a band first gets together, and they spend so much time sitting around trying to decide what to call themselves, and no music is actually made . . .'

247

'Or bread, in their case?'

'I think they baked one loaf. Hannah said she nearly broke a tooth on it—'

'Well, mine's called Dough Farah,' he says quickly.

'Dough Farah?' I repeat. 'Are you a runner, then?'

'A bit,' he says. 'At least, I did Couch to 5k and managed not to die—'

'It's the law, isn't it? For people our age?'

'Seems like it,' Harvey says. 'But no, it was my nephew who came up with it. He's the athlete in the family. We were playing with words, and it seemed perfect—'

'Because it keeps on going?'

'Yeah, exactly.' He smiles, and again I think, what a *likeable* face he has; more interesting than classically handsome, his nose a bit crooked, his mouth seeming to be almost permanently on the verge of a grin.

'If you want to give it a try,' he's saying now, 'you could have a bit of mine to get yours going. That's probably the easiest way . . .'

'Is it?' I ask, trying to keep down another smile. Clearly, he's serious about this bread business. He's already told me that he's up at six on Saturday mornings in order to bake for his regular customers and a couple of local grocery shops. It's just a sideline – IT is his main thing, and he's obviously committed to that – but it seems to bring him a huge amount of pleasure.

'Oh, definitely,' he says. 'But if you want to do it from scratch, the best way I've found is with a little bit of flour and grapes . . .'

Although I'm as likely to carve a model of the Sistine Chapel from ice as I am to ever bake bread – at least while shops that sell loaves exist – I'm enjoying hearing about his methods and processes; his kneading methods and tips on achieving the perfect crust.

'I can give you a demo sometime, if you like.' He catches himself and grins. 'I'm sure that'd be thrilling for you.'

'It would!' I insist. Light rain is starting to fall now, driving us to pack up the remains of our picnic.

'I was going to ask,' he adds, with a note of hesitation, 'would you like to come over for dinner sometime? To my rank little hovel, I mean?'

'I bet it's not.' I beam at him, feeling my heart lift as we stride across the park towards the subway. 'And yes, I'd like that very much.'

When we reach the station it feels so natural when we kiss; not jammed up against a rusting skip but very sweetly, in the middle of the pavement, with the world going on all around us. And while it's not a fervent snog, it's definitely more than quick peck goodbye.

Something stirs in me, quickening my heart. 'I really enjoyed today,' Harvey says.

'Me too. I've had such a lovely time.'

Instead of parting company somehow we've ended up in a hug. He smells so good, I can't help noticing. It's so rare when you're close to someone for the very first time and just want to breathe them in. 'So, dinner,' Harvey adds. 'Is there anything you don't like to eat?'

'Not really,' I reply. 'I like pretty much everything – apart from oysters. I'm not crazy about those.'

CHAPTER THIRTY-FIVE

Hannah, 23

Hannah appears in the crowds at Central station, waving while dragging her wheelie case. I hug her tightly, take her case and we stride across the concourse towards the taxi rank. 'You look great, Mum,' she announces. 'Kind of . . . different. What've you done?'

'Thread lift,' I tease her. 'Everyone's having them, love.'

'You haven't!'

'No, of course not,' I say, laughing now. 'Leena was considering it. I think she was feeling a bit rubbish about everything, but not anymore. She has a new job.'

'Oh, that's great. What is it?'

'She's going to work for a hotel chain, in charge of corporate events and attracting new business. It's in London. She's moving in with her sister to start with—'

'That's brilliant, Mum.' I'm aware of her giving me quick glances as we walk. 'So, what about you?'

'Oh, things are good,' I say. 'I'll miss Leena, of course.

Freddie will too. But he's thrown himself into his course and we all have the feeling that things are starting to happen again. There's even a tiny rumour that there might be a buyer for BudgieAir.'

'So, you could start flying again?'

'We'll see,' I say as we wait in the taxi queue. 'It's happened before and come to nothing,' I add.

'Yeah, I know.' She gives me a teasing smile. 'So, are you seeing someone, then? Is that what's different about you?'

'Um, I wouldn't *exactly* say that,' I say, smiling too as we climb into the taxi. She's only here for two nights. Her visit was short notice and I wasn't offended when I discovered that it had been prompted by her friend's Kaya's birthday party, which she'd decided – at the last minute – that she didn't want to miss. She and Kaya, of perfect gingerbread house fame, have been friends since they were five years old.

Back home, I tell her about Harvey and show her his profile and find myself describing, with a note of pride, how he supplies his loaves to local shops at the weekends – as if I have anything to do with it.

'He sounds lovely,' she says.

'Oh, it's really early days,' I say quickly. 'I've only seen him twice. He's asked me over for dinner. We'd planned for tomorrow but we're going to rearrange—'

'You don't need to do that, Mum,' Hannah says with a frown.

'But *you're* here. I hardly ever see you. I'm not going to be out gallivanting and miss on our time together.'

'"Gallivanting."' We're laughing now, both of us drinking tea and eating toast on the sofa, like we used to, and I'm filled with a surge of happiness at her being close to me

251

again. The gaps between seeing her are so long now that even though she's not a child, growing and changing rapidly, she still looks a little different to me every time. Her hair is still coloured a deep, glossy red, but maybe she's done her make-up differently, or perhaps it's just that she's becoming more and more enmeshed in her London life. 'Tomorrow's Kaya's party,' she reminds me.

'Yes, but—'

'You don't need to sit there waiting for me to come in,' she teases, 'like when I was sixteen.'

'Yes, I know that, Han—'

'Pretending you just *happened* to be up, sitting there looking all casual and not panicking at all. Like, "Oh, hi, love. I was just about to go to bed"—'

'Was it that obvious?' I chuckle, hit with a bolt of nostalgia for those days, even though I was on tenterhooks pretty much every time she went out at night; not because she ever staggered in and threw up on the sofa (well, only once) but because that was my *job*, to worry. That's what mothers do. Mum used to check my breath whenever I came in late, for evidence of booze and cigarettes. I'd spend a fortune on gum and Polo Mints and still notice her nostrils quivering as she checked me out.

'Kaya's just moved into a new flat,' Hannah is telling me now. 'It'll be just as disgusting as the last place but loads of people are going—'

'Oh, who?' I still can't shake off my eagerness for information.

'Just *people*, Mum.' Hannah laughs. 'And I'm planning to stay overnight.' Perhaps in reaction to her mother's impeccable standards, Kaya seems to exist perfectly happily surrounded by takeaway cartons and cultivates mould in coffee cups. 'You don't mind, do you?' she asks, as if catching herself.

'No, of course not, love.'

'So if you go for your dinner,' she adds with a sly smile, 'it doesn't matter if you're out late or anything.'

'Oh, I don't think—'

'Or even if you're out all *night*.' She smirks as, ridiculously, I feel my face glowing hot. 'I'm just saying there's no need to rush home, all right?'

'Okay,' I say quickly. She tails me into the kitchen as I top up our mugs from the teapot. I had already switched my shifts in order to be free for tomorrow night, and at the last minute I'd managed to take today off too. 'We're seeing Dad for Sunday lunch,' I add, 'and Gran's coming too.'

'Oh, great. Dario's?' She beams hopefully.

'Of course,' I say, catching her glow of happiness at not only seeing her dad and grandma but also being reunited with her favourite waiters, always ready with the back chat and jokes, at the old-fashioned Italian we've been going to for years.

'I hope it's not different?'

'Of course not,' I say. 'It's exactly the same as it always was.'

A little later we study a takeaway menu. It's for a local Malaysian that's another favourite of Hannah's. As we deliberate over dishes I'm anticipating a lovely evening, just the two of us, catching up. These times feel so rare and precious these days.

'Dario's will never change,' Hannah says happily, pulling herself up onto the worktop and sitting with her long jeans-clad legs dangling.

'I really hope not,' I say firmly.

'But you have,' she adds. 'You've changed, Mum. You're all glowy or something. And I think you should stick to your plans for tomorrow night.'

Next day I find myself wondering if this is in fact the very *best* kind of date. Hannah and I are wallowing in gently bubbling water – not in a hot tub in the forest but in the jacuzzi at a city-centre hotel spa. The lighting is low, changing gradually from violet to soft pink, and the air is steamy and gently scented. I'd booked us in as soon as I'd known Hannah was coming home for the weekend. We've already visited her gran this morning, which propelled Mum into a flurry of excitement as she pulled out the boxes of chocolate fingers and huge bottles of Coke, plus those pastel iced Party Ring biscuits, which Hannah hasn't eaten since she was ten. 'I know these are your favourites!' Mum exclaimed. 'And I've got Battenburg and Tunnock's Teacakes . . .'

I was relieved that Mum had remembered Hannah was coming, even if it had meant stocking up as if preparing for a global sugar shortage. She didn't seem to remember what her granddaughter does for a job, but that's to be expected. As Hannah says now, leaning back against the edge of the pool with her toes poking through the bubbles, 'Gran's never listened to a podcast, Mum. She probably doesn't understand what they are. And she's not going to know what an assistant producer does.'

Hannah now knows about her gran's growing confusion and the doctors' appointments; she's a grown-up, after all. And she'd noticed changes in her this morning, not just with the Coke and array of sweet treats, but when Mum had wanted to show her the blooming herbaceous border. Brad the pug had been pottering around by himself in Kirsten's

254

garden. Instead of attracting his attention and having a 'chat' with him, as she used to, Mum had shuddered as if he were a rat. Then Kirsten had come out to greet Hannah and Mum had barely managed to be civil before marching back indoors.

'Gran doesn't seem to like Kirsten and Brad anymore, does she?' Hannah says now.

'No. I don't really know what's going on there. She's a bit scared of Brad, I think.'

'No more one-calorie doggy treats?'

'I don't think so, love. And I doubt he'll be getting a selection box at Christmas either.'

'Oh, that's such a shame, Mum. It's so sad to see this happening.'

I take her hand and squeeze it. 'I know, love. We just have to take it day by day. Mum still enjoys lots of things in her life, like her garden and the birds, and I'm thankful for that.'

Our chat moves on to her dad's new girlfriend, and naturally I am required to give a detailed description of Gaby and everything that happened during her brief visit to my flat. 'Did Dad seem happy?' Hannah wants to know.

'Yes, he really did.' Kind of on edge, too, I decide now, although maybe I just imagined that.

'And you liked her?' she asks.

'She seemed like a really nice person,' I say blandly. 'And your dad's looking really well. You'll see. He seems like a new person actually.' I'm not sure why I'm finding the subject of Rod and Gaby a little uncomfortable to talk about and hope Hannah hasn't noticed the catch to my voice.

It's a relief when we move on to her life in London, and her latest project: a podcast called *Just a Number*, meaning that age is nothing more than that. 'We're interviewing women of all ages,' she explains, 'about their experiences of life, their wisdom, all of that. We've had some amazing guests already. People are sick of so much media being targeted at the young.' I can't help smiling at my twenty-three-year-old daughter saying that. She tells me about a well-known actress in her seventies 'who was so feisty, Mum. She was brilliant! She said anyone who treats her as if she's a defective appliance that's ready for the dump can just fuck off.'

I laugh, soaking in her opinions and stories as we move on to talking about her social life. Museums, exhibitions, the theatre; she does far more cultural stuff than I did at her age – and have ever done, in fact. And now she is telling me about how she and Jacob went to London Zoo for a lark, and then another time they got chatting to a man on a narrowboat, who'd been waiting at a loch on the canal, and he'd invited them to jump aboard and chug along through the city with him. Jacob's name is featuring a lot today, but although I'm itching to know if something's developed between them, I also know better than to ask. Any time I have, when other names have come up, she's shrugged and said, 'We're just hanging out, Mum.' As if traditional couple relationships are as dated as consulting the *Radio Times* and three-channel TV.

When I was just three years older than Hannah is now, I'd discovered I was pregnant. 'Don't worry,' was Rod's first reaction. Actually no, it was to turn sheet-white and mutter, 'Fuck, Jen. How did that happen?' Of course we were both well aware of the basics of human reproduction. We just couldn't believe that one night of drunken recklessness was all it had taken. 'It'll be all right,' he'd added then, holding me close. 'Whatever happens it'll be all right.'

If it had happened with anyone else I might not have gone through with the pregnancy. I loved my job, and my life; being a young woman in a big city, as Hannah is now. But this was *Rod's* baby, and I cared for him very much. I loved him, even if I wasn't *in love* with him.

Did that matter? On a layover in Magaluf I sat up late in the hotel bar with Freddie; him on sangria, me on orange juice. I kept thinking about all the cocktails I'd tanked when we'd been away again together on that week's holiday before I'd known I was pregnant. How the only aspect I'd been worrying about was whether things would be okay with Rod the next time I saw him. In truth, I'd hoped we could just forget all about it – like the way you might rearrange the furniture to cover up a mark on the floor.

In that ritzy hotel bar with its golden chandelier, I had a decision to make. We were due to fly back to Glasgow at ten a.m. I'd done the positive test a couple of weeks before and time was running out.

'Can you imagine you and Rod being parents?' Freddie asked.

I had to say no, but only because I couldn't imagine *myself* being one. Being responsible for the safety and comfort of two hundred passengers was fine. But in no way did I feel ready for the colossal responsibility of raising a human being.

'What kind of dad d'you think he'd be?' Freddie's gaze met mine.

'Brilliant,' I said, without even thinking. And right then I knew he would be, and that meant we could do it together. I also knew it would be a bit unusual, as we wouldn't be a couple living together, or get married, or any of that. We could do it our way instead.

'I love him. Just not in that way,' I told Freddie.

That's what I've always said, whenever it's come up over the years. Dear Rod, who's the best father anyone could have. *I love him. Just not in that way.*

And I pictured my own parents, and the frequent flare-ups at home, and how on one occasion Mum had flung a bowl of Rice Krispies and milk across the dining table, aiming for Dad, and they'd scattered everywhere, sticking to the carpet.

And I thought about the shouting I'd often heard at night, when I'd wondered how long a night could last when you were lying there waiting for it to finish, unable to sleep (Phil never heard it, or so he claimed). Then I pictured that sailing trip, around Corryvreckan – cauldron of the speckled seas – when Mum had shouted at Dad for bringing us there. ('Call this a holiday? Why can't we do what normal people do and go to a nice resort?') I'd thought she was being mean, shouting like that when of course she'd been terrified.

Rod and I might not have planned a baby, I decided then in that glittering bar in Magaluf. But we loved and cared for each other and I knew, right then, that I would be able to depend on him forever.

Out of the jacuzzi now, Hannah and I swim lengths in the main pool and finish with a sauna. 'This has been great, Mum,' Hannah says as we get dressed in the changing room. 'Thanks so much.'

'Oh, I loved it,' I say. 'It'll set you up for the party too.' I'm thinking now of the evening that's ahead of me, at Harvey's. My stomach swirls in anticipation as we leave the spa.

Immediately, as is her habit, Hannah fishes out her phone as soon as there's a signal, checking it as we leave the hotel.

'Dad's messaged,' she says. 'He's asking if we mind if he brings Gaby to lunch tomorrow?' She stops and looks at me, pulling a startled face. I knew she was planning to head over to Rod's after lunch (she never visits without seeing Casey, her cat) before catching the train back to London. And I had wondered if she might meet Gaby then.

'Well, *I* don't mind,' I say firmly, thinking maybe he could have checked with me first, when it's a family lunch at the restaurant we've been going to since they used to drag over a highchair for Hannah? It's silly, I know, to feel mildly hurt at being cut out of the equation. But clearly things have changed, and I'll have to get used to the way things are now.

'I s'pose I don't either.' The little crease between Hannah's brows suggests that she does a little. 'But Gran's coming too, isn't she? Will she be okay about meeting someone new?'

'She'll probably enjoy it,' I tell her firmly. 'She seems to love everyone these days.'

'Apart from Brad. And Kirsten . . .'

'I think it's more about Brad really. She doesn't seem to know what to do with him anymore . . .'

'It's so sad, Mum,' she says, then adds: 'You don't think it'll be awkward? For Gran to meet Gaby, I mean?'

'No, not at all,' I say firmly. 'It'll be *great*.'

Back home now, after a hasty stir-fry that I make for her, Hannah disappears to change for Kaya's party, leaving me to get ready for my date. This time there's no need for all those extensive preparations. I kiss Hannah goodbye, then take a taxi round to Harvey's place. He lives in a top-floor flat in a well-kept modern block, red brick and glass reflecting the blue sky, close to the river. Tonight in my bag there's just my keys, purse, phone and a decent bottle of wine. No toothbrush or spare pair of knickers.

I won't be staying over, even if Harvey suggests it, because the last thing I'd want is to be all bleary tomorrow, with a lunch date looming – with Hannah, Mum, Rod and now Gaby too. I have a feeling I'm going to have to be on my toes for that.

CHAPTER THIRTY-SIX

Dough Farah, 5

'Jennifer,' Harvey announces, brandishing the open Kilner jar inches from my face, 'meet Dough.'

'Dough Farah?' Having only just slipped off my jacket, I have already been greeted very sweetly with a hug and a kiss on the cheek, and handed a perfectly chilled glass of white wine.

'Yeah. Smells good, doesn't it?'

'Hmm, yes, it does! It has a kind of . . .' I wrinkle my nose as if assessing a wine, although the kind I buy for myself doesn't taste of nectarines or gooseberries or any of that. 'It's got a yeasty tang,' I remark. Now I've made it sound like a rank gusset. 'Or maybe more like a craft ale?' I add. 'Although I've never actually *had* a craft ale—'

'Hardcore techno clubs, unfathomably expensive beer—'

'So many things I haven't tried,' I cut in with a smile. 'I've led a very sheltered life.'

He puts the jar down and picks up a tea towel and puts

it down again. I'm urged to park myself at the kitchen table while he tops up my wine. (I'd barely taken a sip.) In his favourite café, and lolling about on a blanket in Kelvingrove Park, Harvey had seemed relaxed and entirely comfortable. Yet now he seems nervous, as if this wasn't his neat and orderly flat but a professional kitchen, and I am a notoriously harsh restaurant reviewer.

Harvey's kitchen is bright and airy with an uninterrupted view over the Clyde. There are shiny white brick-shaped tiles and gleaming utensils dangling from a rack. Expensive-looking casserole dishes – Le Creuset, I'd guess – are lined up on a shelf, the kind Freddie and Pablo asked for as wedding presents. (I couldn't believe anyone could be so excited about cooking pots.) On the pale oak table sits a large white bowl piled with lemons. It's like being inside an Ottolenghi cookbook and I was taken aback when Harvey had welcomed me in. While I'd guessed he was joking about his 'rank little hovel', I'd expected something a bit more blokey, more softly worn around the edges, a bit like Harvey himself.

Now he's stirring something in a pot on the hob and bobbing up and down, peering through the oven door, checking on something. When he's not doing that he's wiping down the work surfaces and poking at his laptop to find a 'better' Spotify playlist even though the one that's currently playing is perfectly fine.

'Can I help at all?' I ask, feeling guilty for sitting here observing all this activity. I sip my wine, which definitely *does* taste of lovely things, being several rungs up from my normal plonk.

'No, no, it's fine . . .' Some rapid chopping is happening

now; proper cheffy chopping like they do on TV. 'Maybe I should've done something I could've prepared ahead of time,' he adds, possibly more to himself than to me.

'I wish you'd let me do something . . .'

'No, you're fine! Relax!' He catches himself and pushes back his reddish hair, then wipes a hand across his blue-and-white striped apron that he's wearing over jeans and a grey crew-necked top. 'Bloody hell, I *am* sorry. I'm acting like one of those performance chefs—'

'I think you should chop that tomato so it flies in the air and catch it in your mouth,' I suggest with a smile.

'I've been practising that all day but I'm not sure I can pull it off.' His off-centre grin warms my heart.

'You didn't need to go to all this trouble for me, you know,' I add.

'It's no trouble,' he says firmly. 'It's the simplest thing in the world. It's just, I haven't cooked for anyone in quite a while . . .' Now he's back to his pot again. 'I guess I'm a bit out of practice.'

We're having monkfish and a risotto made with Harvey's own home-made stock. There's something incredibly appealing about a man cooking; I mean, properly cooking, requiring *ingredients*, and not just taking something out of a box and heating it up. As he stirs, Harvey explains that his vegetable stock involves simmering onions, carrots and some other bits and bobs for something like five hours. 'Half-a-day stock,' he calls it, which seems like an awfully long haul to make what is basically vegetable-flavoured water. I'm also learning perhaps a *little* more than I really need to know about making stock. But then, he's an enthusiast, and that's an attractive trait.

'I can't remember when I last cooked for anyone apart from Hannah,' I tell him. 'I must've been in my thirties, the night of the terrible rum chicken.'

He glances round at me. 'Tell me about the terrible rum chicken.'

'Oh, I had Leena and Freddie and a couple of others round, a bunch of friends from work. It was basically chicken breasts in a dish with some kind of weird flavoured rum that'd been on special offer at duty-free. I'd tried it – it was pretty vicious – so I thought I'd use it as a cooking ingredient instead.'

A bemused smile. 'Don't tell me you invented the recipe to use it up?'

'I kind of did, yeah.'

'So, can I ask what it is?' he asks. 'Or is it secret?'

'The recipe?' I chuckle. 'It's basically chicken in a dish of rum.'

His eyes are kind of twinkly and he looks even more attractive now, mussed up from all his kitchen activity. 'So what happens next?'

'It just goes in the oven,' I explain.

'So, you don't burn off the alcohol first or anything like that?'

'No,' I say. 'The alcohol stays right where it is.'

'And there's nothing else added—'

'Nope.' I am laughing now, which sets Harvey off. 'I'm sure you've heard that the best chefs don't overcomplicate things?' I add.

'You're right. They let the ingredients speak for themselves. So, what was it like?' he wants to know.

'Probably the worst thing I'd ever eaten. Freddie said he could still feel it a week later, burning the lining of his throat . . .' I pause. 'If I can't find another client-facing job, I was thinking of writing a cookery book.'

'You absolutely should!' he says, piling salad ingredients into a smart glass bowl. Harvey has relaxed now, and as he carries on tending to things he asks about my continuing job search. 'Nothing else has come up,' I explain. 'But there is a rumour that BudgieAir might have a buyer after all.'

'Really?' he asks. 'You said you weren't sure about going back to flying . . .'

'Yeah, that's right.' Already, he knows that I'm valuing having my life back again, and being able to spend more time with Mum. Now I tell him that I've started to look back at my old job as if it were a particularly demanding husband – requiring so much attention and dedication that it literally left time for very little else. Back then, my flat was badly neglected (standards have improved a little of late) and I didn't see friends socially for weeks, apart from on layovers. 'I just worked and worked,' I tell him, 'and now . . .' I stop and shrug. 'Well, I'm wondering now if maybe there's another way to live.'

'I get that,' Harvey says. 'We don't have to keep slogging away at the same thing all our lives.'

'You like what you do, don't you?' At the picnic he'd described his working life: the big modern city-centre office where he's been for ten years, taking pride in his job, managing 'systems' that I can't even begin to understand.

'Y'know, I do actually.' A note of surprise there. 'If you'd told me when I was eighteen that I'd be happy going into an office every day, with a bunch nice people and a decent boss, I'd have thought you were stark-raving mad.'

'What did you think you'd be doing?' I ask.

He smirks as if a little embarrassed by his youthful

ambitions. 'Working for something like, I don't know, an ad agency or something because that doesn't count as an office, right?'

'You mean a workplace with panoramic views and people darting about with presentations and shouting—'

'Or on stage,' Harvey cuts in, 'being an actor.' He slips into a grandiose voice. 'Wowing the audiences with my Romeo—'

'Did you want to go to drama school?'

'For about a month, yeah, after my performance in *Joseph* had been rapturously received at school. At least by my mum and dad,' he adds. 'They were the only ones who didn't bolt for the door the minute it was over.'

'Were you Joseph?'

'No, the butler. Don't knock it. It's a pivotal role.' I laugh and sip my wine as dressing ingredients are shaken in a jar. Our salad is tossed deftly and Harvey serves dinner. It all looks perfectly delicious but, unusually for me, my appetite seems to have dwindled.

At first I can't understand it because being cooked for is one of my favourite things. But then I start to realise what it is. His jitteriness when I arrived; the flustered jacket swiping ('Let me take this for you!') as if I'd have expired from overheating if I'd worn it for a second longer; then the watching him busying about, and just *being* here, seeing him in his natural habitat with his bowl of lemons, generously pouring wine. It's all combining like the ingredients in this beautiful dinner to crank up his appeal until I'm absolutely certain that I fancy Harvey Jackson an awful lot. So much so, in fact, that I can hardly eat the most delicious meal that I can remember being cooked for me, which is surely a design flaw in the whole business of sexual attraction.

What sense does it make, that someone goes to all this trouble because they like you, and possibly even hope to impress you a little bit? They cook fish to perfection and make a risotto that's not even a tiny bit claggy, which I regard as one of the Wonders of the World along with the Great Wall of China (I only ever cook the kind of rice that comes in a pouch). And you can barely choke it down.

I *do* manage, of course, because I wouldn't insult him by picking at it feebly. The mood is jokey as he promises to send me his risotto recipe, as I've given him mine for rum chicken. 'How does the sourdough thing work?' I ask. 'I mean, what's the science of it?'

He puts down his fork. 'Are you sure you want to know? Some of my mates have banned me from talking about it.'

'Honestly,' I say, leaning forward. 'I really do.'

So he starts to tell me about the flour and yeast spores that fly about naturally in the air, and something about grapes being added, and it all combining to make something happen. 'It's a magical process,' he says. 'Well, of course it's biology really. A biological reaction.'

'It sounds pretty magical to me,' I say. 'D'you have to feed it, like a pet?'

'Yes, but it's very low-maintenance. It just lies there dormant in the fridge. Mine's five years old and theoretically it could go on forever, a bit like me, right now, boring you senseless . . .' He breaks off and grins.

'I'm interested. I really am. So how d'you wake it up?'

'You just bring it out of the fridge and pretty soon, things start to happen. It reactivates.'

I touch my face, hoping I'm not flushing like a beacon here in Harvey's kitchen with him sitting opposite me, wine glass in hand, with a cream candle flickering between us, dinner things all cleared away now. I'm finding it incredibly stirring, listening to him talking about food with such passion. Never mind the running app woman; this is the voice I'd like in my ears as I scamper around the local streets. It would make exercising a whole lot more bearable.

'Don't you have to do anything to it?' I ask.

'No, you just let it sit there and acclimatise and it soon gets going again.' *I can imagine it does.* 'All it needs,' he adds, 'is a little bit of food and love.'

'Right,' I manage, taking a sip of wine.

'It's a very natural process.' He smiles. 'You could try it, you know. I could give you some of mine to get you started, if you like?'

'Oh, I'm not sure I'm ready for the responsibility.'

'But you've brought up a daughter to adulthood, haven't you? I'm sure you could nurture a little bit of culture in a jar—' He breaks off, and I don't know how we switch from discussing fermentation and yeast spores across the table to standing up and kissing gently, or how we move from the kitchen to the squashy charcoal sofa in the neatly ordered, pale grey living room.

It's as if we've been teleported and are now kissing hungrily (no dearth of appetite now). My God – so I still have proper sexual feelings after all. None were involved in that kiss with Neil against the skip that left the rusty mark on my best jacket. That was driven by booze and desolation, not lust. In fact recently I'd started to worry that, as I'd gone so long without any action, I'd never be able to rev up again. Like when you've left your car sitting for ages and, when you go to drive it, it won't start. And you're talking jump leads or possibly even a new battery. But no

– it seems that my libido is still there after all, fully functioning and ready to go.

It was only lying *dormant!* It hadn't withered and died like the poinsettia Mum gave me last Christmas in a big red pot!

CHAPTER THIRTY-SEVEN

I don't care that I'm not neatly trimmed down there, or that my body hasn't been buffed to a sheen. My legs are bristly and I haven't even stashed a toothbrush in my bag. But that doesn't matter. I'm just thrilled that I can still feel these feelings, that my body still *works*.

I'd been so certain that tonight we'd just have dinner and drinks and that would be that. But now our clothes are coming off – his shirt, my dress – and his body is lovely and I couldn't care less that I'm wearing a plain old white bra and unmatching black knickers because he's saying, '*You're beautiful,*' in a slightly overawed voice. It's been so long since anyone's said anything like that to me that my throat catches and my heart seems to stop—

Cheep-cheep!

'What was that?' Harvey looks at me.

'My phone. Just a text notification . . .'

'Sounded like a bird.'

'It's a budgie.'

'How apt,' he says with a smile, then gently moves a

270

strand of dishevelled hair out of my eyes. I could leave it, check it later. What could be urgent at – quick glance at the clock on the wall – just gone eleven on a Saturday night? But it's cut through my thoughts and now some invisible cord is pulling me away from this lovely sexy man with his warm, delicious-smelling body and sticky-up hair.

'Won't be a sec,' I murmur, slipping my dress back on quickly. The cord continues to pull me out of the living room, towards my bag, which is dangling from a brass hook in the hallway. I take out my phone. It's a message from Hannah; a photo of her and her oldest friend, their cheeks pressed together, both looking flushed and tipsy, with the caption: KAYA SAYS HI!!

I can't help laughing. She knows I'm here but she still sent it. I might be a bona fide grown-up woman, on an actual date – but I'm still her mum.

'Everything okay?' Harvey has appeared in the hallway and scratches his head.

'Yeah, sorry about that. Just Hannah.'

'Oh, right.' He gives me an expectant half-smile.

'Just a daft text from the party,' I explain.

'Ah. Hope she's having fun . . .'

'She is,' I say, dropping my phone back into my bag and striding towards him. 'And I am too,' I add.

'I'm really glad.' There's a sense of bewildered excitement at what's just happened, as if we've stumbled off a roller-coaster and don't quite know what to do next. A tuft of Harvey's reddish hair is jutting out like a tiny diving board above his left ear. Neither of us says anything as we wander back through to the living room, where our wine glasses are sitting on the coffee table and my sandals are lying there, having been kicked off in haste. My feet are bare, my red toe polish chipped as I didn't get around to doing a pedicure for tonight either.

We sit down on the sofa, side by side. 'Are you okay?' He looks at me with such kindness that my heart seems to turn over.

I nod. 'Yeah. Yeah, I'm fine.'

He knows, of course. He might not be a parent himself but somehow he still gets it. 'Feel a bit weird, Hannah texting?'

My mouth twists. 'A bit, I suppose.' I laugh quietly and shake my head. 'It's just reminded me, you know. That she's here.'

'What?' He widens his eyes in mock horror and looks around the room.

'No, not *here*. Not in your flat. But here in Glasgow, you know?'

Now he darts a glance towards his second-floor window as if she might have scaled a ladder and be peering in.

'Harvey, I know it sounds mad,' I start, 'but, you know, she's back here for the weekend and—'

'It feels wrong to be here?' he suggests.

'No, not *wrong*,' I say firmly. 'Not at all. She's at that party and she said she'll probably stay overnight. But then . . .' I shrug. 'She might not.'

He looks genuinely puzzled. 'Er . . . right.'

'I mean, she might not want to stay on a lumpy sofa with the party remnants strewn everywhere. Kaya doesn't even believe in having a bin. She just hangs a carrier bag on the kitchen door handle and finally gets around to taking it out when it starts overflowing, or busts all over the floor . . .' Why am I telling him this? He doesn't need a description

272

of Kaya's methods of waste management. 'So she might have a sudden urge to come home to her own bed,' I add.

'Right,' Harvey says. 'And if she did, and you weren't there . . .'

'I kind of feel like I *should* be there, maybe?' His kind blue eyes are focused on me. 'I know it's ridiculous,' I add. 'She's a fully grown adult, she lives in London, she has a job and life there and—'

'But she'd be worried, if you weren't home?'

'No, it's not even that. She knows I'm here at yours tonight. I've told her all about you.'

'Have you?' He looks both surprised and pleased.

'Of course I have!'

'Would she be upset, then?' he asks.

'No,' I say firmly, smiling now. 'She'd be pleased. Delighted, actually. It was Hannah who bullied me into joining the site in the first place. It was all, "Oh, no one meets in the real world anymore"—'

'—It's all algorithms now,' he chips in.

'That's *exactly* what she said.'

'That's what Eddie at work kept saying too. He's one of those people who's convinced that everyone should be doing what he's doing. Like, it's his mission to convert the masses, that we're all dinosaurs, relics from the past, when actually he can't even update his phone without help—'

'Harvey?' I cut in, resting a hand on his knee. 'I'm glad he bullied you into it.'

'Are you?'

'Yes, I really am.'

We sit there, looking at each other for a moment. 'Well, I was actually going to ask if you wanted to stay tonight,' he says, all in a rush, as if he was worried he'd lose his

273

nerve if he didn't blurt it right out. 'You wouldn't have to use my toothbrush,' he adds quickly. 'I have a new one, still in its wrapper—'

'Harvey, I—'

'It was in a package of stuff from a flight,' he cuts in, like I'd prefer to know its heritage. 'You know, with the eye mask, the ear plugs . . . a kind of care package, is that what you call them?'

'Amenity package.' I'm trying to keep down a smile as a ridiculous thought hits me: that maybe – just maybe – Harvey and I will be sharing a rooftop jacuzzi in that Santorini hotel in a few weeks' time. I know I'm jumping the gun. It's mad to think of us going away together when we haven't even done it yet. But then, madder things have happened . . .

'It had socks in too,' he adds. 'I didn't get that. Why would anyone need spare socks on a flight—'

'Harvey.' I rest a hand over his. 'I just want to tell you that obviously, you fly with smarter airlines than BudgieAir, because we didn't do amenity packages.'

'Really? Oh, it wasn't a holiday. It was a work thing, a business conference in Geneva—'

'I didn't know you went to conferences in Geneva?'

He grins. 'I have a very whizzy life.'

'You obviously do. Amenity packages, my God!' He's laughing now, and I'm filled with a surge of warmth for this man, about whom I still have so much to find out. 'And yes,' I add, 'I'd really like that. To stay here tonight, I mean, and use your complimentary toothbrush if you're sure that's okay.'

'Oh. Okay then.' He is beaming now. 'It's just, I thought you felt a bit weird just then . . .'

'It's been a very long time since I've been in this kind of scenario,' I explain. 'I wasn't quite sure *what* I was feeling.'

'Me too. I mean, it's been a long time for me as well.' He leans forward and touches my hair, then kisses me gently on the lips. 'I think we'll be okay, though, don't you?'

I nod and smile. 'Unless they've invented a whole new way of doing things?'

'I don't think . . .' Another kiss, sending tiny sparks shooting around my brain. 'No, I don't think they have—' My phone's ringtone cuts through the air. 'Oh, God. I am sorry . . .' I jump up, figuring that it's bound to be Hannah again. She'll have had a few more drinks, and maybe she's forgotten I'm out after all and is being a good, dutiful daughter, calling to say that she's definitely staying over at Kaya's tonight.

It's unlike her to call rather than message me, though. Maybe she's pocket-dialled me?

By the time I've rushed to the hallway to fish out my phone from my bag, it's stopped ringing. And it wasn't Hannah who called. It was Kirsten, Mum's next-door neighbour. With a dull thud to my chest I realise there's only one reason she's called me so late on a Saturday night.

Something has happened to Mum.

CHAPTER THIRTY-EIGHT

Mum, 79

As I arrive at Mum's by taxi any noticeable effects of several glasses of wine have disappeared, such is the instantly sobering effect of a parental emergency.

Kirsten appears at the door. I've already gathered, from when I called her back, that she'd found Mum heading out just as she'd got home from work and asked her where she was going. 'Just the shops,' Mum had told her. 'There's a few things I need to pick up.'

Kirsten had pointed out that it was ten-thirty at night, and surely it could wait till the morning? 'Tomorrow's Sunday,' Mum had said – correctly, as if it were one of Dr Mahmoud's tests. Kirsten hadn't wanted to upset Mum by reminding her that shops have been opening on Sundays since the 1990s. It probably wouldn't have made any difference anyway as Mum had marched off, clutching her wicker shopping basket.

There'd been tears and a bit of a scene on the high street,

with someone rushing over to check that Mum wasn't being attacked, as Kirsten tried to coax her home. Mum's face is still mottled red, and her eyes bloodshot as I sit next to her on the sofa. Kirsten is in the kitchen, making tea. 'I don't know what *she* thinks she's doing,' Mum mutters now.

'She was just worried about you, Mum.' I place my hand over hers. Her nails have been painted messily in a pearlised pink polish. Mum is all dressed up in the smart outfit she'd worn for Dr Mahmoud, including her heeled shoes, plus her gold clip-on earrings, a cut-glass necklace and a hefty dose of Estée Lauder's Red Door. Mum has always taken immense pride in her appearance when going out in public. Her shopping basket is still sitting close to her feet.

'What was she worried about?' she asks now.

'Well, it's night-time, Mum. You shouldn't be going out on your own.'

'It's not that late,' she says defensively, like a teenager railing against a curfew.

I inhale slowly, picturing Phil eye-rolling me for mentioning a flaccid cucumber in her fridge. 'It's just not that safe. And the shops were shut anyway.'

'Not all of them.' Well, no. There's an all-night garage half a mile up the road.

'What were you going to buy?' I ask. It seems important to try and normalise things, to have an ordinary conversation.

'Just a few bits for you. But it gets difficult carrying everything.'

'Mum, you don't need to do my shopping,' I say as Kirsten reappears with our teas.

'I'll leave you now,' she says quickly, setting them down on the table. 'Brad'll need letting out.'

'Thanks so much, Kirsten,' I say.

'No worries at all.' We hug briefly before she leaves, and I settle back next to Mum. I can hardly believe that, less than an hour ago, I was kissing Harvey in my underwear on his sofa.

'I was just trying to help,' Mum says now, looking a little less confident that her expedition had been such a good idea.

'Honestly, I can do my own shopping, Mum. And I can do yours too. I work in a supermarket now, remember? You wouldn't believe the bargains we have at the end of the day.'

'What like?' She smiles eagerly, and I'm aware of a lump in my throat.

'All kinds of stuff. Chilled goods, ready meals, fruit and vegetables . . . all for 10p.'

'Why aren't you doing that other job anymore?'

'I was made redundant, Mum. Remember?'

'Oh yes.' She nods, as if trying to commit this to memory. 'You've always been like this, haven't you?'

'Like what, Mum?' I ask lightly.

'Independent and capable. Always known your own mind, liked doing things for yourself. I tried to teach you how to tie your laces on those pink trainers you had, remember?'

I smile and nod. They had spongy soles and glittery stripes. I must have been about six and was delighted with them.

'You wouldn't have it,' Mum continues. 'Said you could do it yourself. A right mess, they were, all jumbled up and knotted, but off you went, saying they were fine. It's a wonder you didn't trip and break your arm!' She chuckles, and I squeeze her hand. The feel of it, thin and bony in mine, triggers an ache in me. I glance around the room that was once kept so immaculate but is now accumulating small stacks of clutter on shelves and unused chairs. It feels smaller than it used to. 'I probably get it from you,' I offer. 'You're independent too, Mum.'

'Mmm, that's what *he* said.'

I blink at her. 'Who said that?'

'My friend.'

'Is this the friend you've mentioned before?' I ask, trying to keep my voice light. 'That man, I mean? The one who's been round and phones you?'

'Yes, that's him,' she says, brightening now.

I pause for a moment, aware that I should tread carefully. 'What's his name, Mum?' All casual as if we're chatting about someone new who's moved in over the road.

'Richard. Or Roger. Something like that . . .'

'Oh, right.' I try to figure out how to coax out more information.

'He's coming round next week,' she adds.

'Is he? That's nice.' I glance at her. 'D'you know when exactly?'

'The middle of the week I think he said.'

'Right.' I nod. 'Could you maybe give me a call when he arrives?'

A quizzical look. 'Why?'

'I'd just really like to meet him,' I say, 'if that's all right? He sounds like *such* a nice man.'

Her face breaks into a beatific smile as she reaches for her cup and blows across its rim to cool her hot tea. 'Oh, okay then. That is a lovely idea. I think he'd really like to meet you too.'

By the time we've finished our tea it's just gone midnight. I've suggested staying over, but Mum was instantly suspicious of my motives. 'Why would you want to do that?' she asked, understandably baffled as I have never slept there before. This is the house she bought with her second husband; Brian McGuire of the fried breakfasts, so vast that super-sized plates had to be bought to accommodate them.

As well as Mum's room there's a tiny box room and a proper spare bedroom. Until she seemed to lose interest, or perhaps the ability to make things, this was the nerve centre of her craft empire. Here her sewing machine would whir, and her dressmaker's dummy would be clad in pinned-on pieces. But gradually her interest fell away and now there's a dusty stillness to the room.

'I just thought it'd be nice to keep you company tonight,' I'd said unconvincingly. But once she'd changed into her nightie Mum was virtually bundling me out of the door.

Back at home, I picture Hannah at the party and Harvey in his flat. He'd been full of concern as I'd talked to Kirsten, and offered to come with me to Mum's, which was sweet of him. But I'd just kissed him goodbye, thanked him for a lovely evening and dashed out to the cab. And now he's messaged: *How are things? Hope all OK?*

—*Yes thanks. Mum's fine now. Really sorry to dash off.*

—*Don't worry about that. As long as your mum's safe and well. See you soon I hope? Hx.*

—*Yes hope so too. Thanks again for a lovely evening.*

I'm aware, as soon as I've sent it, that it could have been a message to the chair of Hannah's school's PTA after a fundraiser night. But it's too late to worry about that now.

CHAPTER THIRTY-NINE

It strikes me that our Sunday lunch feels odd because of the things we *don't* talk about.

Although Hannah knows all about her gran's attempted shopping trip last night, the fact that Mum is sitting here with us in Dario's means it can't be discussed. All Rod knows is what I've been able to mutter to him quickly while Hannah and her gran were chatting. Mum's memory and comprehension, and her ability to reason and make decisions might be growing fuzzier, but her hearing could rival a greyhound's. As for Rod, the fact that Gaby apparently only told him this morning that she couldn't make lunch has obviously rattled him somewhat.

'What happened?' I asked as we all sat down at our favourite circular table at the back.

'She didn't say,' he murmured. 'Something just came up.'

'Everything okay with you two?' I asked, but he just shrugged and crunched distractedly on a complimentary breadstick. Of course he wasn't going to go into detail with us. So it all feels a bit peculiar, although Mum seems to be having a lovely time, and is as thrilled as ever with the waiters' attentions, with whom she is flirting enthusiastically. It has also enabled Hannah to spend more time with her gran, and have her parents together for a couple of hours, so I guess it's been a success really.

When lunch is over I hug Hannah tightly before she heads off to spend a little time at her dad's, reconvening with Casey, her cat; then Rod will take her to the station for her train back to London. I drive Mum home, reminding her, as I see her into her house, that she's promised to call me when her friend comes to visit.

'Which day is he coming again?' I ask.

'One day next week,' she says vaguely. 'He wasn't sure.' I'm not convinced she'll call me, or that she's really expecting her visitor at all. But what if she is, and he comes when no one else is there? While Kirsten still pops in from time to time, Mum's pretty frosty with her these days and it's starting to feel like the potential for her to come to harm, or have some kind of disaster, is growing by the day.

Later that night I FaceTime Phil, expecting him to be his usual perky self with his morning espresso. But his eyes look hooded and his face has a greyish tinge. 'You know what I never realised about puppies?' he says, launching right in. 'They're like moths. They never damage the cheap stuff. That's yet another two-hundred-dollar cashmere sweater of Loretta's she's wrecked.'

It's on the tip of my tongue to say, 'Can't you keep things out of reach?' Because that's what Phil said to me after Hannah – who'd been two at the time – had stuffed a piece of gravel up her nose and Rod and I had had to take her to hospital so they could extract it. 'We were in the park,' I'd retorted. 'Gravel was everywhere. How was I supposed to keep it out of reach?' Back then, Phil hadn't yet become a dad. But naturally, when that time came he'd ensure that such incidents never happened because everyone's behaviour would be exemplary and he'd *keep hazardous things out of reach*. I've noticed this over the years, that the greatest experts on child-rearing are the ones who haven't yet had kids of their own.

When their time comes they will of course do it perfectly. They certainly won't have slept with a friend, while drunk, and become accidentally pregnant. 'Christ, you've really gone and done it now,' was Phil's reaction to the news. In contrast, the conception of his two children was meticulously planned so their births would coincide with breaks in Loretta's filming schedule, and also allow her to be pregnant throughout their autumn, winter and spring, rather than in the fierce Australian summer heat.

I'm remembering all of this as Phil chatters on about Nico the puppy, who has apparently developed a habit of eating oven gloves. 'Disgusting, right?' he exclaims. Now an electric guitar is wailing in the background (I'm actually surprised my nephews are up at this hour), driving Phil from his kitchen to the garden in the rain. He hunches, radiating ill humour, against the garage wall.

When he's finally run out of puppy talk I start to tell him how I plan to call social services to see if Mum can be assigned a social worker. 'And I think she might qualify for a visiting nurse,' I continue, 'who'll come round and assess her regularly. Then there's the possibility of carers dropping in to supervise her medication. That is, if Mum will accept help . . .'

'Uh?' Phil's brow furrows. In the pause that follows there's an outburst of high-pitched barking over the heavily distorted guitar. Things are happening in Phil's world. He's mentally calculating how much longer he has to stand here talking to his tedious sister because he wants to finish the call and attend to the puppy – or maybe Loretta is signalling at the back door that his freshly made pancakes are getting cold? I'm conscious of my heart rate accelerating.

It's not that I expect Phil to seem delighted whenever we chat. I'm not one of his celebrity mates inviting him to a party at a waterfront restaurant or on a yacht. I am his younger sister, calling from Glasgow to wreck his day before he's even had his breakfast by dropping in terms like 'dementia helpline' and 'psychiatric nurse'. It's hardly a sparkling start to his day.

I know all of that, and that I'm probably viewed as a gigantic pain in the arse for foisting this stuff on him. Yet it's not just any old stuff; it's our *mum*. And I can't help it that she's ill and becoming progressively worse, and he's in Sydney so we can only communicate via screens. And yes, I also know my nephew Rohan is undoubtedly the best DJ to ever grace Sydney and Nico is the cutest puppy to ever have lived, and isn't it amazing that Loretta found this no-rinse cleaning spritz (with mallow extract) to keep the puppy's coat perfectly snowy white but *right now we need to talk about Mum!*

I actually yell this, causing my brother's expression to turn to one of shock. Because no one ever calls my brother out for anything. At work he has a bevy of glamorous minions who rush out to buy his pastrami bagels for lunch – I don't think he's had to fetch his own lunch since 2007 – and ensure that there is always a large jug of water ('spa water,' they call it) with cucumber, lemon and mint bobbing in it, on his desk. I know this because Hannah and I visited him eight years ago. Although BudgieAir didn't fly to Australia (which would've meant free flights) I'd received a generous bonus that year, which had made it possible.

To their credit, Phil and Loretta had made us extremely welcome and we'd had a wonderful time on the beaches and at Taronga Zoo where Hannah, who was mad about animals, got to stroke a koala. Together with the day her dad brought Casey home, it was probably one of the happiest times of her life. I'd felt closer to my brother then, and grateful that he'd gone to such effort to make our trip special.

However, that was Phil doing what Phil does best: organising, hosting, making fun things happen. And now his face has clouded as he says, 'We *are* talking about Mum, aren't we? I know you're upset but I don't think it's fair to take it out on me—'

'I'm not taking it out on you!'

'Okay,' he snaps, 'so what am I supposed to do from ten thousand miles away?'

Listen, I want to shout. *I just want you to listen and understand what's happening here. I don't want to talk about Nico eating a fucking oven glove!*

'I know you're not here,' I say levelly. 'I know you're *there*. And of course I don't expect you to be able to do anything practical when Mum takes enormous amounts of money out of the bank and lets it blow everywhere, or when she decides she needs to go to the shops at half past ten at night. I know you can't actually do anything about that, Phil. But what I do expect is that we can talk about it, and that you've got time for me, because you know what?' I pause to catch my breath, aware that I'm in danger of losing it now.

Positive, pleasant, professional. We do our best to say yes. Whatever happens, STAY CALM.

'Is this about money?' Phil asks.

'What? What're you talking about?'

'I mean, do we need to pay for a carer or something, if it's too much for you to manage?'

For a moment I can't get any words out. 'It's *not* too much. That's not what I'm saying.'

'Sounds like you are, sis. But look, if we need to pay someone I can cover it. Just let me know what's needed—'

'That's not what I'm getting at,' I snap. 'This is Mum, Phil – not a party than can be sorted by flinging a ton of money at it. It's not a canapé and charcoal lemonade kind of situation.'

'What the *fuck*?'

'And we are getting help,' I rant on, trying to steady myself. 'There's her GP, the psychiatrist, the woman I spoke to at the dementia helpline . . . They've been brilliant. They've all said there's no need to feel alone.'

I pause, waiting for his response. But Phil's attention seems to have been caught by something in the middle distance.

'I said there's no need to feel *alone*,' I repeat sharply.

'Can you stop ranting for a minute?' Phil says with a frown.

'No, I can't,' I shoot back. 'I'm sick of it, Phil. Sick of you implying that I'm over-reacting to every damn thing. You know, a little while ago I had a date. I'd never even met this guy before but we sat there and had lunch, and he was more interested and sympathetic about the situation with Mum than you are—'

'That is *so* not fair,' my brother thunders.

'Isn't it? I think it is!'

'Okay.' His reddened face fills the screen. 'Shall I tell you something, Jen? I've got quite a lot on my plate too right now, in case you're interested—'

'Like what?'

'Like the puppy—'

'No one forced you to get a puppy, Phil. It's not the law to have one. That was your choice.'

'Well, Loretta's choice actually but to be honest she's had fuck all to do with her. She said she'd take time off work – puppy leave – but of course as soon as a job comes in that's out of the window. She's away filming till the end of next week . . .' He exhales loudly as he takes me back into the house where the barking and guitar screeching seem to have ceased.

'Okay,' I start. 'I shouldn't have shouted at you. I just want you to know that it's not about money or anything like that. It's about wanting to *share* it with you. The responsibility, I mean. To know that you understand—'

'Jen, sorry,' he interrupts. 'Something's just happened. We're going to have to talk another time, all right?'

'What is it? Is everything okay?'

'Yeah. No, not really. Not at all. Nico's just chewed a hole in Loretta's Stella McCartney handbag and she's going to go mental when she gets back.'

CHAPTER FORTY

There's no chance to meet Harvey again over the next few days. He's at work during the day and I'm at the shop until late. We message and chat a little, but I suspect I'm seeming pretty distracted as I have also been popping over to see Mum every morning. I'm hoping that, if her friend actually exists and turns up again, then I'll be there and able to reassure myself that he's a pillar-of-the-community neighbour who's just trying to help her out. Either that, or I can march him out of her house.

There are no visitors while I'm there, but at least there have been no more nocturnal outings either. Maybe that was just a one-off.

By the time Thursday night rolls around, and I'm refilling the fresh produce section at work, I'm starting to think perhaps Harvey and I could arrange something for the weekend. Maybe I could even ask him over? I know there's no way I could match his risotto skills. But we could eat out first, and go back to mine for drinks and whatever else might possibly happen. But then, would it be as head-spinningly lovely as it was at his place on Saturday night? I'm a little worried that the spontaneity might be lost; that it might seem like going back to the holiday resort you'd loved, but instead of the sea-facing apartment with the wrap-around balcony you've been landed with one at the back with drain smells and a view of the giant bins.

Maybe Phil is right, I figure as I go to fetch the sticker gun, at least in that I tend to over-worry. I know that Harvey certainly wouldn't be critical of my place, even though there's no bowl of lemons on display. And actually, my flat is okay! I mean, burnt chair aside (which has now, with Hannah's permission, been disposed of) it's perfectly functional if a little basic and plain. I'm mulling all of this over as I start to sticker the veg, vaguely aware of the chatter of customers and the cry of a small child and behind it all, the bland music that I barely register now. But I do pick up on the burst of laughter from the next aisle.

'You're mad, you know?' comes a male voice. 'Whenever I went camping it was tins of beans and spaghetti hoops!'

'We're not having spaghetti hoops, all right?' a woman retorts.

'Why not?'

'Because we're not seven. C'mon, let's get the rest of the stuff . . .'

'It's going to be so late when we get there. It's already half-nine.'

'We could've set off earlier if you hadn't gone out after work.'

'I only had a couple,' the man says petulantly.

I'm aware of them coming closer now, debating their plans as I focus on stickering the packs of mixed vegetables for soup. Without warning the urge hits me – to be going away somewhere fun. To enjoy that delicious sense of anticipation when your weekend is starting on a Thursday night and that bonus day feels like a gift. Mouseman Marc and I had a weekend away, to Dublin, but he'd insisted on spending great swathes of it in a sports bar, chugging down pints of Guinness while watching TV.

Now the couple has wandered past me to peruse the vegetable aisle. At well over six foot, he is powerfully built with broad shoulders and a thick neck. She looks tiny beside him with her fine light brown hair flowing down her back. 'Let's get aubergines,' she says.

'Aubergines?' he exclaims. 'What for?'

'You've never lived if you haven't had them charred over a camp fire,' she announces.

'Oh, haven't I?' he teases.

'Honestly, you'll love them. We can do them a kind of Moroccan way. So we'll need chilli and lemon, and we should get some cumin and coriander—'

'Can we please just get going?' he interrupts. 'This place is depressing the hell out of me.'

'Stop being such a snob,' she chides him. 'I can't believe you don't come here more often. It's virtually on your door-step, isn't it?'

'I just pick up stuff in town after work.'

'Don't lie, Scott. You use Deliveroo—'

'Not every night.'

'Every night I've been over you have,' she says, laughing now. Then: 'Oh, look. There they are. Maybe if we hang about a few minutes they'll be reduced?'

I'm stickering packs of lemons now, intent on getting the job done as I still have some bakery items to attend to. After that it'll be a tidy-up of the section, and then some restocking, before the end of my shift.

'I can't believe you buy reduced stuff,' the man's voice booms out. An elderly customer wanders by, pulling along his tartan basket on wheels, and catches my eye. We both smile. He's a regular in here in his blue overcoat and tweed cap. If there are reduced items in the chilled desserts section he'll always zoom straight for them. He looks a little frail but with the merest whiff of a knocked-down cheesecake he'll virtually break into a sprint.

'Why wouldn't I?' the woman is saying now. 'There's nothing wrong with it. If it isn't sold it just goes to waste. So really, it's best for everyone . . .'

'Unless you get food poisoning from it,' the man suggests.

'No one gets food poisoning from reduced stuff. Especially veg—'

'Yeah, all right. I believe you. Er, s'cuse me!' Realising the man is addressing me now, I swing round to face him.

'Yes?'

'Are you going to reduce these?' He indicates the aubergines which the woman has turned away to examine. She is picking up each one in turn, rotating it under the bright lights as if it's a precious antique.

'No, sorry,' I reply.

'Aw, go on.' There's a whiff of booze on his breath.

'They're not going out of date,' I say with a firm smile.

'They look a bit squidgy to me,' he retorts.

'Scott, they're *fine*,' the woman mutters with an irritated shake of her head.

'Don't worry, I'll get her to do it.' He steps towards me with a swagger. 'C'mon, couldn't you just do it for us?' Towering over me, he flashes one of those let's-just-get-this-over-with fake smiles. He's a man used to getting what he wants, I realise. I can imagine him being shouty to minions at work and irritated if he can't gain immediate access to a treadmill at the gym. I have also figured that he could buy anything he wants in here without worrying about the cost, unlike a lot of our regulars who come in specifically for the reductions, in order to feed themselves and their families. He's just showing off, wanting to demonstrate how effective he is at getting results. Seeming embarrassed, the woman has moved on to the courgettes, which she is selecting carefully for her basket.

'Sorry, they're not being reduced tonight.' I am about to march away and busy myself with other tasks, as Sumi had advised me to when I started here: *'Don't take any nonsense from anyone.'* But as I pass him he jabs at my arm.

'Please don't do that,' I say sharply.

He jabs me again and I jump back, away from him. 'Just sticker the fucking aubergines.'

'Scott!' the woman calls out abruptly.

'D'you mind stepping out of my way?' I ask firmly, at which he takes an exaggerated step backwards in a 'sorry ma'am' kind of way.

'Thank you,' I bark, sensing my cheeks reddening.

'No need to take that tone!'

I stop dead in front of this hulk of a man who could easily shove me into the banana display if he wanted to. We are glaring at each other, as if in a stare-off contest. The woman marches over to join us and, for the first time, I see her face.

'We can afford full-price aubergines, Scott,' she mutters impatiently. She turns to me, her look of apology instantly morphing into shock as she realises who I am.

Gaby doesn't acknowledge it. Gripping her basket firmly, she tugs at his arm and mutters, 'C'mon, for God's sake.

Unless you want to be in here all night?' And off they go, rounding the corner and marching towards the checkout. Apparently they have forgotten to buy aubergines and, minutes later, they're gone.

CHAPTER FORTY-ONE

Over the next few days I mull over what to do.

I could tell Rod I saw her and just leave it at that. I even rehearse it in my mind: '*I think I saw Gaby in the shop the other night?*' I'd leave it hanging there, weirdly, like a rogue Christmas tree decoration. (One year a 'Fuck Santa' bauble appeared – perhaps the work of one of those perfect sons? – on Phil and Loretta's sixteen-foot pine on which only hand-painted glass ornaments, ordered directly from an artisanal maker in the Czech Republic, are allowed.) But what would that achieve?

Of course, rather than hinting I could come out and tell him *exactly* what I'd witnessed in the fresh produce aisle. But it's quite enough to be viewed as the harbinger of bad news by my brother. I'm not sure I want to fall into that role with Rod too.

Anyway, I tell myself as I pull on my top and leggings, with a plan to force myself out on a morning run, maybe Gaby is just friends with the jerk who thinks it's okay to harangue a supermarket employee? Or perhaps he's her brother or her personal hot tub maintenance man? And maybe they'd virtually galloped towards the checkout as if the shop was on fire, not because Gaby had recognised me (after all, I was out of context in there, in my bottle green uniform) but because they hadn't wanted to endure any more time in a discount supermarket than was strictly necessary?

Out on my run I go, keeping an eye out for Jack (thankfully there's no sighting) while mulling the whole thing over some more and reflecting that relationships are bloody complicated; even tiny, fledgling ones, like mine and Harvey's, if you could call it a relationship at all. Because when I come back home a message appears from him which reads: *Hey Jen, hope all's good. Listen, if it's not a good time and you want some space that's quite okay. Love Hx.*

'Oh, right,' I say out loud, staring at my phone. Whatever gave him that idea? Of course, it could be because we haven't managed to meet up since *that* night, when Kirsten's call had acted like a bucket of icy water over us and certainly quashed the heat. Or it might be due to the fact that, since aubergine night, my head's been full of that and I have barely messaged at all. But then, neither has Harvey. Has our lovely thing shrivelled away before it had even properly begun?

I'm remembering now how Mum used to remark how 'weird' mine and Rod's relationship thing was – loving each other *but not in that way* – and implying occasionally that perhaps Rod was the real reason why I was perennially single. She was probably right, in that we've always been there for each other, and having him and Hannah and a job I loved meant I actually didn't need anything else. At least, not enough to go out hunting for it. Certainly not enough to write a dating profile and start worrying about whether it's okay to have pubic hair. (Is it a definite no-no or, like vinyl records, back in vogue?)

Maybe that's why Mouseman Marc had drifted away from me? Because he'd sensed – correctly, as it happened – that I didn't *need* him, especially now that my rodent problem had been sorted? And perhaps being single is just my natural state? After all, I only started dating due to intense encouragement (actually, *pressure* is what it was!) from Hannah, Jacob and Fabs. I went along with it to keep them happy as much as anything else. Then, like eating an oyster, at least I could say I'd tried it.

I peel off my running gear in the bathroom. Standing in my clammy underwear I reread Harvey's message, aware of a growing sense of gloom in the pit of my stomach. Of course there is another explanation for what's going on. No one asks if you 'want some space' unless *they* do, right? At least, that's how I'm interpreting it now. And there I was, picturing us in Greece together, plunging into the Aegean Sea. Talk about getting carried away. I'm feeling kind of stupid now, as I realise that this is probably Harvey's way of retreating politely before things go any further.

Yes, *that's* it, I decide now. He's a nice guy after all. He wouldn't blurt out that there's 'no chemistry' or ghost me. Christ, though – if this is what dating is like, wasn't I right to avoid it all those years? All the disappointments I've had, all those soul-sapping face-to-face meetings and now I've actually been dumped, albeit gently. Rather than being dropped from a great height, and broken to pieces, I've been carefully placed on a shelf.

Well, he's right, I tell myself now as I dump my phone on the laundry basket lid. It probably isn't a good time.

My thoughts switch back to Rod as I tug off my underwear and step into the shower. His relationship is his business, I reflect. I have no intention of flinging a Fuck Santa ornament into his personal life. So I'm *definitely* not getting involved. I stand there, inhaling deeply under the shower's hot blast, feeling pretty desolate about everything – even when I realise that I must have run something like five kilometres without stopping today.

To make doubly sure, I replay the route in my head. Yep, I definitely did it. I didn't even have that woman's encouraging words to boost me on. As I hadn't been able to find my earbuds, I'd just headed out and run and run without even thinking about where I was going, probably because my head was too full of other stuff like Rod and Gaby and Mum.

And I'd done it! I'd completed the programme without even listening to it! So, even if Harvey's not interested anymore, at least something good has happened today.

I towel myself dry, trying to reassure myself that I've made the right decision; about what I'm not entirely sure, as everything still seems a little muddled. But *something* seems to have settled in my mind. Maybe this is for the best, I tell myself. Maybe it's better that Harvey and I are over now instead of me falling crazily in love and it being a real mess when it ends.

At least I can say I've tried, I decide as I curl up on the sofa wrapped up in a bath towel and open my laptop. No one can say I haven't given it my best shot.

Sick of it all now, I go onto Mature Matches with the intention of deleting my profile immediately. But then, filled by a surge of recklessness, I decide to compose a message instead:

Hi Gavin, I like the look of your profile. What a lovely cat you have. Mr Sox! Cute name too. I'm a cat lover myself so I just thought I'd say hi. Jennifer x

Why am I doing this? I have no idea. Maybe receiving that message from Harvey has propelled me into a sod-it kind of mood. In fact the moment I press send I wish I could *un*-send it – because what am I trying to achieve?

A shrill, excessively loud ringing sound fills my flat. It's the landline; a relic from a bygone age that nearly gives me a heart attack as it rings so rarely. In fact the only ones to ever call it these days are those strange, robotic people (who I guess aren't really people) to tell me I can claim for an accident I haven't had. Or Mum.

I charge towards it, still wrapped in a towel with my hair dripping. 'Hello?' I bark, clutching the clunky device.

'Jennifer? It's me. It's Mum. You said to phone you when my friend came round? Well, he's here right now.'

CHAPTER FORTY-TWO

*Roger (or possibly another name
beginning with R?), age unknown*

Mum opens the door with a flourish. She has always disliked anyone – even me – just knocking and barging right in. 'Your hair's still wet,' she remarks. 'You could catch a cold like that.'

I smile. 'I've just been for a run, Mum.' *Never mind my wet hair. Let's see who's wormed their way into your life . . .*

On the drive over I told myself not to jump to conclusions because, if Mum's met someone locally – some kind, genuine man who's been keeping her company – then what's the problem? It could just be an innocent, companionship kind of thing. Yes, she's certainly vulnerable, but that doesn't mean she can't have friends – even new ones who I've never heard of and whose names she can't remember. It's also becoming clear that Mum's condition isn't quite as straightforward as I'd first assumed. I'd expected that things would gradually become worse, her grip on the world loosening until it slipped from her grasp altogether. But it's not like that. In amongst the copious bird seed purchasing and Mum's strange aversion to the little pug next door, she'll suddenly remember something with absolutely clarity – for instance, to call me when her friend, the famous Roger-or-Richard, comes round.

'Jennifer, this is *Robert*,' she says with an excitable glint in her eye. 'And this is my daughter, Jennifer.'

I shake the hand of this unfamiliar man who has bobbed up from a chair at her kitchen table. 'Hello, Robert,' I say. 'How are you?'

'Very good, thanks.' As he sits back down, I assess this curiously tanned, clean-shaven and slightly sweating man who looks to be in his early forties. He is wearing a navy blue suit with a slight sheen to it, a white shirt and a dark grey tie, also sheeny, knotted tightly around his rashy neck. In front of him sits a red plastic folder filled with papers of some kind. Mum is all dressed up in what seems to be her default smart outfit these days: cream blouse, narrow black skirt and heels, plus clip-on gold earrings shaped like those icing swirls on Iced Gem biscuits, and a double string necklace of jet beads. More dressed up even than she was for Dr Mahmoud, Mum has *accessorised* for Robert.

'So,' he says, launching right in, 'I've been chatting with Mrs McGuire for a little while now about her best options.'

'Best options about what?' I ask lightly, taking the seat opposite him while Mum perches close to his side.

'About a new kitchen.' He smiles tersely and opens the folder, as if his time has suddenly become extremely valuable and he would like to get this over and done with as quickly as possible, and would I please melt away into the ether?

I turn to Mum. 'I didn't know you were thinking of getting a new kitchen?'

'Oh, I think I will,' she says, waving a hand to indicate the perfectly good units that were only put in just before Brian died. He was a great one for throwing money at the place, and with Mum living alone these past few years they've hardly been subjected to much wear and tear.

'We've already gone through Mrs McGuire's options,' Robert says, 'and she's keen to take advantage of our special offer than runs out in ten days—'

'Sorry,' I cut in quickly. 'This seems to be all happening very quickly. Could we scroll back a bit please?'

A quick, sharp glare. Something tells me that this Robert and I won't become firm friends. I think it's fair to say he's unlikely to be coming to Santorini with me. 'Well, that's the thing. There is a time issue here,' he mutters. 'But this is what we offer. It's all top of the range.' Begrudgingly, he starts to flip through the pages of his folder. Each A4 sheet depicts various options for fittings and is protected by a crumpled clear plastic sleeve. It looks like a ten-year-old's school project entitled 'Kitchens'. 'Mrs McGuire is aware that we need to move quickly,' he adds.

'Yes, but I'd like you to go through the whole thing with me please,' I say pleasantly. 'I mean, the whole thing, right from the very beginning.'

'Erm, uh . . . sure?' His fuzzy eyebrows shoot up. Mum is watching us with the same kind of rapt attention as when she was being gently quizzed by Dr Mahmoud. There are no raised voices. Robert and I are doing our utmost to remain civil in front of Mum. She hasn't guessed that I could happily slam her toaster onto his head.

'So how did this come about?' I prompt him.

'We were just working in the area,' he starts, but Mum jumps in.

'You came to my door, didn't you? I remember that.' She smiles, clearly enjoying the memory of their first meeting, then turns to me. 'I told you, he was ever so helpful. We talked about my kitchen, didn't we, Robert?' He nods and flashes his teeth like a little beaver. 'And he said there could be a *much* better use of space,' Mum adds. 'I said Bill had done it all. He'd decided what we were going to have. Bill always thought he knew best, didn't he, Jennifer?'

'Yes, Mum,' I say. Her second husband was called Brian but it's not the time to split hairs. I turn to Robert. 'So you tout for business door-to-door, then? That's how your company operates, is it?'

'Well, we just sort of go round the area and see what people need.' Now his upper lip is shiny with sweat.

'And it's all half price,' Mum chips in, eyes glinting.

'You do love a bargain, don't you, Mrs McGuire?' Robert says, emitting oily charm as he regains his composure.

'Oh yes!' He angles himself towards her as they chuckle conspiratorially, as if cutting me from his vision will mean I will cease to exist. But what he hasn't realised is that I have developed a new talent over the past few months. My brother regards me as the harbinger of doom, and what Robert from Sleek Style Kitchens is about to discover is that his day was about to take a turn for the worse the moment I stepped into it.

Maybe that's my thing now; my transferable skill. Never mind *the brightest smile in the sky*. More like: here comes Jennifer Morton, ready to wipe that smile right off your face.

It's tricky with Mum sitting here, all perky and excited about the prospect of having some shoddy new units to replace the eye-wateringly expensive ones that she and Brian had put in. In fact, it takes a great deal of self-control for me to sit there smiling and agreeing that the 'Moderne' range is indeed a fine example of kitchen design. At one point I realise I am actually sitting on my hands to stop myself from lurching across the table and grabbing Robert by the throat. But finally he winds things up, explaining, 'I'll need to take a deposit today, Mrs McGuire, so we can move forward.' From out of his briefcase comes a card reader device.

'Right, of course.' Mum's jet necklace tinkles as she jumps up from her seat. She looks around the kitchen as if unsure of what to do next. 'Will a cheque do?'

He winces, a little crease forming between his brows. 'Card payment would be easier, if you don't mind.'

'Yes, of course. Cheques are quite old-fashioned, aren't they?'

'They are actually these days,' he says with a fake laugh. Ha-ha-ha. What a wheeze this is, sending a seventy-nine-year-old lady in the early stages dementia off to find her handbag so you can charge her for a kitchen she doesn't need, if indeed you ever reappear to fit it. What a brilliant caper you've come up with!

'I'll just get my bag,' Mum announces, causing my heart to clench as she flutters off, leaving a hint of Red Door fragrance in her wake.

A terse silence settles, broken only by Robert clearing his throat, closing his cheap red folder and slipping it into the scuffed black leather briefcase at his feet. 'You're not taking a deposit from my mum,' I inform him.

His eyelids flutter. 'But I'll need to, for the half-price deal.'

'No, you don't understand what I'm saying. You're not doing anything to my mum's house. You've come here and realised that maybe she's a little bit vulnerable and you've kept dropping by, gaining her trust until you've got her to the point where she's about to sign some contract—'

'We don't work that way,' he says, looking aghast at the very suggestion.

'No, I think you do.' I fix him with a stare. 'Can I have your card? Or something with your company name on it?'

'Yes, of course.' Still full of bluster he pulls out a white card from his wallet, cheaply printed with blue lettering, and hands it to me.

'Thanks.'

He glowers at me, then glances down at the card reader as if willing Mum to return with her card and punch in those vital four digits.

'Okay,' I say, indicating it, 'you can put that away now and leave right away because I don't want Mum being upset over this.'

He stares at me, blinking rapidly. 'I think Mrs McGuire can make up her own mind about this. It's her house and she seemed pretty sure—'

'No, she can't,' I hiss at him. 'She can't make up her own mind. She thinks she can, but she can't. That's why you're here and it's disgusting, what you're trying to do. You've been *grooming* her, working on her for weeks—'

'How can you even suggest that?' he gasps, eyes wide. 'I've never been spoken to like this in my life!'

'There's a first time for everything,' I snap, 'and it's stopping right now. So get the hell out of here and don't ever come back or I'll call the police.'

CHAPTER FORTY-THREE

When I tell Rod about Mum's visitor we agree that his ability to target her as a soft touch would almost be impressive, if it hadn't been so despicable. 'You'd never know she was vulnerable if you just talked to her at the front door,' I explain as we follow the narrow path towards the river in Kelvingrove Park. It's a mild and hazy Sunday afternoon, a few days after my showdown with the kitchen salesman, and the hillside is dotted with picnicking groups.

'Yeah,' Rod says. 'I feel bad, actually. I haven't seen her in ages and all this stuff's been going on.' He glances at me. 'How did she react when you sent him packing?'

'She kind of enjoyed it. This might sound awful but I made up a thing about scammers like him, and how we'd foiled him, as if we'd been in on it together and she'd never really intended to pay him anything at all . . .'

'That was clever of you.'

I smile. 'It was all I could think of. You know how Mum hates feeling she's not in control.'

He nods. 'God, yes. But I wish I'd been there when you confronted him. You could've called me—'

'For back-up?' I ask with a smile. 'There was no time and anyway, he left straight away when I threatened to report him.' I pause. 'I'm not even sure if the police would've done anything. I mean, I don't know if it's a crime. If Mum had paid for the kitchen willingly—'

'I don't just mean with the kitchen, Jen,' Rod cuts in, giving me a quick glance as we walk. 'I mean, I could've been around more for you lately. All this stuff you've had to sort out with your mum – all the doctors' appointments, trying to get her some support . . .'

'It's fine,' I say lightly.

'Well, yeah. I know how capable you are but you've been dealing with it all on your own, haven't you? I know Phil's not exactly hands-on . . .'

'It's been kind of a project.' I smile wryly.

'Yeah. You're the project manager,' he remarks, smiling too. We walk on and the silence that settles feels entirely comfortable. If Rod had wanted to talk about Gaby, I'd reasoned a little while ago, he'd have mentioned her by now. I'm not intending to ask how it's going with her. Best to avoid it, I've decided. I have also managed to convince myself that I've been panicking over nothing, and that Scott is probably just some idiot friend of hers. And anyway, as I'd already decided, it really is no business of mine.

We stop at a kiosk and drink coffees while perched on a low stone wall in the pale afternoon sunshine. 'You know, the kitchen thing only happened because of the way Mum is now,' I remark. 'She'd never have been taken in by a scammer a couple of years ago. She wouldn't even have let him into the house, let alone given him tea and biscuits.'

'You mean she's become more trusting?' he suggests.

'Yeah.' I nod and look across the river towards the penthouse flats, sleek glass boxes visible through the tangle of trees. 'Or gullible, unfortunately. It sickens me, how she was nearly taken advantage of.'

'Trusting sounds nicer, doesn't it?' There's a catch to his voice. I study his face for a moment, and want to ask him if something's wrong, but decide to let it go.

'Yes, it does,' I say. 'But it kind of breaks my heart because the person she used to be is slipping away.' He nods and puts an arm around me, and I lean in close. The feel of him, so warm and comforting, causes my eyes to prickle with tears. 'Remember how fierce she used to be?' I add, trying to keep my voice steady. 'Virtually banging the door in the Jehovah's Witnesses' faces? And God forbid anyone should bother her with a catalogue for cleaning products or some kind of door-to-door survey. Now they're all invited in for tea!' I glance up at Rod, expecting to see him smile but his mouth remains set in a horizontal line. He inhales slowly and sips his coffee, wiping a little off his top lip.

'You okay?' I ask lightly.

'Yeah, I'm fine. Absolutely.'

An odd silence falls as he gets up and we start walking on. I fill the space by chattering about my brother (who Rod has always found highly amusing) and the very real possibility that Nico might be returned to the breeder because, in Phil's words: 'I don't think we realised what we were taking on.'

'He's a clever man,' I remark. 'He's just brokered a multi-million-dollar deal for one of his clients with a perfume brand. How could he not have known that puppies poo and pee and chew things?' On and on I go, conscious that

307

Rod is not only saying very little, but is also holding something back. I can *feel* it, shimmering between us. I'd been pleased but surprised when he'd called to suggest meeting today. I couldn't remember the last time we'd done this: hung out together, just the two of us. But now there's tension hanging between us and I can't figure out why that is.

'So, are you still seeing the sourdough guy?' he asks eventually.

'Um, no, I don't think so,' I say.

There's a quizzical look. 'Why's that?'

I hesitate before answering because, in truth, I'm still not really sure what happened. And as I tell Rod about Harvey's message, and the 'wanting space' thing, it sounds as if perhaps I read it wrongly, or too hastily anyway – and then, before I'd decided how to respond, Mum had called and there'd been the kitchen drama to deal with.

'So you didn't message him back?' Rod asks.

I shake my head. 'You know what? I think it's best to just leave it now.'

'But I thought you liked this guy?' He shoves his hands into his jeans pockets as we walk.

'I did. I *do*. But I'm not sure about things at the moment. Life feels pretty full and honestly, I got the feeling that Harvey wants to back away.'

Rod frowns at me. 'Are you sure that's what he meant?'

'No.' I smile ruefully. 'I'm not sure about anything. But if I've messed this one up, it's probably a sign that it's not for me.'

Another quick, sideways look. 'You mean *dating's* not for you?'

'Yeah. Y'know, I used to blame my job for hardly ever meeting anyone, but maybe that was just an excuse. I mean, plenty of flight attendants meet people and get married and all that.' I pause for a moment, trying to figure out what I want to say. 'But maybe that wasn't the real reason, Rod. Maybe it's just me and the way I am and I'm better off single.' I can sense him looking at me in a curious kind of way. 'There's this thing with online dating,' I barge on, 'about time-wasters and game-players. It really gets people's hackles up, that thing of stringing someone along and not being honest. And I'd hate to do that to Harvey—'

'I'm sure he wouldn't think that,' Rod cuts in, frowning.

'Maybe not,' I say lightly. I pause, then add: 'Dating seems so easy for some people, doesn't it?'

He nods. 'Hmm. Yeah, I guess so.'

'Fabs seems to love it,' I add.

'Your new London friend?' A hint of a smile now.

'Yeah. She's seems to have found her soulmate actually. Some theatre guy, a director. Very dapper and handsome – she sent me a photo. He seems completely besotted with her and she says she's maybe ready to get serious with him, to come off all those sites she's on . . .' I break off, figuring that Rod doesn't need to hear about the love life of someone he's never met. 'Sorry, I really am going on today.'

'I like it. You going on, I mean.' A proper smile now. 'And you're right. Dating's not easy at all . . .' We stop in front of an antiques shop. A taxidermied owl in a glass dome gazes at us mournfully.

'Yeah. I mean, even when I meet someone in real life it still goes tits up.'

'What d'you mean?' he asks, so I fill him in on the Jack Sander lunch; how he'd suggested I switched to a *kinder* type of job.

'Jesus,' Rod exclaims. 'What on earth made him say that?'

'I don't know.' I shrug. 'I know I'm not perfect, Rod. Christ, I have plenty of faults. But I didn't melt the polar ice caps.'

'At least, not personally—'

'*I* didn't destroy the ozone layer—'

'You used to use tons of hairspray back in the day,' he reminds me, feigning sternness. 'When you had that massive perm, remember?'

'I might have *lightly set* it . . .'

'Lightly set it? It was like a giant, crispy meringue with its own postcode and ecosystem. It's a miracle it didn't self-ignite—'

'Leave my perm out of this.' I can't help laughing, despite everything. We walk onwards and the silence that settles feels just right. 'So, what were you saying,' I venture finally, 'about dating not being easy? What's going on?'

'It's nothing really,' Rod says.

I glance at his handsome profile and try to figure out what's happening in his life. But his face is unreadable. 'Please tell me, Rod. You know you can tell me anything.'

'Oh, it's just me and Gaby,' he says. 'I kind of blew it—'

'You blew it? But how? I thought you two were really happy—'

'Listen, d'you mind if we go somewhere? Just for one drink?' Rod rakes back his hair and pulls a hopeful, tight-lipped smile. I catch his gaze flicker to the left where a welcoming pub, with gleaming dark woodwork and a gilt-lettered sign, seems to be beckoning us in. 'I mean, unless you're rushing off somewhere?' he adds.

'Of course I'm not,' I say, linking his arm now as we cross the road. 'Let's have that drink. I'm not rushing off anywhere at all.'

CHAPTER FORTY-FOUR

Rod, 51

It feels good, the two of us sitting together in this quiet bar at 5.30 p.m. It's just us, like we always used to be. Not even pre-Gaby or pre our lives suddenly seeming to allow very little time for each other anymore. But way before all of that – before Hannah, even. Way back when it all started.

We were nineteen when we met, Rod and I. My parents lived in Glasgow but had come to the tattered end of their marriage and divorce was imminent. Phil had already gone off travelling. Desperate to start my own adult life, I'd moved into a five-person flat-share in the West End, with peeling wallpaper and grim brown carpets that were sticky with God knows what. But to me it was as exciting as Thailand was to Phil. I juggled college assignments with working in an off-licence and a café.

One afternoon, one of my flatmates' friends came around. It was Rod. I liked that he looked like a regular bloke, rather than self-consciously studenty, as many of us did then. I remember clearly that he was wearing a faded old T-shirt and ripped jeans (they just happened to be ripped; it wasn't a fashion thing) and, yes, I thought he was cute. When his friend went off to do something in his room, I'd offered him a coffee. Of course it was instant back then. No one had those silvery Italian stove-top coffee-makers and I don't think Nespresso machines had been invented. We were chatting easily as I took a carton of milk from the fridge and gave it a quick sniff. It was possibly on the turn, I realised. Borderline.

'D'you take milk?' I glanced round to where Rod was sitting at the table where the sun streamed in. A cluster of coloured glass jars sat close to the window, and another of my flatmates had picked wild flowers from a scrubby grass verge to put in them. They looked pretty, I thought. For some reason I hoped Rod liked our flat.

'Yes please,' he said.

'Sugar?'

'No thanks.' I poured our two coffees and added milk, which immediately curdled, floating in lumps. Shit, it *was* off. I glanced round at Rod, then back at the carton (its use-by date was five days ago, it was basically cheese). My brain whirred with options:

Brazen it out and give it to him as it is.

Fish out the lumps with a teaspoon and continue as above.

Try to stir/mash the lumps in.

Strain the coffee. (Through what, though? A tea towel? *Tights?*)

I'd started to panic because, even though he didn't look like the kind of boy who'd be appalled that we had off milk in our fridge, I still wasn't sure what to do. It didn't occur to me that I could simply confess, pour our coffees away and we could just laugh about it.

I was aware of him glancing at me in his bright and innocent way, which made me relax a bit. Then he caught my look and said, 'Sorry, I actually meant I'd like it black?' I looked at him, and there was this tiny delay in my reaction. Because I wasn't quite sure if he was telling the truth. Then I got it, that he'd guessed about the milk. We started to laugh and our friendship began.

'So,' I say now, 'what's happening?'

'With Gaby?' I nod, and he looks down and fiddles with a cardboard beer mat. 'I know you saw them,' he adds.

Immediately, my heart seems to clench. 'Oh do you?' There's a tinny rattle as coins cascade into the slot machine's collecting tray.

'Yeah, she told me,' he says, 'and I know it was all a bit awkward.'

I exhale, wondering why he hadn't told me this right away when we met today. This never used to happen with Rod and me. We always just blurted out whatever was on our minds. And now it feels as if a barrier has come up, and everything is different. 'It was a bit,' I murmur.

Rod sighs audibly. 'I wasn't even going to say anything. I didn't want you to feel like you'd been put in an awkward position. For not telling me, I mean.'

'Well, I wasn't sure what to do.' I look down at my wine glass. 'I'm sorry, Rod. Maybe I should've called you right away. But I didn't want to get involved or cause trouble when it might've all been completely innocent.'

He looks at me and sips his beer. 'Yeah, of course. You weren't to know what was going on. So what actually happened that night?'

'Well, you know, don't you? They just came into the shop to do some, uh, shopping.' However, that's not enough

313

information for Rod. He wants to know how they acted, what was said, what *he* was like. So I describe the scene: him nagging me to sticker the aubergines and how he'd jabbed me in the arm. How Gaby had grabbed him and they'd rushed off together.

Although Rod doesn't say much, I know what he's thinking. He can't stand seeing someone being verbally abused, or even mildly hassled, when they're just trying to do their job. The waiter who's barked at rudely, as if they're a food-transporting robot and not an actual person; the flight attendant who's harangued when she can't magically reconfigure the seating so two friends can sit together when they haven't pre-booked seats. He hates all of that, and perhaps knowing that Gaby's other man is a jerk makes it slightly easier for him. If she likes a guy like that, then surely she was never right for him anyway?

'He sounds like a complete tosser,' Rod remarks.

I shift in my seat. 'I'm not sure you and him would get along.'

'And trying to get you to reduce stuff? The nerve of it.'

'With some people,' I say, 'it's not that they can't afford to pay full price. It's more, they get a little thrill from grabbing a bargain. It's like a game with them.'

'Yeah, I can imagine.' He nods gravely. 'I'm really sorry you were put in that position,' he adds.

'Oh, it's okay,' I say lightly. 'It happens all the time. Nearly every shift, you get one of those—'

'I don't mean that. I mean, seeing the two of them out together and wrestling with whether to say anything to me . . .'

I study his face, wanting to hug him but unsure of the rules these days. There never used to be rules. 'I did wrestle

314

with it actually,' I admit. 'It's been on my mind the whole time. How did you guess?'

A flicker of a smile now. 'Well, I know you, Jen.'

There's a small lull as we sip our drinks but it feels comfortable, as if any tensions between us have all but dissipated now. 'So . . . is it over with her?' I venture.

He nods. 'She was actually seeing him all along, that Scott guy. Some client of hers. She's been doing PR for his pop-up clothing stores. Admitted that the professional and personal had kind of crossed over a bit.' We exchange a grimace.

'I am sorry, Rod,' I murmur.

'It's okay. It's for the best.' He shrugs. 'You know how you said you're not good at dating?'

'Yes?'

'Well, I don't think I am either.'

'What d'you mean?' I ask, leaning forward.

He runs a finger down the condensation on his glass. 'I kind of flung myself into it, you know? All those weekends at her bus, posting photos on Facebook, asking her to that lunch with you and Han and your mum . . .'

'You were just being keen. Nothing wrong with that, is there? I mean, surely we're both a bit long in the tooth to be playing hard to get?'

He laughs dryly. 'I've no idea, Jen. That's what I mean about not being any good at it. It freaked her out and that was that for her . . .'

I blink at him, confused. '*What* freaked her out? You mean the lunch?'

'Yeah. At least, a "meeting people who are dear to me" kind of lunch. She politely explained that that wasn't her kind of thing at all.'

'Oh.' I take a moment to digest this. 'But Gaby seemed keen on you too. There were pictures of you on her Instagram, all grimy and oily, working on the bus—'

'That didn't mean anything,' he says breezily. 'She posts about ten pictures a day. And I'd kind of got the wrong end of the stick with her. About us, I mean. I'd thought she was just seeing me – *exclusively* as Hannah would say . . .'

'And she wasn't?'

He shakes his head. 'Nope. I mean, we hadn't had the "Are we exclusive?" conversation. I'd just assumed . . .'

'Oh, Rod.' I touch his hand. 'Is that how it works now? That conversation has to be had?'

He chuckles. 'I've no idea.'

'Neither have I. Pretty useless, aren't we? In the ways of modern dating, I mean.'

'Yeah, I guess so.' He picks up his glass. 'She soon straightened me out, though. After the lunch thing she explained that she doesn't like being tied down to one person and that, actually, the two of us were probably looking for very different things.' We look at each other and, without thinking, I put my arms around him and hold him close.

'I really am sorry, Rod.'

'Honestly, it's all right.' He pauses. 'You must've wondered why I was posting all those pictures, though?'

'I did a bit,' I admit, sitting back now as he tells me that, just like Marta at the shop, Gaby had found it hilarious that Rod was so ambivalent about social media. 'A relic, she called me. So I thought, okay, I'll prove that I'm not.' His mouth flickers into an embarrassed smile. 'And I thought there was no harm in *you* seeing what a great time I was having either.'

316

'What d'you mean?' He's completely lost me now.

'I mean,' he says, pausing for another sip of beer, as if to fortify himself, 'I actually found it really difficult when you signed up to that site.'

I peer at him, astounded. 'When I started dating, you mean?'

'Yeah.' He nods and reddens slightly. 'Remember when I sent you that message when you were at that amazing restaurant at Loch Earn?'

'You mean when you asked if you could pick up your blowtorch?'

He nods and reddens even more.

'What is it, Rod?' I ask.

'Did you think I'd forgotten you were on that date?'

'Yes, of course!'

'Well, I hadn't.'

I shift in my seat. There's an old-fashioned jukebox at the pub and it makes a series of clanking noises as a song comes on. 'So why did you message me?'

'I dunno really. I s'pose I just wanted to remind you that I was still there.' He fidgets and looks down, as awkward as a teenager.

I stare at him, trying to figure out what to make of his confession. 'I'd never forget you were there, Rod. What made you think I would? And it never seemed to bother you before, when I was seeing someone.'

'Well, there was only really rat man,' he cuts in.

'*Mouse* man—'

'Anyway, it felt different this time,' he continues, refusing to meet my gaze. 'I s'pose I'd never seen you so focused on it before. On meeting someone, I mean, on being *proactive*—'

'Only because Han and Fabs nagged me into doing it!'

'Yeah, but it freaked me out. I realised things would change. With me and you, I mean. And that's why I signed up too. Why I thought I'd better haul myself into the modern age and do what everyone does. Isn't that what Han says? That everyone does it?'

'Yes, but—' I start.

'Because if *you* were going to meet someone serious, then I reckoned maybe I should too. Or at least try to get over you.'

'What?' I exclaim. Our eyes lock for a moment, and my heart seems to stop. Rod turns away and seems to be busying himself with pulling on his jacket. 'What are you doing?' I ask.

'Nothing.' The jacket is on now and he's up on his feet, his drink unfinished.

'Rod, what's wrong? Please don't rush off. Stay and talk to me.'

My heart is thumping hard as I jump up and try to reach to him, but he's turned on his heels, and mutters something under his breath that I don't catch. Then Rod, my dear Rod, is striding towards the door. I'm poised to run after him, to plead with him to stay, but I realise with a wave of dread that he wants me to let him go.

CHAPTER FORTY-FIVE

Gavin, 50

There are no surprises on this date. Gavin Jones is exactly as I'd expected him to be; the kind of man you'd never even notice normally. He's wearing black jeans and a light blue shirt and whiffs strongly of a spicy aftershave. I suppose he could be considered good-looking with his youthful, virtually line-free skin, bright blue eyes and a full head of thick dark brown hair. But there's a flatness about him, a lack of engagement with life – maybe that explains the absence of laughter lines. When he sees me walking into the coffee shop he merely nods and raises a hand in greeting. He doesn't even smile.

'Hi, I'm Jennifer. You must be Gavin?'

'Yeah, that's right.' The sun is high and bright and the cheery café is filled with sunshine. That is, apart from the shadowy corner where Gavin has chosen to sit.

We go through the motions of exchanging information without giving much away. He lives a few streets away and

319

says he does property maintenance jobs of all kinds. For a good twenty minutes he talks about a guttering job he's just finished, for a man who'd quibbled about the fee. He also mentions an unpaid invoice for something or other and grumbles about the rising costs of something else. He isn't interested in films or books or anything really. He doesn't cook or do anything sporty and he's not interested in travelling. 'I don't like foreign food,' he says.

'But don't you ever have the urge to go anywhere different?' I ask.

He shrugs. 'Everywhere's the same, isn't it?'

By now my attention is drifting, and I'm reminding myself of the real reason I'm here, while also remembering how fun my last date was – with Harvey. And now I'm thinking how passionate he was about so many things, and how I might have misread that last message and behaved badly in not replying. But then, he didn't message again either. Have I somehow made things more complicated than they needed to be? As for Rod, I seem to have hurt him without ever intending to. Somehow, life seems to have become more complicated recently.

While I was out with Rod – a week ago now – it had occurred to me that, once the dust had settled after the Gaby business, I could suggest that he came away to Santorini with me. It would cheer him up, I'd reasoned. Plus, we'd been away together lots of times before (although always with Hannah), and I knew already that we were 'holiday compatible', which isn't always a given, even with the closest of friends. But then along had come his blurted confession – minutes after I'd formulated the idea – and after that it would have been unthinkable. All last week our contact was stilted and sporadic. He's busy with work, I reassured myself. Certainly, they've had some huge orders and I know from Marta, when I happened to run into her in town, that it's been all hands on deck at the shop.

I'm discovering now that Gavin does have an interest, and that's money. He's talked about little else for the past half hour. I can't understand what lovely bright, sparky Sally ever saw in him – but then we all make mistakes. I sat in many a sports bar with Mouseman Marc because, I'm ashamed to admit, I thought that was what a girlfriend did. I mean, I'd never really been one, so how would I know? 'Are you sure about this guy?' Leena had asked once, frowning, when I'd described my latest interminable night out with him.

Gavin doesn't know where I work or what I'm interested in, because he hasn't asked anything beyond which part of town do I live in, and have I ever been married? I catch the eye of a young woman with a blonde crop sitting at a nearby table. *Poor you,* her glance seems to say, *with your crap date.* But it's okay because I knew it would be crap. I didn't suggest meeting because I wanted to get to know Gavin or ever see him again.

Once, I feel, is quite enough.

We get up when our coffees are finished. As he seems to have forgotten that it's something you have to attend to, I end up going to the counter to pay the bill. But that's fine. I've probably never spent a fiver more wisely.

'That was nice,' he says, looking more enthusiastic than when he was in the café. 'First dates are meant to be awkward, aren't they? But that was really relaxed.' His gaze settles on my face for a moment.

'Have you been on a lot?' I ask as we fall into step. 'From the site, I mean?'

He shakes his head. 'Couldn't get anyone to actually meet up. There's a lot of time-wasters on there, want to chat and message all the time. I can't be bothered with that.' He exhales in exasperation then goes on, 'You're the first one. So, how about you? Have you met many people?'

'Quite a few, yeah,' I reply.

'Oh, right?' He gives me a knowing look, which I'm not sure how to interpret. 'What's it been like, then?'

'Varied,' I reply.

'Like, good and bad?'

'You could say that.' I pause, reminding myself that I can *do* this. I can go through with it just as I've planned. 'You said you live near here, didn't you?' I add.

'Yeah,' he says brightly. 'Five minutes away. Why, d'you wanna . . .' He pauses and a lascivious smile flickers across his lips. 'D'you want to come in for coffee or something?' Now a flush has spread across his cheeks.

Ignoring the sensation of bile rising, I reply, 'Yes, okay then. Just a quick one.'

'Really?' His eyes widen. 'Okay then. Let's go.'

He honestly thinks I'm going back to his place for sex, I realise, judging by the bounding gait he's adopted now. I also know it's a mad situation to put myself in, even with the safety measure I've put into place – and that Rod would be appalled (even more than burnt-chair-appalled) if he knew what was happening.

We arrive Gavin's block where he marches in ahead of me and lets us into his ground-floor flat. 'D'you want something stronger than a coffee?' he asks, glancing round at me. 'A vodka or something? Wine?'

'Erm, whatever you're having,' I say, still loitering in his hallway, close to the front door, as he marches through to

322

the kitchen. There's the clank of the fridge door, the sound of something being poured, then the *plink* of ice cubes dropping into glasses.

'Make yourself comfortable,' he calls through. From where I'm standing I can see into a small, cluttered and dingy living room.

'Thanks,' I call back. Christ, he's keen to get things started. No small talk or slow, steady build-up here. In his keenness he hasn't even realised I'm still lurking at the front door, which I've left slightly ajar, with my jacket on. The hallway is littered with taped-up boxes as if he has just moved in.

His phone rings. Still in the kitchen, he takes the call. I step quietly into the living room where more boxes – these ones are open – seem to contain random items like games consoles, a wire chest expander, a pillow and tubs of some kind of protein powder. A bath towel has been flung over a faded armchair. A cigarette packet is lying on the small dark brown sofa and a wilting pot plant is perched next to the TV. It looks like the home of a twenty-five-year-old who has yet to get his act together, not a man of double that age.

'We agreed a price so you can't come back and say you're not paying,' Gavin announces from the kitchen. Then: 'No, mate. It doesn't work like that . . .'

Quickly, I scan the room. No sign of Mr Sox in here and I don't have the nerve to go hunting any further into the flat. I'm certainly not planning to go anywhere near the bedroom. There's more urgent phone chat, although Gavin's voice is growing quieter so I assume he has left the kitchen and gone to another room.

Then all falls quiet. My mouth is dry now, and my heart is thumping urgently, but I'm trying to hold my nerve.

Stealthily, I check behind the boxes and sofa but there's still no sign of Sally's cat. And now Gavin has reappeared, clad not in his jeans and blue shirt but in black tracksuit bottoms and *no top*. I stare at him, realising his chest is glistening. In these brief minutes he must have nipped off to his bedroom or bathroom, and not only changed but *oiled* himself.

He smiles creepily. 'Hey, sorry about that. Just some customer who's trying it on.'

'That's okay.'

He studies me for a moment. 'Relax, Jen. Take your jacket off . . .'

Instinctively, I step backwards, knowing I've taken this as far as I can and that pushing it any further would be madness. I turn and stride back into the narrow hallway, towards the front door, and that's when I hear it.

A tiny miaow.

'Jen?' Gavin calls after me.

Ignoring him, I look around the gloomy narrow space. Then, from behind a large, taped-up cardboard box, Mr Sox pads out. He looks up at me and mews again. 'Hey,' I say gently. I turn back to Gavin, who is staring at me in confusion.

'Don't you want that drink?' he asks.

'No thanks,' I reply. 'I didn't come here to have a drink with you or anything else.'

'What?' He gawps at me.

'I'm actually a friend of Sally's,' I continue. 'Maybe I should've told you that at the start?'

'Huh? A friend of Sal's? I don't get it . . .'

'That's why I met you,' I explain. 'Not because I wanted a date with you but because of Mr Sox. And I've come to collect him for her,' I add brightly.

A stunned silence falls as I'm reminded of confronting the kitchen chancer at Mum's where, out of nowhere, something had reared up in me; a kind of fearlessness I'd forgotten I had since I'd stopped flying.

'What if I won't let you have him?' Gavin blusters, flushing beet red now. He glances down at the cat, who seems to be watching the scene with rapt interest.

'Then I'll report you,' I say.

'What, to the police?' he splutters. 'What are they going to do?'

'They'll treat it as theft.'

'But he's mine,' Gavin insists, eyes narrowing.

'Not in the eyes of the law, he isn't.' *Thank you, Posh Stephen,* I reflect, before charging onwards: 'Who had him originally? Who took on most of the looking after and dealt with the vet, and all of that?'

'Well, Sal did but—'

'Who was Mr Sox's prime carer?' I cut in, not rudely but firmly: *I'm sorry, sir, I'm going to have to ask you to sit down and fasten your seatbelt. If you won't do that I'll alert the captain and we might have to divert this flight.*

Only once did I have to do that but once was enough. The huge, bearded bear of a passenger tried to spit at me (he missed) and punched a man who was trying to restrain him, and our Valencia-Glasgow flight had to land at Nantes.

Do I miss those days? Not so much anymore. But I'd developed a tough shell in order to deal with every eventuality and it seems that's still intact.

'I'm not getting into this with you,' Gavin retorts, shaking his head as if I am quite mad.

'You don't need to get into anything,' I say. We glare at each other as I pull my phone from my pocket and make the call. 'Ready,' is all I say, before finishing it. Perhaps sensing the tension, Mr Sox emits a quiet miaow, and when Sally appears in the doorway he runs to her. 'Oh, my baby,' she cries, scooping him up into her arms.

'For fuck's sake, just take him,' Gavin thunders. 'He's been a pain in the arse since he's been here. Pissing on the bed, crying to be let out at night. Missing you, maybe. I don't know. Do what you want with him,' he snaps, before marching away and disappearing back into the kitchen.

'Thank you, Jen,' Sally exclaims. 'C'mon, let's go . . .' We hurry out of the flat, both of us glancing back in alarm in case Gavin has decided to put up a fight and isn't going to let us get away that easily. But he doesn't follow us and once outside, we head straight for Sally's car from which she extracts a cat box. Once Mr Sox is installed in it we pull away.

'Honestly,' she says, 'I can't thank you enough.'

'I'm just glad it worked,' I say.

She exhales loudly and glances at me. 'You're a brave woman, Jen. I didn't like you putting yourself in that position . . .'

'Well, I won't ever again,' I say, grinning. I look back and talk gently to Mr Sox, not wanting to startle him. But he doesn't seem to be scared. In fact he's purring, as if he'd been waiting patiently to be rescued.

'Without Mature Matches this would never have happened,' Sally marvels.

'Yeah. So at least some good has come out of it.' We both laugh, and I think of Hannah, and how she'd teased me when I'd been so resistant to online dating. 'No one meets in real life,' she'd said. 'It's all algorithms now.'

I didn't want to believe that nothing happens by chance

anymore; that magic is obsolete. Because things *do* just happen. Little miracles happen every day.

As we stop at red traffic lights I pull out my phone. Sally glances over again and registers the Mature Matches home page on the screen.

'Setting up a date?' she asks with a smile.

'God, no,' I say firmly. 'I'm done with all of that. I'm deleting my profile . . .' A couple of clicks and it's done. And from his basket on the back seat Mr Sox lets out a small miaow, perhaps of approval, or maybe because he is happy to be going home.

CHAPTER FORTY-SIX

A Month Later

The Aegean Sea glitters, a wash of almost impossibly vivid turquoise. The sun beats down on the dazzling white houses and churches stacked up on the hills. As I stepped off the plane yesterday, thanking the flight attendant in her smart red uniform, I stopped for a moment to inhale the gently scented warm air. Then, in the airport, Fabs called out my name and hurried towards me. She had flown in from London and arrived a little before me. She'd needed a holiday, I'd figured, after everything that had happened. And she had been delighted to come.

As Mum is now aware, there are scammers out there who appear to be perfectly charming. Of course they do. Otherwise they wouldn't gain your trust.

'I've been such an idiot, Jen,' Fabs had told me over the phone. 'I like to think I'm an intelligent woman and I've never had to rely on anyone for anything. Certainly not

Jacob's dad. And here I am, your classic case of idiot middle-aged – no, *old* woman—'

'You're not old,' I'd insisted, but she'd charged on: 'I'm sixty-one. Okay, I'm middle-aged if I make it to a hundred and twenty, which I very much doubt. Anyway, age isn't the point, apart from the fact that I should've been sussed enough to know what was going on.'

I'd already heard from Hannah how the 'too good to be true' theatre director whom Fabs had met online had turned out to be precisely that. Andrew Crickley had seemed so kind and thoughtful, just as kitchen man Robert had appeared to Mum. 'Nothing's too much trouble for him,' Fabs had told me. Dashingly handsome, he'd festooned her with flowers and was constantly popping round, doing jobs for her in her house and garden. They had been spending heaps of time together and he had even suggested that, when he was out of temporary accommodation and back in his newly renovated house in Maida Vale, perhaps she would like to live with him.

While she'd been a little uncertain about compromising her freedom, Fabs had been edging towards saying yes. Andrew had seemed like the perfect man. There were no red flags. So, when he told her that funds hadn't come through for a play he was directing, she'd offered to step in and help.

'I mean, why wouldn't I?' she'd said. 'It had been cast already. Rehearsals had started. The actors were all young people, around Jacob's age but from disadvantaged back-grounds, pinning their hopes on this being their big break. He'd even shown me pictures of some of them. It was heart-breaking to think that the whole project could crumble due to some admin cock-up. And I could pull together the money, just about. Andrew promised me that when funds did come through – they were only delayed, he said – then I'd be paid back in full.'

Only there was no play. There were no actors either; there probably wasn't even an Andrew Crickley. When he'd disappeared with her £5000 it was as if he had ceased to exist.

'Are you still trying to track him down?' I ask now as we sip crisp white wine and pick at a dish of fat green olives on our hotel balcony.

'No, I've given up for now,' she says. 'It's always better to look forward than backward, don't you think?'

'Definitely,' I say, gazing out onto the shimmering sea.

'Thank you for inviting me here,' she adds. 'It's just what I needed to move on. I don't want to give that bloody man another second's thought.'

'I'm so glad you could come,' I say truthfully. It wasn't that I'd asked Fabs out of pity, in the wake of the 'romance scam', as such scenarios are apparently called. I'd invited her because, after that weird night with Rod, it had struck me that she would be the perfect date for a week in Greece. Yes, that was it, without a doubt; *female* company was what I craved. No weird dynamics and no pressure. 'Just Jen and an Argentinian model in a honeymoon hotel suite,' as Freddie put it. 'And what could be better than that?'

We'd arrived yesterday and had a wonderful evening at the hotel restaurant with a little too much retsina and ouzo. ('It's the law, right?' Fabs had laughed.) We hadn't talked about Andrew Crickley at all. Not that he was a taboo subject; we were just too busy getting to know each other better, filling in the jigsaw piece by piece. I've learnt that as well as modelling Fabs has a raft of side hustles, including making celebration cakes smothered in fondant flowers that look like outrageous hats.

Tonight, as we head out to town for the evening, I'm so glad it's just us two. For one thing, it's thrilling to realise that at fifty I have made a new friend. This hasn't happened to me for years. I still have a few school and college mates, and friends from when Hannah was little, when every toddler group session acted like a platonic speed-dating event for mums. And of course there's Freddie and Leena and all the other Budgies out there. But now there's Fabs, and Helpline Sally, whom Fabs knows all about. Also a cat lover, she regards my recent rescue mission as nothing less than heroic and has chivvied me into retelling it no less than three times.

'It was pretty fitting for your last date,' she says now, as our waiter arrives with freshly caught swordfish, salads and the most incredible home-made bread. She knows I have come off the site. Fabs, too, has deleted her apps and called time on dating – at least for now.

'Like I said to Sally, I'm glad it was useful for something,' I tell her. Now Harvey flickers into my mind. I still haven't messaged him and it feels way too late to do anything about that now. He's probably met someone else, and written me off as one of those game-players. So I'm trying to take a leaf out of Fabs's book. She doesn't dwell on things or chew things over. She's done her utmost to track Andrew Crickley down, contacting theatrical organisations and unions, plus a whole raft of theatres and, of course, the police. Now she's accepted that it's time to move on. I should be more like Fabs, I decide, and just get on with my life.

After dinner we stroll around the town, following the narrow, twisty streets that meander between whitewashed houses and twinkling bars. There's a hubbub of chatter and laughter and, as we wander down towards the beach, the steady whoosh of the sea.

Much later, giddy on cocktails now, we climb into the enormous bed. It strikes me that there's definitely nothing 'wasteful' about staying in a honeymoon suite when all you want to do in it is chat and giggle, drink wine and eat snacks. In fact I can't think of a better use for it.

Next day we hire mopeds and scoot off up into the hills, stopping off at a charmingly faded café where we are the only customers. Music is playing softly from a record player. The elderly owner seems to be transfixed by Fabs, and festoons us with complimentary almondy cakes and incredible honeycomb ice cream. Later that night, we stop off at a bar perched on the shore where again, she is the centre of attention.

'So, are you girls here to celebrate something?' asks a red-cheeked British man. He's around our age with neatly cropped short grey hair and is wearing a brown corduroy jacket over a linen shirt and jeans. There's something country squire-ish about him.

'Yes,' she replies, turning to me. 'We're celebrating life, aren't we, Jen?'

Corduroy man has been joined by a friend of a similar age, who's sporting an extravagant moustache and a straw boater hat. Both are sipping beers from long, tall glasses and are hovering close to our table. When they ask if they can join us, we agree. They want to know all about us, and keep stressing that we look 'nothing like your ages!', as if this is the ultimate compliment. When they discover that I used to be a flight attendant, they are almost falling over themselves to find out more.

'Did you get to keep your uniform?' Corduroy man gives me a wink.

'I did actually, yes . . .'

'You know what I want to know?' the other one chips in. 'If they have hidden cameras in aeroplane toilets.' Fabs and I splutter, and he clarifies: 'I mean a spy camera to see if people are up to stuff in there.' Of course they want to know all about the mile high club because everyone does.

The talk moves on to the men's fledgling business, which they run together in Kent; it turns out that they're brothers who are setting up an insect farm. 'It's a new, entirely sustainable form of protein,' corduroy man explains. This triggers copious insect talk, which is interesting to a point (certainly more than plug-in radiators anyway). However, Fabs and I have already perfected a way of communicating without words. So, at a pause in conversion, we exchange a glance, wish the brothers much success with their insects, and leave.

There's a warm breeze as we stroll back to the hotel. 'This is wonderful,' Fabs says, linking my arm. 'Aren't we lucky to be here, Jen?'

'We really are,' I say.

'This is all down to your cleverness at selling those little budgie toys!'

I beam at her. 'Well, I did have some talents—'

'*Do*,' she corrects me. 'You do have talents.' A bemused smile now. 'When you've had enough of the shop, there's always insect farming.'

'You know, I'd never thought of that!' I delve into my bag for my phone when it cheep-cheeps with a text notification. Hannah has sent me a photo of her, Jacob and Mum in Mum's garden, in front of the cluster of bird feeders.

Their three smiling faces are pressed together. *Having fun here*, her message reads. *Managed to persuade Gran that she's not going to run out of bird seed anytime soon! Lots of love xxx*.

My heart lifts. She and Jacob are staying with Mum for the week, to keep an eye, of course – because it's becoming more evident that it's dangerous for her to live alone, even with carers dropping in daily to supervise her medication. However, Mum doesn't know this. She still thinks she is managing just fine.

Hannah's solution to how we would 'manage' the situation while I was away with Fabs struck me as nothing short of genius. She would interview her gran for their *Just a Number* podcast, gently coaxing out her stories of being a midwife from the 1950s onwards. Mum was thrilled to be asked. 'I'm going to be on a podcast!' she told Kirsten, proudly, over the fence. As soon as that had been agreed, Mum had seemed perfectly happy for Hannah and Jacob to spend the week with her. 'I can look after you while your mum's away in Greece,' she'd said, as if Hannah was still nine years old.

I'm about to slip my phone back into my bag when I spot another unread message, this time from Freddie:

Hey, Toots, thought you might be having too much fun to be checking the news. He's right; I haven't. *But thought you might be interested to know Budgie are back in business again and they're recruiting!*

Oh amazing, I message back. *You interested?*

Not me, Toots. Loving what I'm doing now. There's no going back for me. But I was thinking about you?

CHAPTER FORTY-SEVEN

I wasn't expecting anyone to meet me at the airport. But there he is, holding up a sign with my name on it, as a joke: MORTON. Rod and I hug and I'm filled with relief and happiness. 'You needn't have come,' I tell him as we make our way to the car park. 'I could've got a taxi—'

'I just thought it'd be nice to meet you,' he says.

I glance at him, trying to read his expression. 'Well, thanks. It's really sweet of you.'

'So, how was it?'

'Brilliant,' I say truthfully. 'Honestly, we loved every minute. Fabs was totally the right choice . . .'

Rod grins. 'So you *can* pick a good date, then?'

'Looks like it,' I say.

He colours slightly. 'I also wanted to say sorry,' he adds, 'for being so weird these past few weeks. Since we had that drink, I mean. So I thought I'd come and say it in person—'

'You were just upset,' I murmur, 'and I'm sorry you felt that way.'

'I'm not proud of myself,' he says quickly, 'and honestly, you have nothing to be sorry about. I felt pretty stupid afterwards. That's why I've hardly been in touch lately.' Rod lifts my case into the boot of his car. 'For once in my life I didn't know what to say to you.'

I inhale slowly as we stop and look at each other. 'I didn't know what to say to you either. But there was nothing to feel stupid about, Rod. You just told me how you'd been feeling and there's nothing wrong with that.' I pause. 'Haven't we always been honest with each other?'

'Yeah, we have. The thing is . . .' he starts, as we climb into his car. 'I mean, the thing that really triggered all that was when you joined that dating site.'

'Really?' I say.

He nods as we pull out of the car park. 'I mean, how pathetic to feel all jealous and insecure just because finally you seemed set on meeting someone?'

'There's nothing pathetic about that.' I glance out at the flat horizon, remembering all those times, in our early days, when I'd had a yearning for something more with Rod, but shied away from making a move because I was terrified of spoiling what we had.

We travel in silence for a few minutes. 'Did you mean it?' I ask eventually. 'What you said in the pub, I mean?'

'About trying to get over you?' His mouth sets in a firm line. 'Well, yes. And when you joined the site and started seeing all those guys . . .'

'"All those guys"?' I repeat.

'Yeah, your hordes of admirers.' A flicker of a smile now. 'I was scared I was going to lose you. And even if I didn't, I panicked that we wouldn't be like *us* anymore.'

'Rod,' I say, 'we'll always be like us. You do know that,

336

don't you? I mean, even if one or both of us ends up with someone?'

He nods. 'You're right.' Then, after a pause, he adds, 'You know how we always explained things to Hannah? Why we weren't a couple, I mean?'

'Yeah,' I say quietly.

'We said we loved each other, but not in that way.'

'Uh-huh.' My eyes are misting now and I swallow hard.

'Well, it wasn't really true,' he continues. 'I mean, I love you in *all* ways – as Han's mum and my best friend. All of that and everything in between.' He gives me a quick look. 'If that doesn't sound too corny.'

'It doesn't sound corny,' I say, aware of a tightness in my throat.

'And the fact that we're not *together*-together doesn't diminish any of that,' he adds. 'But really, in this completely roundabout and incoherent way . . .' He pauses and laughs. 'What I'm trying to say is, I've always been a bit in love with you.'

I look at him and smile, then glance at the sky again. It's one of those weatherless days; neither sunny nor dull but something vaguely in between. 'You wanted us to be together?' I ask. 'Right at the beginning, I mean?'

'Yeah.' A small, dry laugh. 'At least, I thought I did. I wanted what was best for the three of us really. And I didn't want to screw things up.'

'Well,' I say, 'there were times when I really wanted to be with you too.'

'Really?' A proper laugh now. 'Fucking hell, Jen. What were we like?'

'We were fine,' I say, feeling my heart lifting. 'We did

337

the right thing, I think. Getting together might've ruined things . . .'

'Or,' he cuts in, 'it might have been absolutely fucking fantastic.' We both laugh, and if he wasn't driving I'd throw my arms around him right now.

'Oh, God,' I wail, in mock horror. 'We missed our chance, didn't we?'

He looks round quickly and smiles. 'Maybe. But you know what? I also like things just the way they are with me and you. I mean, I *really* like that, more than anything. And while you were throwing cocktails down your neck in Santorini—'

'Hey, it was a cultural trip! We went to see some ancient ruins!'

'—I thought about us a lot,' he says.

'I did too,' I say truthfully.

'And I realised I don't want anything to change between us,' Rod adds. 'Ever, I mean.'

My heart seems to swell as I look at him. 'Rod, I'd hate anything to change between us too.'

'And you know what?' he adds. 'This is going to sound mad, after the last time I saw you, but I've been thinking about this as well. And I'd be really happy for you if you met someone wonderful.'

Another silence falls. 'You really mean that?'

He nods. 'Yes, honestly. Not that you'd need my permission of course.'

'No, I realise that,' I say, unable to keep down a huge smile now. 'But it's just nice to know because I'd hate to hurt or upset you . . .'

'You won't,' he said quickly. 'I don't think you can actually. I mean, you can wind me up, you never listen to anything I say . . .'

'What are you talking about?' I ask, feigning defensiveness.

He glances at me and grins. 'Can I just say . . . blow-torch?'

'No need to cast that up again,' I say as we turn off the motorway. It's the journey I've done myself thousands of times over the years, coming home from the airport after a shift. Often I'd be dog-tired after a long flight, desperate to pull off my uniform and fall into bed. But today, as the late afternoon sky starts to brighten and the sun appears, I am filled with a sense of newness and so much energy that it feels as if it could burst out of me. So, as soon as Rod has dropped me off and headed into town to work, I change into my vest and leggings, pull on my trainers and go for a run.

CHAPTER FORTY-EIGHT

At first I'm not sure if it's him in the distance. There are so many runners around here, from the serious types who are training for races, constantly checking their watches to monitor their pace, to the beginners just starting out with that running app I used to listen to.

I suppose I'm somewhere in between. While I wouldn't say I love running exactly (not in the way that I love, say, *wine*) I do love the feeling it gives me: heart pumping, endorphins swirling, making me feel truly alive. And that's how I feel today as the man grows closer and I see that, yes, it *is* him. Jack Sander is bounding towards me on the long, wide street.

I have no desire to stop and chat. However as we're heading towards each other there's no way I can avoid him – unless I can vaporise or slip neatly through the gaps in a drain. Then, just as I'm trying to gather myself together and appear calm and unrattled as we pass, something peculiar happens. Having clearly registered that it's me, Jack turns in a wide arc and runs away (actually, he *sprints*) back in the direction he came from. A few seconds later he's darted down a side street, out of sight.

The bloody nerve! I'm outraged at his rudeness – even though I *really* didn't want to chat – and now I'm thinking, sod that, Mr-hot-water-sipper. I will not be blanked in such an outrageously obvious way! These are my streets too, and we should be grown up enough to be able to at least acknowledge each other when we're out.

I don't know where it comes from, the burst of energy that ups my pace as I charge along and veer into the side street to see Jack way off in the distance. 'Jack!' I call out. 'Hey, Jack!'

He glances round, looking momentarily alarmed as I run even faster in order to catch up with him. 'Jen, hi! How're you?' Acting all surprised as if he hadn't seen me a few moments earlier. Shabby acting, Mr Sander.

'I'm good,' I say. 'Really good. But don't stop because of me . . .'

'Uh, okay . . .' I can see tension in his jaw as we start to run together, side by side. 'You look well,' he offers, giving me a quick look.

'Thanks.' I smile, registering that I am not only keeping up with his pace but capable of talking simultaneously. A few months ago I could barely *breathe* and run. 'I just wanted to say,' I add, 'that there's no need to avoid me if you see me, okay?'

'Oh. Oh, right!' He flashes a tight smile as we start to head up a slight incline. Then, all in a rush: 'Look, Jen, I'm sorry for being such a jerk that time. About your job, I mean. I thought about it afterwards and spoke to a couple of friends and, well, I didn't really need them to tell me that I'd been out of order . . .'

341

'I'm not worried about that now,' I say truthfully.

Another quick, awkward smile. 'I realised the last thing you needed was a lecture from me. I mean, what the hell do I know?'

'It's okay, honestly.' Onwards we run at a steady pace. Weirdly, I'm not worrying about what he might be thinking about my running style, or whether I'm holding him back, because he could zoom ahead if he wanted to. Anyway, I don't need Jack's approval and I don't really care what anyone thinks, because it feels good, doing what I'm doing. I feel stronger these days, in *all* ways.

'Your running's really come on,' he adds with a trace of genuine surprise. 'Honestly, Jen. I'm really impressed.'

'Thanks. I'm enjoying it,' I say truthfully.

'You don't do that looking-down-at-the-ground thing anymore?' A teasing smile now.

'No.' I grin at him. 'No, I'm over that.'

'Glad to hear it.'

'It just seemed safer to look where I was going instead.'

We run in silence for a while, which feels fine and natural. 'We could go out for a run together sometime, if you like?' he says finally. 'I promise I'm not trying to get you on board as a client.'

I consider this, and how thrilled I'd have been a few months ago when nine a.m. meant fox o'clock and I would always be primed for a sighting. 'I believe you,' I say, 'but I actually enjoy running on my own.'

'Yeah, some people prefer that,' Jack remarks. 'They're happier doing their own independent thing.'

I take a moment to absorb that, thinking, maybe that's it, and I've always been content by myself. But that doesn't mean there's no space in my life for anyone else; even for someone new to come into it. There's always going to be room for that special person, I realise that now. I can *do my own independent thing*, as Jack put it, and still have an open heart.

And that's what spurs me on, after we've said goodbye, and I run on home. This time, instead of pulling off my clothes and jumping straight into the shower, I grab my phone and scroll to the number I've been wanting to call all these weeks, but for some reason, I haven't.

A fear of rejection, maybe? Or trying to cling onto my pride? Sod that, I decide, barely stopping to think before I compose the message:

Hi Harvey, hope things are good with you. I'm sorry I haven't been in touch. I think I just needed to clear up a few things in my head. But if you'd like to meet for a drink sometime, that would be great. Love, Jen x.

I read it over just once and then, with my heartbeat accelerating, I press send. A few minutes later my phone rings.

'Jen?' Harvey says. The sounds of his voice lifts my heart. 'How are you? What've you been doing?'

Where do I begin? By saying that I'm wondering if we could start over and see what happens? I try to put this into words, telling Harvey that, really, all of this is new to me and, while it might be too late for us, I'm not afraid to try.

I look out through my living room window onto the bright October afternoon. The pavement is covered in leaves, gone mushy now, but it strikes me suddenly that it's the perfect day for a picnic and for starting all over again. 'D'you fancy that?' I suggest. 'A picnic in the park, like the one we had before?'

'Well,' Harvey says, feigning hesitation but I can tell he's smiling, 'I have just baked what's probably my best-ever loaf . . .'

I'm smiling too. 'I'd love to try it,' I say, knowing now that I don't need to say sorry and that everything is going to be okay, however our story turns out.

EPILOGUE

Eight Months Later

Mary, 80

Sheila, 84

Mum loves everyone now. Every time I visit her home I am introduced to new people – staff members and fellow residents – whom she describes as 'so kind and nice'. And today, with eyes shining, she announces, 'There's someone I want you to meet.'

'Oh, who's that, Mum?' I ask.

A mischievous grin. 'Her name's Sheila and she's a right character. I've told her all about you. C'mon, let's not keep her waiting . . .' She leads me from the lounge to the bright, airy conservatory where a lady with wavy white hair is engrossed in the crossword in a newspaper. 'Sheila, this is my daughter, Jennifer,' Mum announces. 'She works in a supermarket!'

'Hello, Sheila,' I say as she greets me with a warm smile and a proper firm handshake. 'Lovely to meet you.'

'You too, love. Which supermarket d'you work at?'

'Actually, I'm starting a different job now,' I explain. I turn to Mum. 'I have some exciting news . . .'

'About a job?' she asks, and I nod. 'But I thought you liked it at that shop?'

'I did,' I say, 'but I had an interview this week and they called me today to say they want to offer me a job. It's with an airline, Mum. Remember I worked for one before?'

She nods. 'Er, I think so. What were they called again? The one with the bird emblem?'

'BudgieAir,' I reply, 'but it's not them.'

'Aw, I am sorry, love.' Her mouth forms a flat line.

'No, it's okay, Mum. I actually fancied a change. It's a new airline that's just started flying out of the UK. They want to do things differently. There's a uniform, obviously, but they want to get away from all the make-up, the done-up look we used to have. There'll be no approved lipstick shades and flight attendants won't have to wear heels. They want a fresher, more modern approach—'

'So you're going to be flying again?' she asks excitedly.

'Actually, no. I'm going to be a trainer, teaching classes to people who want to become flight attendants. I'll be helping to send whole new crews into the skies.'

'You know how to do *that*?' Mum looks aghast, as if I've announced that I am about to be let loose to perform heart surgery in a hospital.

'Yes, Mum.' I laugh and squeeze her hand. 'I did it for a very long time myself, remember?'

She is studying me intensely, then her thoughts seem to wander. 'Have I ever shown you our garden?'

'Yes, but I'd love to see it again . . .'

'There are lots of birds out there. I feed them all. There's blackbirds and finches and . . . what are the other ones?'

'Tits?'

She giggles naughtily. 'Yes, there's a few of those around here.' There's another giggle, which sets Sheila off too, and now they're chuckling away together as if sharing a private joke. Then a blackbird lands on the neatly clipped hedge outside, catching Mum's attention. 'You always wanted to fly, didn't you, Jennifer?' she says.

'Yes, Mum. I did. But a change is good, I think. We all change, don't we?'

She nods as Sheila gets up and the three of us stroll out to the garden together. It is beautifully kept with a small, freshly mown lawn and borders exploding with colour. I think Mum actually believes that she takes care of it all by herself. There's certainly a note of pride in her voice as she points out the early summer flowers: the lacy white hydrangeas, the butter-yellow roses and dazzling red hot pokers.

Mum doesn't notice at first when Harvey appears at the conservatory doorway and comes out to join us.

'Hi, Mum.' As he hugs Sheila, he catches my eye and smiles. I introduce him to Mum, even though they have met before many times. I have met Sheila too but each time I visit I am introduced as if it's for the very first time.

Now Mum's attention has been caught by the soft rattle of the tea trolley that's being wheeled into the conservatory. 'Shall we go in, Sheila?' she says as if Harvey and I have ceased to exist.

'Where's my crossword?' Sheila asks, looking round at the bench beside her.

'You left it inside,' Mum says.

'Oh, did I?'

'Yes, don't worry. We can go and get it. I'll help you finish it.'

Sheila beams at me. 'Your mum keeps me right.'

Yes, I'm sure she does . . . I can't help smiling as she links her arm through Mum's. Then, just as they are about to head indoors, Mum adds, 'You know what this garden needs? A bird table and some feeders. Could he do it?' She indicates Harvey, who's standing there with a bemused look on his face.

'Who?' Sheila asks, frowning.

'Him. The handyman.'

'That's not the handyman,' Sheila exclaims, laughing now. 'That's Harvey. He's my son!'

'Oh, is he?' Mum beams at him flirtatiously. 'Sorry, Harvey. I didn't realise.'

'That's quite all right, Mrs McGuire,' he says.

'Call me Mary . . .' Off they go now, lured by cake, leaving Harvey and me to stand there for a moment. Then we follow them in, and there are hugs goodbye but I have a feeling that Mum and Sheila are more interested in the cherry bakewells than us right now. Teas are being poured and china plates handed around, and although Euan, Mum's favourite carer, asks if we'd like to stay for tea, we thank him and say maybe next time.

Harvey takes my hand as we leave. 'Your mum seems to be settling in so well,' he says.

'Yes, she loves it,' I say, aware of a rush of gratitude for Mum's new family here, and to Harvey too – and the magic that makes things happen when we least expect it. The sun is high and bright, and an aeroplane trail slices through the brilliant blue sky above us as we step out into the beautiful afternoon.

Acknowledgements

Huge thanks to Cara Chimirri, Rachel Faulkner-Willcocks, Helen Huthwaite, Becci Mansell, Ellie Pilcher, Helena Newton (copyeditor supremo) and the whole fantastic Avon team. A big shoutout as ever to my wonderful agents, Caroline Sheldon and Rosemary Buckman, and to my dear friends Jen, Kath, Cathy, Wendy R, Wendy V, Susan, Jennifer M and Maggie. A dazzling sun salutation to Lisa Woolley for all the walks, chats and inspiration. For 20 years I've belonged to a writing group in Biggar (unofficially named The Coven). While our meets are on Zoom these days my writing friends are always inspiring. Thank you Tania, Vicki, Amanda, Pauline, Sam and Alison. Here in Glasgow I don't know what I'd do without Elise Allan's creativity coaching group. Big thanks to Elise, Christobel, Annie, Anne and Mif. When writing I'm always indebted to those who help me with research. Huge thanks to Liz Silvester and Jackie Brown for your (sometimes hair-raising) insider stories on online dating. And to Sharon Shuppert and John Smith, both former flight attendants, who gave me a fascinating insight into life in the skies. For the purrfect cat names thanks to Kirsten Bennett for Mr Sox and to Lisa Ward Weir for Casey. Special thanks to my son Sam who not only did a much-needed proofread for me, but also hoovered out the bits that were deemed too embarrassing to print. Finally heaps of love to Dexter and Erin, to my dad, Keith, for always cheering me on, and to my husband Jimmy who kept me (mostly) sane during the writing of this book.

Follow me on Instagram@fiona_gib
twitter@FionaGibson
facebook.com/fionagibsonauthor

Suzy Medley is having a bad day . . .
. . . when a shabby terrier turns up at
her door . . .

FIONA GIBSON

The
DOG
SHARE

Two
strangers.

One
dog.

It's complicated!

Can one unruly dog change her life forever?

Sometimes life can be bittersweet . . .

When life gives you lemons, lemonade just
won't cut it. Bring on the gin!

When the kids are away . . .

'Warm, funny and poignant' *Daily Mail*

THE MUM
WHO GOT
HER LIFE
BACK

An empty nest has
never been so much fun!

Fiona Gibson

The laugh-out-loud *Sunday Times* bestseller
is back and funnier than ever!

Everyone has a last straw . . .

An unmissable novel, perfect for fans of
Milly Johnson and Jill Mansell.